PRAISE FOR *THE LIVIA LONE* SERIES

"An absolutely first-rate thriller . . . Emotionally true at each beat."
—*New York Times Book Review*

"An explosive thriller that plunges into the sewer of human smuggling . . . Filled with raw power, [*Livia Lone*] may be the darkest thriller of the year."
—*Kirkus Reviews*, starred review

"[An] exciting thriller . . . Eisler keeps a firm hand on the throttle of what could be the first of a rewarding series."
—*Publishers Weekly*

"Livia is a complex and sympathetic character . . . Readers of hard-boiled fiction, heavily tinted toward noir, may see in Livia something of Carol O'Connell's Kathy Mallory, also a cop with an abuse-filled past and an appetite for revenge."
—*Booklist*

"Eisler offers up an astonishingly raw tale that is dark and disturbing, but one that you will want to finish. Both the compelling narrative and the fascinating—yet seriously flawed—heroine are indications that Eisler is at the top of his game."
—RT Book Reviews

"Barry Eisler is back, and then some. [*Livia Lone*] may be the best and strongest work of his storied career . . . *Livia Lone* moves like a freight train . . . Jump on what appears to be the start of a terrific new series."
—Bookreporter

T0059109

ALL THE
DEVILS

ALSO BY BARRY EISLER

ALL THE DEVILS

BARRY EISLER

THOMAS & MERCER

Text copyright © 2019 by Barry Eisler
All rights reserved.

Published by Thomas & Mercer, Seattle

www.apub.com

Amazon, the Amazon logo, and Thomas & Mercer are trademarks of Amazon.com, Inc., or its affiliates.

ISBN-13: 9781542094238 (hardcover)
ISBN-10: 1542094232 (hardcover)

ISBN-13: 9781542094221 (paperback)
ISBN-10: 1542094224 (paperback)

Cover design by Rex Bonomelli

Printed in the United States of America

First edition

For Danny, Evan, and Pete
You can't make new old friends—and I'm glad
I'll never need to.

Hell is empty

And all the devils are here.

—William Shakespeare, *The Tempest*

Prologue

One Month Earlier

Boomer pulled up behind the collapsed wall and cut the lights. Even inside the minivan, the rotting sulfur smell was enough to make his eyes water. He might have gagged, if he hadn't been used to it.

He opened the door and stepped out, his boots crunching on what sounded like gravel but what he knew instead were the pulverized bones of a million poisoned fish. The air was furnace hot: past midnight and still almost a hundred degrees. But what the hell, it was a dry heat. Besides, it had been hotter in Iraq, and back then he'd endured it on combat patrols while loaded with eighty pounds of gear.

He closed the door. Other than the ticking of the engine, the night was completely still. Around him stood a few derelict structures glowing faintly beneath a low crescent moon: A broken-down trailer. A windowless storefront. The skeletal frame of a roofless house. Fifty yards farther on was the edge of the stagnant water, a vast sinkhole of darkness. Miles across, on the eastern shore, he could make out a few scattered lights. Hard to imagine anyone still living around here. But if you were desperate enough, it was amazing what you could endure. Even the stench of the Salton Sea.

He heard footfalls coming from his left. He turned and squinted. It was too dark to make out a face, but he recognized the silhouette well enough.

"Snake," he called out. "You son of a bitch, is that really you?"

The moonlight glinted off a smile. "You dumb bastard, who else?"

And then there he was, close enough to really see now. The same compact, wiry frame, the same coiled-danger vibe that had put the fear into almost everyone. Snake.

Boomer laughed and started walking toward him. "I can't believe it. Get over here, you crazy fuck."

They hugged, tightly, old comrades in arms. Then Boomer stepped back, still holding Snake's shoulders. "Seriously, I can't believe you're out. What's with the encrypted messages and coordinates? And why here, why not a bar?"

"Come on, man, it wouldn't do for Congressman Bradley Michael 'Boomer' Kane the Third to be seen associating with a convicted felon. Plus, you know, this is our place."

Boomer ignored the last part because yeah, it was their place. Or at least it had been. "General court-martial," he said, releasing Snake's shoulders. "Not a civilian proceeding. No such thing as a felony in the military."

Snake laughed. "Shit, now you even sound like a congressman. Anyway. Abusive sexual contact. Conviction and dishonorable. Is what it is."

"You were smart to plead it down. Aggravated sexual assault, you'd have another ten years still ahead of you. Maybe more."

"Whatever. For you, it's the same guilt by association."

"Like I give a fuck."

"That's your call, if you want to make it. But I wasn't going to take the choice away from you."

Boomer was moved by the man's loyalty. And after so much time, too. "Thanks, brother."

"It's nothing."

"You need anything? Money? Place to stay?"

"Nah, I'm good."

"Bullshit you're good. Almost seven years in Leavenworth, don't tell me you're good."

"Don't I look good?"

Boomer laughed. "All right, I'll give you that." They were quiet for a moment, and he added, "I didn't even know you were out. I should have been following more closely. I'm sorry. Paroled?"

Snake nodded. "Model prisoner. All I did was read, jerk off, and work out. Not necessarily in that order."

Boomer laughed again. "Yeah, business before pleasure."

"Don't you know it, brother. Anyway, don't worry. I know you got a lot on your plate. Fucking congressman, seriously, I can't believe it."

"Yeah, sometimes I can't believe it, either."

"Your old man must be proud."

Boomer preferred not to talk about the admiral. Or even think about him, if he could avoid it. "Hard to know what that asshole thinks," he said. "Never exactly been generous with the praise."

They were quiet again. The night was so still, the sky studded with stars. It felt good, being with Snake again. Just the two of them, away from all the bullshit.

Snake said, "Brings back memories, right?"

"Being out here?"

"Yeah."

Boomer couldn't deny it. Not that he wanted to. "Sure does."

"Remember the one we brought here from El Centro? Eight years ago?"

Boomer nodded, feeling wistful. "That little Latina, Camila. Damn, she was tasty."

"You know I called her."

Boomer looked at him. "Seriously?"

Snake shrugged. "We took her cellphone, remember? I figured she'd have the same number when she replaced it. So I memorized it. Stole a phone and called her after I got out."

"How'd she sound?"

"Sweet."

"What'd you say to her?"

Snake smiled. "What do you think I said?"

Boomer smiled back, thinking of the best song ever. The soundtrack he'd been playing since high school, that he and Snake liked to play even now. "Let the good times roll."

Snake laughed. "Ah, I hate to be so obvious. But yeah. Sang her a verse."

"What'd she say?"

"Oh, you know."

Boomer punched him in the shoulder. "Come on, man, tell me!"

Snake laughed again. "She gasped. Sounded like she was going to choke. Brought it all back, I could tell."

Boomer's mouth felt dry. "And then?"

"Ah, she hung up. But she knew it was me. Knew I was still thinking of her, just like she's still thinking of us. And she always will be, too. Especially anytime she hears that song."

They were quiet for a moment. Boomer realized he hadn't felt this happy in a long time.

"You miss it?" Snake said.

Boomer sighed. "Only every day."

"Guess you can't, what with being a public figure and all."

"Yeah, it has its disadvantages. Plus it wouldn't be the same without you."

"Or as easy."

"Exactly. Look what happened to you the first time you decided to have some fun on your own."

Snake smiled. "Got news for you, brother, it wasn't the first time."

Boomer realized he should have seen that coming. "Whatever. When the shit hit the fan was when I wasn't there to have your back."

"Fair enough. Good lesson for me, I'll tell you that."

They were quiet again. If it hadn't been for the stink, it would have been a beautiful night. All those stars, and the silence, and the endless, empty desert.

Snake said, "How's the Senate race coming?"

For some reason, it made Boomer feel embarrassed. "What, you've been reading about me?"

"Told you, nothing else to do in the joint. Better than jerking off about you."

Boomer laughed. "Yeah, I wouldn't advise that. Anyway, I guess it's going all right. Some ups and downs. Bumps in the road, you know how it is."

"Read you got a 'Me Too' problem. Chick from high school saying you raped her at a party. Big football jock forcing himself on a little cheerleader. Classic."

"Yeah," Boomer said. "Can you believe it? Twenty-plus years ago and she's bringing it up now."

What that bitch Noreen was trying to do to him was so unfair. His advisors were always telling him it was okay to be outraged about it with the media—what man wouldn't be, in the face of such a vile lie? But a lot of that was acting. Because, come on, sure it was vile, but it wasn't exactly a lie, either.

Snake looked at him. "Is it true, though?"

"You're asking me that? Hell yes, it's true."

Snake laughed. "Just messing with you, man. Portrait of the young artist, am I right?"

Boomer shrugged. "Guess you could say that. Bitch sure is causing me some headaches, though."

"Heard she got a bunch of death threats. Had to go into hiding, some shit like that."

"So it seems."

"Damn, Congressman, you must have some seriously devoted constituents."

"Maybe. Don't know if it's going to help, though. She's still giving interviews."

"I don't know. Don't think she's given one in, what, three days now, is that right?"

Boomer looked at him, knowing Snake was up to something, not sure what it was. "What are you not telling me, man?"

Snake pointed toward the water. "I'm parked over that way. Come on. Want to show you something."

They walked southeast, away from the ruins, their boots crunching on the fish-bone beach. In the pale light, Boomer could make out what looked like a panel truck parked at the edge of the water.

They stopped at the back of the truck. Snake pulled open the doors. It was too dark to see inside.

Snake took a mini-light from a pocket, adjusted it to a low setting, and shone it into the back of the truck.

On the floor, behind a row of bench seats, was a woman, trussed and gagged, wearing nothing but a diaper, her eyes wide and terrified.

It took Boomer a moment to understand. "Is that . . . Fuck, is that her? Noreen?"

Snake nodded. "Early Christmas for you, brother."

Boomer's heart started pounding. "Are you kidding me? Christmas? This is going to kill me, man, are you out of your fucking mind?"

"Kill you? How?"

Christ, Snake really was crazy, and though it was one of the things Boomer loved about him, this was too much. The campaign would never survive this. Hell, *he* would never survive this.

"You can't just . . . We can't just disappear someone who's been doing interviews, publicly accusing me of raping her! I'm the first guy the cops are going to talk to!"

"Talk to you about what? You left your phone home like I told you, right?"

"Yes, but—"

"Then you were never here. And Noreen was never here, either. I got a little dinghy in the truck. Picked it up for twenty-three bucks at a Walmart outside Yuma. Weights and chains, too. The usual."

Noreen made some muffled, desperate noises from behind the gag. Snake looked at her. "Remember what I told you about talking, honey. You want me to pull another fingernail?"

But apparently, Noreen was afraid of more than just losing another fingernail, because she shook her head frantically and kept on trying to say something.

"That's a shame," Snake said. "You wouldn't know it, but she's been good for days. The whole ride out here. Only had to pull one nail, right after I picked her up. 'Hiding,' my ass. I'd like to see the bitch who can hide when it's me looking for her."

"You don't get it," Boomer said. "I've got press in my face all the time. Maybe they haven't noticed yet because she's supposed to be in hiding, but at some point, someone's going to report her as missing. And the media's going to be up my ass about it. 'Isn't this just a tad convenient for you, Congressman Kane, your accuser going missing?'"

Snake continued to shine the mini-light at Noreen's face. "Well, brother, I'm just a dumb former GI and ex-con besides, and you're an esteemed congressman and all that, but the way I'd play it if some jerkoff reporter ever suggested Noreen disappearing was convenient for me? I'd say *hell no, it's not the least bit convenient, because her disappearance denies me the opportunity to face my bullshit accuser and clear my good name.*"

Boomer looked at Noreen's face. It was surreal seeing her after all this time, naked and trussed, not least because how many times had he fantasized about something exactly like this since she'd gone public ten days earlier?

"And don't you have contacts?" Snake said. "People who can plant rumors with the media? You know, the disappearance is a stunt she's pulling, to focus attention on you and because she knew her allegations were going to be proven lies. No apologies. You don't give ground. Attack back. Go on offense, brother. Like we always did. And it always worked for us before."

Boomer kept looking at Noreen. Actually, she'd held up pretty well. Even with the diaper, he could tell she'd kept the skinny hips that had attracted him in the first place. The kind that always attracted him. Her tits looked good, too. Maybe partly from the way Snake had trussed her. "Shit, man," he said absently. "You wrapped her like a damn present for me, didn't you?"

Noreen squirmed and tried to say something again. It came out *"Mmmmmmph!"*

Snake laughed. "No one cares, sweetheart."

Boomer rubbed his chin. Now that he thought about it, Snake did have a point. The papers said Noreen was living, where—in Denver, that's right. Boomer hadn't been anywhere near Denver. Hell, other than Fort Carson over ten years earlier, he'd never even been in Colorado. His schedule was always full, his whereabouts easy to prove. If Noreen had disappeared three days ago in Denver, he couldn't possibly have been involved.

Snake said, "You need me, brother. Don't tell me she's the only one."

Noreen shook her head violently. *"Mmmmmmph!"* she said again.

Boomer kept looking at her. It was nice how scared she was. He felt himself getting hard.

He reached out and brushed the back of his fingers against Noreen's cheek. She jerked away as though from an electric shock. He laughed and gripped her by the jaw. Looked into her terrified eyes.

"Noreen," he said. "You really missed me. What do you think, let the good times roll?"

"Mmmmmmmph!" Noreen said. *"Mmmmmmmph!"*

"You want me to inflate the dinghy?" Snake said. "Get this done?"

Boomer turned Noreen's head from side to side. She struggled but couldn't do anything to stop him from moving her the way he wanted.

"I don't know," he said, smiling. "I feel like . . . the night's still young, right?"

Snake laughed and clapped him on the back. "Brother, you read my mind." He reached into a pocket and pulled out an iPod. "Brought some music, too. Just in case."

Damn, if Snake wasn't the best friend ever. Boomer smiled into Noreen's eyes. "All right," he said. "Let's do it. Let the good times roll."

1

"Detective Lone," Chief Best said in her slightly breathless drawl, coming out from behind her desk and heading toward Livia. "Well, aren't you the prodigal."

Livia wasn't sure how to respond, so she stayed at the door and just said, "Chief Best." She saw the embrace coming and, when it arrived, managed not to stiffen. Off the mat, she didn't like to be touched.

"Charmaine, please," Best said, releasing her. "At least when it's just us girls. Come in, come in. Can I offer you some coffee?"

"Water's fine."

"Oh, that's right." She glanced at her admin in the outer office. He was already on his way to the cooler. "Thank you, Lloyd," she called after him.

They walked over to a corner sitting area. Best gestured to the couch, which faced the wall-to-wall window, and took one of the chairs facing inward herself. Livia sat. In the distance, she could see the choppy surface of Elliott Bay, gray in the fall Seattle rain. Offering the view was ostensibly courteous. But of course it was also a way of reminding Livia of the chief's inherent power. It wasn't a coincidence that the wall adjacent to the window was covered with framed photographs of Best—something of a celebrity as SPD's first black female chief of police—with the governor, the mayor, and a dozen other VIPs. There was a reason detectives liked to interview suspects in the station rather than at the suspects' homes, and though chief of police was more chief than police . . . well, once a cop, as the saying went.

"Forgive me," Best said, leaning forward in her chair the way interrogators did to promote a feeling of shared interests. "I've been meaning to congratulate you in person, but it's sometimes hard to get out from under all the political bullshit. Anyway, I'm glad—though not at all surprised—you were cleared in the officer-involved. As open-and-shut a case of a cop righteously defending herself as there could possibly be."

Best was talking about the ambush a month earlier at the martial-arts academy where Livia taught women's self-defense. Livia had killed both attackers with her duty weapon. And because Seattle PD was still operating under a settlement agreement following a DOJ finding of a pattern of excessive force, the investigation had been especially thorough. Still, in the end, the recommendation to clear had been unequivocal, and the Force Review Board had agreed.

"Thank you, Chief. Charmaine."

Lloyd came by with a glass of water, set it down, and left, closing the door behind him.

Best paused for a moment, maybe waiting to see if the silence would induce Livia to add anything. When it didn't, Best said, "Of course, whoever killed those snipers across the river from your apartment could likely have claimed self-defense as well."

Livia nodded, feeling increasingly wary. The "whoever" had been Dox, who she called Carl, the former marine sniper she had partnered with in Thailand and who was now . . . she didn't know what to call it. A friend, certainly. But also a lot more. Carl had anticipated that the same people who'd come at her at the martial-arts academy might deploy a team outside her place as well, and had preempted them.

Livia didn't want to engage, but she knew Best was going to press, and continuing to dodge would have looked suspicious. So she said, "I guess nothing new on who they were, or who might have sent them?"

Best shook her head. "No. Ghosts, just like the two at your self-defense class. No ID, no DNA matches, nothing in the IAFIS. And no one claiming the bodies. Ghosts."

The IAFIS was the Integrated Automated Fingerprint Identification System, a database of criminal and civilian prints maintained by the FBI. And the "ghosts," Livia knew, had been sent by OGE—Oliver Graham Enterprises, recently renamed Percivallian—the world's largest private military contractor.

Livia took a sip of water. "I guess it's not surprising at this point. We can probably assume they were sent as part of the attempted cover-up of that Secret Service child-pornography ring."

"A ring you uncovered. And then blew wide open. You are a force to be reckoned with, Livia."

Livia knew the chief was probing. That was no surprise. It was what might be behind the probes that concerned her. She set down the water glass. "Just doing my job."

Best offered a slight smile. "Well. I think we both know you go far beyond just that."

Livia felt a nervous tightness in her gut. The chief's comment could have been based on almost anything—from nothing more than vague unease; to suspicions about the rapists Livia had tracked down and killed over the years; to how she and her little sister, Nason, had been trafficked as girls from their Lahu village in Thailand, and how Livia had escaped from the people behind it, and discovered what they'd done with Nason, and taken her revenge on all of them, her revenge and Nason's, too.

But all she said was "Charmaine, you're very kind."

Best blinked, maybe surprised her comment had elicited so little. "No," she said after a moment. "I'm really not. I look at you, and I see a cop fearless and determined enough to go after the Secret Service if that's what justice requires. To take on the FBI when they try to cover things up. And who finds a way to expose everyone implicated, surviving multiple assassination attempts in the process. You have nothing but my gratitude and admiration. It's just frustrating we'll likely never learn who was behind your assailants."

Not from me you won't.

"I wish we could learn more, too," Livia said. "But I'll settle for seeing the people involved with that ring punished."

Whether that would happen, of course, remained to be seen. Three exceptionally rich senators and the head of the FBI's Criminal Investigative Division had a lot of resources they could fight back with, and so far they seemed determined to do so.

Best nodded. "Fair enough. And I'll settle for knowing that now that the cover-up has failed, you're safe. Donna was right about that. I owe her an apology."

Donna Strangeland, Livia's lieutenant, had wanted to go public with their suspicions early on, as a way of protecting Livia. Best had overruled her. It interested Livia that the chief hadn't yet gotten around to the apology. It seemed she wanted to have this chat with Livia first.

"Well," Best said, coming to her feet. "I'm glad we got to talk. You are an officer to watch, Livia Lone."

Livia waited until she was alone in the elevator to blow out a long breath. Obviously, Best suspected—but what, exactly? More importantly, what did she know? And why was she holding back?

Well, anytime a cop interrogated a suspect, the questions unavoidably revealed aspects of the cop's case. Maybe Best's reticence was no more than that. The chief had wanted to sweat her, hadn't gotten much, and had ended the interview before revealing more than she wanted to.

But that didn't mean Best wouldn't keep working the case. Or that there wouldn't be more interviews to come.

2

Boomer leaned back in his chair, trying to appear nonchalant. He hoped it was working. It was embarrassing to admit even to himself, but his father always intimidated him. And it had gotten worse since the old man made veep. Now when he came to visit Boomer's San Diego office, there was always an advance Secret Service team checking for bombs, sweeping for bugs, making Boomer feel like a hick. Three of them were combing the room now, and Boomer wondered for a moment whether they'd been told to lay it on extra thick for Boomer, just to remind him of who was the boss.

When it was finally over, the agents walked out, not bothering to close the door behind them. So the old man didn't have to knock. He just strolled right in like he owned the place.

"Admiral," Boomer said, resisting the urge to stand. It was what everyone had starting calling him beginning when he'd gotten his fourth star—even Boomer and his sister. For whatever reason, the title had stuck after the old man had retired from the navy and run for Congress. Reporters called him Mr. Vice President now, but people who knew him from back in the day still used Admiral. Which the prick obviously liked, otherwise he would have issued cease-and-desist orders a long time before.

"Bradley," the old man said, closing the door behind him. He tugged one of the two chairs facing Boomer's desk a foot to the left and then, apparently satisfied, sat in it. Why did he have to do that shit? He just couldn't help himself, he always had to demonstrate some kind of control over other people's spaces. It was like a dog scent-marking its territory. The prick was well into his sixties now, and though he still had the trademark ramrod posture and hit the gym at least three days a week, Boomer could have kicked his ass all over the room if he'd wanted. Which made the damn . . . meekness he felt even more humiliating.

The old man glanced left and right, then at Boomer. "I like what you've done with the place."

Beyond hanging new pictures, Boomer hadn't changed a thing since inheriting the seat six years earlier. *Are you just fucking with me?*

"What are you talking about?" he said, looking around in case he was missing something. "It's practically the same as when it was yours."

The old man smiled. "That's what I like."

He should have seen that coming. He would have, too, if it had been anyone else. But the old man always made him feel like a dumb, awkward kid again.

"Anyway," the old man went on. "I'm in town for a fundraiser. There's money here, but nationally California's a lost cause."

Boomer nodded, waiting for him to get to whatever had really brought him.

"Well," he said after a moment, looking at Boomer closely. "Your polls are looking good, anyway. You think that 'Me Too' woman is going to come out of the woodwork again?"

Boomer looked into the ice-blue eyes. They were especially startling in contrast to the prematurely white hair, and they were a key part of the intimidation effect. When the old man stared, it made you feel you were hooked up to a lie detector. Something you couldn't fool. Something inhuman.

"No," Boomer said. "She's a liar. The whole thing was a stunt engineered by my political enemies and intended to smear me."

The old man gave an exaggerated nod, a pantomime of understanding. "Yes, I believe I've heard that verbatim in several of your television interviews."

Boomer suppressed a surge of irritation. "How many times did you tell me when I took over your seat that I had to stay on message?"

"Quite a few, as I recall. Though I don't recall telling you to sound like a robot, either. It's a delicate moment. Be careful not to come across as callous."

"My media people tell me the opposite. That sensitivity will make me look weak. Even guilty. That outrage at being slimed and slandered is better."

Among those media people, of course, was unofficial advisor Snake. And damn if the crazy bastard didn't have good PR instincts. The professionals had been more detailed in their advice, of course, but substantively everything they'd been telling him tracked perfectly with what Snake had counseled that night at the Salton Sea.

"'Slimed and slandered,'" the old man said. "I remember that from the television interviews, too. The alliteration is catchy, I'll give you that."

"I'll be sure to pass along your praise," Boomer said, trying for defiant, but succeeding mostly in feeling petty.

The old man ignored the jibe, reinforcing Boomer's sense of feebleness. He fixed Boomer with the ice-blue stare. "Are there going to be others?"

Boomer almost said, *How can I answer that, when there are obviously no depths to which my opponents won't stoop in trying to slander me,* which was what his media experts had gamed out in preparation for just such a question. But of course, the line would only elicit another criticism about the dangers of sounding too scripted.

So instead, he just shrugged. "I don't know."

"Because I went to great lengths when you were in high school, cleaning up after your peccadilloes. Noreen Prentis was only one of them. If any more are going to recrudesce, I need to know."

Jesus, the old man and his Naval Academy vocabulary. "I don't know," Boomer said again.

"What are you going to do if it happens?"

"I'll handle it." He was tempted to add, *Like I handled Noreen.* But that would have crossed a line Boomer knew he had to maintain.

"I need you to keep me posted. It's not just you who stands to be affected by this. It's not just me. It's the president as well."

He paused to let that sink in, then continued. "You need his support in this race, Bradley, and if he decides you're radioactive because another half-dozen Noreens are going to start telling their stories, he'll distance himself. If we want to turn out your base in this state— and God knows we need to—we can't have that happen. Do you understand?"

"I understand." Damn it, he hated the way the old man could get him to revert to practically saluting.

"You've made a lot of choices I didn't agree with," the old man said, the eyes boring in. "Skipping college, when you would have been a legacy at Annapolis—"

"I don't have to do everything the way you and Gramps did," Boomer said.

But all it did was make him feel petulant. And give the asshole an opportunity to ignore him.

"And then the army instead of the navy," the old man continued. "Special Forces instead of an intelligence rating."

"It's called an MOS in the army."

"I know what the heathens call it. My point is, it's worked out well for you. You needed the discipline, obviously. And you acquitted yourself admirably. Three Purple Hearts—"

"Enemy Marksmanship Badges."

"—and a Silver Star for heroism in Fallujah. Got a smart name for that one?"

Boomer didn't. Besides, he didn't know where the old man was going with all this, and wasn't even sure why he was pushing back.

"You think I don't know it hasn't been easy, Bradley? What do you think it was like for me at Annapolis, with my own father an admiral?"

Boomer might have said, *Why do you think I didn't want to go there,* but what would have been the point?

"But I climbed higher than he did," the old man continued. "I stood on the platform he built, yes, but I climbed higher. That's the only way to get out from a father's shadow. Do you understand what I'm telling you?"

Boomer shook his head. "No."

"The platform I built, and that you're standing on, is the vice presidency. And if you want to escape from my shadow, you'll have to climb even higher. But you can, son. You can climb that high. As long as you're cognizant of the one thing that can stop you."

For whatever reason, the old man's words weren't encouraging Boomer. They were scaring him. "What?" he said.

"The past," the old man said. "The person you were. Who you no longer are. And who you can no longer be. You're not Hal anymore, Bradley. You're Henry. Remember that. And you can climb higher than almost anyone. Not just anyone in this family. Anyone in history."

Boomer nodded. He felt a little sick. "Okay."

"So if you have reason to believe there are any other skeletons threatening to tumble out of your closet, you need to tell me."

"I don't."

The old man waited a long beat, then stood and started to move toward the door. He had his hand on the knob when he turned back to Boomer and fixed him with the stare. "And while you're at it. Be sure you don't make any new ones."

With that, he turned again and left, closing the door behind him.

Boomer sat for a few minutes afterward, just breathing, willing away the queasy feeling.

Not for the first time, he wondered how much the old man knew. A little, or a lot?

It didn't matter. How to handle it was the same either way. He went to a wall safe, opened it, and took out a burner. It was time to call Snake.

3

Livia sat in front of her laptop, reviewing case notes, her loft illuminated by nothing but the glow of the screen and the ambient light from the container facilities across the Duwamish. It wasn't uncommon for her to be up in the wee hours. She'd struggled with insomnia since she was thirteen, when the men had taken her and Nason. She was used to it, and for the most part no longer fought it. Instead, she would roll off her futon, make herself a snack of yogurt, granola, and berries, and work at the computer, comfortable being awake and alert while the world around her slumbered. And then, as a line of pink began to glow outside the windows, she'd feel tired again and catch another hour or two before heading out to the office.

But tonight, even the work wasn't helping her unwind, and she finally gave up, knowing she had to take care of the thing that was keeping her from sleeping. That she'd been struggling with since getting back from Paris.

She threaded her way among the grinders and lathes and other disused machine tools the building owner stored in the space, opened her safe, and took out the satellite phone. She had bought it per Carl's recommendation, so she supposed it was appropriate that she would use it to call him now. Still, she felt sick about what she knew she had to say.

She walked along the perimeter of the loft to the windows on the north side. She wasn't worried about snipers. There was no line-of-sight to the loft from the north, and besides, the outside glass was too grime coated to see through. She stopped, closed her eyes for a moment, and focused on her breathing, the way she always had before wrestling and judo matches.

It's the right thing. Stop thinking about it and just do it. At least then you won't have to dread it anymore.

But what if the regret was worse than the dread?

She had no answer to that.

She started to turn it all over again in her mind, and stopped herself. She'd been through it more times than she could count. It always ended the same way.

She powered up the unit, blew out a deep breath, and punched in the number.

Two rings, and then the Texas twang: "Hello."

She squeezed her eyes shut, surprised at the pang his voice produced. For a bad second, she thought she might cry, and furiously suppressed the feeling.

"Hey," she said.

"Labee," he said, and she could so clearly imagine his grin. "How are you? Is everything all right?"

"Yeah, mostly. I mean, not like last time."

Last time had been two would-be assassins at one of the martial-arts schools where she taught women's self-defense, and a plane brought down to kill the FBI contractor she'd been working with. She'd called Carl then because she was desperate, so desperate she hadn't even been able to deny it. And while she knew it had been the right thing to do, and a lot of good had come out of it, it had also led to a lot of . . .

complicated things happening between them. Including a plan to meet in Portland. Neutral ground—not her Seattle, not his Bali.

"I sure was hoping you'd call," he said. "I mean, I would have called you, but like I told you in Paris, I know you need your space."

"Yeah." She didn't know what else to say.

There was a long pause.

"Of course I'd like to be wrong," he said, "but . . . I'm getting the feeling this call might be your way of . . . reiterating that."

She grimaced. He loved to play the hick, and the routine could be as disarming as it was convincing, but in fact he was so insightful it sometimes unnerved her.

She tried to think of what to say. What came out was "I'm sorry."

Another pause. "It's all right," he said. "I mean, I won't deny I'm disappointed. And I don't mean to push, but . . . damn, was it just me? I mean, I thought Paris was special. And not just because the two of us killed a whole bunch of bad people again."

She laughed softly. That was another thing about him. He could always make her laugh. Even when she was sad. Even when she was terrified.

The way she was right now.

"Was I wrong?" he said. "I mean, if it was just me, if you don't feel the same way. I know it would be hard for you to say it. But I hope you'll believe me when I tell you, you'd be making it easier on me by being honest."

Just tell him about Chief Best. That you're under a microscope. You have to lay low. You need time. That's all. You just need time.

She understood why she was so afraid. Every wave of happiness she'd ever managed since the men had taken her and Nason had always been followed by an immediate undertow of fear. Fear that whatever she had, whatever was the source of that moment of pleasure, or joy, or delight, it would be ripped away from her again. The way everything else she had taken for granted had been ripped away: her home, her autonomy, the little sister she loved and for whom she had bartered her own teenaged body to try to protect.

She hadn't been this afraid in longer than she could remember. Which she supposed was a measure of . . . how happy Carl made her.

Then tell him that. Just tell him. He's so patient with you. You can trust him.

"Remember you once told me you realized after Thailand you were waiting for me to call?" she said.

"I do. And I was."

She raised her free hand to her mouth, the knuckles pressed hard against her lips.

"Don't anymore. I'm sorry."

She clicked off before he could answer.

Shut down the phone.

Then slid to the floor, her back against the wall, and sobbed, her body shaking with the force of it.

4

Later that morning, Livia was taking care of paperwork in her cubicle at headquarters when her cellphone buzzed. She looked, didn't recognize the number, and answered. "Hello."

"Hey there. Let's not use names just now, okay? I'm close by. I need an hour of your time. Maybe less. Are you at the office now?"

She recognized the confident baritone. B. D. Little, Homeland Security Investigations. The man who had offered her a position with a joint task force investigating Thai human trafficking, a position she'd then used to track down and kill the men who years earlier had taken her and poor, doomed Nason. It turned out Little had known what she would do. Wanted her to do it. And wanted her to do more. He had a tragedy of his own, and Livia was one of the ways he sublimated.

But there would be other ways, too. If she knew anything, she knew that. Little had become an asset, yes, but he was also always a danger.

"Yes," she said.

"Good. There's a Starbucks on the northwest corner directly opposite from where you work. It has four upholstered chairs by the windows. I'll leave a cellphone under the seat cushion of the one closest to the windows and facing the baristas. Get it. Turn off your own phone before you go. Better yet, don't turn it off, and leave it where you are now. I don't want any connection between your phone and the one I'm giving you. Nothing to worry about, just being careful."

Livia had more than enough experience with Gossamer portable cellphone trackers to understand the nature of the precautions. But this level of electronic security was more than Little usually engaged in.

She glanced around. The neighboring cubicles were empty. Still, she kept her voice low. "Five or ten minutes okay?"

"Yes. You'll see that Signal is installed on the unit, and that there's a number programmed into it. Use the number to call me right away, will you?"

Signal was an end-to-end encrypted messaging-and-calling app. What the hell was going on? "Okay."

"The unit I'm calling you from now is a burner. I've used it many times to dial random people. So if anyone ever asks—and they won't—this call you just got was some kind of telemarketer. Okay?"

Livia's training included undercover operations with the anti-gang unit, the instructors for which were former CIA and FBI. Beyond which, she had her own secrets, and knew how to protect them. So she didn't appreciate Little's security primer. But the call was so strange, and his tone so urgent, that she decided to let it go.

"Of course," she said.

"Thank you." He clicked off.

She turned her phone to silent, slipped it into a drawer, and stood to head out. As she eased into her windbreaker, Lieutenant Strangeland came from around the corner. Not for the first time, Livia wondered if the woman was mildly psychic.

"Livia," Strangeland said in her incongruous Brooklyn-transplant accent. "Got a minute?"

"I was just going to grab a coffee across the street. Want me to bring you one?"

"Ah, I'll go with you. Could use a little air. But what do you mean, across the street? No Caffe Vita?"

Strangeland knew Livia was particular about coffee. The lieutenant, by contrast, was all about the caffeine.

"It's raining," Livia said. "Figured I'd just hit Starbucks."

"A little rain getting in the way of a gourmet hot beverage? That's not like you."

Livia should have realized the lieutenant would spot the anomaly—cops couldn't help themselves, and Strangeland was one of the best. But there was nothing suspicious about a quick coffee run, and therefore the question was nothing to worry about.

Livia smiled. "You making fun of me?"

"Only a little. Starbucks works. I'll grab a jacket and meet you in front of the elevators."

Livia headed down the hall. Strangeland coming along wasn't a problem, exactly, but on the other hand, it wasn't good luck, because Little was expecting her call right away. Well, he'd understand that anytime you did something clandestine, the shit-happens factor was always a lot higher. He'd just have to wait. And Livia would have to wait to learn what he wanted.

It was raining harder than Livia had thought, which was fine, as it supported her excuse for the departure from the gourmet-coffee routine. They dashed across the street. As soon as they were inside the Starbucks, Strangeland lowered her hood and said, "I was out yesterday or I would have asked sooner—what did the chief want?"

Yeah, psychic. Or very well informed. "I was going to tell you. Just wanted the coffee first."

"Haven't had any yet?"

Another minor anomaly, and again Strangeland was all over it in an instant.

Livia glanced at the chairs Little had described. They were empty.

"Am I hearing this right?" she said. "You're telling me there's such a thing as enough coffee?"

Strangeland chuckled. "Just don't over-caffeinate if you're facing any follow-up from the chief. Anything she doesn't have under her thumb, she doesn't like."

"You're talking about me?"

Strangeland raised her eyebrows. "Does she have you under her thumb?"

The lieutenant obviously meant the comment at least half in jest, but even so, the notion of being under someone else's control made Livia want to push back hard. Still, she managed to dial down her response to a simple "No."

"Correct. So no, she doesn't like you, she doesn't trust you, and worst of all, she can't figure you out. Why do you think she brought you in without me this time?"

"Yeah, I picked up on that."

"Well, I hope you survived the interrogation."

"I think I did."

"Good. Why don't we enjoy our coffees here, and you can fill me in."

"Sure. Black venti big enough?"

Strangeland chuckled. "Yeah, but I'm buying. And no need to ask, I'll ruin your tall with plenty of milk and plenty of brown sugar. You get us a place to sit."

Livia made a beeline for the corner. But the chairs Little had described were all too far apart from each other to be suitable for the kind of private conversation Strangeland obviously had in mind. Maybe if the place had been full, but it was actually half empty—the rain momentarily depressing the usual Seattle turnout. In fact, there was a perfect open table right in the corner, and it would look odd if Livia didn't take it. And with Strangeland already keyed in on two anomalies, Livia didn't want to risk yet another.

She went over to the empty table and took the chair with a view of the room. Strangeland was focused on paying, but all she would have to do was glance over to catch Livia getting up to retrieve Little's burner. And the island with sugar and milk would keep the lieutenant facing in the same direction.

Nothing to do but wait. And hope no one sat in that chair.

5

Snake sipped his milkshake, glancing up as a couple of teenagers came in from the rain. Just after three o'clock, so Portland schools were getting out. The McDonald's was pretty empty—a geezer Snake made as retired; a broken-down-looking dude who was obviously homeless; and a third, younger guy, staring worriedly at a laptop, who Snake made as recently unemployed—but it looked like there would be a little more traffic now.

Of course, Snake wasn't here for the teenagers. This wasn't the kind of terrain he and Boomer liked for hunting, and it wasn't the right time of day.

He liked the milkshake, though. Vanilla, his favorite. He pulled the straw halfway up through the hole in the plastic cap and licked it clean, then pushed it back down again.

Snake was in town to take care of a woman named Hope Jordan, another of Boomer's high-school conquests. Boomer had told Snake, when they'd finished with Noreen Prentis at the Salton Sea, that there had been other girls in high school who might not have been exactly willing. But Boomer was rich, and popular, and from a powerful family, and most of the girls had convinced themselves afterward that they'd wanted what happened, or at least that it had been their fault and they'd be better off staying quiet. Some of them had even kept on dating him. But there were three, Noreen and Hope and one other who was next on the list, who'd confronted Boomer with words like *consent* and *traumatized* and even *rape*. And nearly caused a major scandal, until Boomer's old man had intervened.

Boomer had resisted at the Salton Sea when Snake had offered to take care of the other two. But Snake knew his friend. Sometimes Boomer could be reluctant at first, but usually he came around. Going down to Campo for a little weekend hunting trip two weeks after the Salton Sea, and taking that sweet little Native American girl, was probably what made the difference. Just reminded Boomer of what they could get away with, and how much Boomer enjoyed it. Made him feel like *Why take chances when my old buddy Snake can make all my problems go away?*

So Boomer had given Snake Hope Jordan's particulars, along with a newer version of one of the cellphone trackers the two of them had used to hunt insurgents in Iraq. And that very morning, Snake had read a text to Hope from her husband, who helpfully reminded her to pick up some kind of muscle-building supplement when she went to Whole Foods later that day. There was only one Whole Foods anywhere close to their house, and Snake had swung by to familiarize himself with the terrain. He liked the parking garage and decided he would do it there. With the tracker, timing his arrival right would be easy.

The hell of it was, Hope hadn't even gone to the press yet. But Boomer thought she might. And what was the man supposed to do, wait for another Noreen and then have Snake deal with her after? Preempting a problem was risky enough. Another woman dying or disappearing immediately after launching accusations against Boomer would have been too much. It was always better to get out ahead of a problem rather than reacting to it after it had already happened.

It had been interesting hearing Boomer reminisce about high school. They'd never talked much about Boomer's childhood, and Snake realized now it was because Boomer was embarrassed by his privileged upbringing. Which was nice, in a weird way, but also kind of funny, because number one, Snake couldn't give a shit, and number two, hell, if he'd had a chance, he would have been happy to grow up privileged himself. It was just that there wasn't a lot of privilege going around in Aliquippa, or in any of the other dying steel towns in western Pennsylvania. The mill that used to support most of the area had closed not long before Snake was born, and locals had a habit of talking about the better times Snake had never known: this or that business that had previously occupied one of the boarded-up buildings on Franklin Avenue, and how there had been three supermarkets instead of a single convenience store, and how once upon a time they hadn't even needed metal detectors at the local high school.

Snake didn't know who his father was, and as far as he was concerned, he didn't have one, just a succession of stepfathers his mother periodically shacked up with. It hadn't been so bad when Snake was little, because his mother, Darla, was pretty and so had more of a choice of men. But no one stayed pretty for long in Aliquippa, especially single mothers with accidental kids and no job skills, not that it mattered much because there weren't any jobs. So Darla had to start fishing in increasingly polluted parts of the pond, and she got good at overlooking just about anything as long as the man in question was putting a little food on the table. Snake learned fast that no matter what he went crying to her with—a bloody nose, a split lip, once two black eyes so bad he could barely see for almost a week—she'd ask what Snake had done to provoke Tyson, or Mick, or Freddie, and tell him whatever it was, he needed to apologize.

Looking back, though, Snake wasn't sorry. His childhood had made him tough. He'd been in his first fight at five, and it was pretty much constant after that until he started training at a local boxing gym at twelve. One of the old-timers, a former merchant mariner named Thomas, had shown him what he could get away with when the referee was out of position: axe punches, guillotine punches, hammer punches. And dirty tricks, with names like the pile driver, the foot breaker, the nodder. It wasn't long before no one wanted to fight Snake anymore, and if he felt like some trouble, he needed to find it in other neighborhoods.

Darla had named him Stephen because she thought Stephen Spencer was a classy name and hoped he'd try to live up to it. So it was funny that two weeks into basic, he'd been christened Snake. During pugil stick training, Snake had beaten a big Georgia cracker named Boyton. Ashamed and in disbelief that a little guy like Snake could have knocked him on his ass, Boyton demanded a two-out-of-three. Snake was happy to oblige, and dropped the dumb fuck even faster the second time.

Snake had known what was coming from the way Boyton kept glaring at him afterward. And right on schedule at chow time, Boyton stalked over to Snake in front of the other recruits, probably thinking that with the padding off now and no rules, he'd get his manhood back. Boyton leaned in, getting in Snake's face, and said, "You think you're tough, you little turd? I'll show you—"

But he hadn't gotten further than that, because Snake jellied his nose with a headbutt, then popped a knee into his balls, then just danced around him, nailing him at will, pounding him to the ground like a lumberjack chopping down a redwood. Boyton was so fucked up from the beating that command placed him in Fitness Training Company, a.k.a. Fat Camp, for rehab. The drill sergeant who witnessed the whole thing wrote it up as a training accident. And everyone started calling him Snake, because he'd hit that headbutt fast as a cobra.

But Boomer . . . Boomer had grown up in a different world. Prep schools, quarterback of the football team, champion wrestler, and with two generations of admirals before him—Bradley Michael Kane Sr. and

Bradley Michael Kane Jr., making Boomer Bradley Michael Kane III. Snake thought having a *III* after your name was actually pretty hilarious, and luckily Boomer didn't mind his giving him a hard time over it. And for all the privilege Boomer was embarrassed about, he was as tough and mean in combat as anyone, even Snake. He'd gotten the nickname in high school because of how hard he'd hit when the football team was playing defense, and it had stuck in the military because of his tendency to blow shit up first and ask questions later. They were a good team. Flexible, mean, fearless. And they had each other's backs. Compared to that, why would Snake give a shit about the man's childhood—his or anyone else's?

Maybe what embarrassed Boomer was that his old man, and the family money and connections, provided a kind of safety net. But why not? Where Snake grew up, there weren't any safety nets—hell, there wasn't any safety, and people tended to settle their problems directly. Certainly no one had ever asked many questions about where young Snake was getting all the bruises and black eyes. But in Boomer's world, people complained and gossiped and sometimes even pressed charges. So as far as Snake was concerned, Boomer was lucky his old man had been able to buy the silence of a few girls Boomer had done. Or threaten them into it, what difference did it make? But then Noreen had gone public all these years later, and now Boomer was worried about the other two on top of it.

Well, he wouldn't have to worry for long.

6

Strangeland set their coffees on the table, shed her jacket, and sat facing Livia. "Okay," she said. "Tell me about the chief."

Livia took a sip of her coffee and nodded her appreciation. She'd been drinking coffee with milk and turbinado sugar since her stepuncle, Rick, had first made her a cup, all the way back when she was a teenager living with the secret of abuse. The combination would always be the taste of the lifeline that Rick, a Portland cop, had subsequently provided her. And a reminder of what she had to live up to.

"For one thing," Livia said, "she thinks I know more about those dead snipers across the Duwamish than I'm letting on."

"She press you on that?"

"No. Just probed, then dropped it."

"Dropped it for now, you mean."

"Yeah."

Strangeland sipped her coffee. "I told you at the time, the amount of evidence you had on hand to prove you weren't there when those snipers were shot—multiple eyewits, credit-card receipts, surveillance-camera footage, cellphone data—might strike someone like Chief Best as so good it had to be planned."

Livia didn't respond. She had known Strangeland would press that point. It seemed the time was at hand.

"And even beyond all that," Strangeland continued, "there's the question of whether you're just supernaturally lucky, or whether it's more like you have some kind of guardian angel. Some serious off-the-books firepower you can call on when the shit hits the fan."

Again Livia didn't respond. The least-worst move was just to wait.

Strangeland took another sip of coffee. "Now don't get me wrong, I'm glad you had all that proof you weren't there. But I don't believe in luck. At least not supernatural levels. So, putting myself in the chief's shoes, I gotta figure you have someone watching your back. Someone good enough to anticipate those two snipers, punch their tickets, and walk away clean."

Livia nodded. "I know how it looks," she said, having gamed out this conversation in advance. "But there's another possibility."

Strangeland raised her eyebrows.

"We might never be able to prove it in court," Livia went on, "but you and I both know those snipers were sent by Oliver Graham and OGE."

"Sure. Working with Arrington at the FBI, trying to cover up the Secret Service child-pornography ring you uncovered."

"Yes. So, look. You know how bureaucracies work. Half the time, the left hand doesn't know what the right hand is doing. Or the left hand knows, or finds out about something, and doesn't like it. There are always factions. And in an organization like OGE, where the factions are all former spooks and Special Forces, they're probably going to do more than just send out interdepartmental memos or whatever when they're not getting their way."

"You're saying the OGE right hand sent those snipers to kill you, and the OGE left hand sent someone else to kill them?"

"Not saying it. Just speculating."

Strangeland didn't respond. She didn't even sip her coffee. She just sat and watched Livia, letting the silence work on her the way the lieutenant would let it work on a suspect.

When it became clear Livia wasn't going to be drawn out, Strangeland drummed her fingers on the table and said, "Is that also your explanation for Oliver Graham getting kidnapped and assassinated in Paris? Factions?"

Livia shook her head. "LT, I really don't know."

"Because, just putting myself in the chief's shoes again, it might start to look like people who come at you—even exceptionally powerful people, capable people—wind up dead. So I don't know. Maybe Chief Best will be mollified by your exculpatory evidence regarding the snipers. But she might wonder whether you have that kind of evidence regarding Oliver Graham, too. She might even hope you don't."

Livia kept her composure. Having gamed this out from the lieutenant's perspective helped. But only so much.

"In fact," Strangeland said, "she might even wonder where you were while you were on administrative leave during the FIT investigation. She might, for example, wonder whether you were in Paris when Graham was killed there. Did she ask you that?"

Livia kept her face expressionless. "No."

"Well, if you were in Paris, and if you were traveling under your own passport, you better hope Best doesn't know someone in CBP who can check immigration records for her."

Livia didn't know whether Best had a friend in Customs and Border Protection. Either way, she couldn't decide whether she should be reassured about Strangeland not asking about Paris, or concerned.

They were quiet for a moment. Livia said, "I didn't kill Graham."

Which was technically true—an exceptionally lethal former black-ops soldier named Larison was the one who had pulled the trigger—but Livia had been there, and she'd been part of it. And having seen the child-torture videos Graham had been trying to conceal and exploit, she certainly would have done it herself if Larison hadn't.

"Yeah," Strangeland said, way too good a cop to be deflected by something as weak as that. "But you didn't kill those snipers, either."

They were quiet again, sipping their coffees. A young guy, an office-worker type with a security keycard dangling from a neck lanyard, sat in the chair where Little had hidden the phone. Of course.

Strangeland said, "One more thing you might want to hope the chief doesn't look into."

Livia was cool under pressure. Cold, even. She'd developed the trait over a lifetime: as a state-champion high-school wrestler; as an Olympic alternate with the US judo team in college; as a survivor, a cop, a killer.

But she could feel the lieutenant's probes, and her pauses were beginning to have an effect. She understood the pressures: suspects almost always knew better than to talk, but they told themselves that silence made them look guilty, and so they talked anyway, and talking made them talk more, inconsistencies prompting even more inconsistencies in an attempt to fix what should never have been broken to begin with, until finally the lies unraveled and the truth spilled out.

She reminded herself of who she was. The lieutenant could make whatever she wanted of her silence. What mattered was not damning herself with words.

Strangeland was looking at her. Livia raised her eyebrows questioningly. Strangeland waited another moment, perhaps in recognition of Livia's cool, then nodded.

"You better hope she doesn't start looking into where else you've been in the last year or so. Like, say, Thailand, while you were trying to decide whether to join B. D. Little's international anti-trafficking task force. Or what might have happened while you were in Bangkok and just after. If she does, she might find out about a shootout and an explosion at the Rot Fai Night Market. A dead trafficking kingpin named Rithisak Sorm who was apparently burned alive. Another named

Leekpai. About a half-dozen dead Royal Thai police, one of whom also seems to have been burned alive. And a war between Thai and Ukrainian trafficking gangs that's still going on."

Livia nodded. She shouldn't have been surprised at how much the lieutenant knew. In a weird way, it was almost a relief.

Of course, that, too, was part of being a good interrogator. Making the suspect believe you knew more than you really did. That you knew everything. That therefore there would be no harm in confirming a few trivial details.

Livia dropped her head and looked at the table. No matter what happened, she wasn't going to help anyone make a case against her. Ever.

"LT," she said, "I'm not sure what you're getting at. I wish you'd just tell me."

This time, Strangeland didn't wait. She just sighed and said, "I'm telling you that pretty much anything I can put together, so can the chief. The difference is, knowing you were in Thailand, it occurred to me to check the *Bangkok Post* online and see if anything interesting might have happened while you were in town. If the chief doesn't know you were there, she won't make that connection. We'll see."

Livia didn't look up. She'd worked so hard and been so careful. But still it felt like it was all closing in around her.

"The other difference," Strangeland went on, "is that I'm your friend. I have your back. And I love you, Livia. I love the cop you are and the person you are. You quote me on that, I'll deny saying it. And it won't show up in your fitness reports. But you're an officer worth protecting, and I'm damn well going to try to protect you. I don't need to know everything about you. I don't *want* to know. What matters, I already do know."

Livia looked at her, and realized instantly it was a mistake. Pressure she could take. Cruelty she could endure. But kindness always undid her. She looked away and blinked back the tears.

"But the chief," Strangeland said, pretending not to have noticed Livia's reaction. "That's another thing entirely. You're one of her officers. Her subordinates. In the world as she understands it, she has more power than you. She has power *over* you. And yet you've got some sort of mysterious connections, or capabilities, most people could only dream of. That's not going to make Chief Best happy for you. It's going to make her fear you. Cops don't like mysteries generally. But the mystery you present to the chief . . . she's not going to just accept it. She's not going to let it alone. She's going to look to take you down."

Livia blew out a long breath. Then another. When she felt composed again, she looked at Strangeland. "What does that mean for the people who have my back?"

Strangeland smiled. "I told you. Best and I already have our issues."

"Yeah, but this is going to make it worse."

"Well, you're not wrong about that."

"What can I do?"

Strangeland shrugged. "You make it sound like it must be something complicated. But it's actually pretty simple. You take it easy for a while. Just be a cop. Be *just* a cop, you understand what I'm saying? No more exotic travel destinations. No more officer-involveds. No more bodies near your apartment. Just make cases. Speak for your victims. Put rapists in prison, where they belong. That's all you have to do. Nothing else. Meaning just that. Nothing. Else. Rope-a-dope for long enough and even Best will get tired. You follow?"

Livia nodded. "Thanks, LT."

"Don't thank me. This isn't just for you. People know I'm a fan. Meaning heat for you becomes heat for me. And I don't like heat. It's why I moved out here, where it's rainy and cold ten months out of the year."

Livia smiled. "I thought you moved out here for Mia." Mia was Strangeland's wife, a trauma surgeon Livia had met while staying at their house after the martial-arts-academy attack.

"Yeah, well, maybe that too. But you get my meaning."

"Completely."

"You told me after Thailand you'd exorcised your demons. Was that maybe a little optimistic?"

Livia looked away. "Maybe."

"Then get help if you need it. A department shrink if you feel comfortable going that route. Outside the department otherwise. I'd say talk to me, but that's obviously not going to happen."

Livia looked at her. "I wouldn't do that to you, LT."

"Yeah, I know. I guess I appreciate it. Or at least where it's coming from. Anyway. Keep your cards close. If you get pressed, play it the way you just played it with me. It doesn't matter what Best knows, only what she can prove. Now give me a minute—I need to use the ladies' room, and then we ought to get back."

Strangeland grabbed her jacket and walked off. As soon as she was inside the restroom, Livia got up and walked over to the guy in Little's chair, who was texting on a cellphone.

"Excuse me," Livia said.

The guy looked up and gave her a weirdly knowing smile. "I thought I saw you noticing me," he said. "And I won't lie, I noticed you back."

"I'm flattered," Livia said, thinking *Why is nothing ever simple?* "But it wasn't you I was noticing. It was the chair. I was sitting here earlier, and I think I might have lost my cellphone in the cushions. You mind if I have a quick look?"

The smile broadened. "I will if you give me your number."

Livia briefly considered dragging him out of the chair and throwing him into a table. But she had to do this smoothly. She didn't want Strangeland to see another anomaly. Maybe she should just come back later. Of course, the longer she waited, the greater the chance that someone might stumble across Little's phone.

"Let me look first," Livia said. "Make it fast and we'll see."

The guy came leisurely to his feet, then turned and started digging under the seat cushion. "Hmm, not finding anything," he said.

Livia edged a shoulder in front of him, dropped her level, and pivoted her hips. The guy went stumbling backward. "May I?" she said, as sweetly as she could.

"Well, sure," the guy said from behind her, obviously confused about how the little Asian woman had moved him so far and with no apparent effort. "I mean, you don't have to get pushy."

Livia pulled the seat cushion off the chair. Immediately she saw a clamshell unit wedged under the back cushion. She grabbed it, stuffed the seat cushion back in place, shoved the burner into a jacket pocket, and zipped the pocket closed. She turned and gestured to the chair.

"All yours," she said.

The guy looked at her, his expression uncertain. Part of him had probably decided he didn't want her number after all. Another part was probably telling him that if he didn't insist, he was being a pussy or whatever. After all, didn't he have a right to ask for her number? And hadn't they made a deal on top of it?

"So . . . you going to give me your number?" the guy said, the dumb in him winning out over whatever smart there might have been.

Livia glanced at the name on the keycard hanging from his neck. "Trust me, Bryce," she said. "You don't want it. Thanks for helping me find my phone. You have a good day."

She looked up. Strangeland had come out of the restroom and was watching. *Shit.*

Livia headed over to where she was standing. "What was that about?" Strangeland asked, eyeing the guy.

Livia kept moving, and Strangeland turned to follow. "Nothing. Bored guy, hitting on me."

Strangeland chuckled. "You must get that constantly. I'll tell you, it's one of the advantages of getting old. They leave you alone."

"LT, you're not that old."

Strangeland chuckled again. "Yeah, I was never that young, either. Not as young as you."

Back at headquarters, Livia tried to concentrate on paperwork. She'd go out again in a bit to call Little. Too soon after getting back from a quick coffee run would present another anomaly.

But she was having trouble focusing. She was too concerned about what Best might be up to. About how much Strangeland seemed to know, and how knowing it was putting the lieutenant in a compromising position.

Most of all, about what the hell Little wanted.

7

Snake hung back at the edge of the Whole Foods parking garage, placing a few food items he'd picked from the trash into a shopping bag as though this was the most important task in the world. The dirty hoodie, jeans, and boots he was wearing were versatile: near a work site, they might say day laborer; in a park or near a trail, they indicated hiker; picking through trash, they could only mean homeless.

Of course, Snake wasn't relying on just the hood to obscure his features. He never went anywhere without some additional items for disguise—facial hair, prosthetic nose, eyeglasses, you name it. A little makeup like that, a hoodie, a bunch of sweatshirts under a jacket to add thirty pounds, a pebble in your boot to change your gait . . . and your own mother could walk right past you and not even realize it.

He had to admit, the instructor the army had brought in to teach urban disguise had known her shit. "We always approach disguise like an onion," the woman, a CIA specialist named Kim, had explained. "Whether we're building it or peeling it off. Enough layers one way or the other, and you disappear—and another person takes your place." Snake had been skeptical at first, but seeing how much the woman could do with just a few simple tricks had been a revelation.

A revelation, and so useful, too.

Of the various possibilities, homeless was Snake's favorite. Civilians didn't like to look at homeless people—it embarrassed them about their own good fortune. So as long as you avoided eye contact yourself, which was typical behavior for the homeless when they weren't actively panhandling, you were practically invisible to passersby. Cameras would pick you up, sure, but with what he'd learned from Kim and practiced on his own, the cameras just recorded someone else.

He glanced up, and there she was—Hope Jordan, no question, the same woman he had checked out in the online photos. Short brown hair, slender, legs looking good in a pair of yoga pants. Boomer's age, of course, but she looked younger. Took good care of herself, like Noreen had. Snake had to hand it to Boomer, the man had good taste.

The shopping cart the woman was pushing had a kid in it, a little boy, it looked like, maybe two years old, his legs dangling through holes at the front of the cart. Snake wasn't surprised. Married, late thirties . . . he'd figured it was possible she'd have a kid with her when she did the grocery shopping, or maybe two. It didn't really change anything. Might even be an advantage.

She pressed a button on a key fob and the hatch of her car, a Volvo SUV, opened with a beep. She spent a minute getting the groceries inside, then pressed another button. As the hatch closed, she pushed the cart over to a designated return area, the little boy still in it. A good citizen, not leaving the cart in an empty parking space like so many people did. And a good mother, too, not wanting to leave her little boy alone in the car while she returned the cart, not even for a minute. That was good to know.

She hoisted the boy out of the cart and carried him back to the car, pressing another key-fob button on the way. A double beep. She opened the rear passenger-side door and spent a minute strapping the little boy into a car seat. Snake looked around. There were a few other people coming and going, but no one paying any attention to their surroundings. After all, what could ever happen in a suburban Portland grocery garage?

The woman closed the back door and started around to the other side. No new beeps. Meaning she'd unlocked all four doors to get her boy in, and hadn't bothered relocking them after. But why would she? All that unlocking and relocking and unlocking would be a pain in the ass. She was too careful to leave the boy alone, sure, but locking the doors again when all she was doing was getting in the car herself? That would have been too much. Once she was inside the car, though, that might be a different story. Some people were pretty quick to lock the doors the second they were inside. Especially if they had a kid with them.

Snake ghosted in, making sure to time it right. The woman opened the driver's door, stepped in with her right foot, lowered herself, sat—

As Snake reached the front passenger-side door, he could see her through the window, turned to face her own door, grabbing the handle, pulling it toward her—

Snake opened the passenger door and popped inside, the Ruger Boomer had given him pointed at her. It was the SP101 chambered in .22 LR—not as quiet as a suppressed pistol, of course, but quiet enough, and with the advantage of not ejecting shells the police would collect later.

The woman finished closing her door by reflex and spun toward Snake, flinching when she saw him and gasping, her face contorting in panic. Snake leaned away, reached across his body with his left hand, and pulled his door closed. Keeping the Ruger low and close to his torso, he said, "Don't make a scene. I want you to withdraw money from an ATM. That's all."

There were a lot of variations, but social engineering always came down to giving the person something to hope for, something to believe in. The impression that what was happening was just a transaction, a kind of contract with an acceptable price and a reasonable expectation of performance by the other party. Sure, the other party was offering terms at gunpoint, but under stress most people clung to their everyday beliefs, including the belief that their fellow humans could generally be counted on to carry out promises. The alternative—an acceptance of imminent mortal jeopardy, and a recognition that the only way to avoid it was the risk, the utterly unfamiliar notion, of fighting back—was hard and scary. By comparison, clinging to everyday beliefs was easy and comforting. The instructors who had schooled Snake in the fine arts of extraordinary rendition, otherwise known as kidnapping, had taught him this and more, and he'd learned it was all true.

The woman glanced at the gun, her eyes bulging. The Ruger wasn't particularly large, but Snake knew what she was seeing: something the size of a cannon, the muzzle pointing directly at her heart.

"I'm just an old friend," he said quietly, calmly. He glanced back at the kid. The kid was holding a toy, some kind of puzzle, but he was looking at Snake. Snake gave him a reassuring smile, then looked back at the woman. "That's so nice that we ran into each other. Old friends, right? And you're going to give me a ride to the bank. Okay? Just a ride to the bank."

She nodded.

"Good. I don't want to scare anyone. And I won't hurt anyone unless you give me a reason. You're not going to do that, are you?"

She shook her head. Her hands were shaking.

"Say it."

She swallowed. "I won't give you a reason."

Fuck. He felt himself getting hard. It was the way she obeyed so quickly. And how afraid she was. It was her son, he knew. She'd do anything to protect her little boy. The thought made him harder.

"That's good. Then fifteen minutes from now we'll be done with this. What's your name?"

"H-Hope."

"Okay, Hope. Put your seatbelt on. Come on, go ahead."

She couldn't do it—her hands were shaking that badly. She stabbed the buckle at the insert three times, missing consistently. She started to hyperventilate.

"Hope," Snake said. "I told you, don't give me a reason, and you and your little boy are going to be fine. Right? Go ahead, you can do this."

She nodded, blew out a couple of long breaths, and managed to get the seatbelt buckled. Snake buckled his, too. He would have preferred to leave it off for greater freedom of action, but he'd seen a movie once where a woman had convinced the guy holding her up to take off his seatbelt, and then rammed her car into a tree. The seatbelt and the airbag had saved her. The guy had gone through the windshield.

"Good girl. Now press the door-lock button."

She did.

"Okay, start the car. Come on."

She pressed the ignition button and the car started up smoothly.

He loved this. Was Simon Says the best game ever?

"Make a right when we get to the street," he said. He didn't want her to have to cut across traffic yet—she was still too shaky. Better to give her a minute to get her shit together.

She glanced back at her boy as though to make certain he was still there. Then she blew out another long breath, put it in reverse, and started backing up.

Half a minute later, they were out on the street. She'd gotten the shaking under control, probably in part from having the steering wheel to clamp on to. The windshield wipers had come on automatically. Snake liked the rhythmic *thump-thump, thump-thump* they made as they swiped away the rain.

"Good job," Snake said. "We're going to make a left now. On Forty-Fifth Street. Use your turn signal."

"But my bank—"

"We're not going to your bank. There's a branch I like better. Turn signal, Hope. Now."

She did as he said, and a moment later, they were heading north on a quiet, tree-lined street, nothing but neat lawns, driveway basketball hoops, and wet leaves raked into neat piles alongside curbs.

Snake had reconnoitered the area, of course, and the place he was taking them was a construction site—a halfway-done McMansion project that had obviously come to a standstill some time earlier, probably because someone ran out of money and the contractor had stopped work. The site was at the end of a cul-de-sac, lots of trees, all the houses set way back, a long gravel driveway. Private. Discreet. The kind of spot he and Boomer always looked for when they were traveling and couldn't go to the Salton Sea. It had actually gotten to the point where Snake would get aroused just driving by one of these places, he didn't even have to have a girl with him.

Although today, of course, he did.

He reminded himself it was supposed to be just a carjacking gone bad. That's what he and Boomer had discussed, and it made sense. But . . . fuck. He was so turned on. Had he known what maybe he was planning? He'd told himself he scouted the site just to have a quiet spot to kill her. But now he wondered.

You're a bad man, he thought. He would have smiled at himself, but she was doing well and he didn't want to scare her.

They came to the end of the street. "Left here," he said. "Use your turn signal. Then bear right."

He knew she wanted to ask where they were going. But she didn't. She was too afraid. Oh, goddamn. He was so turned on.

She followed his directions for another few minutes. Snake looked back at the kid. He was playing with his puzzle or whatever.

They came to the driveway of the construction site. "Pull in," Snake said.

The woman glanced in the rearview at her boy. "Where are we?" she said, one kind of fear getting the better of another. "What are we doing here? You said a bank. The ATM."

She was shaking again. Her instincts were okay, actually, she just should have listened to them sooner. It wasn't her fault, though. Not really. It was how the brain worked. She knew this was bad now, even worse than she'd admitted to herself at the beginning. The problem was, she'd made it this far by cooperating. And now her brain was saying, *I'm cooperating, and I'm not dead. So cooperating must be the right thing to do. If I keep doing it, it'll keep me alive.* It was a loop, and once it started, it was hard to get out of. She would have been better off saying no right at the outset. Negotiate, fight, whatever. No one should ever go to a secondary crime scene. The only reason a bad guy wants a secondary crime scene is rape, torture, or murder. Or some combination. And yet. Even people who understood all that had a hard time accepting it when it counted. The brain. What could you do?

Yeah, it really wasn't her fault. A weird part of him wanted to tell her that. Well, maybe he still would.

"I need to pick up my stuff," he said. "Then the bank, then I'm gone." He motioned with the Ruger. "Go on. Pull in."

She did. They rolled along, rain pattering on the roof of the car, the wipers going *thump-thump, thump-thump*, gravel crunching under the tires. The driveway slowly looped to the back of the site. The framing on the exterior of the house was mostly done, but the garage doors hadn't been hung yet. Three gaping holes in the back of the unfinished structure, the interior too dark to see clearly from the car.

Snake gestured with the Ruger. "Drive in. Out of the rain."

The woman shook her head. "You can have my purse," she said, her voice getting higher. "My wallet. I'll tell you my ATM number. You can take the car, go to the bank yourself—"

"Pull in," Snake said, his tone deadly calm. "I'm going to get my stuff, and then we'll go to the bank together. You're not going to give me a fake ATM number."

"The number is 5-9-5-9. I'm telling you the truth."

Snake glanced at the boy. He was looking up from his puzzle, his expression concerned bordering on frightened. He'd picked up on his mother's distress, obviously. Well, it didn't matter now.

Snake looked into her eyes. Since getting in the car, he'd been trying to project a reassuring, businesslike vibe. But he dropped that now. He wanted her to feel the fear. All of it.

"Pull into the fucking garage, Hope," he said. "You really don't want to make me ask again."

The boy started crying. The woman did, too. But she crept forward, out of the gray daylight, into the shadowy space before them. The patter of the rain ceased. The wipers stopped, too. In the sudden silence of the car's interior, Snake imagined he could hear the pounding of her heart.

He took out the iPod and hit "Play." *Sorry, Boomer,* he thought, so hard now it hurt. *I promise, man, this will work, too. Maybe even better.*

8

That night, Livia walked with Little along a dim path in Fremont Canal Park, a strip of green paralleling the narrow waterway separating the neighborhood of Fremont from Queen Anne in Seattle.

Little hadn't been irritated about the delay. His primary concern, he said, was that they be cautious. And even though they'd been talking on two burners, he'd used oblique references to make her understand the meeting point would be the Theo Chocolate factory in Fremont, just before closing time. From there, it had been a short stroll to the dark beside the water.

They walked in silence, their breath fogging in the chill air. Livia waited, wondering what this was about, not wanting to seem eager by asking. Finally, Little stopped and looked at her, his gaze intense behind the trademark green plastic-framed eyeglasses.

"Thank you for meeting me," he said. "And I'm sorry for all the precautions."

Livia checked behind them. The park was deserted.

"What's going on?" she said.

There was a long pause, punctuated by nothing but the lapping of water on the muddy bank to their left and the crunch of dead leaves beneath their feet. Livia had the sense Little was collecting himself.

"I told you about my daughter," he said.

Little's daughter was named Presley. About ten years earlier, when she was fifteen, she had disappeared while walking to the neighborhood grocery store to buy popcorn for a movie she was going to watch with her parents. Little had shown Livia a photograph from his wallet. A beautiful black girl with a radiant smile, her arms wrapped around her beaming father's neck.

"Yes," Livia said, feeling wary.

"I told you what it's like," he said. "With resources like mine, and still not able to find her. Or to find out . . . what happened to her."

They came to the end of the park. Beyond them, the grounds of the Lakeside Industries asphalt plant were spotlighted in frozen white. Little stopped in the shadow of some trees and flipped up the collar of his suit jacket. He left the jacket open, though. Buttoning it would have slowed access to the pistol Livia knew he carried in a waistband holster.

Little turned and looked at her. In the mottled darkness and light, his eyes were large and seemed haunted. Livia took in the bags under them, and realized the man seemed not just tired, but older than when she'd last seen him, only a month earlier.

"The men who took her," he said. "They're back."

"What do you mean?"

But what she meant was *What do you want from me?*

"The night she went out to rent that movie, Presley was on her way to the grocery store about a half mile from where we lived. A creek on one side. Houses set far back on the other. Just getting dark, and people home from work. Not much car traffic at that hour on that winding neighborhood road, and even fewer pedestrians. A perfect time and place to snatch a teenaged girl, if that's what you were of a mind to do."

Livia said nothing.

"It might have been a lone wolf," he went on, "choosing his time and place, but still getting lucky no one noticed him lurking, or got a plate or a vehicle description, or saw him dragging a struggling girl into a car."

His voice broke and he paused. She remembered him saying to her: *How many people, Livia, how many people could look you in the eye like I am right now and say, "I know what you've been through? What you're going through"? Well, I can. And I do.*

He wasn't wrong. The problem was that it went both ways.

He cleared his throat. "But it wasn't a lone wolf. It wasn't someone impulsive, or lucky."

Livia watched him warily. "Why do you say that?"

"Because for four years after, I practically lived inside ViCAP and databases like it. Over time, I identified seven similar disappearances. A pattern. And the pattern didn't involve a singleton. It's two men. And they're not lucky. They're methodical. This is no hobby for them. It's what they do."

ViCAP was the FBI's Violent Criminal Apprehension Program, a database the Bureau had established in 1986 and ran out of Quantico.

"Why do you think two?" Livia said, the cop in her momentarily pushing aside her other concerns. She didn't have to ask why he assumed it was men. It was virtually unheard of for this kind of crime to be committed by a woman.

"Because one wouldn't be enough to pull it off so consistently. Too much luck required. You wouldn't be able to control the terrain—monitor for potential witnesses and other problems. And it would take too long. You'd have to subdue a struggling kid, restrain her, keep her from crying out, get her into your vehicle. Then drive off. Maybe you could get away with it once. Twice. Hell, three times. But not eight. And it's almost certainly more than eight, because you and I both know if there were eight in ViCAP, there are probably another dozen that didn't get filed."

Livia knew he was right about that. ViCAP was a good idea, but so many local cops didn't bother to upload their cases that using it was hit or miss, more often the latter.

"Why two men?" Livia said, already knowing the answer. "Why not three?"

"Not impossible, but unlikely. Three's an unstable number. And the chances of three men being this evil and still managing to trust each other and work together so efficiently over time doesn't feel right to me. You see it differently?"

She knew he was trying to draw her in. Unfortunately, he didn't need to.

"No, from what you've told me, I see it the same. But . . ."

He looked at her. "Don't you worry about my feelings. Ever. It's your insights I need."

She nodded, wondering what he wanted in addition to the insights. "It would be a lot faster, and a lot easier, to kill the victim at the point of contact. That would be unusual, but it's not impossible, and if that's how it happened, you could be talking about a singleton."

Little shook his head and clenched his jaw. His nostrils were flared, heat in his eyes. He looked like someone barely keeping it together. Someone dangerous.

"No blood," he said. "No shell casings. No sound of gunshots ever reported. Killing someone that fast and leaving nothing behind would itself require too much luck over time. They're not killing their victims right away. They kill them later."

Livia nodded. "Agreed as far as it goes. But you're basing all this just on what you learned from ViCAP?"

"Of course not. When something looked similar to what happened to Presley, I made phone calls to local law enforcement. Most of the time, what I'd learn from the call suggested a false positive. But when the details sounded sufficiently promising, I'd travel to the crime scene. Talk to the family and other potential leads. Walk the terrain. They all happened at about the same time of day—just as it was getting dark. Always on a quiet neighborhood street with few houses and a convenience store or bodega the girl was heading to on foot. Nothing ever found. No DNA at the scene. No body recovered. Just eight girls, each on an evening walk to the neighborhood store, vanished into thin air. Taken by the only people on Earth who know what happened to my little girl—because it's the same two men who did it."

Livia zipped up the neck of her fleece. "You mind if we keep walking? I didn't realize we were going to be outside."

He shook his head as though to clear it. "I'm sorry. Just . . . forgot myself."

They headed the other way, the leaves crunching again, the water to their right now. Yeah, he was strung out. She had to handle him with caution. Someone drowning will grab on to anything, even a rescuer.

"Don't worry about it," Livia said. She glanced at his midsection. "You have a little more insulation than I do."

He chuckled. "Don't I know it. Wasn't always this way, you know. But yeah, my college football days are behind me."

"You said the men are back. What do you mean?"

"I mean, the disappearances went on for four years after Presley. Two predated her. Five came after. And then they just . . . stopped. Like someone threw a switch."

"You check arrest records?"

He glanced at her. "You talking down to me?"

"Just being thorough."

"Good answer. Anyway, hell yes I checked arrest records. It's the first thing I thought of. Anyone, anywhere arrested for anything remotely like kidnapping teenage girls. Nothing fit. Whatever made them stop, it wasn't that."

"And now it's started again?"

"Yes. And no, you don't have to ask. I searched again—this time, in every goddamn database there is for records of imprisonment *and* release. I searched for everything. I searched for fucking tax evasion. Anything that could explain these two, or one of them, being out of business because they were in prison for the seven years in question. And there's nothing that matches. Whatever stopped them, it wasn't because they were doing time."

They walked in silence for a moment while Livia considered. "Tell me about the latest disappearance," she said, deliberately using *disappearance* instead of *victim* to maintain a degree of critical distance. She was aware the expression of interest might encourage him, but she didn't see an alternative. What concerned her more was how easily he was drawing her in. He knew her past, knew what buttons to push. And he had a lot on her. So far, he'd never used it. But how well would reluctance hold up against desperation?

"Another teenaged girl," he said. "Two weeks ago, in Campo, California. And she fits the pattern."

Livia didn't think the pattern Little had described was nothing. But she didn't think it was enough to believe the perpetrators were the same, either. The problem was, Little *wanted* to believe. And how could he not? He was desperate for a link to Presley, a salve against the omnipresent background agony of just not knowing. She'd lived that horror for sixteen years, and knew how it could distort cognition. The trick would be finding a way to push back that would get past Little's defenses.

"I know what you're thinking," he said. "I'm strung out. Desperate. Seeing lakes in the desert because I'm dying of thirst."

She should have realized he'd be smart enough to see it from her perspective. "Only because I know how it is," she said softly.

"Fair enough. But there's more. The one in Campo was a Native American girl. Of the other eight, four were black, three were Latina, and one was Native American."

"That's more of a pattern, okay, but—"

"Hear me out. Every one of the nine—because it's nine now, and it's going to be more if we don't do something about it—has been taken from a lower-income neighborhood. What do you make of that? Combined with the fact that all nine are minorities?"

Livia caught the *we*. Ordinarily, that kind of forced teaming pissed her off, but given Little's state, she decided to let it go.

"Well," she said, "if I were abducting teenaged girls and didn't want more police attention than absolutely necessary, I'd probably steer clear of white girls from affluent neighborhoods."

"Exactly. The last thing you'd want would be to take the daughter of a man who was rich enough or connected enough to bring unusual investigative resources and stamina to bear."

"In which case, they got unlucky with you."

"Not until I catch them they didn't."

There was a furtive movement near the embankment. Little stopped and peered over, his hand slipping inside his jacket. A skinny, whiskered man wearing a shoulder pack eased back into the gloom.

Livia put a hand on Little's shoulder. "Homeless," she said. "Come on."

They kept walking. Livia glanced at him. "I need to pressure-check. Okay?"

"I told you. More than okay."

"When a teenaged girl disappears with no evidence of a crime, the most common reason is—"

"Is that she's a runaway. But there are upwards of two million runaways every year. They don't get entered into ViCAP. Anyway, believe me, I've ruled out hundreds of runaways. Usually with no more than a few phone calls. I talk to local law enforcement, talk to the parents, the teachers, the coaches . . . You know how it is, you can read between the lines pretty quickly most of the time. But these nine, including Presley, they weren't troubled. No alcohol or drug use, no suicidal tendencies, no mental illness . . . none of the risk factors. They were good kids, with good grades, good relationships with their parents. Some of them were athletes, they had part-time jobs, they were applying to colleges. One of them—literally—was a candy striper. They weren't runaways. They were stolen. By the same two men."

They walked in silence again. Yes, Little was motivated to believe, and his theories had to be discounted accordingly. But was she motivated by the opposite? She didn't want to be involved. Couldn't afford to be, after her conversation with Chief Best and the advice—or call it a plea—from Strangeland. Was she looking for a way to downplay Little's theories to slip loose from whatever he wanted of her?

"Look," Little said. "You could replicate my work. Start with ViCAP. Cross-reference with the National Center for Missing and Exploited Children. Identify teenaged girls who disappeared without a trace. Screen out the runaways. You'll be left with the same nine I'm looking at. Each of which shares too many parameters with the others for coincidence to be the explanation. Or even if I have one or two false positives, hell, even if *half* are false positives, there's a pattern here. Can't you see that? Even discounting how emotional I am, can't you see it? You were emotional about your sister, but in the end weren't you still able to find out what happened to her?"

In any other circumstances, someone invoking Nason's memory as a means of manipulation would have set Livia off. But she felt Little's pain so acutely that his attempt barely riled her.

"There were things I could see," she said, trying not to remember. "And a lot I was missing."

"Fine. I'm sure it's the same for me. That's why I need your help."

She realized he'd anticipated her response, and she'd walked right into the setup. Little's pain was so close to her own trauma that it was throwing her off her game.

"I'm not the most objective person when it comes to missing teenaged girls," she said, still looking for a way out.

"I don't want your objectivity. I want your ferocity."

And there it was. "For what?"

"I can't investigate the girl from Campo. I made some calls, calls that confirmed she fits the pattern. So I applied for leave and was granted it, and then they shut me down."

"Shut you down? Who?"

"My boss, Ronald Tilden, the head of HSI's Human Smuggling and Trafficking Center. He knows my past, and my obsessions, and he's never denied me leave before. Something's going on."

"Come on, B. D.—"

"Don't *come on* me, Livia. I'm not being paranoid. You think I don't know how messed up I am? I've been living it every day for almost a decade. It doesn't mean my instincts no longer apply. I could tell something was up. 'We need you here, B. D., I have some unspecified bullshit I'm going to send your way.' Oh, and 'The budget's too tight for anyone not assigned to Islamic terrorism,' which doesn't make any goddamn sense either because I was asking for leave, not a per diem. On top of which, he looked scared."

"Scared of what?"

"How the fuck do I know? Someone got to him, that's all I'm sure of. Maybe it was the indictments I backed for those child-pornography senators. That earned me a lot of enemies, especially because everyone knows, even if they can't prove it, that I was behind some of the leaks that made the indictments politically impossible to stop. Maybe it's something else. I don't know yet."

"This is why . . . the burners? All the precautions?"

"Yes."

"You think someone is monitoring you."

"Yes. Otherwise, why would they shut me down?"

"Why would anyone want to interfere with your investigation of a missing teenaged girl?"

"Why would anyone have interfered with your investigation of a child-pornography ring? Because the investigation threatened other interests that at the outset you couldn't see. But this is actually good news. Because the fact that someone has taken an interest, that someone's trying to stop me . . . it could open up a whole new avenue to investigate. This might be the most important development I've ever had, don't you see?"

It was impossible to say how much of what he was telling her was real, and how much was the result of something in his mind beginning to unravel. She understood—there were times during her sixteen-year search for Nason that she had come to doubt her own sanity. But those doubts hadn't been without reason.

She considered. Maybe there was a way to help him without putting herself at risk. "The pattern," she said.

"What about it?"

"I once heard about an intelligence program. Something the CIA and maybe the NSA use to monitor everything people buy other than with cash, and everyplace people go, and who they meet with—unless they and everyone associated with them leave their cellphones at home—and everything people search for on the Internet, and everyone people know and interact with through social media. It's a powerful tool."

She didn't add anything about how she knew the program was powerful: it had been instrumental in her hunt for a serial rapist who had previously been a ghost. She understood that at some point, her contact at the CIA, Tom Kanezaki, was going to ask for something in return for having used the program to help her. She didn't care. Whatever it was, it would be worth it.

"You're talking about Guardian Angel?" Little said. "Previously known as God's Eye?"

Livia glanced at him. Maybe she shouldn't have been surprised, but still, how widely was the program used not just for counterterrorism, but by law enforcement?

"Yes," she said.

"I already tried. The problem is, the program's only a few years old. And all the data involved with the first eight disappearances is older than that. All I have to feed the program is the disappearance at Campo. But the program can't do anything with single data points. It needs multiple points, so it can identify patterns. So yes, if we can't learn anything about what happened in Campo the old-fashioned way, it'll likely happen again somewhere else. And then Guardian Angel could be useful. But by then, another girl will be gone."

Well, so much for that. She wondered how Little would feel about other girls disappearing if it helped him find out what happened to Presley, or got him to the men who took her. She could imagine. But probably it was better not to know.

"So your plan was to go to Campo," she said. "And interview local law enforcement, and the family, and the teachers, the way you do. Walk the terrain, try to uncover a new clue that could provide a break-through about Presley."

"Exactly. And now I can't. I managed to concoct a reason for visiting the HSI Seattle field office, but Tilden already called me there once. Probably he's got people in the office keeping an eye on me, too, making sure I'm in Seattle and only Seattle."

Livia stopped walking. She felt trapped. She looked down the embankment at the dark, rippling water. She could hear the sounds of traffic on the Fremont Bridge, but the park still felt deserted.

"You want me to go to Campo for you."

"Yes. There's no one else I can ask. Whose discretion I trust, or their ability."

"Well, your timing sucks," she said, still looking out at the water. "After Paris and OGE and all that, my chief has a target painted on my back. She's watching me, practically baiting me, trying to put together enough pieces to take me down. My lieutenant has her own suspicions, and she told me I have to lay low for a while—and not just for my sake. For hers, too. I can't get involved right now. I'm sorry. I can't."

"Livia. Look at me. Please."

She realized that refusing to meet his eyes had shown her ambivalence. Her weakness.

She blew out a breath and looked at him.

"Please," he said again.

"Damn it, B. D., I'm not going to be any use to you if I get fired. Or put in prison, for that matter."

He was shaking his head before she'd even finished talking. "You know what it's like," he said. "You know. You reach a point where you'd give anything, you'd give your life, you'd put out your own eyes or set yourself on fire just to know, just to know what happened. Where is she? What happened to her? Is she alive? Where's her body? Just let me bury her, just let me be tender to her one last time."

His voice cracked. Damn it, she wanted to help him. She did. But she couldn't. Not now.

"You know what it's like," he said again. "All that hurt, that pain, that agony, I can't even lock it away, I can only cram it into a room with a heavy door that doesn't have a lock. And I lean on that door every damn day, trying to keep it shut, and if I relax for even a minute, the door bursts open and the pain comes flooding out."

She turned away again. He'd recognize the weakness, she knew, but if she kept looking into his pleading, agonized eyes, she was going to crack.

"Please, Livia. I'm begging you. Please. Help me find what happened to my little girl. Please."

She didn't answer.

"I helped you, goddamn it. You owe me now."

No. That kind of pressure was the wrong move. She gave him a steady stare. "You didn't help me. You used me."

"The one doesn't preclude the other. Without me, you wouldn't have been able to track down the rest of the men who took you and

Nason. You wouldn't have been able to kill them. The way they deserved to be killed."

"This is what you wanted from the beginning, isn't it? Or at least what you hoped for."

"I wanted you on my side, yes. But if I owe you for that, I paid up front."

She looked away again. God, she needed a workout. To train. To cut loose.

"A nonstop to San Diego," she heard him say. "And then an hour's drive to Campo. Just one day."

She sighed. She realized she'd been fooling herself. It wasn't in her to say no to something like this, no matter the risk. It was how she kept faith with Nason.

She hoped she wasn't rationalizing recklessness. She supposed she'd find out.

She looked at him. "What if I don't find anything?"

He held up his hands in supplication. "Then you don't find anything. Just this trip to Campo. That's all I'm asking."

She knew he believed that was true. Just as she knew it wasn't. He was asking for much more than that. More, probably, than either of them yet realized.

9

Boomer paced along the concrete of San Diego's Ocean Beach Pier. It was late, but the night was breezy, warm, and dry, and there were still a few people around, mostly kids toking up or making out or both. Boomer had the family Labrador with him. He wasn't much of a dog enthusiast, but the wife and the kid loved the thing, and it was certainly great cover for action if you needed to be out at night. Just a good citizen walking the dog, the kind of neighborhood event cops found not just unremarkable, but even reassuring.

Boomer didn't feel reassured himself, though. He was pissed, and even a little scared. Local Portland news networks were running stories about a gruesome rape-murder—a woman and her toddler son—in the Beaumont-Wilshire neighborhood, which was close to where Hope Jordan lived. The networks hadn't yet reported the victims' names, but it would have to be a hell of a coincidence. Especially because there were no other reports of, say, carjacking killings, which was how Snake was supposed to do it.

He came to the ocean end of the pier. The wind was gusting hard this far out, and he paused, looking out over the endless dark water, listening to the waves breaking below him. Yeah, he'd always liked the pier. He'd spent a lot of nights here as a kid. On the pier, or underneath it. Sometimes he wished he could go back to those days, when everything was easy. When he could do what he wanted. Or better yet, Iraq. That was the best time, the best ever. He and Snake had been like gods there—respected, feared, unstoppable.

But life didn't work that way. It sucked, but all anyone had was the here and now. And somehow, you had to find a way to make the best of it.

He was about halfway back when he saw Snake strolling toward him. Boomer gave a subtle nod, relieved. They hadn't wanted to risk any form of electronic contact, and Boomer realized now the radio silence had been making him nervous. He walked over to the railing and leaned against it, looking out over the water, the pier's lights to his back.

"Hey, brother," Snake said, stopping alongside him.

The dog, on Boomer's opposite side, whined. Dogs didn't like Snake. Boomer gave the leash a quick jerk. "Knock it off."

Snake ignored the dog. "Sorry I'm a little late. Long day."

Boomer glanced at him. "But good?"

Snake chuckled. "Hell, yeah."

"I saw some weird shit on the news. A rape-murder. Woman and her kid. Nothing about a carjacking, though. What's going on?"

"Yeah, I had to . . . improvise a bit."

Boomer knew he didn't have a right to be pissed. After all, Snake was doing him a favor. Or not a favor, exactly, because they each owed each other. But a solid, anyway. So it seemed unfair to gripe about the details. Still . . .

"Had to?" Boomer said. "Or wanted to?"

Snake sighed. "Maybe some of both. Nothing wrong with a little party, right?"

Boomer couldn't help himself. "This isn't the party, man, this is the cleanup. It's not the toast, it's the fucking hangover!"

Snake smiled. "Well, hair of the dog, then."

"Dude. We talked about this. We agreed on the objective, and on the parameters. What the fuck?"

"Come on, man. It still gets you what you need."

"How?"

"By looking like an ordinary crime, not an assassination. Sure, it could have been a carjacking that went wrong. But instead . . . it was a carjacking that got out of hand. And then went wrong."

"What about the kid?"

Snake shrugged. "Way I see it, part of the narrative. Heinous, sure, but still an ordinary crime. This is why we did it before she started shooting her mouth off, right? So no one would ever think to connect it with you. Or with Noreen. But even if they did, and they won't, you've got nothing but alibi. You were nowhere near Portland."

Boomer shook his head. "I'm supposed to thank you for killing the kid?"

"Look, if you think about it, doing the kid made sense. Even if someone thought you might want to schwack the mother to shut her up, what kind of monster would do the kid, too? It would be too much. People won't want to believe it."

Boomer shook his head again. He knew Snake wasn't wrong, exactly, but still. "You shoot them?" he asked.

"What am I, stupid now?"

No, Boomer thought. *Just crazy.*

They were quiet for a moment. Snake said, "Come on. I know the gun was untraceable, but the less evidence, the better, just like always. I strangled the mother. Smothered the kid. So, you know. Desperate guy, carjacks a soccer mom in her Volvo SUV, he's planning to rob her, makes her drive someplace secluded, and things just . . . escalate. If you think about it, it's not that different from what really happened."

Boomer looked at him. "Are you really trying to convince me you did that bitch, and killed her son, as some kind of favor to me? And not because you wanted to?"

"Why does it have to be one or the other? Sure, I wanted to. I mean, honestly, man, you had good taste. There was something about her. The way she kept complying, you know what I'm saying? 'Please, just don't hurt my little boy. I'll do anything.' Well, she did. She did everything."

Boomer couldn't deny, he liked the sound of that. Yeah, he remembered Hope. She'd been fun.

"So how about you thank me?" Snake said. "I mean, I just had your sloppy seconds with no complaints."

Boomer couldn't help but laugh at that. "It's not sloppy seconds twenty years later, man."

Snake laughed, too. "I'm sorry, brother. I know it wasn't what we planned. But I didn't get carried away. I saw a better way to do it—a way to get you what you need, and get me something, too. So everybody wins, right?"

The dog whined again. Boomer looked at it and jerked the leash. "Knock it off."

Boomer knew Snake wasn't being completely honest. Maybe he hadn't gotten carried away completely, okay, but he'd started with what he wanted and reverse engineered the rest. But his points about how it would look to investigators, and to anyone inclined to think the worst of Boomer, were actually pretty good ones. Boomer wondered if he would have gone along if Snake had suggested doing it this way up front. He decided he probably would have.

"Well?" Boomer said. "Are you going to tell me?"

"Tell you what?"

"The parts that weren't on the news."

Snake laughed. "Hell yes, brother, I was hoping you would ask."

10

Just over twelve hours after her meeting with Little, Livia was on her way to Campo.

She'd stayed up much of the night reviewing Little's file on the nine missing girls, Presley of course among them. Then she'd slept briefly, made an early appearance at headquarters, and caught a morning flight to San Diego, spending most of the time in the air researching the town. Campo was an unincorporated community on the Mexican border, a little over 2,600 people, mostly white and about a third Hispanic. There was a small Native American population and two nearby Native American tribal areas, one that included a casino. The biggest employer was the Border Patrol. The navy ran its Mountain Warfare Training Camp a few miles away. And the town was the southern terminus for the Pacific Crest Trail, which continued all the way to Canada. Nothing that leaped out at her. Nothing notably in common with the other places the girls had disappeared from. It was all right, though. The initial research was about providing a foundation. For real insight, you almost always had to get up close and personal.

She rented a car and drove the fifty miles from the airport, most of it along a winding road cut through the arid hills. Visibility was bad because of the California fires, but once she was east of San Diego she could tell there wouldn't have been much to see anyway, just mile after mile of rock and dirt and scrub, punctuated by tiny towns that announced themselves with not much more than a roadside gas station and a momentarily slower speed limit: Dulzura. Barrett Junction. Canyon City. The whole area felt remote, even abandoned. She tried to picture the landscape through the eyes of the men she was hunting, but couldn't yet see it the way they would have.

And then, there it was: the Campo Green Store, a low-slung wooden building that, truth in advertising, was painted forest green. According to the sign, purveyors of groceries, liquor, beer, and wine. Where, two weeks earlier, fifteen-year-old Hannah Cuero had picked up a box of pancake mix and some berries for the breakfast her mother planned to make the next morning, and then vanished into thin air on the walk home.

Livia parked, stepped out of the car into an incongruously large lot, and checked her surroundings. The midafternoon sun was obscured by haze, and the mountain air was cool. A hill rose behind the store, nothing but boulders and chaparral and a few stunted trees. The area was quiet, and it was hard not to feel that the silence was in recognition that something had happened here recently, something terrible.

She shook off the feeling and walked inside. A gray-haired woman behind the cash register wished her a good morning. Livia returned the salutation and wandered the aisles, not looking for anything in particular, just letting her mind relax and open up, imagining herself as Hannah, trying to feel like that lost girl. There, the pancake mix. Pick it up, grab some berries, and head home because it's getting dark and there's homework still to be done . . .

She bought a bottle of water and went back to the car. Ordinarily, she would have engaged the proprietor in conversation, tried to see what she could learn from the local scuttlebutt. Maybe the woman had even rung up Hannah's purchase on the evening in question. But she needed to keep a lower-than-usual profile for Little's sake. And for her own.

Hannah's house was only a minute's drive from the store: a white clapboard. It wasn't much, but it had been painted recently, the tiny lawn was trimmed, and there were neat rows of desert flowers along the walkway. A red SUV was parked nose-out in the gravel driveway. Like the house, it was clean and obviously well cared for. Livia went past, drove around the town for a half hour, and then parked back at the Green Store.

She stood in the lot for a moment, considering. There were any number of places two men could have positioned themselves. On the road itself, of course, or along the Pacific Crest Trail, which paralleled and looked down upon it. In fact, it wasn't clear whether Hannah had been walking on the road or the trail, which would have offered something of a shortcut, when she was taken.

Livia had already driven the road, so she decided to take the trail. She set out, briefly marveling that this narrow slice of dust and sand continued north for another 2,600 miles, all the way to Canada. Well, like everything else, it started somewhere. And had an endpoint, too.

As soon as she was clear of the store, she decided she had made the right choice. If you were hoping to snatch a girl, the trail would offer more possibilities. If the girl were on the trail, too, you'd have her that way. If you saw her on the road below, you could cut through the scrub and be on her in seconds. Either way, just before grabbing her you'd call your partner, who would move in from somewhere close by in a vehicle. Teamwork like that would require planning, practice, and precision, but it could be done. And had been done, if Little was right. Again and again, by the same two men.

Little hadn't called the Cueros to tell them to expect her—he'd been concerned someone could be listening in on their calls, and he'd repeatedly told her to watch her back. It all struck Livia as paranoid, and his precautions, which were already circumscribing her ability to investigate, were going to make the whole trip a waste if it turned out no one was home. Well, there was that SUV in the driveway. That was promising. Anyway, she would know soon enough.

The trail crossed the road a short distance from the Cuero house. Livia stopped and looked around. Little had told her to be surveillance conscious. She doubted anyone was going to be watching the house, but it couldn't hurt to check. She saw no cars anywhere, parked or moving. Just the quiet, empty afternoon street.

But still, that feeling of . . . aftermath. A silence born of sorrow.

She came down off the trail, went to the door, and knocked. A minute passed. Then the door opened—a woman of about forty, with dark hair pulled back in a ponytail. She was pretty, and would have been more so but for the utter exhaustion in her eyes.

"Mrs. Cuero?" Livia said.

The woman nodded slowly. "Can I help you?"

"I apologize for disturbing you, ma'am. My name is Livia Lone. Detective, Seattle PD. I don't have any information on your daughter, I'm very sorry to say. But I'm investigating another missing girl, and it's possible there are some commonalities with Hannah. If you don't mind, I'd like to ask you a few questions that might help with my investigation."

The woman frowned as though perplexed. Her fingertips rose to her cheek and remained there for a moment, as though to confirm her own presence. Livia sensed she was medicated, probably with Valium. Well, how could she not be? Two weeks ago, she'd been a mother, with a daughter, living a life that followed predictable rules. Now, every morning, she woke into a nightmare.

She looked at Livia, her eyes wide and beseeching. "Could you help find Hannah?" she said.

"I don't know, ma'am. But I'm certainly going to try."

The woman nodded, but only once, and quickly, as though more than that would have been to give in to a hope she must have found terrifying.

"My husband is at work," she said. "Border Patrol. They were very generous, but he couldn't take any more time off. But . . . please, come in."

Livia stepped inside. The woman closed the door and led her past a small living room. That was good. Kitchens were always for the real conversations. Living rooms were where people tried to hold you off.

There was another woman, sitting at the kitchen table, who from the resemblance Livia made instantly as the woman's sister. She stood when Livia and Mrs. Cuero came in. "My sister," Mrs. Cuero said. "Staying with us for a while."

"Arbel," the woman said, offering Livia her hand.

They shook. "Detective Lone, Seattle PD. Livia."

Arbel offered a pained smile. "No new information about Hannah?"

Livia shook her head, pushing away a pang. Sisters looking out for each other wasn't something she could allow herself to feel. "I'm afraid not. But her disappearance might relate to a case I'm working on."

"Can I offer you anything?" Mrs. Cuero said. "Coffee? Tea?"

Livia realized the woman still hadn't introduced herself. It wasn't surprising. Just putting one foot in front of the other would be effort enough. "Just water, ma'am, if you don't mind."

Livia spent three hours with Mrs. Cuero and Arbel. They looked at photo albums, at report cards, at artwork from as far back as the first grade, some of it framed and hung on the walls because Hannah had hoped to be an artist and her parents wanted to encourage her. It seemed Little had been right: Hannah presented none of the risk factors of a typical runaway. Her parents were involved in her life; they knew her friends; they had her Facebook and cellphone passwords. And they'd already been through all her online accounts with the San Diego County Sheriff's Department, who had also interviewed Hannah's schoolmates and her younger brother. There were no leads. Nothing suspicious. And though Livia would have liked to do her own interviews, including the father, she sensed nothing deceptive or otherwise off about Mrs. Cuero or her sister. She had hunted enough freaks and sniffed out enough lies to know a good family from one with secrets. This was one of the former.

She would have wished otherwise, but her wishes didn't matter. From all she could see, Hannah hadn't run away. Nor had she been abducted by a predator she'd met online or was otherwise acquainted with. Most likely, Hannah was taken by a non–family member unknown to her. A stranger. The rarest form of abduction, and also the hardest to solve.

When Livia left, the sun was already low in the sky. She gave Mrs. Cuero a card and told her to call anytime, for anything. It was frustrating to leave without having done a real investigation, but her hands were tied. By Little's concerns, and by the need to get back to Seattle before anyone noticed she'd been away.

She'd left her phone off since landing in San Diego—Little's admonition about being watched, combined with her own cellphone-tracker paranoia—so she turned on the car's GPS and chose a slightly different route back to the airport: Buckman Springs Road, the northern loop instead of the southern. Just outside of town, she saw a sign: *Mountain Warfare Training Camp Michael Monsoor*. She might have swung by just to satisfy her curiosity, but there wasn't time.

She drove on along the two-lane road. She passed a few small agricultural plots amid the arid terrain, but soon even these isolated settlements were gone, and it was nothing but the road again, winding through rocky hills and stunted trees and dry grass, with not even a telephone line in sight.

As she came to a bridge spanning a dry arroyo, she saw a gray Taurus approaching in the rearview, the magnetic light on its roof flashing blue. She checked the speedometer and saw she'd been a few miles over the limit, but not enough to warrant a traffic stop. Especially not by an unmarked car. She felt a twinge of unease. She gave a wave of acknowledgment with her right hand to obscure the brief disappearance of her left, which had dropped for an instant to ease her fleece aside and undo the strap securing the Glock in her belly-band holster.

The bridge had no shoulder, so there was no place she could safely stop. Immediately on the other side, the road curved right, with a wide gravel turnoff she could have pulled onto. But she kept going. The turnoff was too secluded a spot, too hidden by a clump of trees, and too much where she might have been expected to pull over.

A quarter mile down, she came to a long straightaway. She took her foot off the gas and coasted onto the shoulder, the gravel suddenly loud beneath the tires. When the car had rolled to a stop, she put it in park, released the seatbelt, cracked the window, and turned on the hazard lights. Then she put her hands on the steering wheel and watched through the rearview.

The Taurus drifted in behind her and stopped about a car length away. Closer than she would have expected for a tactically correct traffic stop. And it was parked in line with her car, rather than offset. Like the distance, the lack of an offset wasn't unheard of—cops had different traffic-stop preferences, and some cops were just plain sloppy—but still.

She watched in the mirror, her heart beating hard, her hand ready to go for the Glock. But the situation was dicey. If she mistook a real stop for something illegitimate, she might wind up shooting a cop. If she mistook it the other way, the one shot might be her.

A midthirties white guy got out. Fit looking, short hair, clean shaven. She saw no telltale bulges, but he was wearing a dark windbreaker that would offer a variety of concealment possibilities. He might have been a cop. Hard to know without more. His hands were empty, that was good. But he'd gotten out awfully quickly. Not much time to have called in the stop—to describe the vehicle, suspect, and location—and certainly not enough time for dispatch to have run the plates.

He started walking toward the driver-side window. That was also odd. The more tactical approach would have been the passenger side. There were cops who favored a driver-side approach—mistakenly, in

Livia's view—but they almost always parked their own vehicle farther to the left to create a zone buffered from traffic in which they could safely reach the stopped car.

And there was something else off. He was too confident. Cops were relentlessly drilled that there's no such thing as a routine traffic stop. They were shown dashcam videos of "routine" stops with the approaching cop shot at without any warning. Cars thrown into reverse and officers rammed. Officers grabbed while reaching through the window for something and dragged down the road. Any halfway-tactical officer approaching a stopped car knew to do so cautiously, even if his tactics were weak. But this guy—this guy in plain clothes and an unmarked car, who had stopped her for going maybe five miles an hour over, who had switched on his flashers just the right distance from the secluded spot where someone a little less careful would have pulled over—this guy was sauntering up to an unknown car as though he knew exactly what to expect.

She breathed slowly and deeply, keeping cool, watching through the sideview now. His hands were still empty. She wanted to draw the Glock. But damn it, if she were wrong . . .

"Hello there," he said, looking in at her through the driver-side window. No badge that she could see—not hanging from his neck, not affixed to his belt. His palms were on his hips, a quick trip to a concealed weapon. She didn't like that, but it was what a prudent cop would do, and the main thing was that for the time being, his hands remained empty. She'd play it cooperative. If he went for a weapon in the face of that, she'd have to draw hers. She was tempted to preempt him, but that would be too likely to provoke a gunfight, with her trapped inside the car and him outside and mobile. And even if she dropped him, ballistics could match the rounds to her duty weapon.

There was another option, though. The Somico Vaari in her cargo pants. Tough as an axe, sharp as a razor. She had a hole cut in the right hip pocket to make room for the sheath, which was clipped in place inside. Catch the edge of her pinky on the overhang built into the pommel, and she could deploy the knife even faster than she could the gun.

With no ballistic evidence left behind after.

"Hi," she said, with a friendly smile.

He nodded. "Do you know why I pulled you over, ma'am?"

"I don't, Trooper . . . ?"

Trooper was a title of address for state cops. Whatever this guy was, he wasn't with the California Highway Patrol.

"Johnson," the guy said. "Ma'am, I'm going to need you to step out of the vehicle and follow me back to my patrol car."

No correction regarding the mistaken title. On top of which, an unmarked wasn't a patrol car. And no request for license and registration? Either this guy was the most clueless cop ever—

Or he was no cop at all.

But if he, or someone else, had somehow seen her at the Cuero house, and followed her as she left town, they must have known, or at least suspected, that she herself was a cop. If she pretended otherwise, he'd recognize the subterfuge. The better bet was to pretend she believed his act.

"Happy to, Trooper Johnson," Livia said. "Just so you know, I'm on the job. From out of town, and I don't have my duty weapon with me. Okay to exit the vehicle?"

The guy stepped back toward his own car and nodded. "Good to go."

"Good to go" sounded more military to her than cop, but it was hardly a sure thing. What was more telling was that the guy was prepared to accept at face value her assurance that she wasn't carrying. For a normal cop, a driver's spontaneous "I'm not carrying" declaration would be the opposite of reassuring. Yet this guy was good-to-going her without even having asked for ID.

Well, whoever he was, it didn't seem this was just about killing her. If it were, he would have already tried his luck. No, he wanted information, probably of the *Who are you, what were you doing at the Cuero house, what do you know, what do you suspect* variety, and he'd have to extract that information before killing her. Which was why he wanted her in his car, and was most likely thinking to cuff her and then planning to drive to a secondary location where he could take his time and be completely in control.

A.k.a. the last thing on Earth she would allow, ever.

For an instant, she marveled at how readily she had accepted that this man intended to kill her. Apparently, the two attempted hits she had survived in connection with a government-run child-pornography ring had eradicated whatever vestigial urge she might have had to question her intuition. Or dismiss it as paranoia.

She heard a vehicle approaching and waited. A second later, a white Ram 2500 went by from behind them, the bottom panels covered with dust and dirt, probably from off-roading. As soon as it had passed, she opened the door with her left hand, keeping her right free and ready to go for the Glock if the guy even twitched. But he didn't. He just watched her with a matter-of-fact expression, which she supposed was his approximation of what a cop looked like after pulling over a driver. She reminded herself that just because he didn't know anything about traffic-stop tactics didn't mean he didn't know anything else.

She stepped out, her heart beating hard, turned toward him, and swung the door closed with her left hand. He was about five feet away—closer than a cop would have stood, farther than she would have liked for purposes of the Vaari. She saw no weapon shape anywhere around his waist. Could be an old-school shoulder rig. More likely, something at the small of his back.

The sound of the passing truck faded, and the area was suddenly silent.

He gave her a quick look up and down, his gaze pausing on the slight bulge under her fleece. He brushed his windbreaker back with his right hand, resting his knuckles on his hip. Yeah, she'd been right. A small-of-back holster, now just a few inches from his hand.

"I thought you weren't carrying," he said.

She felt her heart rate kick up another notch. "I'm not."

He flexed his right hand. "What's that under your fleece?"

"A camera."

He flexed his hand again. "Show me."

She looked in his eyes. "Are you even going to tell me what this is about?"

If he'd been a real cop, a good cop, he would have stepped offline by now and had his own weapon out. Hell, a good cop wouldn't have allowed her out of the vehicle without a thorough check in the first place.

She saw a flash of concern in his eyes. Yeah, he wasn't supposed to just kill her. He was supposed to interrogate her first. But in that moment, he was wondering if he could safely manage it.

Spoiler alert, motherfucker. You can't.

"Show me," he said again.

"Sure," she said. "Just as soon as you tell me what department you're—"

He went for his gun. Smart to do it while she was in midsentence. But she'd been ready for the trick, and saw him tense for an instant, so she was moving in even before his hand started sweeping around to his back. She closed the distance in less than a second and slammed his gun arm back with her left hand, the Vaari already out and tight in her right. She plunged the eight-inch curved steel blade up through his abdomen all the way to the hilt.

He shrieked and folded in half as his body reflexively tried to jerk away from the cold metal suddenly inside it, and his arms snapped together in front of him, barn doors closing after the horses have stampeded out. She gripped the right sleeve of his windbreaker with her left hand, pivoted counterclockwise, and blasted his legs out from under him with *hiza guruma*, a simple judo knee sweep, using the Vaari to push him into the throw rather than the more customary lapel grip to pull him. He landed hard on his back.

She yanked out the Vaari, twisting it on the way, and kept control of his right arm to make sure he couldn't reach for his gun again. But maintaining the grip probably wasn't necessary. His knees were fetaled in, his face contorted in agony, and his mouth flapped open and closed as though he were a fish on the deck. She was pretty sure the knife had sliced through his spleen, ruptured his diaphragm, and penetrated his left lung. Meaning the diaphragm was in full spasm, the lung collapsing, and the spleen, the most vascularized organ in the body, dumping blood inside him.

She watched him, still holding the arm. His body began to shudder. She listened. She heard a vehicle coming toward them from up the road and around the bend. *Shit.*

She sheathed the Vaari, took hold of the back of his windbreaker, and dragged him between the cars. She was lucky—he wasn't big, and the gravel acted as a kind of dry lubricant. He shook as she dragged him but didn't struggle, a thick trail of blood from his wound marking their passage.

They made it between the cars just as she heard the vehicle enter the straightaway. Keeping low, she kept tugging him back until she had pulled him next to his passenger-side front tire. There was a gravel embankment at the edge of the shoulder, dropping to a weed-covered ditch below. She scooted over the side, pulling him after her. He rolled down limply and came to a stop faceup, one leg draped over the other in a weird pantomime of ease.

The vehicle slowed. Shit, had the driver seen her? She didn't think so, but . . .

She pulled herself up the embankment and did a quick sneak and peek. The vehicle was the white Ram 2500 that had passed just a couple minutes earlier. She couldn't be certain, but the same model, the same color, the same dust and dirt as though from off-roading, was good enough for her. The driver hadn't been interested when he'd passed the first time; what would have brought him back? And why would he be slowing . . .

The truck passed their position, did a U-turn, and eased past again. Then it pulled onto the shoulder in front of her car and stopped, the engine idling.

What the hell is this?

A cellphone started buzzing. She glanced down. It was coming from the guy, his pants or his jacket. The ground around him was soaked in blood—she must have hit the spleen, as she'd thought—and he was obviously past hearing his phone, let alone answering. Still, was it loud enough to be audible from inside the truck? She didn't think so, but if someone got out . . .

She dropped back, grabbed the guy by the arm, and hauled him over onto his stomach. She tugged the windbreaker up, and there—a small-of-back holster, as she'd thought, the butt of a Glock protruding. She yanked free the gun—*the 19, good*—checked the load—*9-mil, good*—proned out, and started a low crawl along the embankment. She didn't want to be directly below the cars, and she especially didn't want to be directly below that pool of blood on the shoulder. It would be the first place someone would look, and she damn well wasn't going to get into a gunfight while lying in a ditch, against someone holding an elevated position.

A few yards away, a clump of rocks rose above the shoulder. She came out of the low crawl into a crouch and moved faster.

The cellphone stopped buzzing. She heard the truck door open. Boots on the gravel. She clambered clockwise up the rocks, her heart hammering, controlling her breathing. She forced herself to go slowly, to watch her foot placement, to trade speed for stealth.

She heard a man's voice: "Frank?"

Eight steps crunching the gravel. A pause. The voice again, softer this time: "The fuck?"

The footfalls hadn't been coming toward the embankment. They had gone past her car and then stopped. Meaning he hadn't seen the body. But he had seen the blood. And his brain was trying to sort it all out: *Did Frank kill her? Where did he take her? Why isn't he answering?*

Wait, is that her *blood, or is it—*

Livia burst from around the rocks. "Do not move!" she bellowed, closing the distance, the Glock she'd taken extended in a two-handed grip.

It was another fit-looking, jeans-and-windbreaker white guy, facing away from her, staring at the pool of blood between the cars as she'd expected. He was holding a pistol at low ready in a right-handed grip— he must have decided when he saw the blood and didn't see Frank that a holstered weapon was the wrong way to go.

He ignored her command, bringing the gun up and around, spinning clockwise toward her—

She pressed the trigger—and a second time, a third, a fourth, rapid-fire. Her sights on his torso, shifting left as she moved, using the first guy's car for cover and forcing the new guy to turn farther to try to acquire her. The guy twitched as the rounds hit home, and he stumbled toward the embankment, still turning, still trying to get in the fight. He managed a wild shot. A second. She reached the side of the car, dropped her level, focused her sights on his face, and put two rounds into the side of his head. His knees buckled and he flopped to his back, his torso going over the edge of the embankment. He hung like that for an instant, and then his legs disappeared as he slid down the other side.

Livia stayed behind the cover of the car's engine block, checking her flanks. She blew out two long breaths, forcing herself to stay calm, stay tactical. Then she dashed along the embankment until she was ten yards beyond the guy's position. She wasn't going to take anything for granted—it was unbelievable what a person could sometimes survive, even head wounds.

She snuck a look down and saw the extra care wasn't necessary. One of the rounds had gone into his temple and blown out an eye. His face was a mask of blood.

She wanted to search the bodies and the cars. If she could find out who they were . . .

No. She needed to go. Now. All it would take was one passing civilian driver, glancing at the three vehicles on the shoulder, noticing the blood. Or a random hiker on the nearby Pacific Crest Trail, hearing the shots and coming closer to investigate. Or a motorcyclist with a helmet-mounted GoPro, recording her license plate. And she didn't even want to think about a cop coming by. She had one chance—maybe—to walk away clean from this, and every second she lingered, that chance got smaller.

Time for just one thing: a quick glance into each vehicle. No dashcams—windshield, rearview, dashboard, all clear. Thank God.

She ran to her car and got back on the road. She kept expecting to see another set of flashers behind her. But ten uneventful minutes later, she was heading west on Interstate 8, one car among countless others. She checked herself as she drove. There was a lot of blood from the guy she'd hit with the Vaari, but it wasn't too obvious on her dark fleece and jeans. The smell was actually more noticeable than the sight. Shouldn't be too hard to find a rest stop to clean up, then a store for bleach wipes and a change of clothes. The Vaari sheath was contaminated, and she'd need some kind of new one, even if it was just temporary. Then stop at a few places to dispose of the sheath and the other contaminated items. And the gun.

And then back to the airport. Turn on her cellphone. Hope she hadn't been missed.

And then she could get to the most important thing of all: Little. Because she realized now, with a simmering rage she was having difficulty keeping from boiling over, he hadn't just used her. Or even just manipulated her.

He'd fucking set her up.

11

Charles "Chop" Opperman, the commander of the navy's Mountain Warfare Training Camp Michael Monsoor, put through the call from the secure unit on his desk. The news wasn't good, and he wasn't looking forward to the conversation.

One ring, then the admiral's voice: "Yes."

"Admiral. Chop."

"Go."

Chop didn't hesitate. Everyone knew the admiral liked his news fast. And his bad news faster.

"My guys observed a visitor to the house. A woman. They followed her and engaged her. The woman got away, and my guys are dead."

A pause. "Who was she?"

Christ. Not a thought for the two dead men. "I don't know yet."

"They were using video to monitor the house?"

"Yes."

"Is there a recording?"

"I assume so."

"You assume?"

Chop felt a burst of irritation that was instantly eclipsed by fear.

"Sir. My priority was recovering the vehicles and the bodies."

A pause. "Of course. Are there going to be questions?"

"None that should cause problems. The bodies . . . It seems the two men had an accident involving white phosphorous."

White phosphorous was a self-igniting incendiary weapon. The burns it produced were so horrific that numerous laws governed the deployment of the substance against civilian targets.

"I'm sorry, Chop. That's unfortunate."

"It is, yes. Their families are being notified. But there won't be any . . . forensic inconsistencies. The burns were extensive."

"Then you should be able to focus now on retrieving a recording, yes?"

Chop felt the irritation again, and the fear. "Yes, sir."

"Good. Upload it to the secure site. I have people who should be able to identify the woman."

Chop was concerned the admiral was relying on him to upload something that might not even exist. "Admiral, the two men who were in charge of the op . . . they're gone. I don't know for certain if there's a recording. Or, if there is, whether I can access it."

"You'd better hope there is, Chop. Because if there isn't, you'll have to send men to the house, and uncover the identity of this woman by interrogating whoever in the house she met with."

Chop clenched his jaw. "Yes, sir."

"I'll look forward to that video," the admiral said, and clicked off.

Chop set down the phone. It felt like the admiral had been smiling when he delivered that parting shot, and Chop hated it. But what was he going to do, disobey? Fight back? Even if there had been a time for that, it was too late now. Better to be a realist. The survival rate was better.

He hoped the video could be recovered. He really didn't want to send a team to the Cuero house. It would be indecent.

12

Just past midnight, Livia met Little at Fremont Canal Park again.

She'd been lucky: cleaning up and getting rid of her clothes and the other contaminated items had gone smoothly. And no one had missed her at headquarters. She'd even slept deeply on the plane back to Seattle, knocked out by the parasympathetic backlash to the adrenaline rush of combat. Which was good, because she was so furious at Little—and at herself—that it would have been dangerous to confront him exhausted and not fully in control.

She waited in the shadows by the asphalt plant at the edge of the park until she saw him walking up the path. She listened. Other than his footfalls, the park was silent.

She ghosted back to the tree line, then circled around to his rear, satisfying herself that he hadn't been followed. She knew Little wasn't as surveillance conscious as, say, Carl and Rain and the rest of the team she'd worked with in Paris. And she knew now he needed to be.

Not that she was in a great position to throw stones. Look what had almost happened to her outside of Campo that very afternoon. But that was the point.

"Hey," she said, coming up behind him.

He spun, his gun arm stopping halfway to his waist, his eyes wide in the glow of a distant streetlight. "Damn," he said. "You trying to give me a heart attack?"

She looked at him for a moment, watching his breath turn to vapor in the cool night air. "Just being careful. Like you said, remember?"

"Did you learn anything?"

"You tell me."

He frowned. "What does that mean?"

"Who were the men who ambushed me?"

"You were ambushed? What do you mean?"

She looked at him. She had a good nose for deception, and he seemed genuinely surprised. But a suspect could always tell the truth if you didn't ask the right questions.

"Outside of Campo," she said. "A few miles south of Interstate 8. Two cars and two bodies by the side of the road. Don't tell me you haven't already checked with the San Diego County Sheriff's Department. You knew what was coming."

He shook his head as though confused.

She took a step closer, trying to tamp down the anger. "Did you check with the sheriff's department?"

A beat. Then, "Yes."

"Then you fucking knew."

"Livia, I . . . there are no bodies. No cars. No reports of anything like that at all."

She looked at him, trying to process that. "There's no way those two vehicles have been sitting on the shoulder since it happened, next to all that blood on the ground, without someone calling it in. Without a highway patrol passing and checking it out."

"Blood on the ground . . . what are you talking about? Somebody came at you? You killed them? Please, tell me."

She shook her head. "No, Little. You don't get anything from me until you come clean."

"About what?"

"You knew," she said, coming closer. He was six inches taller and outweighed her by at least a hundred pounds, but he took a step back. "You knew someone would be watching. You knew I would walk right into it. You used me to draw them out."

He held up his hands as though in surrender. "I told you I was being watched. And that you had to be careful."

She flexed her hands, resisting the urge to grab him by the lapels and throw him onto his back. "You told me knowing I wouldn't listen. That I'd discount it as paranoia—a mirage, like you said, produced by desperation. You only told me so you could cover your own ass. So that when I confronted you later, you could wave it in my face like some kind of get-out-of-jail-free card."

"Livia, listen to yourself. You're—"

"Fuck you. I'm done." She turned and started walking down the path.

"Livia!" he called out from behind her.

She kept walking.

"Livia!" he said again.

She heard his footfalls, coming fast, overtaking her. "Goddamn it, would you just—"

She sensed his right hand coming in to grab her arm an instant before it landed. She snatched his sleeve at the wrist, dropped, blocked his right leg at the knee with her thigh, yanked his arm forward, and threw him with *tai otoshi*. He was already off balance, his momentum carrying him forward, and there was nothing he could do to stop himself from sailing past her. She resisted the urge to drill him into the ground, keeping the arm and pulling up at the last moment to protect the back of his skull. If she'd wanted to, she could have transitioned to an arm bar and broken his elbow. She resisted that urge, too.

She stepped back and looked down at him. "Don't touch me."

He lay there, sucking wind. "Yeah," he said after a moment. "Like I said, my football days are behind me."

He got his legs under him and stood, a little stooped and still catching his breath. "We cool now?" he said.

"No, we're not cool. I told you. Come clean or we're done."

"But you know I'm right. You know those men are out there. You know—"

"Shut the fuck up *right now*," she said. "Or you're going for another ride. And this time I won't be gentle."

They stood there, staring at each other, both breathing heavily. She hated that he knew what buttons to push. And that he wasn't hesitating to push them. Because, okay, was she really going to walk away from this just to prove a point? Just to show him that he couldn't control her? Whoever had made a run at her in Campo, whoever had taken Hannah Cuero, whoever was protecting the perpetrators . . . was she really going to let them prey on new victims?

He put his hands on his hips and blew out a long breath. "Okay," he said. "I didn't know. But . . ."

"But you knew it was possible. Maybe even likely. Otherwise you wouldn't have checked in with the San Diego County Sheriff's Department."

"I told you. My boss, Tilden, is watching me. And I thought . . . if someone is watching me, and being that careful, it's not impossible they'll be watching the Cuero house, too."

"And you let me walk right into that."

"Not exactly. I told you to be surveillance conscious. And wait, wait, I'm not saying that to get out of jail free. You're right, I knew you'd discount it. But I also know the way you can handle yourself. Look what you just did to me."

She said nothing. She realized that, as furious as she was, she couldn't blame him. Not really. Would she have put someone else at risk to find out what had happened to Nason?

She hated to admit it, but putting someone else at risk might have been the least of it. If she'd had to make that choice.

"The men you killed," he said. "It wasn't them, was it? The ones who took my daughter?"

She looked at him. Maybe he didn't deserve an answer, but she couldn't be that cruel.

"I don't know," she said. "But . . . I don't think so."

"Why not?"

"The men who are doing it . . . they don't stick around after. This was something else."

"What?"

Yeah, that was the question. She realized it wasn't Little she was furious with. It was herself. She should have seen all this beforehand. And the worst part was, she *had* seen some of it. She just hadn't put it together. She'd told herself Little was traumatized, desperate, over-reaching. And she'd gone to Campo and interviewed Mrs. Cuero at least half thinking she was doing it just to humor the man and get him out of her hair.

And then she realized something else. She'd been so focused on what she might have left behind at the scene, and getting rid of the evidence, and how she was going to confront Little, that she hadn't thought back to the Cueros. And now that she was . . .

"Surveillance," she said. "Whoever came at me on the highway must have tracked me from the Cuero house. I didn't spot surveillance, but they wouldn't have had to be present. They could have been watching the house remotely, a video camera in a tree, a telephone pole, wherever. They could have logged me going in and coming out, and rolled up behind me a few miles out of town, without my realizing until it was too late that they'd followed me. Which is pretty much what happened."

"That makes sense."

She shook her head. "You don't get it. I gave Mrs. Cuero my business card."

"What? Why?"

Because I didn't really think there was anything to your theories. Because I assumed you were so stricken you were just being paranoid.

"What was I supposed to do?" she said. "'Hi, Mrs. Cuero, I can't tell you who I am or under what authority I'm here or why you should let me into your house and open up to me about the most traumatic, horrifying thing imaginable, but please spend hours with me talking about your daughter and maybe I can help'?"

"Okay, but—"

"What time did you check in with the San Diego County Sheriff?"

"About an hour ago."

"And they had nothing? No reports of a roadside homicide?"

"Not a peep. Not even a speeding ticket."

"Then someone moved those bodies. Which means . . . some kind of nearby manpower. If I'm right about the video, there might be a recording. Of me, maybe of my rental car. And even if there's no recording, all they have to do is ask Mrs. Cuero who was visiting. And based on the way they came at me, I don't think these people are in the habit of asking nicely. And maybe they won't want her talking afterward. They want to clean up loose ends, like they just cleaned up the bodies and cars by the side of the road. Have you thought about that? You didn't just put me in danger. You put me in *continuing* danger. And not just me. That poor girl's traumatized mother and aunt, too. Do you even care?"

"They'll be fine. No one's going to—"

"That's the same bullshit rationalization you told yourself to get me to go out there. Who the fuck are we dealing with, Little? Enough manpower to monitor the house, send two at me, sanitize the crime scene right afterward, and you're telling me the Cueros are safe now? Do you understand how out of your mind you are on this? Forget about me. What are you going to do if something happens to the Cueros? You think that's what Presley would want?"

His face darkened and his gun hand clenched. "You don't *ever* get to—"

"Yes I do! Because you dragged me into this, and now I can't get out even if I want to! I'm stuck with you, you asshole, and I need to know you're going to be enough in control of yourself to not get innocent people killed!"

He stared at her, his eyes furious, clouds of vapor that could have been smoke jetting out of his nostrils. Then his expression softened and he looked down.

"You're right," he said. "I'm sorry."

They stood there for a moment, neither speaking. Little looked up again. She couldn't read his expression.

"What?" she said.

"I really am sorry."

"Yeah, but you're glad, too."

"That's part of what I'm sorry for."

She nodded. She hated it, but she actually understood.

"What's your theory?" he said.

"About who attacked me?"

"And who was behind them."

She considered. "Well, we know we're dealing with significant local manpower, right? The surveillance, the attack, the cleanup."

"Agreed."

"I'm no expert on Campo, but from what I've seen, I can imagine only three things that could explain that. The San Diego County Sheriff's Department, the Border Patrol, and the navy Mountain Warfare Training Camp."

He nodded. "Agreed again. You like any one of them better than the others?"

She thought about the vague sense she'd had that she should drive by the naval base, her frustration that there wasn't time. And the way "Trooper Johnson" had performed his traffic stop.

"I don't think they were law enforcement," she said. "I don't think they were accustomed to doing any kind of vehicle stops or searches."

"So not the sheriff's department. Not the Border Patrol."

"If I had to guess. So. Can you find out anything about that naval base?"

He nodded. "You better believe it."

13

Admiral Kane hung up the secure phone. For a moment he just sat, rubbing his chin. The situation was quite a conundrum.

He leaned back, put his feet on the desk, and steepled his fingers. He needed to devise a plan, something that would quickly and cleanly prevent things from spiraling further, and he didn't have much time. The life of a vice president wasn't quite as demanding as that of the president himself, but more than a few minutes alone without some aide disturbing him was a rarity.

Chop hadn't managed to recover any video. If there was a recording at all, it seemed Chop's men had hidden and probably password protected it. So, given that the men in question were now dead, the video had functionally been rendered a dead end, too. Meaning that learning who had visited the Cuero house and then killed Chop's men might have involved a regrettable interrogation of Hannah Cuero's parents. But Chop, to his credit, had devised an interim solution that had worked just as well. He'd sent a team to black bag the Cuero house. They'd found a card, right in the kitchen, secured to the refrigerator with a little magnet. A Seattle sex-crimes police detective named Livia Lone. A quick search of CBP records revealed that Detective Lone had flown round-trip from Seattle to San Diego the very day Chop's men were killed. It was her. It had to be.

And what was even more interesting was, Lone was connected to Little.

Kane had known about this man Little for a long time—ever since Kane, on a hunch Bradley might have relapsed into some metastasized version of his degenerate high-school habits, had asked an FBI contact to use the Bureau's ViCAP database to check into possible disappearances from areas around the country to which Kane knew Bradley had been deployed.

The results were extremely unsettling.

Kaila Jones, a black teenager, had gone missing from Guthrie, Kentucky, a small town close to Fort Campbell, Bradley's unit's base. Nothing so remarkable about the disappearance of a teenaged girl, at least statistically, and the story probably wouldn't even have made the news. But the girl's parents both worked on the base, and they insisted that their daughter would not have just run off. They were certain she had been abducted. And there had been other disappearances, too, all from towns near and at the same time of Bradley's various deployments.

And worse, Kane wasn't the only person with an interest in these disappearances. It seemed a Homeland Security investigator named Benjamin Dixon Little spent almost every evening, sometimes until nearly dawn, querying ViCAP about missing teenaged girls. Indeed, Little had taken a particular interest in the very girls whose disappearances coincided with Bradley's stateside rotations. Little's own daughter had gone missing, it seemed, and the man was obsessed with finding whoever had abducted her.

Kane put his elbows on the desk and massaged his temples. He had attributed Bradley's high-school behavior to boys-will-be-boys excesses, and blamed the girls involved at least as much as he blamed his son. Girls should know not to lead a young man on, that it was hard to stop once things got started. A young man's sexual impulses were strong, even overpowering, and the discipline required to manage those impulses could take time to develop. Everyone understood this. He didn't know why so many people were intent on denying it.

And maybe Bradley's behavior was occasionally a bit more than average. But that just meant his impulses were stronger. His discipline, more lacking. Kane had sensed this even before discovering his teenaged son's stash of pornography. The material had been . . . extreme. Kane had burned all of it, leaving a note in its place: *If I can find it, so can others.*

He and Bradley had never discussed that note, or what it referred to. And that was fine. Kane had never found any other material. Problem solved.

The main thing was, he always knew Bradley would grow out of the boyhood behavior. If he was given time. If his environment could be properly managed. If the occasional girl who decided to deal with postcoital shame or regret by accusing a boy—who was no more culpable than she—could be persuaded to keep quiet.

As betrayed and even humiliated as he'd felt when Bradley announced he was eschewing Annapolis and joining the army, Kane thought there would at least be a silver lining: The rigor. The discipline. The responsibility. It was a cliché, but the army, Kane had believed, would make his son a man.

And then Kane had received a call from Bradley's commander in Iraq. A reluctant call, full of apologetic circumlocutions. It seemed that Bradley, along with one of his teammates—a low-class specimen named Stephen Spencer, known among the men as "Snake"—had developed a habit of taking advantage of young girls during raids on houses suspected of harboring insurgents. Bradley's commander didn't condone the practice and wanted it to stop, but out of respect for Bradley and his heroism, he preferred to avoid overt action.

Kane had understood that by "respect," the commander had meant "fear." Which was good. Fear was a more valuable currency than respect.

Fear was what had caused the commander to quietly notify Kane, rather than risking public action against the son and grandson of former admirals, one of whom had gone on to become a congressman. Fear bought Kane time to engineer a solution. And he had time: Bradley was finishing a six-month tour, shortly to rotate back to Fort Campbell.

And then, a month later, Kane had awoken in the night with a strange intuition—more akin, really, to a premonition. He'd called his FBI contact. Learned about the disappearance near Fort Campbell. The other disappearances. And Little.

At that point, it seemed Little had managed to make no connections. Apparently, Bradley was being careful, the childhood *If I can find it, so can others* lesson perhaps having been learned. But the situation was untenable. Eventually, Bradley would make a mistake, or this man Little would get lucky, or both.

Well. Depriving Bradley of his illicit materials had worked once before. Kane understood he simply needed to do it again. The difference being that this time, he would leave no note. Bradley wouldn't even know what had happened. His son would simply find himself no longer in the presence of what tempted him, and, absent that temptation, he would finally grow up.

And it had worked. Snake had gone to prison and was no longer a baneful influence. Bradley left the army, won the special election for the seat Kane was vacating, and went on to win two more elections on his own thereafter. Kane's Quantico contact continued to keep him posted. Little was still indulging his nocturnal ViCAP hobby, but there were no new entries that might be attributed to Bradley. Which was exactly as Kane had foreseen. After all, he knew firsthand that being a congressman didn't leave much time for extracurricular interests.

But now Snake had been paroled. Surely it was no coincidence that shortly thereafter, the Campo girl, Hannah Cuero, had gone missing.

Nor was it a coincidence that the little accusatory slut Noreen Prentis had herself disappeared.

It was ironic, he supposed. It seemed Bradley was cleaning up one kind of mess—the one he had created as a boy. While leaving it to his father to clean up another kind, the one Bradley had gone back to creating today. Well, *plus ça change*. The fact that it was ironic didn't make it any less pressing.

Kane's contact at HSI had filled him in about the connection between Little and this Seattle police detective. It seemed Little had involved the woman in some sort of anti-trafficking task force in Thailand. Maybe that had been a favor. Or else Little had something on her. And it seemed they were likely connected in another way— the recent indictments of three senators, including Walter Barkley, the now-erstwhile presidential frontrunner—for involvement in a child-pornography ring. Lone had been part of a joint FBI-SPD task force investigating the ring. And Little had received documents about Secret Service ring members, documents Little claimed were from an anonymous Justice Department whistle-blower. Little had then used those documents to press for indictments.

Whatever the nature of their connection, what mattered was that the woman had been willing to do Little an exceptional service—traveling to Campo to investigate in his stead.

He wondered for a moment how much Little would have told her. Quite a bit of how Kane might proceed depended on that.

Everything, he decided. Little would have told her everything. Because how else could she have hoped to conduct a meaningful investigation in Campo?

The more he considered, the more difficult the situation began to seem. Lone's reputation and her record were outstanding, and obviously the woman was formidable. Chop's dead men were testimony to that. On top of which, it seemed she had recently survived some sort of assassination attempt in Seattle, killing her two attackers and being cleared in the investigation that followed. Kane sensed the woman might present more trouble even than Little himself. Murphy's law in action, he supposed. Kane's connections at HSI had managed to quarantine Little, and in doing so had caused Little to infect someone else with his suspicions and his knowledge. Meaning that now Kane had to deal with two adversaries, the new one even more dangerous than the first.

The conundrum was that removing them both would be national news. Either an assassinated cop or an assassinated HSI investigator would be a lot. But both, and at the same time? That would be newsworthy indeed. Especially because people at SPD would know about the Thailand task force, and the child-pornography ring, and therefore about the Little-Lone connection.

Yes, it was a delicate situation. Moving against one would warn the other. Moving against them simultaneously would be so damn attention-getting. And reducing attention was the point of the entire exercise.

On the other hand . . .

If they were both involved in that anti-trafficking task force . . . and had exposed the child-pornography scandal that caused the resignations, and in the fullness of time possibly the imprisonment, of three senators . . . then they both had enemies. Powerful enemies.

Most importantly, common enemies.

And Little was in Seattle right now. The HSI people were keeping extra-close tabs on him, making sure he got nowhere near Campo. None of that had done any good in the end, but perhaps some good could come of it.

The right personnel would be essential this time. Chop's men had obviously not been equal to the task. Either because they were sloppy, or because they had underestimated the woman, or both, it didn't matter.

The naval mountain-warfare center had been close to Campo, and Kane and Chop went way back. That combination, along with the security advantages of siloing different aspects of Kane's activities, had led to a bad call. He wouldn't make a mistake like that again. This time, he would use picked men. He would brief them carefully: *Don't underestimate these two—especially the woman. And forget about interrogation—this is no longer about intelligence gathering, it's about neutralization. Not a kill-or-capture, just a kill.*

But damn it, there would be a lot of attention. He had to find a way to mitigate that. He couldn't use his own people. He needed an intermediary. A fall guy.

And then it hit him. He'd heard the rumors. That Oliver Graham Enterprises—OGE, these days doing business as Percivallian—had been involved with the child-pornography ring. That OGE had even caused the civilian plane crash in which an FBI contractor investigating the ring had died. If that were true, it might be that the attack Lone had survived in Seattle had also been an OGE operation. Certainly it was hard to believe Oliver Graham's subsequent abduction and assassination in Paris was unconnected to all that. In fact, now that he was thinking about it, he wondered where Lone had been when Graham died. In Paris? CBP could confirm that.

If she had been in Paris, it would hardly be proof. But it would be further evidence that this woman was not just formidable, but also formidably connected.

It didn't really matter, though. Whether the woman was involved with Graham's death, whether OGE had been involved with the plane crash and the various attacks . . . the rumors would be enough to get people looking in the wrong direction. Which, from Kane's perspective, would be the right direction.

The more he thought about it, the more he liked it. If Lone and Little were to die violently now, OGE—or, rather, Percivallian—might easily be the primary suspect. Especially with a few judicious leaks to favored contacts in the media fueling the proper speculation.

It felt right. He'd been focusing so much on how to take care of it discreetly. But with enough misdirection, discretion might not really matter. In fact, misdirection might be even better.

OGE. Kane knew plenty of people there. They'd done work for him before.

He swung his feet to the floor, picked up the secure unit, and punched in a number.

14

Livia flipped up the hood of her Gore-Tex jacket and started heading toward Lake View Cemetery in Seattle's Capitol Hill neighborhood. Fremont Canal Park was fine, but she thought more than two meetings in the same place might be unwise, and had proposed the change before finishing up with Little the night before.

She'd made sure Lieutenant Strangeland had seen her that morning—at roll call, of course, but also afterward. The lieutenant hadn't commented on the previous day's absence. Livia could have handled it—her detective's schedule was flexible enough, and irregular enough, to explain time away from the office. But it was better that she didn't have to.

The cemetery was a little under three miles from headquarters, most of it uphill, and she walked fast, sweating despite a steady downpour, needing to burn off the stress. She hoped Little had learned something. They had to come to grips with this thing, whatever it was. Get off defense and on offense. And not just for their own sakes. For Mrs. Cuero's, too.

No matter what, she had to make sure her own name stayed out of it. She couldn't afford the scrutiny. How long had it taken her to revert to the very behavior Strangeland had specifically warned against? She might have laughed if she hadn't been so worried, because there hadn't been even a day's hiatus. She'd had that talk with Strangeland not ten feet from the burner Little had deposited. The next day, she'd killed two men who ambushed her. And here she was, on her way to meet Little again, her own phone back at headquarters in case anyone was trying to track it.

She was still angry at him, though maybe not quite as intensely as she ought to be. He hadn't been completely wrong when he said she owed him, for one thing. Without the files he'd given her, she never would have been able to track down the rest of the gang that had trafficked her and Nason. Yes, he had his own reasons for sharing those files, but it was also true she had benefited. Enormously.

But whether or how much she owed him was really the least of it. The truth was, she couldn't help herself. Not knowing what had become of someone you loved, not even knowing whether she was alive or dead . . . She couldn't think of anything worse. She'd lived that nightmare for sixteen years. If she could help assuage someone else's similar anguish, she had no real choice. And how could she resent Little for something that was ultimately intrinsic to her?

She entered the cemetery on the northwest side through a hole she knew of in the fence. It was noon, and she was a half hour early. But one of the things she'd learned in Paris from Carl's partner, Rain, was that arriving at a meeting on time was generally a bad idea. In fact, it was one of the world's most effective ways of letting the opposition set up an ambush. And while she wasn't concerned about Little in that regard, she understood that the habits you practiced in low-danger environments would shape your behavior in high-danger ones as well.

She walked the perimeter clockwise, noting nothing out of place. A few dog walkers, a few retirees trudging along, out for their daily exercise despite the weather. On a clear summer day, there would be more people—the cemetery was named for its spectacular view of Lake

Washington, after all. But in the cold autumn rain, she and Little would have it mostly to themselves. The main attraction was the Brandon Lee and Bruce Lee gravesite, where at least a few tourists could generally be found paying their respects. That was where she and Little would meet. It would give him what she knew spies called "cover for action," and from there the two of them could stroll anywhere—the adjacent GAR Cemetery, Boren Park, Interlaken Park . . . This part of the city was quiet during the day, and heavily wooded, and would offer plenty of options for privacy.

She was in the southeast corner, next to a maintenance structure, when she saw Little walking in from the entrance, holding an umbrella aloft. She smiled. For whatever reason—maybe because it rained on and off so often—Seattleites tended not to bother carrying umbrellas, preferring rain jackets and hoods instead.

She headed north, then ghosted in behind him. He seemed to be alone. But as careful as he was about cellphone security, in Virginia he would have led two OGE operators right to their position if Rain and Larison hadn't spotted the problem and dealt with it. That had been a good lesson for her, and she thought it was worth employing now.

They were almost at the Lee gravesite when he glanced behind him. He saw her, gave a nearly imperceptible nod, and kept going. Okay, he was checking his back, albeit not as often as she would have liked.

There was a tall row of thick shrubbery facing the two markers. Little disappeared around it. Livia continued on to the circular road behind the monument and approached from that direction. She wasn't concerned about anything in particular. It was just better not to come from the direction someone was expecting.

She moved up alongside him and they stood quietly for a moment, facing the markers, a couple of martial-arts pilgrims visiting the site.

"All good?" she said after a moment.

"Yeah."

"Anything about the naval base?"

He glanced around. "Maybe. All I could get was a report of a training accident."

"What kind of training accident?"

"I don't know. The executive officer I spoke with told me his commander wasn't available."

"Why?"

"The XO wouldn't say, other than that the commander was attending to the aforementioned training accident. When I asked him for more about this training accident, it turned into a pissing match about the nature of my interest, military and civilian jurisdiction, etc."

"Under the circumstances, aren't your questions going to be a red flag?"

"Under the circumstances, do you think I care?"

They were quiet for a moment. Livia said, "What do you make of it?"

"Oh, they're hiding something."

"Something like two bodies?"

"Yeah. Along with the effort to make it seem like the men in question died on the base in a 'training accident' rather than by the side of the road at the hands of a cop they were trying to abduct. That's what my gut tells me, though for the moment I don't have anything resembling proof."

A man walked by on the road behind the markers. He was wearing a boonie hat and an old-school trench coat, and he held an umbrella over his head with one hand and an aluminum attaché case by his side in the other. He glanced at them as he passed, his expression neutral, detached.

Livia watched as he headed back toward the cemetery entrance. "How did you get here?" she said to Little, feeling uneasy.

"I drove."

The man disappeared behind some trees.

"Are you sure you weren't followed?"

Even as she said it, she realized the question was pointless. Even if he claimed to be positive, she wouldn't trust his judgment.

He glanced around. "I was careful."

"Because that guy felt odd to me."

"Odd how?"

It was too much to discuss right then, and she wasn't sure she could articulate all of it regardless. Some of it had to do with things Rain had told her in Paris—about how not to get noticed in an urban environment. Some of it involved the incongruities. The umbrella suggested he was from out of town. But why bother carrying it if he was also wearing a hat? At best, it was suspenders and a belt. Sure, maybe explainable. And maybe his presence was explainable, too. But if he was an out-of-towner here for homage to Bruce and Brandon Lee, why had he not lingered close by? His glance at them would have been explainable if he'd thought, *Oh, there are people here, I'll wait until they depart before paying my own respects.* But he'd just looked at Little and her and then headed out. And anyway, why would he be toting around an aluminum attaché case on a walk in the rain?

"We need to move," she said. "Now."

"Are you sure?" he said, but she was already walking fast toward the hole in the fence where she'd come in.

She came to the hole and waited impatiently. When he'd caught up, she pointed through the hole to the street below them. "Climb down," she said. "Go right. Then another right on East Howe, and right again on Fifteenth. Back to the entrance where you came in."

"Where are you going?" he said, breathing a little hard.

"Same place, other direction. Just do it. Be watchful, okay? I think someone followed you."

"I'm pretty sure—"

"Just do it," she said. She turned and ran through the trees along the western perimeter, vaulted over the chain-link fence in the southwest corner, then sprinted east along the muddy, tree-lined path that cut between the cemetery and Volunteer Park just south of it.

What was that? she thought. *It was something. I know it. But what?*

She came to the end of the path and slowed, hanging back behind a clump of trees for concealment. A few cars passed on Fifteenth, their tires splashing rainwater onto the sidewalk. Otherwise, the area was deserted.

She darted across Fifteenth, continuing east on Galer, then made a quick left on Grandview. Heading north now, parallel to the cemetery but one street over. To her left were small apartment buildings; on the right, single-family houses. No traffic. No pedestrians. There were cars parked on the right side of the narrow street, but she ignored them. If this was an ambush, no one would have expected her over here.

She stopped at the end of the street, crouching along a low concrete wall, and peeked left along Garfield. The street rose on a steady incline to the cemetery across Fifteenth. More parked cars. Nothing out of place.

She looked right. The street declined steadily until it was out of sight. Again, nothing.

But she hadn't been wrong. She knew it.

Where did he go? What was he doing?

If he, or a team, had followed Little, why the walk-by in the cemetery?

To confirm. Your presence, your identity, your location. And then—

She crept left on Garfield, staying low along the concrete wall, parked cars to her right offering some concealment from Fifteenth Street and the cemetery. She saw movement through the trees on the other side of Garfield. A flash of something metallic.

The Louisa Boren Lookout. A little urban oasis with views of Lake Washington and the Cascades. She ducked lower, alongside one of the parked cars, looked more closely, and—

It was him. Standing next to one of the columns of the sculpture on the lookout—a twenty-foot-high collection of rusting steel-covered monoliths. Lurking under one of the horizontal blocks. To get out of the rain? While staying close to the cemetery, where he'd confirmed her and Little's presence? Why?

The man knelt, facing the cemetery, and set the attaché case on the ground. Worked an integral combination lock. Opened the case. Began manipulating something inside it.

The weather was bad, true, but even on a gray day no one on the lookout would stand—or kneel—facing the street. The spot was all about the views, and the views were all in the other direction. But this guy wasn't here for that. His mind was on the cemetery, and his posture was mirroring his focus.

She didn't consciously consider what she was doing. It was all instinct. She just melted back along Garfield, moving downhill until the man and the sculpture were out of sight. Then she cut between two houses and onto a jogging trail in the heavily forested park behind the lookout. She moved counterclockwise until she was past his position, then crept up the wet hill, careful with her footing in the mud and wet leaves. All she could hear, other than the steady drumbeat of the rain, was an occasional car passing on Fifteenth Street, the sound of water spray and tires on wet pavement, above her position.

The last ten feet of the climb were too slippery to proceed upright, and she dropped to a crawl until she reached the top, level with the sculpture but positioned on the other side. As expected, she couldn't see him from here. Which meant he couldn't see her.

She crept closer, her boots squishing softly on the wet grass. Her heart was pounding hard and she breathed deeply, all the way in, all the way out, taking the tension down a notch the way she always had in wrestling and judo competition. She lowered the hood so she could see better.

She came to the closest pillar and paused next to it. Concealment—and cover, too, if it came to that.

She dropped her hand to the belly-band holster, undid the strap, and gripped the Glock. But she would use it only if she absolutely had to. It wouldn't matter if she was cleared in another officer-involved. Cleared or not, she'd be under even more of a microscope, and examined by even more people. She doubted this time she could survive it.

She took one more deep, silent breath, pushed it out, inhaled again, and eased clockwise around the pillar.

She saw him an instant before he did her. He was still kneeling, focused on something inside the open attaché case. Then his head snapped around as he detected movement in his peripheral vision. She saw recognition in his expression—his eyes wide, his mouth open, everything equal parts fear and surprise. He slammed the case shut and jumped back, his hand whipping around to his waist, digging inside the trench coat—

She moved in fast, much faster than he could backpedal, blasting straight into him with her right side at the same instant she grabbed his right sleeve and left lapel. The shock of the impact knocked him back, and his arm came forward, his hand out, and in her peripheral vision she saw the gun, but she was already spinning counterclockwise, bending at the hips, yanking out and up with the sleeve hand and launching an uppercut into his chin with the lapel grip, her right leg reaping upward directly into his balls. *Uchi mata*—but for the testicle impact instead of the inner thigh, a classic judo throw and one of her favorites. His body somersaulted, his legs whipping past, both heels slamming into the overhang of one of the steel blocks, ringing it like a gong. Then he was past her, his head rocketing toward the ground, and she drove her knuckles into his throat as the back of his cranium took the impact, and she heard a loud crunch, felt something like a glass rod breaking behind his Adam's apple. Her right leg was still raised and her momentum threatened to carry her past him, but she got a hand out on the ground and blasted a knee into his liver, arresting her momentum. She groped for his wrist, found it, and yanked it high, but the gun was gone, lost on impact, and he was seizing now—whether from the cranial impact or the blow to the throat, she didn't know—his body twitching, his arms flapping, his heels making a weird rhythmic pattering noise on the wet ground. She rolled off him, stood, and checked her perimeter, her hand on the butt of the Glock. No one. Nothing but the steady downpour.

She saw Little running down the street, arms pumping, the umbrella closed in his left hand, keeping his right free. She waved parallel to the ground in a *slow-down* gesture—it was done, now the trick was to avoid attention. Her heart hammering, she glanced around at the mud and wet grass. There, the gun. She picked it up—HK45 Compact—and shoved it into one of the pockets of her cargo pants.

Little came in under the sculpture, knelt, and held his fingers to the man's neck. The seizing had stopped and the man's face had gone blue. Little looked at her. "He's done. Get out of here."

"What are you going to—"

"I'll drag him into the underbrush and come back for him," he said, glancing left, then right. "If he's found, or I'm found with him, I'll take the heat. Just go. Now."

She knew he owed her. But she hesitated.

"Damn it, Livia, for once in your life would you just listen?"

He was right. Either both of them could take the risk, or one.

She raised her hood. "How do I reach you?"

"Meet me at Fremont Canal Park. Midnight."

"No. We've already been there too many times. And you were followed, Little, do you get that? You need to watch your back. Change hotels. Turn off your cellphone. You need to figure out what weakness they exploited, and fix it."

"I do turn off my cellphone. And you can't be sure—"

"You're used to tracking people electronically! It's natural that's the way you think, that's the area you're careful about. But the old-fashioned shit still works, and if someone couldn't track your phone with a Gossamer, they'd resort to something more traditional. Do you get it? When the lights go out, candles still work."

He opened his mouth as though to argue, then closed it and glanced around again instead. "You're right. I'll be extra careful. Do you still have the burner I left for you?"

"Yes."

"Okay. I'll get a new one, just in case, and I'll text you from some-place where I'm not staying long. Turn on the burner whenever and you'll know the text is from me. You tell me a time to meet. That's all. Nothing else over the phone."

"Where are we meeting?"

"You tell me."

She thought for a moment. Somewhere central, so Little could get to it easily, but reasonably discreet. Someplace she could see in multiple directions at once.

"The reflecting pool at Cal Anderson Park," she said.

"Reflecting pool. Cal Anderson Park. Got it."

She nodded and leaned down to grab the case, thinking to examine its contents later. But what if there was a tracking device?

She knelt and opened it. There was a large tablet computer affixed to the top. In the bottom section, a keyboard, dials, and toggles. And foam protective casing, surrounding something that might have been a hummingbird, if it hadn't been obviously mechanical.

Little took hold of the lapels of the guy's coat. "What is it?" he said.

She stared at the contents of the case, having a hard time accepting the truth of what she was seeing. Then she looked at Little.

"I'm not sure," she said. "But I think . . . it's a drone."

15

Little watched as Livia walked off. When she was across the street and had broken into a jog, he turned back to the matter at hand.

Whoever he was, the guy was clearly dead. He'd stopped moving, his mouth was a rictus, and above the collar of his shirt his throat had blossomed into a giant purplish balloon, like the neck of some exotic tropical frog. Little wasn't sure what Livia had done—broken the guy's neck or crushed his larynx. Not for the first time, he felt a flush of admiration, and gratitude, and even a degree of envy.

He used his grip on the lapels of the guy's coat to drag him toward the dense underbrush on the west side of the overlook. When he reached the edge, he stopped. Livia had disappeared from view.

He looked around. Some cars going past on the street in front of the cemetery. No pedestrians. The guy had clearly chosen the sculpture for the concealment it offered, and between that and the weather, Little was pretty sure no one would have noticed any of what had just happened.

He thought for a moment. There had been no gunplay, so no ballistic evidence to worry about. In fact, given the amount of rain, he doubted there would be forensic evidence of any kind at the scene. So no real reason not to leave the body where it lay. It would be discovered, and then the local cops would run the prints, search his clothes. Maybe they had his face in a database, or his DNA.

You could learn something. Maybe a lot.

But then a coroner would fix the time and manner of death. And Livia had told him the kind of shit she was dealing with at the office—shit he couldn't deny he had made substantially worse. He imagined her getting back to headquarters soaking wet and covered in grass stains and mud. Would anyone think to connect that with what got found here? Especially given her martial-arts skills and the broken neck.

No. He couldn't just leave the body. He had to do something to disappear it more permanently. He circled around, got his hands under a thigh and shoulder blade, and braced to roll the guy over the edge.

A voice spoke up in his mind, loud and insistent:

Leave him. Let the local cops find his corpse. Let them investigate. Do you want to solve this fucking thing? Do you want to find the men who took Presley?

For a long moment, he was frozen, stranded in some awful purgatory, trapped between decency and desperation.

He knew he was in a bad place. Maybe not even completely in his right mind. Livia had sensed that, and she hadn't been wrong.

But he'd never been this close, so fucking close to knowing. Just *knowing*. If he could just know what had happened to that sweet girl. Just that and no more. He'd be satisfied. He'd be grateful.

But please, God, give me an hour alone with the ones who did it. Yes, please, God, give me that. Please.

He tried not to imagine what he would do to them. Sometimes he swam in those fantasies—of a MAPP-gas blowtorch, an eighteen-inch butcher saw, a twenty-volt hammer drill—and sometimes, the fantasies threatened to drown him. There were weekends he would stop at a hardware store, handling the wares, imagining how he would use them. He had spoken to butchers and construction workers and forensic pathologists, drawing them out about the various tools they used, the applications, the advantages and disadvantages, the reasons they preferred one over another.

There were times things like that could soothe him. Give the helpless, boiling rage a direction, bleed some of it off. Sometimes he fell asleep to extraordinarily precise and detailed fantasies about what he would do to the men, what instruments he would use, the ways he would employ them, how careful he would be not to make a mistake that could end things prematurely, so that the punishment he inflicted could be both maximally excruciating and maximally long.

If he ever caught them. If he ever had the chance.

And now, maybe, maybe, maybe . . . he did. But he had to focus on the mechanics, not the endgame. Work the evidence, step by step. Do everything he could to push away all the emotion and just . . . investigate.

If he could do that, he would find them. He would.

Then leave the body. Let the police do their job.

He wanted to listen to that voice so badly that he actually groaned from the effort of overruling it. And then he began to cry.

I'm sorry, he thought. *I'm sorry. I'm sorry.*

He didn't know who he was apologizing to. Presley, for restraining himself? Or Livia, for having almost betrayed her?

It didn't matter. He felt like he had walked to the very edge of a horrible, dark abyss, and looked over, and somehow . . . held back.

This time.

He patted the guy down. But for a Tracfone, which was almost certainly a burner from which Little would learn nothing, his pockets were empty.

He jammed his hands deeper under the shoulders and both legs, then half lifted, half shoved the body over the edge. It tumbled down the side and disappeared into a tangle of brambles.

He remained there for a moment, breathing hard. Then he stood, opened his umbrella, and walked out to the street. He was parked just around the corner. He'd come back after dark, drag the body into the trunk of his car, and dispose of it somewhere more permanent. The whole Seattle area was shot through with rivers and lakes. All he had to do was find the right one and dump the body there.

Of course, he'd need to punch it full of holes first, to ensure that it would stay sunk. That meant a trip to a hardware store.

He laughed out loud at the thought, and wondered if he might be going crazy. And maybe he was. Because he didn't even care.

16

An hour later, Livia was back at headquarters. She'd wanted to go to her loft in Georgetown to change out of her wet, grass-stained pants, but she'd already been gone too long. So she'd jogged back from the cemetery, stopping at a Safeway to buy a shopping bag in which she could carry the HK and the attaché case. She was paranoid about tracking devices, but the drone, if that's what it was, had an obvious battery, which she removed, and the tablet was powered off. She bought a few innocuous items for cash and loaded them into the bag on top of the gun and the case.

Naturally, she was just out of the elevator at headquarters and on her way to her cubicle when Strangeland popped out of her office. The lieutenant looked her up and down, then raised her eyebrows. "You fall into Puget Sound?"

The bad luck was so predictable it could have been funny. Livia gave her a sardonic smile. "Something like that."

"Seriously, what happened? You look like you dove for third base out on Safeco Field."

"Got caught in the rain. Took a dumb shortcut."

"Where?"

"Community Garden."

That would be the Danny Woo Community Garden, an acre or so of terraced plots tended by elderly Asian residents of the International District. A half mile southeast of headquarters, it was a nice place for a stroll, at least when the weather was good.

Strangeland laughed. "What, you growing your own kale now?"

Livia didn't like the laugh. It was too disarming. And the conversation had already gone on too long. "Yeah," she said. "Don't tell anyone, or they'll all want some."

Strangeland could have pushed it if she'd wanted, and though Livia had answers, they wouldn't have been great ones. But maybe the lieutenant didn't really want to know, because all she said was "Just be careful you don't catch a cold."

Livia recognized the subtext. For a second, the enormity of what she'd just done, what had almost happened at the overlook, crashed through the barricades and into her consciousness.

She shoved it away. The trick was to not think about it. Little would either handle the body or not. It was up to him now. The best thing she could do was focus on being a cop. Her job. Her calling.

And weirdly, she supposed, the safest thing she did.

She checked her cellphone. There was a message from Mrs. Cuero, wanting to know if she'd found anything.

Yeah, she thought. *Though I'm not sure what.*

But she would try to tell the woman something. Eventually. The thought of leaving someone marooned in the kind of hell she herself had endured over Nason was unbearable.

There was another message, this one on the office line. A woman responding to information on the SPD blotter about a rapist tied to three attacks through new DNA evidence. A man matching the blotter description had offered the woman a ride in his SUV late at night in Capitol Hill a year earlier. The woman had declined the offer and nothing had happened, but it sounded to her now like the same man.

It was good news. So as not to infect the testimony of potential witnesses, the department hadn't made it public, but the man they were looking for had a signature line he used when offering his victims a lift: *Hey there, you look like someone who could use a ride.* Within the department, they were even calling him the Hey There Rapist. The hope was that other women would recall being offered a ride by a man fitting the physical description and using the line, and that eventually, someone would remember a key detail, or some new facet of the pattern would reveal itself, which would lead to an additional piece of evidence, and eventually to Mr. Hey There himself.

Livia called the woman. She was named Amy, and she worked as a waitress at a place in Capitol Hill called the Pine Box, so named in part because the building was previously a mortuary. Amy had to be at work at three, but yes, she could meet now. Ghost Note Coffee, right around the corner from the Pine Box? Perfect. See you there in fifteen minutes.

Livia headed out, the shopping bag in hand. She made sure to pause outside Strangeland's office on the way to the elevators. "Might have a lead on the Hey There Rapist," she said. "Woman who says a man matching the description tried to give her a ride a year ago. Going to interview her now."

Strangeland glanced at the shopping bag, then nodded. "Let me know what you find," she said.

Livia nodded and moved off. She'd caught the glance at the shopping bag. Yeah, Strangeland had questions. For now, the lieutenant preferred not to ask. But that might change. Livia couldn't let it.

In the basement garage, Livia shut down her phone, got in her Jeep, and headed out—northeast on James, left under the I-5 overpass onto Seventh Avenue, then Hubbell, and finally Pike. She pulled into an alley across from the Starbucks Roastery, dumped the innocuous items and the HK from the shopping bag, hit the power button on Little's burner, and photographed the contents she'd taken from the attaché case. Then she logged on to the Starbucks Wi-Fi, brought up Signal, and called Kanezaki.

He answered instantly—a habit she remembered from the previous times they'd worked together. "Hello."

"You recognize my voice?" she said.

There was a pause. "I think so."

"Good. I have something that might interest you."

"Okay."

"I don't know exactly what it is. I thought you might."

"Is this for my benefit, or yours?"

Carl had warned her that information was Kanezaki's coin of the realm. And that anything he offered, he would expect to be paid for.

"I don't know yet," she said. "I'm hoping both. Can I text you photos?"

"Go ahead."

She did. A moment went by. Then he said, "Where the hell did you get that?"

She felt a little adrenaline surge. He hadn't even tried to conceal the astonishment in his tone.

"You know what it is?"

"Uh, yeah. Where did you get it?"

"A man who I think was planning to use it against me somehow."

"What do you mean, 'somehow'?"

"I mean, I don't know what it is. A drone?"

"Yeah, it's a drone. Called an Azrael. I hope you've been handling it carefully. There's an explosive in the nose. Fragmentation charge."

"What?"

"Who's the man you took it from?"

"I don't know. He was following me. I doubled back on him, and he was preparing something inside an attaché case. When he saw me, he went for a gun."

Kanezaki didn't respond, and for a bad moment, she wondered if she'd made a mistake in contacting him. For all she knew, the man she'd killed was one of Kanezaki's colleagues. He'd helped her catch the park rapist, and Carl trusted him, but . . .

She forced the thought aside. She'd consider those angles later. For now, she'd committed to a throw. Backing off halfway was a good way to get thrown yourself.

"Here's the thing," Kanezaki said. "That drone is a prototype. There are three in existence. Very tightly controlled program. Even I'm not supposed to know, and I'm not going to tell you how I do."

Well, she didn't need to know that. She assumed it was because Kanezaki made it a point to know everything. She wondered briefly if he'd ever been betrayed. If so, it had made a lasting impression.

"You guys use these for . . . assassinations?" she said.

"We don't use them for anything yet. But yes, they'll be the next thing in 'dispositions,' as we prefer to call them. Drones started off as surveillance platforms. Naturally, someone got the idea that maybe they could be missile platforms, too. And then 9/11 happened, and some S&T guys—CIA Science & Technology, the geek squad—literally bolted a couple of Hellfire missiles to the wings of an early model of Predator and blew up a truck full of high-value targets in Yemen. That was the first salvo in the drone wars, and the focus after that was loiter time, accuracy, and firepower. The Predator was succeeded by the Reaper."

She thought of how Carl would have made fun of all the scary names . . . Hellfire and Predator and Reaper. She could only imagine what alternatives he would propose. It made her miss him. And the way he could make her laugh. And how safe he made her feel.

"But that was yesterday's game," Kanezaki went on. "Today, it's all about miniaturization."

"I knew about the bird-sized ones," she said. "It's how Dillon tracked Carl—Dox—in Thailand. But this one . . . I mean, any smaller and it would be more like a dragonfly than a bird."

Kanezaki said nothing, and she realized insect-sized drones must already be in development.

"How does it work?" she said.

"What do you mean?"

"I mean, you fly it close to the target, and blow it up?"

"Pretty much. A Hellfire missile destroys the whole building. What we're talking about . . . much smaller footprint. It's ineffectively lethal from farther than five feet out, though maybe it could blind someone. But fly it up alongside the target closer than that, and . . . done."

"What about two people standing close together, talking?"

"Sure, fly it right between them. Precise and discreet as a sniper rifle, and with a lot less required training and skill. Plus it's more versatile, because it's standoff. You don't need line-of-sight. It can go anywhere— around corners, through windows, you name it."

"You said there are only three," she said.

"That's right."

"Can you tell me who would have access?"

"Can you tell me what you're involved in that would make someone with access want to use one against you?"

"I'm not sure yet."

"Okay, tell me what you know."

She didn't distrust him, exactly, but she didn't like going first. On the other hand, she didn't see an alternative. He'd dangled enough to make her realize that, and he'd done it well.

She briefed him. When she was done, he said, "Whatever the involvement of the naval base, this drone wasn't them. They don't have access. They don't even have knowledge."

She caught just a hint of professional pride in the assertion, and hoped it was a consequence of his confidence, rather than the cause.

"Okay," she said. "Then who?"

"I don't know."

"Can you find out?"

There was a long pause. She thought he was going to tell her no. Or name some impossible price—kill someone, betray someone, she didn't know what.

But all he said was "Maybe. Will you give me the Azrael?"

That wasn't even hard. "It's yours," she said.

"Okay. Keep it with you. Like the president keeps the nuclear football, okay? I don't want that thing lost. Or to fall into the wrong hands."

"I get it."

"Call me back in thirty minutes."

She hesitated, then said, "Thank you."

"Don't thank me yet," he said, and clicked off.

17

Kanezaki took the stairs to the basement. From there, it would be a good quarter-mile walk to the tech lab. He was always looking for reasons to visit the various fiefdoms at Langley. If nothing else, it meant a little exercise. He needed it, too. These days he spent way too much time at his desk.

The call from Lone had been the weirdest he'd received in longer than he could remember. And mixed up as he was with Rain, Dox, and the rest of his off-the-books assets, Kanezaki was no stranger to weird calls.

He knew about the Azrael program. Give the geek squad their due, they came up with cool names, and associating the miniaturized drone project with a biblical angel of death was a great way to ensure continued funding.

Which wasn't to say that Azrael was just a marketing boondoggle. The geek squad had made astonishing progress with battery life, and what had started as tether powered, and then laser powered, had now reached almost an hour of entirely self-contained battery-operated flight time. The implications were enormous—not just for the war on terror, but also with regard to surveillance, both foreign and domestic—which was why the program had to be kept under such tight wraps.

And yet, someone had made the call to let one of the Azrael birds out of its cage. Who? And why? From what Lone had told him, all she was up to was investigating a series of disappearances of teenaged girls. Which was of course a horrible thing, but it wasn't geopolitics.

Well, whatever it was, it must have threatened someone high up. Someone with Azrael clearances and then some. Okay, he could imagine that. What he couldn't imagine was, why would someone want to use something so sophisticated, and with such a specific signature? At a minimum, it felt like overkill. And it also entailed what seemed unnecessary risk, because the remnants of the drone would almost certainly be discovered with the bodies of the Seattle cop and Homeland Security investigator the drone had been used to assassinate. That would point in directions a simple bullet or a regular bomb never would.

He walked along the windowless corridor, the cinderblock walls painted an incongruous powder blue, the overhead fluorescent lights so harsh they almost called for sunglasses. Walking the various subcellars at Langley was always vaguely disorienting, akin to being in the belly of a Las Vegas casino. It could be high noon or the middle of the night or anything in between. No clocks, no windows, just the artificial brightness and the echoes of your own footfalls on the linoleum as you walked by the endless walls, and rounded undifferentiated corners, and passed locked door after identical locked door, nothing but the stenciled numbers beside them to give you even a clue about where you might be.

He wondered why he was helping her. Well, he wasn't sure he *was* helping her yet. He might not be able to uncover anything useful. But still, he was trying.

Some of it had to do with what he might learn from her. Misuse of an Azrael drone in a domestic assassination was the kind of thing he liked to know about. Lusted to know about, if he was being honest. Some of which had to do with the way his then-boss, Tokyo Station

Chief Biddle, had tried to set him up for a fatal fall way back when Kanezaki had been a young, dumb CIA recruit. He would never forget that lesson, and he would never relax in his efforts to be forewarned and therefore forearmed. And never stop surrounding himself with people he knew he could rely on. Which was odd, because it was his colleagues he distrusted and his assets, people like Rain and Dox, who he knew had his back. Maybe it wasn't just Biddle's betrayal. Maybe it had to do with growing up *sansei*, spending time in America and Japan, and feeling like an outsider in both. He wasn't sure.

So why was he inclined to help Lone? Dox, he supposed. He knew there was a strong attachment between the big sniper and the Seattle cop. And because Dox was one of his most valuable assets, it made sense to do right by Lone as a way of keeping Dox in his debt.

All that was true. And yet . . .

The woman made him uncomfortable. She was too much of a zealot. Everything was black and white to her. It was bad enough that she herself was oblivious to shades of gray. Worse, he sensed she judged anyone with slightly more nuanced perception to be morally reprehensible.

She lived in a simple world, he knew. Protect children. Protect women. Protect anyone who couldn't protect themselves. Investigate rapists and child abusers, make a case, make an arrest, put a bad guy behind bars.

It almost made him envious. She could accomplish good in the world without engaging in constant moral triage. But intelligence wasn't like police work. In Kanezaki's world, sometimes good ends meant very bad means. He didn't like it. But he didn't see a way to avoid it, either. All he could do was try to be as honest with himself as possible.

Still. Lone herself was so clean, while he felt increasingly . . . tainted by the work he did. If he stayed too long at sea, would he lose sight of shore? Would he forget a shore even existed? He worried about that sometimes.

Periodically, when he was called upon to do something . . . questionable, he would ask himself whether Tatsu would approve. Tatsu, Rain's friend from the Keisatsuchō, the Japanese FBI, who had died from cancer years earlier. He had treated Kanezaki as a son—an honor under any circumstances, and particularly given that Tatsu's own son had died in infancy. Kanezaki had never known anyone who swam in so much muck while himself somehow remaining fundamentally clean. Tatsu hadn't been just a mentor. He had been a model, too, and Kanezaki was determined to be faithful to the memory of his example.

Which, he supposed, might be the real reason he was willing to help Lone. He had children now, a little boy and girl. It was his job to make the world safe for them, whatever it took. But Lone protected them, or at least children like them, in her own way. Her own uncompromised way. And if he helped her, and she was good . . . maybe it would offset some of what he knew was bad about himself.

He smiled ruefully. Maybe he should talk to an agency shrink. Open up about his doubts. But there were people he had crossed who might learn of it, and use it against him. And he wasn't ready to turn over the asylum to the lunatics. Not yet, anyway. Better a white-knuckle drunk than to let anyone find out you were attending meetings.

So okay. He would help her. And, in doing so, help himself. He was like someone whose job was driving a rig to haul away toxic waste. The job was critical, of course, but the rig caused a lot of pollution in its own right. But if he could find a way to purchase a carbon offset . . . well, that would be good, wouldn't it? And then, if his kids ever had questions about the things he'd done and the life he'd led, maybe the offset would help them understand.

He hoped so.

He came to the entrance to the lab—an oversized double steel door. He picked up the phone intercom next to it and punched in a number.

He heard a series of electronic chirps, and then a woman's voice, doing a faux Russian accent: "This is KGB."

He smiled. "One day, that's going to get you in trouble."

"Intelligence is risky business, comrade."

He laughed. "You got a few minutes for a walk?"

"You bet," she said, dropping the accent.

A moment later, he heard the clack of an electronic lock, the whir of hydraulic cylinders retracting. Then the door opened, and a young woman with long auburn hair and startling green eyes came out, dressed as always in a white lab coat. Maya. Two years earlier, Kanezaki had pulled some strings to get her a position with the geek squad straight out of Caltech. And promoted her within the organization since. She was a good kid. It was strange to think of himself becoming for someone else what Tatsu had been for him, but life was a wheel and you had to roll with it.

The door closed. "You look pale," Kanezaki said. "Don't they ever let you play outside?"

She smiled. "Who wants to play outside, with the toys we have down here?"

He inclined his head, and they started walking. "It's actually one of those toys I wanted to ask you about," he said.

"Uh-huh. I wondered what you were doing down here."

His office was on the seventh floor now—the executive level. And seventh-floor people didn't typically frequent the basement. He didn't mind. Most of the assets he'd developed in the building worked on the lower floors. Some of them weren't even officers—there were contractors, even admins. The people who made the organization run. Whose contributions and knowledge were typically overlooked. And who, for these and other reasons, were the easiest to recruit. He hoped no one would ever hold it against him. He was a spy. The way he saw it, recruiting was what spies were supposed to do.

"I heard a rumor," he said. "One of the Azrael birds flew off recently."

She looked at him, her expression a mixture of concern and surprise. He knew she wanted to ask. He also knew she wouldn't.

"I thought you guys were still testing them," he added. "Who would even qualify for a borrow?"

"I don't know on whose authority," she said, glancing around. "But I can tell you the guy who checked it out was a green-badger."

CIA employees were issued blue badges. Green denoted a contractor.

"You guys checked out a prototype assassination drone to a contractor? Who? Why?"

"All I can tell you is he was with OGE. Or Percivallian, or whatever they're calling themselves now. Under a contract with ICE. You know we got the ICE drone program up and running. And still provide updates and technical assistance."

"Yeah, but that's just surveillance drones."

She looked at him and said nothing.

"Jesus," he said.

Again, she said nothing.

"Okay," he said. "When was it checked out?"

"Just yesterday."

He thought for a moment. The situation was crazy. It was irregular enough to have a prototype out in the wild. Given to a green-badger was another level. And as part of an ICE operation . . . even beyond the fact that the drone was apparently intended for the assassination of a local cop and a Homeland Security investigator, it made no sense at all.

"I know you don't know who authorized it," he said. "But tell me who could have."

She sighed. "Tom, what are you getting me mixed up in?"

"You're not getting mixed up in anything."

"People know we're friends. You helped get me the job."

"And you know what you tell me goes no further. I'm not even asking you for a name, Maya. I get you don't know that. I just want to know parameters."

"You going to tell me why?"

"Would you want to know even if I could?"

She chuckled. "Probably not."

"Then who?"

"All I can tell you is this. You know those Azrael birds are closely watched and tightly controlled. If my boss let one go, the request would have had to come all the way from the top."

"The DCI?" That was the director of central intelligence, the head of the whole organization.

She laughed. "Not even close. The boss has been running the lab since before 9/11. He dances circles around directors. Says they come and go, and he's not wrong."

"Then who? DNI?" That was the director of national intelligence, who ran the entire intelligence community—CIA, NSA, everything.

"Higher," she said. "I'm talking SecDef. Vice president, maybe. Or POTUS. That's it."

Kanezaki couldn't see it. What interest would the secretary of defense, the vice president, or the president of the United States have in killing a Seattle cop and a Homeland Security investigator? And even if one of them did, why risk a trail that would lead back to ICE, or OGE, or CIA?

"Anything else you can tell me?" he said.

She shook her head.

"Not even any theories?"

"None at all. You know no one tells me anything. Not even you."

"But you see a lot. You could be a hell of a case officer, Maya, if you ever want to get out in the field."

She smiled. Probably she thought he was trying to flatter her, though in fact he'd meant it.

"All right," he said. "Thanks for the help. Keep me posted? If you learn anything else."

"Don't I always?"

"Well, when I ask, anyway."

"Like I said."

He kept walking, past all the unmarked locked doors. It was good he'd developed ways to get behind some of them. But it seemed he was going to need to figure out how to get inside a few more.

18

It was past two in the morning, and Livia was in her loft, in front of her laptop. This time, it wasn't just the usual insomnia. It was the man at Lake View, and the drone, and most of all what she'd learned from Kanezaki afterward. So although it felt distinctly surreal, she found herself researching the secretary of defense, vice president, and president.

She quickly confirmed that none of them made sense. True, the first of the disappearances had occurred ten years earlier, before the three men had the retinues and security details that followed them everywhere today. But even if back then they might have had the latitude to get away with periodically hunting and abducting teenaged girls all over the country, these days they didn't. Which meant they couldn't have been responsible for Hannah Cuero, at least not directly.

Livia wasn't remotely naïve enough to believe powerful men were incapable of such crimes. If anything, she believed they were especially disposed to them. After all, it was a US senator and his industrialist brother who had been behind her and Nason's abduction, and everything that had happened after. But it wasn't motive that was giving her pause here. It was means and opportunity. The Lone brothers had employed a Thai trafficking network to abduct girls for them, and then deliver the custom-ordered victims as specified—for example, to Senator Lone's soundproofed Bangkok hotel suite.

The one he died in, she thought, taking a moment to indulge a cherished memory.

She knew it was possible some similar means and opportunity could be at work with one of the three men she was looking into now. But her gut wasn't buying it. The point, for whoever was behind these abductions, *was* the abductions. What came after also, certainly. But if all you wanted was venison, you could buy it. Going into the forest to kill a deer was about something else.

But someone had checked out that Azrael drone. And according to Kanezaki, that narrowed the list of suspects to these three.

One of them had a son, though, right? She didn't follow politics much, but she knew that. Vice President Bradley Michael Kane Jr. and his namesake, Congressman Bradley Michael Kane III.

Who, now that she was thinking about it, had recently been accused of rape by a woman he'd known in high school. A woman who had then been forced to go into hiding because of death threats.

Livia searched for news about Congressman Bradley Michael Kane III. Yes, the woman was named Noreen Prentis. A month ago, she had accused the younger Kane, whose nickname was apparently "Boomer," of raping her at a party while they were in high school. Boomer denied the allegations, and Prentis claimed to be receiving death threats for speaking out—threats corroborated by police. And then she'd disappeared. There had been a flurry of reporting about that, but it had quickly died down. Her family claimed she was missing, but police found nothing. Some people suspected the worst, and blamed Boomer's unhinged constituents. Boomer's supporters, enraged about a conspiracy against him, accused the woman of being a publicity seeker and engaging in a stunt. But the consensus seemed to be that she'd panicked, whether because of the spotlight or the death threats or both, that she had gone into hiding, and that her family's claims that she was missing were intended to bolster the story. Apparently, a Ukrainian journalist named Arkady Babchenko had done something similar, faking his own demise in response to death threats. A few talking heads were citing Babchenko as a kind of precedent.

Livia's gut wasn't buying that. A faked disappearance wasn't impossible, but it felt far-fetched.

Still, if something had happened to Noreen Prentis, there was no evidence of foul play. She'd just vanished. Which wasn't an easy thing to pull off.

Unless, of course . . . the person or people involved were good at it.

Because they had a lot of practice.

She felt a tingle of excitement and tried to ignore it. The trick was to stay clinical. Detached. You had to consciously avoid confirmation bias and other psychological traps. Work the evidence as it presented itself.

She went to Boomer's official website and immediately felt her excitement deflate. He'd done six tours with Special Forces in Iraq. Most of the girls in Little's file had disappeared in the States while Boomer had been off at war. It couldn't have been him.

But wait a minute. How much did she really know about overseas military deployments, and about when soldiers rotated back home? No one was deployed to combat for six straight years. What if she could prove Boomer's stateside rotations had coincided with the disappearances of the girls in Little's file?

How could she get that kind of information?

Her mind immediately served up the answer: *Carl.*

She could imagine calling him, explaining the situation, explaining everything . . .

No. Out of the question. She shoved it all aside.

Kanezaki, then? No, she had asked too much of him already. She didn't want to be further in his debt.

And then she thought of someone else. And was surprised to realize it felt right. Surprised to feel she trusted him.

At least as much as she trusted anyone.

She took the satellite phone from the safe, walked to the north windows, and powered up the unit. Then she punched in a number from a coded list and waited for the call to go through. It didn't matter that it was the middle of the night. The guy she was calling was in Bangkok.

She got a ring, then another, and then his gravelly voice. "Hello."

Fallon. A Kanezaki asset she and Carl had worked with against a transnational trafficking network in Thailand. Also a former marine with some kind of medical training, and an unusually capable guy generally. He had patched her up after she'd damn near died killing Rithisak Sorm, the man behind her and Nason's abduction.

"Hey," she said. "It's been a while. You recognize my voice?"

"I think I do," he said. "This phone is encrypted. Beyond GMR-2. If yours is also, we should be good to go."

"It is, and we are. How are you?"

"Ah, I can't complain. Interesting times around here. Quite the gang war we seem to have instigated between Thai and Ukrainian traffickers."

She'd read about all that online. "Good," she said.

"Yeah, it would be nice if they'd all just burn each other up. But no matter what, at least we lit the match. Thanks again for bringing me in on that. I was getting bored. Hell, I guess I am again. Hasn't been the same around here since you and your crazy friend left town. How's he doing, anyway?"

She felt the emotion rolling in, and willed it back. "I think okay."

"Oh, you haven't been in touch."

"Not really."

"Ah. I thought . . . well, never mind. How are things on your end? Staying out of trouble?"

"Not exactly."

"Anything I can do to help?"

"Maybe. How much do you know about US Special Forces in Iraq?"

"A bit. What do you want to know?"

She knew Fallon well enough to understand *a bit* probably meant *You're talking to an encyclopedia.*

"I'm looking into a Special Forces soldier," she said. "Deployed to Iraq. Six tours, 2006 to 2013. I want to know how often during that time he would have been stateside."

"Depends. Unlike regular forces, who were doing yearlong tours, initially SF was doing six months in, six months out. The six months back at group would cover their home time and vacation, professional career schools, and then a train-up before heading back over. But the pace was too demanding. Guys just burning out and giving up. So now it's six in, twelve out."

"So a guy deployed to Iraq from 2006 to 2013 . . . he would have been back in the States for at least half that time?"

"Generally speaking, yeah, I'd call that a safe bet."

She felt the excitement building, and pushed it away. "That's helpful," she said. "What I could use now is something more detailed. If I gave you a name, would you have a way of finding out specifically when he was stateside during those years, and specifically where he was deployed? You said 'back at group,' and I'm not sure what that means."

"Just back with his unit at their base in the States. And yeah, I think I could help."

"Oh, okay, got it. The person I'm looking into is Bradley Kane. The third."

There was a pause. "You mean . . . Congressman Kane."

"Yes."

"The one who's running for senator now. Whose father is Vice President Kane."

"Yes."

Another pause. "Well, I guess it wouldn't be like you to be going after small fry."

"I guess not."

"You want to tell me the nature of your interest?"

"I don't want . . . it could compromise you."

"If I start asking favors of people involving digging up Kane's military records, I'd say that's already a touch compromising, wouldn't you?"

Shit, she hadn't thought of that. The mechanics of how he would get the information, if he could, and the trail doing so might create.

She didn't see any downside for herself. Or for her investigation. Whoever she was up against already knew about her. And about Little. They wouldn't know she was looking into Boomer, true, but if Fallon were inclined to spill about that, he already could. Giving him the big picture wouldn't make any difference.

And maybe . . . maybe it would be better if someone knew the whole story. Just in case.

Yeah, just in case.

She told him.

He listened intently, interrupting here and there only to ask for clarification. When she was done, he said, "Are you worried?"

"About what?"

He grunted a laugh. "Well, I guess that answers my question. About yourself."

"A little bit."

"A little bit is not enough here."

"I know what I'm doing, Fallon."

"I think you know *why* you're doing it, yes. But listen. The closer you get to this, whatever it is, the more resistance you're going to run into. From what you've told me, they've underestimated you so far. I'm guessing that part of the dance is over."

"If I can place Boomer Kane in the vicinity of each of those nine disappearances, I can make a case."

There was a pause. Fallon said, "Look, you're the cop, not me. But what you've described sounds like a case built on nothing but circumstantial evidence. Otherwise known as a weak case. And as a friend— and I hope you won't feel I'm presuming in calling myself that—I'd advise you that a circumstantial case against a guy with Boomer Kane's background and capabilities, with a former admiral and current vice president for a father, who can send experimental fucking assassination drones against you—a circumstantial case against a guy like that sounds a lot like a suicide wish."

She gripped the phone tightly. "Someone has to speak for those girls."

What she meant was *I have to.*

Another pause. He said, "I get that. And . . . I respect it."

She remembered how Fallon had reacted when she had told him she and Carl were going after a Thai child rapist, and that they needed Fallon to translate. The way his face had hardened. How he had insisted translation services were going to be the least of it.

And what he'd done afterward.

She had to wait a beat before she trusted herself to speak. Then she said, "Thank you."

"Can I ask you something?" he said.

"Yes."

"The information you need . . . you know Dox could get it for you. And if you need help with more than just the questions . . . well, I'm in, but I'm an old fart. If I were you, Dox is the guy I'd want riding shotgun."

She squeezed her eyes shut. "You can't tell him."

"I won't, if that's what you want. What I'm saying is, I think you should."

"This isn't about me, do you get that? It's about those girls. That's all I need help with. So just . . . look, can you get me what I need?"

She hadn't meant to be so short with him. She was asking him a favor, potentially a big one, and he had already told her he was inclined to help. But the notion that she needed protection, a bodyguard, anything like that . . . she couldn't stand it.

There was a long pause. He said, "Those kinds of records are centralized. I doubt I can get you the records themselves, but I know a guy who'll give me the dates and places."

She felt a surge of relief. "Good."

"But let's say your hunch is right, and Boomer's home times line up with the disappearances. What are you going to do at that point?"

"I'll figure something out."

"Have you thought about the press?"

She hadn't, actually. "What do you mean?"

"If you can place this guy in the vicinity of nine missing girls, and this missing woman, too, Noreen Prentis, that seems like a story, no?"

She smiled. Fallon knew a lot of things. How newspapers worked apparently wasn't one of them.

"It's an interesting idea," she said gently. "But it would have the same shortcomings as a prosecution based solely on circumstantial evidence. Especially given the power and prominence of the family involved, there's no newspaper that would touch it without evidence that would stand up in court. That being the case, court is where I'd rather take it."

"Yeah, I guess that makes sense."

"Thanks for trying, though."

"Well, I wish it had been worth a little more. But let me check in with my guy. He's on the East Coast and an early riser. Can you leave your phone on?"

"Yes."

"All right. Let me see what I can find. You watch your back, okay?"

19

Kane couldn't believe what he was hearing. "What do you mean, the operator is missing?" he said, gripping the receiver of the secure unit and working to stop himself from shouting. "And why am I only getting this report at nearly oh-five-hundred the following day?"

"I wanted to be sure I had all the facts," Gossett said. "I didn't know what went wrong. And I still don't. The operator checked in right after visual confirmation of the target. Should have been all over less than five minutes after that. But nothing happened. We can't raise him, and we've lost contact with the drone, too."

Kane took a deep breath, knowing nothing productive would be achieved by anger and recriminations. He reminded himself that Gossett was a good man. Loyal. Reliable. He'd worked under Kane in the navy, and had performed discreetly and capably in various projects since leaving the service for OGE five years earlier. Something had gone wrong, which happened, and the sensible thing was to figure out what, rather than trying to blame who.

But still. Jesus God almighty.

"I'm . . . not sure what you're telling me," Kane said. "Was the drone used? Are the targets still alive?"

"No reports of deaths or explosions on police channels, so it seems safe to conclude the drone hasn't been used."

"But you lost track of it."

"That could mean a number of things. One is that it accomplished its mission, which of course would entail a loss of the tracking signal. Two is that it was placed in a Faraday container. Three is that someone removed the battery. Again, given the lack of police activity, I think we're talking about either two or three."

Kane shook his head in disbelief. Was this woman supernatural? The two men in Campo were competent, but all right, they underestimated what they were up against, and tied their own hands by attempting a more difficult capture mission rather than a straightforward kill. But this . . . this should never have happened. Half the point of the drone was about deploying something the target would never see coming and would have no way to stop. Had Lone, or Lone and Little both, absconded with the drone? If so, the operator was certainly dead. But then what had they done with the body?

"You said the operator checked in after visual confirmation," Kane said. "Whose confirmation?"

"His own."

Kane tamped down the anger again. "Why would you have the operator personally confirm? If the operator can see the target, the target can also see the operator. Which defeats the whole standoff advantage the drone is intended to create."

"Agreed, sir. But the operator insisted. He used to pilot drones out of Creech, and had some issues with faulty intel leading to collateral damage. Since then, he's insisted on personal visual confirmation. It's never been a problem before."

Kane wanted to shout, *You mean you've always been lucky before.*

No. Fix the problem, not the blame.

"Besides which," Gossett went on, "again, he checked in after the confirmation. Whatever happened, happened after."

"Yes," Kane said, knowing he should drop it but too angry to resist, "but probably because the target spotted him during the confirmation phase and got off the X. Maybe even set up a counter-ambush. Damn it, Gossett, not that I'm any kind of fan of the army, but this is right out of the Ranger Handbook: 'If an enemy is following your rear, circle back and attack along the same path.'"

"You told me the targets were law enforcement, not military."

"I told you the woman, at least, is obviously formidable. What about force protection? Was anyone doing any kind of overwatch of the operator?"

"Sir, you specifically told me—and I quote—you wanted 'the smallest possible footprint.' A dozen operators would have been a dozen points of vulnerability. A dozen potential leaks."

"What about the team you used for surveillance of the man?"

"Their knowledge didn't extend beyond the surveillance. Again, sir, respectfully, this was in keeping with the mission parameters you yourself laid out."

Kane blew out a long breath. Gossett had a point. Of course, the notion of a dozen was an exaggeration. Two additional operators—hell, even one—might have made the difference. All Gossett had to do was double-purpose the surveillance team he'd put on Little. It would have been a small additional risk for a significant potential gain.

On the other hand, it was equally true that Kane could have laid all that out in advance. But he hadn't. Because he had believed the drone was a sure thing, and that anything but the smallest possible team would involve unnecessary risks.

"You're right," Kane said. "I'm sorry if it sounded as though I was . . . leveling recriminations. I'm just trying to understand what went wrong. And what our liabilities might be, if any."

"Beyond the targets still being alive."

"Yes, of course. On balance, I think it was mostly a lost opportunity. Which is, of course, a shame, but no one is going to know what that drone is. And if they ask, they'll get stonewalled in all directions."

"Do you want any follow-up?"

"No, for now, stand down. I'm sure I'll be in touch."

"Roger that."

Kane hung up. As soon as he was off the phone, his anger bloomed again, and he waited for it to pass.

He'd screwed up, there was no denying it. Whether a plan had made sense at the time, in the end it was success or failure that mattered. And his plan had failed. Spectacularly.

For so long, he'd been very . . . conservative in his approach to managing Bradley's problem. Discreetly intervening when Bradley had behaved foolishly in high school. Blocking Little unseen later on, when the man's obsessions threatened to lead him to Bradley. Separating Bradley from the influence of that creature Snake. And easing Bradley into a position of political responsibility—Kane's own congressional seat—where Bradley would finally be forced to become a man, and to once and for all put aside childish things.

But then Snake had been released from Leavenworth, and Hannah Cuero had gone missing, and Little had reacquired the scent. All Kane's careful measures, his graduated responses, suddenly for naught. He wished he had been less circumspect to start with. Of course, proceeding that way against Snake—a decorated Special Forces soldier, after all—and a Homeland Security investigator would have entailed risks he preferred to avoid, and that he judged unnecessary. But now, with the benefit of hindsight, he couldn't deny that if he had eliminated Snake and Little at the outset, the entire situation would have been nipped in the proverbial bud.

He realized now that in moving against Little and Lone the way he had, he had been overreacting to shortcomings born of his previous cautiousness. Which of course was its own form of mistake.

What he needed was an approach that made sense based on where things stood, not one that he was unconsciously designing in reaction to past successes or failures.

When he felt calmer, he began to consider the situation. There was a silver lining, he supposed. Given that something had gone awry, it was best that no one but Gossett knew what was supposed to have happened. Well, Gossett and the presumably dead operator, which amounted to the same thing.

A paranoid thought gripped him: *Could they have arrested the operator?*

Little and Lone were law enforcement, after all. If they had the operator in custody, and a goddamn Azrael drone along with him, it could be a lot. The drone itself would be denied by everyone. But testimony from a live operator about what the drone was intended for . . . That could implicate Gossett.

Gossett would probably hold firm, at least if given assurances of a presidential pardon, which Kane could almost certainly arrange. But still.

He breathed deeply, in and out. He was being paranoid. That was all right, up to a point, but too much was never helpful. Because Lone had left those two bodies in Campo, hadn't she? What aboveboard cop does something like that? She obviously had a lot to hide. Whatever had made her leave those bodies at the scene in the first place, of course, but now the bodies themselves.

He thought about that. He'd been assuming that whatever she was hiding was tied only to Campo. But the more he thought about it, why wouldn't it be more . . . far reaching than just that?

What? What else is she hiding?

He thought about Bangkok. That seemed to be her initial connection with Little. The anti-trafficking task force.

He started Googling news from Bangkok. It seemed a long shot, but he tried "Bangkok Lone."

The first entry was Senator Ezra Lone, who had died in Bangkok a year earlier.

Kane stared at the screen. *What the hell?*

He knew about Ezra Lone, of course. Supposedly it had been a heart attack. The scuttlebutt, though, was that the man was a predatory pedophile, who had been over there on a child-rape junket when someone had shown up at his hotel suite and butchered him, his aide, and some high-level cop with the Thai national police force. Neither government wanted any of that coming out, and the powers that be had cooperated in devising a "heart attack" cover story that included a Bangkok morgue that had conveniently caught fire, destroying any evidence that might have contradicted the official narrative.

Which, at the moment, sounded a hell of a lot like Chop's white phosphorous training accident.

Kane had never made the connection between Livia Lone and Ezra Lone. It was a reasonably common name, and because Detective Lone was Asian, he had assumed her name was of Chinese extraction. But now . . .

It took him five minutes of additional research to learn that Livia Lone had been trafficked to America from Thailand, rescued in a police raid in Llewellyn, Idaho, and fostered in the home of local magnate Fred Lone. Whose brother was . . . Ezra Lone.

Kane shook his head, trying to make sense of it all.

Fred Lone, it turned out, had also died of a heart attack—when Livia Lone had been a junior in high school. And Livia, according to the press reports, had been some kind of local wrestling and judo prodigy.

He leaned back in his chair, his head swimming, suddenly nearly certain Fred Lone's heart attack had been another "heart attack."

This woman . . . what the hell was she?

Well, at a high level it seemed clear enough. The brothers had abused her when she was a child. She acquired martial-arts skills.

She killed Fred Lone and then had to bide her time with the brother, because a senator was a little harder to get to than someone whose house you lived in. She'd found a way eventually. If the stories about what had happened in Ezra Lone's hotel suite were true, the killer was certainly capable. After all, one of the dead was a Thai cop, and Lone's aide was a former American soldier. If the stories about the condition of the bodies were true—the Thai cop castrated and choked with his own severed sex organs, the aide's face shot to pieces, and Ezra Lone gutted like a deer—the killer had also been extremely . . . motivated. Consumed by molten hate, and carrying out the most savage, primal revenge.

He'd always assumed those lurid rumors were tall tales—exaggerations, at least. No longer.

How the hell had she gotten away with it?

Some skill, obviously. She's a cop, she'd know how to clean a crime scene, how to throw off an investigation. And some luck. The authorities on both sides didn't want *an investigation.*

And good God. This . . . avenging angel, or whatever she was, was now after Bradley. With a partner from Homeland Security motivated by the disappearance of his own daughter, presumably at Bradley's hands.

Kane needed to call his CBP guy to confirm Lone had been in Bangkok when the senator had been butchered. But the confirmation would be redundant. He knew it was her.

And he needed to get Bradley help. Counseling. Something. He wasn't getting better on his own.

Kane felt a surge of helpless rage. He'd worked so hard to get Bradley clean. And now this creature Snake, who was like an evil drug pusher, had gotten Bradley hooked again.

But that would come later. For now, the priority was neutralizing Little. And even more so Livia Lone.

He pushed aside his distress and tried to think clearly. Tactically.

It seemed this woman had been getting away with quite a few killings. Fred Lone in Llewellyn. Ezra Lone and his entourage in Bangkok. Oliver Graham in Paris. Chop's men outside Campo.

In fact, in some ways it was a shame Chop had cleaned up the Campo mess. It might have been interesting to let the local police take care of it. And see if it could be tied to Lone. There was more than one way to take someone out of commission.

Which gave him an idea.

20

Livia was lying on her futon and just beginning to doze off when the phone buzzed. She sat up instantly and clicked the answer key. "Yeah."

"You ready?" Fallon said.

Instantly her heart was pounding. "You got it?"

"Didn't I tell you I know a guy?"

"Let's do it this way," she said, jumping up and heading to her desk. "First, just tell me the times he was stateside. If those windows don't match the disappearances—if he was fighting in Iraq when those girls were being abducted in America—he's not who I'm looking for." She sat, woke up the laptop, entered her passcode, and opened Little's file.

"Got it," Fallon said. He started ticking off the dates when Boomer had been rotated back to the States. By the time he was done, Livia had eight out of eight matches. Hannah Cuero was number nine, but of course that was only a month ago, when Boomer had long since left the military.

"What's the overlap?" Fallon said when he'd finished.

She looked at her notes. "One hundred percent."

"Jesus."

"Yeah. Every time one of the girls disappeared, Boomer was in the States. Three times he was in the States and nothing happened. Or at least, nothing got entered into ViCAP—the FBI database."

"Which I guess wouldn't really mean much."

"That's right. For whatever reason, he could have been inactive for some periods. Or local law enforcement just failed to enter a missing girl into the database, which happens all the time. What matters is, not a single report of a disappearance while he was in Iraq. That alone would be a hell of a coincidence."

She looked at her notes. Names, dates, locations of disappearances.

Trying to tamp down her excitement, she said, "Now let's narrow it further. On those occasions when Boomer was in the States, can you tell me where he was?"

"I can't account for all his movements, but I can give you some parameters."

"Whatever you have."

"Okay. Just about every time, his fort would be the first place he'd go, because weapons need to be put up and gear put away—plus people like to see their families once in a while. The army has forts and marines have camps, by the way. Anyway, for Boomer, who was Fifth Group, we'd be talking Fort Campbell, in Kentucky near the Tennessee border. Any hits near there?"

She checked her notes, opened a mapping application, and felt another adrenaline dump of excitement. "One. In 2007. Guthrie, Kentucky. Which looks maybe a half hour from the base. When in 2007 was Boomer back at Fort Campbell?"

"All of October, all of—"

"That's it. October 10, 2007. A girl named Kaila Jones. Was that Boomer's first rotation home?"

"Yeah, it was. Why?"

"Because he must have realized after that he couldn't hunt near the base again without establishing a pattern. Couldn't shit where he eats.

After that, I'm guessing . . . he would use other opportunities to hunt. Farther afield. Vacation time, things like that."

"Well, everyone gets thirty days' leave a year and can go wherever they want in the world. No requirement to take all those days consecutively, so if his unit lets him, and he's not engaged in training or daily garrison operations, he could use a week here or there, or a two-week block here and a week there, etc. If you don't use leave one year, it carries over to the next. You can accrue up to sixty days before you find yourself in a use-it-or-lose-it situation. But my guy doesn't have access to records of Boomer's individual vacation days."

"Shit."

"Hang on. There is something called block leave, when everyone has to take leave at the same time. Units like it because it keeps the cycle of deployment, home, train-up, and redeployment manageable and orderly."

"And your guy had records of that?"

"You bet. You ready?"

She was glad he was volunteering what he'd learned before she gave him the dates and places of the disappearances, which was the right way to do it. Not that she thought Fallon would feed her false information, but this way was always better. On a multiple-choice test, people could fake knowledge. On an essay, not so much.

"Go."

Fallon gave her six different instances of block leave. Three were negative. Three others overlapped with disappearances.

"Three hits," she said, struggling again with her excitement. "Charleston, San Antonio, Minneapolis."

"It sounds like the timing supports your theory. But if you want to place Boomer in the vicinity during those times, rather than just knowing he had the opportunity, I think you'd need credit-card receipts or cellphone records or whatever. For now, it sounds like all you have is that Boomer *could* have done it. I mean, you know he doesn't have an alibi, at least not the alibi of being on base, but the absence of an alibi means he can't prove he didn't do it, not that you can prove he did, right?"

"Right. But let's keep going. There were four other girls. I guess those he could have done while taking regular vacation time? For which your guy wouldn't have a record?"

"That's right."

"Any other times he would have been off base for a few days at a time or longer?"

"Plenty. For one thing, there's a forty-eight-hour pass, which isn't treated as formal leave. If the forty-eight-hour pass aligns with a weekend, well, congratulations, now you have a four-day pass. For these, you're not supposed to go far, because you have to be ready for recall if necessary. Though honestly, you think SF guys really do what they're told? More like what you think you can get away with."

"Okay, this is great. It sounds like he would have had more opportunities than I was first thinking."

"Hey, we haven't even gotten to the training, for which my guy *does* have records."

"Off-base training?"

"Exactly. There are more SF courses taught at sister service posts than you can keep track of—physical surveillance at Fort Bragg in North Carolina, combat diver training at Naval Air Station Key West, the military freefall jumpmaster course at Davis-Monthan Air Force Base in Arizona, winter operations training at the Northern Warfare Training Center at Fort Wainwright in Alaska . . . Those are just a few, and Boomer's been to all of them and more."

"Give me the names of those bases again," she said. "One at a time."

He did. She plugged each of them into the mapping app. None was in the vicinity of a disappearance.

Shit.

"No go on those," she said. "Okay, give me the rest."

Fallon went through each of Boomer's training deployments. Each one came up negative.

"I'm getting the feeling he doesn't operate when he's training," she said, looking at her screen. "Either because he's too busy, or because he's being careful not to create a pattern that could be checked against military records, or both."

"That makes sense. Well, again, he'd have plenty of opportunities during regular leave and short-term passes. And maybe during language training."

"Language training?"

"Oh, yeah. Fifth Group would mean most likely Arabic, Dari, Farsi, or Pashto. Most of that is taught at Bragg, but Boomer was one of the lucky ones—he got sent to the Defense Language Institute in Monterey in 2006."

"No match for that."

"Okay, one other possibility. Civilian training."

"What do you mean?"

"Aside from the official courses we've been talking about, SF guys also attend a lot of schools taught by civilians with special skills. Shooting schools, driving courses, climbing schools, man-tracking schools, pack-mule courses, self-defense schools, lock picking, B&E . . . you get the idea. If an SF team can write a good concept letter and get it approved through command, it'll get funded, and guys will get some cool training. Your tax dollars at work."

"Did your guy have any of those records?"

"Not a complete record like he had for the block leave and the official training, but some."

"Go."

"Okay, stick-and-knife stuff like kali with a guy named Mike Killman, former SF. A warrior monk type I've trained with myself."

"He's named 'Killman'?"

"Yeah, a Wordsworth kind of thing, I guess. That was in Fayetteville, North Carolina, right next to Fort Bragg."

"No matches. Probably he didn't like Fayetteville because it's near another Special Forces base."

"Okay, next is something called Guerrilla Jiu-Jitsu with a guy named Dave Camarillo in San Jose, California."

There had been a disappearance in Santa Cruz, a half-hour drive from San Jose. "I know Dave," she said. "I used to roll with him when I was in college. When was Boomer there?"

"December 2010."

She felt a flush of excitement. "Bingo. That's five matches. What else?"

"Radical Mixed Martial Arts with someone named Rene Dreifuss in New York City."

Another guy she had rolled with. "When?" she said.

"March 2011."

"Bingo. A disappearance in Summit, New Jersey, same time. That's six. *Six.*"

"My God."

Her heart was pounding. "Yeah. It's him."

She stared at the screen for a moment as though expecting more information to materialize on it. But holy shit, she had him. She fucking *had* him.

Something occurred to her. "What's up with the martial-arts training?"

"Lot of SF guys are into it. MMA, jiu-jitsu, modern combatives, you name it. Why?"

"They any good?"

"Are you kidding?"

She hoped Boomer was good. Maybe she'd get to see for herself.

They went through the rest of the civilian training. There weren't any other clear matches. But it didn't matter. The vacation times could have explained the rest. In fact, she expected there were even more—abductions that hadn't been entered into ViCAP.

She thought for a moment about Little's certainty that it was a two-man team.

"Can you check one more thing for me?" she said.

"I hope so. What?"

"For the six matches we have. Could your guy cross-check and see which members of Boomer's unit were also deployed to Fort Campbell on October 10, 2007, when Kaila Jones disappeared from Guthrie? And also on leave for Charleston, San Antonio, and Minneapolis? And who also went with Boomer to train with Camarillo in San Jose and Dreifuss in New York?"

"You think Boomer had an accomplice?"

"I know he did. If I'm lucky, there will be only one other guy who matches the time on base when Kaila Jones disappeared, and those three block-leave periods, and the training."

"Give me a half hour. Let me see if I can reach my guy."

Twenty minutes later, Fallon called her back.

"His name is Stephen Spencer," he said. "People call him Snake."

21

Boomer and Snake sat at the edge of Ratkay Point, passing a bottle back and forth, listening to the waves break on the rocks below them, watching the moonlight rippling across the endless dark Pacific. It was Snake's bottle, and Boomer knew he shouldn't because he'd driven, and especially with the campaign and everything else going on he couldn't risk a DUI. But damn, it was so good to relax this way, like old times, when it was nothing but upside and without all the fucking pressure and problems.

Snake took a swig of the whiskey, then let out a long sigh. "It's up to you," he said, handing back the bottle to Boomer. "But the way I see it, it's all going according to plan. You're winning. So why would you want to stop before you've won?"

So I can quit while I'm ahead, Boomer thought. But that wasn't a concept Snake had ever understood.

Boomer took a pull from the bottle. His fourth? Fifth? He'd lost count, and shit, they'd been here, what, fifteen minutes? He really should stop. But he was feeling so good. The ocean breeze on his face. The moonlight. And that . . . fuzz the whiskey was bringing down at the edges of his vision and hearing was just what he needed, leveling everything out, putting it all in perspective. He wished they were on leave somewhere, and that he didn't have to worry about driving and maybe getting pulled over, and that they could just keep drinking and bullshitting until everything went away and he didn't have to remember any of it.

"Look," he said, handing back the bottle before he could take another swig, "what you did with Noreen . . . brother, that was epic. And Hope, too. But that reporter spooked me, you know? Asking if I wanted to comment on the 'coincidence.'"

"Shit. Barely a coincidence, if you ask me."

"Come on, man. Two girls from my high-school class, a week apart—one accuses me of rape and disappears, and the other gets raped and killed?"

"But we knew that was going to happen. You can prove you've been in California campaigning the whole time."

"Yeah, but that's not going to stop people from speculating."

"How'd the reporter even know what high school Hope went to?"

"She didn't say. But I know there's a private Facebook page for people from my class. I'm not on it because who has time anyway, but a few people from back in the day reached out when Noreen went public. Just telling me they remembered her, she was crazy, stay strong, that kind of stuff. So I figure, when you did Hope, someone she's still in touch with must have heard the news, and told some other people, and the next thing is, the whole class is talking about it and maybe someone contacted a reporter. Christ, it's like in high school again, the fucking gossip."

He reached for the bottle. Snake handed it over and Boomer took a swig. Oh man, it tasted good. And felt even better. He hesitated, then handed it back.

Snake took a swallow. "The reporter print anything?"

Boomer shook his head. "No."

"See? They know they don't have shit. And if they step out of line, your old man will sue them so hard for defamation he'll bankrupt their asses."

Boomer shrugged. "Still not good to have people talking." His voice sounded odd in his ears. A little slurred and far off. "Far off and far out," he said aloud, and laughed.

"Who gives a fuck what people talk about? It's what you do that matters."

Boomer looked at him. "Politics isn't like that, brother," he said, the laughter dying away. "What people talk about is half the game."

Snake took another swallow and handed back the bottle. "Okay, fine. But you said it yourself—since Noreen, your campaign contributions are through the roof, and your supporters are so fired up they're going to swarm down from the bleachers and storm the fucking field over the conspiracy against you. What happened to Hope Jordan hasn't put a dent in that. Why would it? If anything, it'll help."

Boomer took another swallow. He meant for it to be a small one, but then it wasn't.

"Tell you what," Snake said, the words a little slurred. "I'll take care of the third one the way we took care of Noreen. What was her name again? Sherrie something, that's right. Yeah, Sherrie. Disappear her ass into thin air. Then if anyone wants to speculate, it'll look like some kind of . . . opportunistic move. Like something . . . maybe coordinated with Noreen's vanishing act, and taking advantage of, you know, politicizing Hope Jordan, trying to turn a family's tragedy into a weapon to use against you. Right?"

Boomer took another swallow. Smaller than the last one. That was good. He was still in control.

"Or look at it this way," Snake said, emphasizing the point with a finger jabbed toward Boomer. "Say I don't do Sherrie. And she goes public, like you're worried she will. Well, then you'll have lost your chance. A second woman comes forward and then disappears, and a third one overall . . . the speculation, the talk, it'll boil over. And it'll be hard to get it to simmer down. You'll look back and think, 'Ah, shit, my old buddy Snake, he was right. Told me I should get out ahead of this thing, take the small risk for the big gain instead of the big risk for the small gain. God, I only wished I'd listened. Not much of an education in that one, true, but I gotta admit, he's no dummy, either.'"

Boomer laughed. Was there anyone on Earth who understood him the way Snake did?

Snake stood, moved closer to the edge, unzipped, and pissed over the cliff. The rocks were too far below to hear the piss hitting, and besides, the surf was too loud.

Boomer looked at Snake's back, faintly visible in the glow of the far-off streetlights. He realized all he'd have to do was stand, take a step forward, and give a hard shove. People sometimes fell here. There were signs to warn visitors—*Danger* and *Unstable Cliffs* and *Visitors Have Fallen Here and Died*—things like that.

He shook his head. What the fuck was he thinking?

A moment later, Snake zipped up and sat again. Boomer handed him the bottle.

Snake upended it, swallowed, then blew out a long, satisfied breath. "Yeah," he said. "I'll disappear the third one. Anyone wants to talk about it, it'll look like someone taking advantage of the narrative to undermine you. In which case, your supporters go ballistic, the election's in two weeks, and you're the new senator from Califuckingfornia. After which, who gives a shit?"

The sound of the breaking waves was smooth now, hypnotic. It seemed to merge with the ripples of moonlight on the water, the dark sky overhead, the nice, fuzzy cocoon behind Boomer's eyes and all around his body.

"All right, man," he said. "I mean, fuck it. You've been right so far. Shit, you give me better PR advice than my own damn advisors."

Snake looked at him, and Boomer could see real gratitude in his eyes. That someone valued him not just for his skills, but for his brains, too.

Then Snake slid over so they were right next to each other and threw an arm around Boomer's neck, mock-headlocking him. Boomer felt Snake's hot breath on his face, smelled the whiskey on it.

"You know it's because I love you, man," Snake said. "Right?"

Boomer nodded.

"Where does she live?" Snake said. "Sherrie, I mean."

"Kanab," Boomer said, looking out at the dark water.

"Kanab? What the hell's Kanab?"

"It's . . . southwest Utah. A little north of the Grand Canyon."

Snake laughed. "Are you kidding me? That's like, what, an eight-hour drive from the Salton Sea?"

Boomer laughed, too, knowing where the crazy bastard was going with this. And not giving a shit at all.

"I got an idea," Snake said. "When I pick her up, I won't waste her. I'll drive her to you, like the pizza-delivery man. Right? Like I did Noreen. I mean, as long as you share a slice, right?"

Boomer laughed. Yeah, Snake was crazy, but . . . there was no one Boomer loved more.

"Can you get there?" Snake said. "I mean, with the campaign and all."

Boomer looked at Snake. What did they call it? Serendipity, that's right. "Fundraiser in Palm Springs," he said. "Night after tomorrow."

"Fuck me running, that's an hour away, brother, it's perfect!"

Boomer kept on laughing, knowing he was too drunk to drive, no longer even giving a shit. About a DUI, or anything else. "Good old Salton Sea," he said.

Snake tousled his hair. "Fuck yeah," he said, laughing. "Let the good times roll."

22

It was just getting light when Livia rode past Cal Anderson Park on the Ducati. Little had texted her from a new number, as promised, and she had texted back with a message that they should meet in an hour. But she wanted to get there first.

She parked the bike in the lot between Broadway and Nagle, dismounted, pulled off her helmet, and looked around, her breath turning to vapor in the cool morning air. Just a few parked cars, their windows covered in dew. She secured the helmet to her backpack and slid her left arm through one of the straps. This way, she could drop the pack instantly if there was a problem, while keeping her right hand free to access the Vaari or the Glock. Then she did a quick walk around the perimeter, making sure no one came in behind her. Not that she was expecting anyone—she'd passed the I-90 interchange at about a hundred and thirty.

She stopped at the east side of the lot. It was elevated and had a nice view of the reflecting pool across Nagle and of the surrounding park. From here, she'd be able to see Little coming from a long way off. And she'd have plenty of time to spot anyone tailing him.

As it happened, Little arrived early, too, just ten minutes after she did. That was good. It suggested he was being careful, even paranoid. Slow, maybe, but not ineducable.

He entered the park through the northwest corner, from Denny. Probably he'd taken the Link light rail to Capitol Hill Station. Hopefully he'd gotten off a few times on the way, and stood on the platform to make sure no one was trying to stay with him, and then jumped back on in the other direction. Maybe beforehand he'd used a taxi or two, as well.

She watched him walk the perimeter of the park, checking his back along the way. Yeah, he was being careful. No one came in behind him. Okay.

She headed down to the street and took the stairs up into the park. Little was coming around the bend when she got to the edge of the reflecting pool and nodded when he saw her. She waited until he'd reached her position, then fell in alongside him, walking clockwise around the pool, the two of them scanning as they moved.

"You don't have to mention it," Little said. "I was careful. Cabs through empty neighborhoods, changing trains after waiting on deserted platforms, hoofing it around corners and waiting to see whether anyone was trailing after me. Serious old-school shit."

"What about—"

"No phone with me. Well, the new burner just in case I had to reach you, but with the battery removed. They must have had a team on me when I went to the cemetery. I'm not saying that to distract from my own culpability. I should have been more careful about the possibility of physical surveillance. You were right. I've gotten to thinking everything is electronic these days. It isn't."

It was a relief that he'd shaped up. And she was glad, and impressed, that he wasn't making excuses.

"What about the body?" she said.

"You know the Lake Youngs Reservoir, east of the airport?"

"Of course."

"Let's just say you might not want to go swimming there for a while."

"You dumped the body in the reservoir?"

"That's right."

"That reservoir gets a fair amount of maintenance. SPU—Seattle Public Utilities—manages it. And the body's going to float."

"Not after what I did to it."

She stopped and looked at him, part relieved, part concerned.

And, she couldn't deny, part impressed.

"You put holes in it?" she said.

"With a screwdriver, yes. The entire chest cavity, abdomen, soft tissue . . . wherever gas could collect. It'll stay sunk."

She kept looking at him, trying to process this part of him that she hadn't accounted for until now.

"What?" he said.

"Just . . . that's grisly work."

Little grunted. "The way I see it, that man was protecting whoever took my little girl. Whoever did to her what they did. So no, it didn't feel grisly at all. In fact, he's lucky you killed him before I had him alone. You studied sublimation in your college psychology courses, didn't you?"

She nodded.

"Well, punching holes in his corpse was a poor substitute for what I wish I could have done. But it was something. And I hope you can believe me when I tell you I was thorough. Anyway, no one's going to find him. And even if they do, there won't be any trace of you on him, if there ever was. He's just gone. One more down. Now, were you able to find out anything about that drone?"

They started walking again. She tried to think of how to tell him. She was concerned the information would be so momentous he wouldn't be able to control himself. That he would fly to Southern

California, go straight to Boomer Kane's office, and try to tear him apart with his bare hands.

Well, she had to tell him, one way or another. Best to just get it out. And then try to rein him in.

"The drone is the least of it," she said. "I think I know . . . who took Presley."

He stopped and seized her arm. Instinctively she broke the grip and grabbed his sleeve in return, but stopped herself from doing more. "I told you, don't fucking touch me," she said, shoving him back.

"Who?" he said, leaning forward, his arms frozen halfway to her, the fingers hooked as though desperate to clutch something. His eyes were narrowed and his lips drawn back, his face a mask of pure, primal rage and hate. Then he flinched and shoved the back of a fist against his lips, his expression shifting instantly from rage and hate to grief and terror. His eyes welled up. "Is she alive?" he whispered, and his voice broke.

Livia shook her head. "I don't know. But I don't think so."

Instantly the grief vanished, replaced by rage again. "Then who? You tell me who, goddamn it, who!"

For one second, she hesitated, afraid that the instant he heard the names, he would take off running. But no. He'd want to hear it all, every scrap of information. She'd have a chance to talk him down.

She told him everything. By the time she was done, it was full daylight, and the park was lively with morning joggers and tai-chi practitioners.

"I can get to this man Boomer," he said when she was done, his tone icy calm. "Oh, yes I can. But the other one . . . Snake . . . Do we have a nexus beyond Boomer?"

"Apparently not. No family. No way to know where he'd go when they let him out of Leavenworth."

"Well, he went to Boomer, we know that much. That's what happened to Hannah Cuero. At least we know why they were quiescent for seven years. And why I wasn't able to uncover a connection in all my searches of prison sentencing. I was looking at federal and state institutions. Didn't occur to me to look into military prisons, for an offense committed in an overseas combat zone. It's my fault. I fucked up."

She understood his guilt. She'd dealt with a lifetime of it over Nason. The guilt existed independent of logic and had no basis in facts. So trying to reason with it was mostly futile. You just had to learn to endure. To recognize the guilt's presence, and try not to pay too much attention no matter how loudly it demanded you listen.

Still, she found herself saying, "No one would have thought to look into military prisons for offenses committed overseas. And even if you had, Snake's conviction was for something called abusive sexual contact. Different crime, different MO. It wouldn't have meant anything to you even if you'd seen it earlier. It wouldn't have made a difference. Not to Presley. And not to Hannah Cuero."

Little took off his glasses and with his free hand scrubbed his face. Maybe he appreciated the gesture. But he was never going to buy what she was selling.

"Why only Snake?" he said after a moment. "Why didn't they lock up Boomer, too? His old man?"

Livia nodded. "That's my guess. My contact said there were rumors that the two of them were taking advantage of young girls during raids. But the girls would never come forward."

"Easy to understand why."

"Sure. It's a war zone. Open your mouth, and your rapists come back and kill your family."

"So what put Snake away?"

"According to my contact, it was the testimony of men in his unit."

Little laughed harshly. "Half a loaf. Score one for unit integrity, I guess. Why just the one count?"

"My contact didn't know. But you know how it works. Someone made some kind of deal. One count, a lesser offense, Boomer not involved, the witnesses agree to cooperate."

Something was tugging at a corner of her mind. Some . . . connection. She could feel it but not see it. She tried to bring it closer, into the ambit of her vision, but Little interrupted. "If Boomer is my nexus to Snake, that's fine. Getting the first is my route to the second. Same way that drone operator knew he could get to you. By following me."

She didn't like where he seemed to be going. "What are you planning to do?"

"Leave of absence. Use all my resources to get on Boomer like the proverbial stink on shit. Wait for Snake to make his presence known."

"Homeland Security going to be okay with that?"

"Homeland Security's not going to know a damn thing about it. If Tilden won't approve my leave, I'll retire, effective immediately."

"You pull the plug like that, Tilden will know exactly what's behind it."

"If Tilden tries to get in my way, he can personally greet Boomer and Snake when I send them to hell after him."

"You're going to kill your boss now?"

He looked at her, his eyes flat. She realized she had been too optimistic in thinking she'd be able to talk him down.

"I told you," he said. "It's like the drone operator. Anyone who's protecting the men who took my little girl, knowingly or otherwise, should thank whatever God they pray to that I'm willing to focus on the principals."

"Okay, fine. But abruptly retiring is already a neon sign that you've finally found the men you've been looking for and are going to kill them. Killing your boss first? That's beyond just a sign. You'll be trying to get to Boomer and Snake ahead of a federal law-enforcement manhunt focused on you."

"What do you propose instead? That I try to make a case?"

She said nothing. The truth was, she was conflicted herself. And she wasn't sure they even *had* a case. Or could find a way to make one.

"No," he said. "Out of the question. You know as well as I do that we have nothing but happenstance and circumstantial evidence against the war-hero congressman scion of the goddamn vice president of the United States. Even if I were interested in that fight, and I'm not, I'd know I couldn't win it."

"Look—"

"No, Livia. I'm not sending them to prison. I'm sending them to hell. With some parts missing. You understand?"

"I do understand. I do. But we're talking about different things. You're talking about what you want. I'm talking about whether it will work."

Little didn't respond. She couldn't tell how much he was listening, or whether he was listening at all.

"Think about this," she said. "Even if your leave were approved, and you didn't have to quit, or kill anyone. Tilden would still know. You think you're going to get to Snake through Boomer? All your enemies, every operator intent on protecting these scumbags, will be thinking the same about you. 'Stay on Boomer, and Little will walk right into the ambush.'"

He clenched his jaw and looked away. Yeah, he was listening. But trying not to.

"Little," she said. She suddenly remembered Carl, sitting behind her on the big Kawasaki as they raced out of Pattaya and shouting over the engine roar, *I know you want Sorm bad. But you gotta also want him smart.* The memory conjured his presence so powerfully she actually looked behind her. But there was no one there.

"Little," she said again. "Look at me." She paused, then added, "Please."

He looked at her. His eyes were wet.

"I know," she said, returning his gaze. "I know."

He shook his head—whether to deny that she could understand what he was feeling, or at the grief and horror his obsessions were barely holding at bay, she didn't know.

"We're going to speak for Presley," she said. "We're going to speak for all those girls. We are."

He shook his head again, but less vehemently this time. "How?"

"By being smart. And patient. As smart and patient as you've been for ten awful years. Because all those smarts, and all that patience, is what brought you to this moment. To this threshold. Of course you're not going to rush across it. You're not going to let anyone bait you into that. You're going to be deliberate. And methodical. And you're going to win. Because you're still Presley's father, and you're not going to let her down."

His face contorted and a fresh stream of tears ran down his cheeks. "I already did."

"No," she said, and she felt her own eyes fill up. "It wasn't your fault. There was nothing you could do to stop it, and you would have given anything, everything, if you could have. But what you can do, what you're *going* to do, is make sure no one stops you from being her father now."

He took off his glasses, looked down, and blinked. Tears fell to the ground. Then he closed his eyes, pinched the bridge of his nose, and forced out a long breath. When he put on his glasses again, he looked more in control.

"How?" he said again.

She looked at him intently and said, "Like this."

23

Chief Best watched the mayor pacing back and forth as though he owned Best's office. If she hadn't been seated behind her desk, he probably would have taken her damn chair. But she knew better than to tell him to sit his ass down on the couch and show some respect. Mayor Martin Woods looked at every reasonably prominent Seattleite as a potential political rival, and couldn't help engaging in various domination rituals when he was with them. Best didn't know whether the behavior was intended to remind the potential rivals of who was boss, or to remind Woods himself. Either way, it was better to let the man self-comfort. Because hell yes, Best was a rival. The difference was, she knew better than to let someone see it coming.

Besides which, the occasion for his visit was delicate. And presented some potential opportunities, as well. So why interrupt the man's flow?

"All right," she said. "You don't know who the caller was." It was a short summary of what he'd just spent nearly a minute fulminating about. Every cop knew that feeding back a summary was a powerful elicitation technique. Mayors, it seemed, not so much.

"No idea," Woods said. "The call was blocked. And how the hell did he get my cellphone number?"

Best made it a habit to ignore rhetorical questions, so she said nothing.

Woods paused in front of her desk and ran his fingers through his perfectly cut steel-gray hair.

Come on around to my side, she thought. *You know you want to.*

On cue, he circled to her side of the desk, leaned against the wall so she would have to turn to look at him, and crossed his arms. "You're the cop," he said. "What do you make of it?"

She shrugged. Not at the question, but at how little his body-language games mattered to her. She cared less about a man being rude than she did about his being predictable.

"You know as well as I do that Officer Lone has enemies," she said. "Two assassination attempts. And that was before the child-pornography ring she was investigating turned out to involve Secret Service agents and senators. So—"

"I'm not saying she doesn't have enemies. Of course she does. I mean, you think the guy who called me was a friend? I'm asking if you think there's anything to the caller's accusations."

She knew perfectly well what he was asking. She just wasn't going to answer until he said it.

"I'm not sure," she said, not so much because it was true, but because it was tactical.

He looked at her. "Really? I mean, this caller had extremely detailed information. Dates of travel to Bangkok and Paris. A connection to both a dead senator and a murdered military contractor, both of whom died while she was vacationing in their neighborhoods. Did you know about any of this?"

"No," she said, glad she was able to say so truthfully. "I remember reading last year about Senator Lone's heart attack. And about Oliver Graham's abduction and assassination last month."

"You didn't know Detective Lone was there when both those deaths happened?"

"Assuming that part is even true? No. I didn't know. And regardless, as I just noted, Senator Lone died of a heart attack. You think my detective caused that?"

"The caller said it wasn't a heart attack. And he said her stepfather, the senator's brother, had a heart attack, too, when Detective Lone was being fostered in his home."

"Well, I'm no doctor, Martin, but it sounds to me as though heart disease might run in the Lone family."

"I just told you, the caller said it wasn't a heart attack."

"Respectfully, Martin, the caller could have told you the moon is made of green cheese, and if he had, I hope we wouldn't be having a conversation now about whether he meant Jarlsberg or Havarti."

He frowned, obviously not appreciating the sarcasm, but also not having a good response to it. She wondered why she was pushing back. She wanted something on Lone, didn't she? And Woods was offering it up. But if Lone was akin to a bird with a tendency to fly places she shouldn't, Woods was more like a poisonous snake. The one was annoying. The other was dangerous.

After a moment he said, "So you think the call was bullshit."

She shrugged. "We seem to agree on the obvious—that whoever contacted you did it in an attempt to hurt Detective Lone. Given the motivation, I think it would be foolish for us to assume the person would slavishly adhere to the truth."

"He must have known we'd confirm the dates."

"Oh, I'm sure he was counting on that. And I imagine the dates will indeed check out. But the other thing he would have been counting on is that when we learned he was being truthful about one thing, we'd assume he was being truthful about everything else. Is that what you're doing?"

"I'm not assuming anything. I just want to know what your detective has been up to."

She caught the *your detective*. As in *your responsibility. Your scandal, if it comes to that.*

She waited, letting the silence draw him out.

"Because what are we talking about here?" he said after a moment. "Secret contracts with the feds? Some kind of assassin in the department? What?"

"Are those your theories?"

"Those are my questions. And I have another: Is any of this going to bite us on the ass? And if so, what are you going to do about it?"

She looked at him. "I don't know Detective Lone all that well. But I'll start by having a conversation with her lieutenant, Donna Strangeland. I'm sure Donna can shed some light on whether we have La Femme Nikita on the payroll."

"Don't make light of it, Charmaine. I understand your detective has enemies. We all do. But payback is one thing. Blowback is something else. I don't have to tell you, your department is under a spotlight because of the DOJ settlement agreement. You don't want that spotlight shining on you, you better find a way to point it somewhere else."

That's your specialty, not mine, she thought.

But what she said was "I'll talk to Lieutenant Strangeland."

24

Livia was in her cubicle, working on a chart. Something was nagging at her about Boomer and Snake—the intuition she'd felt when talking to Little at the reflecting pool, but couldn't quite grasp. Something was there, she knew, and if she diagrammed out the dates and places of the disappearances, maybe the visual would bring into focus whatever was shifting in the shadows of her mind. So far, though, the chart wasn't helping. She didn't see a pattern she could make sense of, or anything else other than opportunism—two men who didn't care where or when, as long as their crimes were committed far from their regular whereabouts.

It wasn't helping that she couldn't find anything online about Snake, and had to go on only what she had learned from Fallon. She wondered about the abusive-sexual-contact conviction. She'd looked up the charge in the Uniform Code of Military Justice. Apparently, it was a step down from rape and sexual assault, and she assumed Snake had pled to it rather than risk a longer sentence. Whatever he'd actually done in Iraq, it seemed a safe bet Boomer had done it with him. After all, what they'd been doing in the States had stopped when Snake had gone to prison. And started up again shortly after he'd been paroled.

But why had Snake taken the fall then, and not Boomer? Had Boomer just been lucky? Had his father pulled strings?

What she wanted most of all was information about what the two of them had really been doing in Iraq. Rape? Murder? She wasn't interested in what Snake had been convicted for, or even what he had been charged with. What mattered was what they had actually been *doing*, and how Snake had been caught. Why sexual assault in Iraq, but kidnapping in the States? Or were they taking girls in Iraq, too, and the army had charged Snake only with what a judge-advocate prosecutor thought could be proved, like Al Capone and tax evasion?

Well, Fallon was working his contacts, and though she doubted anyone in Boomer's or Snake's old unit would talk to her, there was always a chance. And depending on what she learned, she could also try the army judge advocate who had been in charge of the prosecution. If she could fold together what they were doing in Iraq and what they were doing in the States . . . she didn't know. Maybe she could make a case. Maybe she could predict their next move.

She was lucky her caseload was light at the moment. She was scheduled to give testimony at a domestic-abuse trial later in the week, and she had appointments with witnesses in two assault investigations, but her interview of Amy the waitress hadn't gone anywhere. The woman remembered the man calling out to her, *Hey there, you look like someone who could use a ride,* which was encouraging because it matched reports from the man's victims. But Amy hadn't been able to recall anything new, anything Livia didn't already have. On top of which, the overall haziness of the woman's recollection would get picked to pieces by a good defense lawyer: *How can you remember so clearly something that happened over a year ago? Was the vehicle's interior light on? Oh, you didn't clearly see the man inside? Weren't you tired after a long shift? Had you had anything to drink before heading home?* Etc.

But there had to be other women the man had approached. For every burglarized house, there were fifty more the burglars had cased and rejected. And for every woman who was raped, there were fifty others who'd been stalked, or assessed, or approached by a rapist who'd decided for whatever reason to go hunt elsewhere.

It would be that way with Boomer and Snake as well. What she knew about them so far would be only a tiny fraction of the truth.

She had that sense again, that feeling of seeing the contour of something but not being able to make out the details.

What?

Little knew as well as she did that serial crimes had three high-level aspects: victimology, modus operandi, and signatures. There was overlap, of course, but generally speaking, the terms referred to the kind of victims a given rapist or killer preferred, his method of committing the crime, and the fetishes he indulged that weren't useful for the commission of the crime itself.

The victims Boomer and Snake favored were black and brown girls. The method was what Little had pieced together—the quiet neighborhood street with few houses, the walking-distance convenience store, time of day around sunset. Okay.

But what was the signature? There was almost always something. A kind of rope. Poses the rapist would force his victims to assume, or a pose in which the killer would leave a body. Words rapists would force their victims to say. Or words they would use themselves, like the Hey There Rapist. By contrast, Boomer and Snake's crimes seemed characterized almost by the *absence* of a signature. No DNA at the scene. No body recovered. Just nine girls, vanished.

It didn't make sense. There was something she couldn't see. It felt like . . . a shadow. But she couldn't find a way to illuminate it.

She did a quick online search for news about Boomer. And was surprised to see an article in a Portland newspaper. A gruesome double murder: a woman named Hope Jordan, raped and strangled to death, and her two-year-old son, suffocated. Authorities were searching for a homeless man witnesses claimed to have seen in the parking garage where Jordan and her son were thought to have been abducted. The article was almost entirely about the crime. But the last paragraph noted a tragic coincidence: Jordan had been a high-school classmate of Congressman Bradley Kane III, now locked in a tight race for the senate in California. Boomer.

Livia stared at the screen for a moment, trying to process it. Noreen Prentis had accused Boomer of raping her in high school, and then disappeared. And now another woman, Hope Jordan, had been raped and murdered. After being abducted. She hadn't disappeared, like Noreen Prentis, like those nine teenaged girls. But maybe this time, the disappearance wasn't the point.

She felt a hot surge of hate. She didn't mind hate. In fact, she welcomed it. She had lived with hate most of her life. Hate was what had given her the strength to save herself from Fred Lone, and later to avenge Nason. Justice was her vehicle, but hate was the fuel it ran on.

But she needed to navigate, too, and for that, hate was too powerful. So she waited until the hate had receded and she could think clinically again.

Had Jordan accused Boomer, too? If so, surely the article would have mentioned it. She searched for other news about Hope Jordan. But there was nothing, only the report of her death.

How had a reporter even found out where Jordan had gone to high school? It was an unusual area to inquire into about a victim who had graduated twenty years earlier. And why would the paper have printed it? It would be guaranteed to draw flak from Boomer, and maybe even from his father, too.

Because someone thought it was newsworthy.

Maybe. Who was the reporter? She checked the byline: Helen Matlock. She clicked on the name and saw that Matlock was the paper's crime-beat reporter.

Why would Matlock have included that information about Boomer? It was the last paragraph and read like a parenthetical, but it was in there.

Matlock knew there was a connection between Prentis and Jordan. She was afraid to be more direct, or her editor wouldn't allow it. So they printed just the simple fact. In the hope that it would lead others to start digging more deeply.

Again, maybe.

She thought about Rick. Her step-uncle was retired now, but he still had contacts in the Portland Police Bureau. He might be able to shed some light. And unlike some of the other routes she might use for information, she knew she could trust him. Both to be discreet and to always have her back. He'd taken her in after his brother-in-law Fred Lone's "heart attack," after all. And though she knew he suspected a lot, he had never even come close to asking.

She took out her cellphone and speed-dialed him. Two buzzes, then his voice. "Livia."

She heard the smile, and it made her smile back. "Hey, Rick."

She'd never called him "uncle," even when she'd first met him at thirteen. She'd hated his sister, Dotty, who knew perfectly well what her husband, Fred Lone, was doing to the little Lahu refugee girl the Lones had agreed to foster in their home. Even now, she never asked about Mrs. Lone. One day, she expected Rick would mention that the woman had died. Livia would of course tell him she was sorry. But that would be a lie.

"How's everything?" he said. "Been a while."

She smiled again. He always said that, even if it had been less than a week. Though this time, he was right—it had been a month since she'd told him about the attack at the martial-arts academy, and of course about being cleared in the officer-involved investigation that followed.

"Everything's fine," she said. "Just busy. How's Gavin?"

Gavin was Rick's partner—another now-retired Portland cop, and another man who had been kind to her, and trustworthy, when she had been a traumatized teenaged girl.

"We're good," Rick said. "Taking it easy. Drinking too much beer. We miss you. You should come down."

That might happen sooner than you'd guess, she thought, though she didn't know how she would manage another disappearance right now.

"I'd like that," she said. "In the meantime, I have a question."

"Shoot."

"I read online about a rape-murder in Beaumont-Wilshire. A woman named Hope Jordan and her two-year-old son."

"Yeah. A bad one."

"Anything you can tell me about it that's not on the news?"

"If I were still with the bureau, probably. But these days . . . not so much. What's your interest?"

"Did you know Jordan went to high school with Bradley Kane? Boomer, the congressman, not the vice president."

"I didn't."

"The article mentioned it. And I was wondering . . . how the reporter found that out. And why it was included. It struck me as strange, so soon after the crime."

"That would be a little strange. You want me to ask around?"

"Yeah. And if PPB has any leads, I'd like to know. Security-camera feeds, witnesses . . . anything."

"Not that I'm ever sorry to hear from you, Livia, but you mind if I ask why you're not liaising with PPB directly?"

She hesitated, then said, "I'm looking into an associate of Boomer's. A war buddy of his named Stephen 'Snake' Spencer. And maybe Boomer himself."

"Jesus."

"Yeah. So you can understand, for now, I want to keep it on the down-low. Is that okay?"

"More than okay. Let me do some digging."

"Thanks. Talk to the reporter if you can. Helen Matlock. I want to know what her angle is with Boomer."

"I know Matlock. Half the homicides I investigated, she showed up before the cops did."

That sounded promising. "Can you call her?"

"Yeah. Let me see what I can find out, from Matlock and the bureau. I'll call you back."

She clicked off. It was frustrating, to know there was so much more but to not yet be able to see it. Or use it. She reminded herself of how much progress she'd made, and how fast. She knew Boomer and Snake had taken all those girls. And killed those women. All she had to do was find a means to prove it.

Or, if she couldn't, make them pay another way.

25

Livia had just gotten off the phone with Rick when Strangeland came by. She glanced at Livia's diagram, the places and dates of the girls' disappearances. "Something I should know about?" she said.

Livia shook her head. "I don't want to bother you with it yet."

The lieutenant had accepted that kind of explanation before. She knew that when it came to rapists, Livia played a long game. But this time, she said, "Let's talk."

Shit.

Strangeland turned and headed in the direction of her office. Livia got up and followed her in. She closed the door without asking—if Strangeland hadn't wanted privacy, she would have said whatever was on her mind at Livia's cubicle.

Strangeland leaned back against her desk, facing Livia. Cop to cop. That was good. If the news was bad, the lieutenant would have delivered it sitting, the desk between them.

"I just got back from Chief Best's office," Strangeland said.

Livia didn't allow her expression to change. But she felt her heart rate kick into a higher gear. Maybe she'd been wrong about the news not being bad. "Okay," she said.

"It seems Charmaine had a visit from the mayor. Who is currently agitated following receipt of an extremely disturbing phone call about you. Specifically, about you being in Bangkok when Senator Ezra Lone died there, and in Paris when Oliver Graham was kidnapped and assassinated."

Livia felt an unfamiliar wave of dizziness. *This is it,* she thought. She'd always known it would all catch up to her. And now it was actually happening.

But if they were going to take her down, they would have to work for it. She would never help them.

"Okay," she said again, and she was gratified to hear the coolness in her own voice.

"Charmaine asked whether I thought there was anything to these anonymous allegations. I told her I didn't know."

She waited, and when Livia didn't respond, she went on. "She told me that was a problem. That I should know, because you're my detective and my responsibility. I agreed with her."

Again, Livia said nothing.

"Charmaine told me she had a difficult play to make here, especially because the department is under scrutiny from the DOJ, and we can't afford a scandal, and was it a mistake that you were cleared in the officer-involved last month, etc., etc. She asked for my candid opinion of you. Not what's in your fitness reports. The bottom line. Do or die."

Livia's heart was beginning to pound. She clenched her jaw for a moment and worked to control her breathing. Then she said, "What did you tell her?"

Strangeland looked at her for a long moment. Then she said, "I told her you are one of the finest cops I've ever had the privilege to serve with. That you are fearless, even heedless, in the pursuit of justice. And that you need people who have your back, not who are trying to take you down. Meaning Charmaine and I can either be your sister cops, or we can be politicians, but we can't be both."

Livia clenched her jaw again. This time she kept it clenched. She didn't say anything. She didn't trust herself to speak.

"I wasn't wrong before," Strangeland went on. "When I told you Charmaine has it in for you. She still does. But you know how it can be with a domestic-violence call. A man's beating the shit out of his wife, and when a cop shows up and intrudes upon their domestic spat, the woman turns on the cop."

"Because it's none of the cop's business," Livia managed to say.

"Yeah, that's the mentality. You know what Charmaine told me?"

Livia shook her head.

"She said, and I quote, 'I'm not a fan of Detective Lone. I don't like her mysteries, I don't think she respects authority, and I don't trust what she's up to. But that's between her and me. I'll be damned if some anonymous cowardly asshole telling tales to the mayor is going to turn me against my own officers. So tell Detective Lone she's got forty-eight hours to put the toothpaste back in the tube.' She says if she can't jerk around a mayor for at least that long, she doesn't deserve to be chief of police."

Livia nodded, her jaw still clamped shut. She felt the wetness in her eyes, but there was nothing she could do.

"Is that enough time?" Strangeland asked.

Livia nodded again.

Strangeland returned the nod. "It better be. Because if you don't take care of whatever this bullshit is before then, Charmaine is going to crucify you. And by you, I mean both of us. Now, do you need anything from me?"

Livia brushed a sleeve across her cheeks and shook her head. "Just the time you already got me."

Strangeland nodded. She reached out and squeezed Livia's shoulder. Livia didn't flinch.

"All right, then," Strangeland said. "Go make me proud."

26

An hour after the meeting with Lieutenant Strangeland, Rick called Livia. "Nothing from the bureau," he said. "A witness who thinks she saw a homeless man in the parking garage where cellphone records indicate Hope Jordan and her son were taken. The witness thinks the homeless man was white and wearing a hoodie. Doesn't remember enough beyond that to even work with a sketch artist. And no security-camera video footage."

"Forensic evidence?"

"Clothing fibers. Other than that, nothing. Jordan's attacker seems to have used a condom. And the interior of her car was wiped down with bleach."

Livia wasn't surprised. "Does that sound like an impulse crime to you?"

"No, it does not. I read up on this guy Boomer. The other one, there's no online information. But they're both Special Forces veterans. Those guys get some pretty esoteric training, including renditions, that kind of thing. Boomer, I figure, must have an alibi, with all the campaigning in California. But the other one, Snake, sounds like a ghost.

Did you know he did nearly seven years in Leavenworth for a sex crime in Iraq?"

She wasn't surprised Rick had found a way to look into it. "Yeah, I did."

"You think Snake's our guy?"

"I'm sure of it."

"Can you tell me how you know?"

She thought of Little. If Rick fed Snake's or Boomer's name to his contacts in Portland homicide, things could go in directions she hadn't had time to consider. Things could be uncovered. Maybe the two dead men outside Campo. Maybe the one from the cemetery. She wasn't ready to go there. At least not yet. And besides, what would PPB do with the information, really? Open up an investigation into a sitting congressman and son of the vice president, on the say-so of a Seattle cop?

"I can't yet," she said. "I need a little more time first. But I'm glad you know. Just in case."

"Don't talk like that."

She hesitated, then realized if she waited she would invent reasons to stop. So she said quickly, "Rick, listen. I'm not being morbid. Just prudent. But if anything were to happen to me, you could get in touch with a guy named Mark Fallon in Bangkok."

"Bangkok?"

"Yes. Bangkok. You can find him on the Internet. Mark Fallon—'Tips Tours & Trips.' Mark with a *k*, Fallon with two *l*'s. He can tell you more."

She had never wanted to close that loop, but as soon as it was out, she felt better. If something happened to her, Fallon would tell Rick what he had told her. And Rick would find a way to make Boomer and Snake pay.

Assuming Little didn't get to them first.

"Livia, you need to tell me what's going on here."

"I have. And I'll tell you more. I promise. But I can't have your people involved yet. Not with me. Okay? Let me make a case against Boomer and Snake my own way."

"The Snake guy is at large. How do you know—"

"I only need forty-eight hours, okay?" She didn't say that she only *had* that much time. It amounted to the same thing.

"Why? How do you know that?"

"You have to trust me on this, Rick. Look, what would your people do, anyway? You said it yourself, Boomer has alibis falling out of his pocket. Along with a father who'll bring holy hell down on any local cop who even dared mention his name in connection with Hope Jordan and her son. And Snake isn't in any databases. Believe me, I've checked. If you give your people his name, they'll be looking for a ghost, if they even look at all. What I need is to figure out his next move. Did you talk to the reporter? Matlock?"

"I did."

Livia felt a surge of hope. Or maybe it was desperation. "What did she tell you?"

There was a pause. "I think you ought to talk to her yourself."

27

Livia's conversation with Matlock was brief. The woman had clearly been fishing for more information about the nature of Livia's interest, and when Livia explained that she wasn't at liberty to reveal details of an ongoing investigation and then went silent in the face of further probes, Matlock gave up. But, to her credit, the woman didn't retaliate by holding back herself. Instead, she'd given Livia the number of Hope Jordan's sister, and assured Livia the sister would want to talk. Matlock had offered nothing more, but the logical inference was that Matlock's source on the Jordan-Boomer high school connection was the sister. Her name was Grace, the parents apparently having been fond of names that were also virtues. She had a 619 area code—Southern San Diego County. Livia called her.

"Grace Jordan?" Livia said to the woman's voice that answered.

"May I ask who's calling?"

"Detective Livia Lone, Seattle PD. I was hoping to talk to Grace Jordan."

A pause, then, "This is Grace."

Okay.

"Ms. Jordan, I got your name and number from a mutual acquaintance, Helen Matlock. I'm very sorry about your sister Hope and your nephew, and I apologize for intruding at what I know is a terrible time."

Another pause while Grace digested those bona fides. She said, "Thank you. It's not an intrusion. Did Helen tell you about Boomer Kane?"

Livia suppressed a surge of excitement. "She didn't tell me anything, ma'am, other than that you might want to speak with me."

"She didn't . . . wait, why were you in touch with Helen? Are you investigating Boomer?"

"I'm a sex-crimes detective," Livia said, thinking it would be enough under the circumstances to bait the hook. "I can't go into detail about the investigation that's behind this call, but I'd be grateful for anything you can share with me about Boomer."

Grace didn't even hesitate. "I'll tell you exactly what I told Helen Matlock," she said. "Boomer's a rapist. He raped Hope when we were in high school. He raped Noreen Prentis. He raped Sherrie Dobbs. He bragged about it in his yearbook entry. But Helen Matlock wouldn't print any of that. Are you going to do anything?"

Livia suppressed another surge of excitement. "I wouldn't be calling if I weren't. Can you tell me, Who is Sherrie Dobbs?"

"Another woman we went to school with. In my class, two years younger than Boomer. Everyone knew what Boomer was. People used to whisper about it, tell girls to be careful. The stalls in the girls' room were covered with warnings about him. But everyone was afraid of his family. His father. The admiral. Who's now the fucking vice president."

"You don't seem afraid."

"I'm terrified, Detective Lone. My sister was just raped and murdered, and my two-year-old nephew murdered along with her. And I know why, even if the Helen Matlocks of the world won't print it."

"You think Hope was going to speak out?"

There was a pause. Livia heard the woman breathing, and realized she was crying. She waited, not letting herself feel anything. That would happen later, whether she wanted it or not. For now, her best weapon was her detachment. For as long as she could maintain it.

"She was afraid to," Grace said after a moment. "She was in touch with Noreen. And with Sherrie. Hope and Sherrie wanted to corroborate Noreen's story by telling their own. They were scared because Noreen was getting all those death threats, but they were going to. But then . . . Noreen disappeared. And we all knew what that meant."

"You don't believe Noreen went into hiding."

"Do you?" Grace said, practically spitting the words.

"Not for a minute."

"Then why did you ask?" Grace said, sounding taken aback.

"I already know my own opinions," Livia said. "I want to hear yours. That's how I'm going to learn something new. Something I can use."

"Against Boomer?"

"Against whoever took your sister and your nephew from you," Livia said. "No matter who they are. Or how connected. Or how powerful."

A long, silent beat went by. Grace, her voice cracking, said, "Promise."

Livia waited, then said, "I fucking swear."

Another beat, during which Grace must have been collecting herself. Livia said, "What did you mean when you said Boomer bragged about it in his yearbook entry?"

"There was a song he liked. 'Good Times Roll,' by the Cars. Boomer wrestled, and the team used to run out to the song before matches. But Boomer had it on a Walkman, too. And he . . . he plugged in two sets of headsets. So he could listen while he . . . did it. And make them listen, too. Years later, Hope would hear that song on the radio and start crying and throwing up."

"He mentioned the song in his yearbook?"

"Yes. And if anyone ever asked, of course he would say, 'Oh no, that's just the wrestling song, what are you talking about?' But he knew what he was doing. Laughing at Hope. And Noreen. And Sherrie. Reminding them."

Livia thought of what Ezra Lone had said about Chanchai Vivavapit, who she would know always as Skull Face. The man who had forced her onto her knees on that boat, telling her it was the only way he would spare Nason. And who had raped Nason into catatonia anyway.

And really, I think he missed you. The way he talked about you . . . you were special to him.

Special because of the way Skull Face had traumatized her. Infected her. Become a part of her. Skull Face had loved that. Loved that she would never be able to forget him. That he would always matter to her. She didn't need to be familiar with all the studies and psychological profiles to know there were men so broken that for them, a woman's anguish felt like a bond.

She pushed the feelings back and forced herself to stay clinical. "So after Noreen disappeared, Hope and Sherrie . . . they were afraid to step forward?"

"Yes. And they thought . . . they felt guilty that they'd taken so long to make up their minds. Because maybe if they'd spoken out sooner . . ."

The woman's voice trailed off. Livia said, "I understand. What about Sherrie? What's she doing now?"

"I tried to get her to talk to the press. But she won't. She's terrified. I told Helen Matlock everything, everything I'm telling you, and look what she printed. 'Hope Jordan graduated from high school with Congressman Kane.' It was nothing."

"It wasn't nothing," Livia said. "It brought me to you."

"Why didn't she print all of it?"

"I don't know. But I'd guess her editor was afraid to. You said it yourself—Boomer's family was frightening when you were in high school, and that was when his father was only an admiral. Now he's the vice president.

No editor is going to print secondhand allegations about a rape that happened twenty years ago. Especially not when the allegations involve a sitting congressman with a vice president for a father. For what it's worth? My guess is that Helen Matlock went to bat for you and did the best she could. A simple, indisputable fact at the bottom of the article. No inaccuracies, no malice. In the hope that someone who was investigating Boomer would come across the article. And follow up on it."

There was a pause. Grace said, "Someone like you."

Now that they were talking, Livia knew there was less upside, and more downside, to being coy.

"Yes," she said.

"All right," Grace said. "Maybe I had Helen wrong. But what are you going to do now?"

"My first priority is making sure Sherrie Dobbs is safe. Can you put me in touch with her?"

"I don't think . . . wait, not to sound paranoid, but how do I know you are who you say you are?"

Livia had been hoping the woman would ask something like this. "You don't sound paranoid. You sound smart. Why don't you look up the number for the Seattle Police Department, call it, and ask to speak to Detective Lone. They'll put you through to me. I could give you my landline direct-dial, but I'd actually rather you look up the number yourself. I want you to feel comfortable."

"You really don't mind?"

"Grace, I like when women are careful. Do whatever you like. I'll wait."

Five minutes later, her landline rang. She picked up. "Livia Lone."

"Detective Lone," Grace said. "Okay, it's you."

"We're good?"

"Yeah. I called Sherrie. She's freaked out, but she wants to talk to you."

Livia had hoped that was why the callback took so long. "Should I call her?"

"She's going to call you."

28

"Hope Jordan?" the admiral said, his voice practically a snarl. "And her two-year-old son? Are you out of your fucking mind?"

The old man was up in Boomer's face. Boomer wanted to push him back—he wasn't a kid anymore, and this was his own house, his own damn study, on top of it—but he was too shocked. And, as much as he hated to admit it, too afraid.

"I don't know what you're—"

"Don't you fucking lie to me!" the old man spat, getting even closer and jabbing an index finger an inch from Boomer's nose.

This was bad. Boomer didn't think he'd ever seen his father this angry—red faced, sputtering, looking about a second from hauling off and taking a wild swing. And swearing, too, which the admiral almost never did.

The old man retracted the finger, but otherwise didn't back off. "It was your degenerate friend Snake, wasn't it?"

Boomer blinked. How did the old man know about Snake? *What* did he know?

"Wasn't it?" the old man demanded again, louder this time.

Boomer slid past, half expecting the admiral to reach out and try to stop him. *Swear to God, put a hand on me and I'll lay you out,* he thought. But luckily the old man must have thought better of it.

Boomer stopped in front of the liquor tray set out on a credenza. There was a bottle of a special Jack Daniel's—mostly empty, even though Boomer had filled it, what, three days earlier? He started to pour a careful measure into one of the glasses on the tray, then thought *Fuck it.* He filled the glass halfway, set down the bottle, and promptly drained half of what he'd poured. He closed his eyes and shuddered.

Fuck me sideways, I needed that.

He turned and looked at the old man, the warmth of the whiskey blossoming in his gut, spreading to his chest, his arms, his balls. His father's surprise mention of Snake had unnerved him, no doubt. But for some reason, a second later it was actually . . . calming. Maybe it was just being reminded that he wasn't alone against his father. That if the old man wanted to throw down, he'd be throwing down on Boomer and Snake both. And hey, ask all the dead hajis they'd left behind how that would turn out.

He surprised himself by smiling. "You want some?" he said, holding out the glass. "It's good."

The admiral looked him up and down, not even trying to hide his disgust. But Boomer thought he saw something else in the old man's expression. Something surprising, even shocking.

Fear.

Once he'd recognized it, he wondered how he hadn't spotted it sooner. After all, Boomer knew all about fear. He'd seen it—hell, he'd caused it—in more faces than he would ever be able to remember. And relished it, too.

But he'd never seen it in his father before. And now that he did, it gave him an additional jolt of confidence and satisfaction that made the warmth of the whiskey seem like nothing.

He tilted back the glass and drank what was left in two big swallows. He exhaled forcefully, then belched, knowing the admiral hated that sort of breach of etiquette.

The old man sneered, the fear momentarily masked. But it had been there. "Is that how you're going to handle the pressure?" he said. "Crawl into a bottle, and hope it all just goes away?"

Boomer smiled again, suddenly feeling better than he had in a long time. "Sure. Why not? You'll take care of the mess for me. Don't you always?"

"I changed a few of your diapers, too, Bradley, when your mother was too busy. I didn't expect you'd still need me doing it at damn near forty."

Boomer laughed. And it felt so good to laugh that it made him laugh more. Ordinarily, the admiral could cut him to the bone just by telling him what a disappointment he was. But that fear he'd seen in the old man's eyes . . . Christ, it was really beautiful. He wished he'd seen it years ago. Wished he'd seen it when he was a kid.

"What do you want, Admiral? You flew all the way out here on Air Force Two just to reminisce about the good old days when you sometimes wiped my ass for me?"

He thought that was pretty funny, actually. And seeing the old man's eyes bulge in horror at the vulgarity made it even better. Boomer laughed again.

"You think this is funny?" the admiral said.

Boomer could tell the old man was trying to sound stern. But he could see the fear again. God, how was it he'd never seen it before?

"No," he said, smiling. "I think you're funny."

The old man shook his head. Boomer had never seen the admiral at such a loss before. He didn't know what to make of it. All he knew was that it made him happy. He poured the rest of the bottle's contents into the glass.

"You know what would have been funny?" the admiral said from behind him. "If I'd never cleaned up your messes. Never bailed you out. Never changed your diapers, either literally or metaphorically, and left you marinating in your own foulness instead."

Boomer turned around. He looked his father right in the eyes and shrugged. "So don't clean up my mess."

The admiral blinked, and there it was again, the fear, even more of it now than just a minute earlier.

"Seriously," Boomer said. He raised his glass in a mock toast, then took a huge swallow. "Take a vacation from changing my diapers. Knock yourself out. Get back on Air Force Two and fly back to Washington and do whatever the fuck you want."

The old man didn't just look scared anymore. He looked borderline terrified.

"Oh, wait," Boomer said, smiling. He realized his voice was slurred. Good. "You won't do that. And I know why. We both know."

"Really," the old man managed, his tone withering, but Boomer was feeling great now, and the admiral's condescension, which was ordinarily potent as Kryptonite, was suddenly as feeble as the punch line of a dumb joke.

"Yeah, Admiral, really. Remember all those times you told me when I was a kid how when you owe the bank a million dollars, it's your problem?"

The admiral was silent, and God almighty, had there ever been a more beautiful sound than that?

"Yeah," Boomer went on. "But when you owe the bank a billion dollars, you told me, that's the bank's problem. Well, you know what I just realized? You're the bank. And I owe you a billion dollars." He started laughing at the perfect, hilarious truth of it, and the more he thought about it, the harder it made him laugh.

The old man watched him. He looked *sooooo* scared.

"You need help, Bradley. Surely you can see that."

Boomer raised the glass in another mock toast. "Sure, Admiral, I know I can count on you. A billion dollars is a lot." He laughed again and took a nice big swallow of whiskey.

The old man stayed silent, his jaw clamped, his nostrils flaring. One of his eyes twitched.

"I want to believe you had nothing to do with it," the old man said. "Really, I want to. Not a two-year-old boy, for God's sake. Tell me it was just that creature Snake. And we'll figure out what to do."

That pissed Boomer off. "He's not a creature. He saved my ass in Iraq a dozen times, and he didn't do it because he's a bank and I owe him a shitload of money. He did it because he's my friend. My best friend."

"Really? He murdered a little boy because he's your friend? How heartwarming."

"What do you want, Admiral?"

"Tell me where he is."

"I have a better idea. Why don't you go fuck yourself instead?"

The old man's face reddened. "Can't you see what he's doing to you?"

"He's protecting me!"

"He's not protecting you, he's enabling you! You think I don't know? About all those girls? Not the ones in Iraq. The ones here."

Boomer looked at him, the whiskey buzz instantly gone, and all the confidence, the hilarity, gone with it. He realized he was scared again, the way he always felt with the old man.

And the admiral seemed to sense it, too, because he smiled. "That's right. I know. The only thing that kept you clean was that degenerate being behind bars. The moment he got out, he infected you again, with that girl in Campo. Hannah Cuero."

Boomer flinched. "You don't know what you're talking about."

"No? Who do you think protected you from him? Who do you think put him in prison, you stupid, blind, spoiled little shit?"

Boomer blinked. He tried to think clearly, but nothing came. "What?" he managed.

For a second, the admiral seemed to catch himself, but then maybe he decided it was too late to back down, because he blew out a long breath and said, "I had to separate him from you, Bradley. From what he was dragging you into in Iraq, and then every time you were back in the States. And it worked, for God's sake, surely you see that? Surely you can see the malignant influence—"

"You put Snake in Leavenworth?" There was a red haze blurring his vision.

"I did what any father—"

"Got him a dishonorable? Took away his freedom, his reputation, his life? Almost seven years, you . . . oh my fucking God, I . . ."

He took a shaky step forward. The admiral stepped back.

Boomer wanted to throttle the bastard so much his arms were shaking. Somehow he managed to say, "Get out." It sounded like a growl.

"Tell me where to find—"

"GET OUT!" Boomer roared.

The door to the study flew open, one of the Secret Service guys swinging it with one hand, his other inside his jacket.

"It's all right, Ken," the admiral said to his man, holding out a hand. "We're fine."

Boomer glanced at Ken, then back to the admiral. "And take your limp-dick security guys with you," he said.

Ken was staring at him. Boomer swiveled his head like a machine gun on a turret and gave him a smile that was more a grimace. "You want to have a go with me, Ken? Go ahead, pull your piece. I'll shove it so far up your ass you'll give the muzzle a rim job."

"It's all right, Ken," the admiral said again. "Thanks for checking. We just need another minute."

"Yeah, Ken," Boomer said, still smiling at the guy. "Be a good boy. Do what you're told."

Ken broke the eye contact and nodded at the admiral, then closed the door behind him.

The study was suddenly silent. Boomer and the admiral stood facing each other. After a moment, Boomer smiled again. Hosing down Ken had been good for his spirits.

"You think it was a problem when all I owed you was a billion?" he said, the smile widening. "You better hope I don't tell Snake you pulled strings to get him sent to Leavenworth. If I do? You'll find out what a problem really is."

29

Livia was on the phone with Sherrie Dobbs. Who was, as Grace Jordan had claimed, freaked out.

"Look," Dobbs said. "Grace said she had a good feeling about you. Which I appreciate. But unless you tell me you're going to arrest Boomer Kane, what can you do for me?"

"It's not just Boomer," Livia said. "It's his war buddy, the guy people apparently call Snake. Stephen Spencer. Who has no fixed address and can't currently be located."

"Well, even worse, then."

"Regardless," Livia said, "I can't arrest anyone if I don't have a case. And I can't make a case if no one will talk to me."

"What is there to talk about? Grace already told you. Boomer raped me in high school. And Noreen, and Hope. And now he's killing us. To keep us from telling the truth about him."

"Have you thought about going public?"

"Of course. But look what happened to Noreen. Death threats. She had to go into hiding. And Boomer killed her anyway."

"But Hope kept quiet."

"And Noreen didn't!"

"I know. What I'm trying to say is, I can't be sure, but my sense is that after Noreen publicly accused him, Boomer decided he couldn't take a chance on Hope corroborating Noreen's story by telling her own. So he staged what could be passed off as a random carjacking that escalated to rape and murder."

"If you're trying to reassure me, you should know it's not working."

"I'm trying to get you to see something you might be missing. I think Boomer decided he could endure whatever speculation might come about the 'coincidence' of Hope's death. But that he decided he wouldn't be able to risk moving against her if she had a chance to speak out first. If I'm correct about that, it stands to reason that he would apply the same calculus to you. That it's the fact that you *haven't* spoken out that's putting you in more danger now."

"More danger. There's danger either way."

Livia couldn't argue with that. She said nothing.

There was a long pause. Dobbs said, "You don't get it. I haven't even told my husband about . . . what Boomer did to me. What he did to the three of us. I'm eight months pregnant, we just bought a new house . . . I'm on bed rest, I can't even help out at our bakery, my husband's doing it all alone right now and it's hell just to make ends meet. Do you have any idea what this would do to our life? The media circus? The accusations? The death threats?"

Better death threats than death, Livia thought. But she wasn't looking to one-up the woman. Just to persuade her.

And protect her.

"I understand," Livia said.

"I doubt it."

Despite herself, Livia felt a trickle of irritation at that. "You don't know me," she said slowly. "If you did, you'd know that, yeah, I understand."

A pause. Dobbs said, "I'm sorry."

"At least let me come see you. And my partner, a Homeland Security Investigations agent."

"What's that going to do?"

"We could advise you on security, for one thing. And if you can tell me more about Boomer, you might help me make a case."

"A case about raping some high-school girls twenty years ago who no one wants to hear from because Boomer's a war hero now and his father is vice president?"

"Why do you assume the case I'm trying to make is only about what Boomer did twenty years ago?"

Another long pause. Dobbs said, "Oh my God."

"That's right, Sherrie. Rapists don't stop raping on their own. They stop when someone stops them."

She realized her tone had gotten more heated than she'd intended. *Easy*, she thought. *Easy.*

"So the only question," she went on, "is whether you're going to make me try to stop Boomer on my own, or whether you'll help me."

Another long pause. Sherrie said, "When can you get here?"

30

In the limousine on the way back to San Diego International Airport and Air Force Two, Admiral Kane poured two inches of a twenty-five-year-old Macallan from a crystal decanter into a matching tumbler. He added a drop of water, swirled the mixture, and took a big swallow. Hypocritical, he knew, after he had chastised Bradley for his own weakness. But there was no one around to see it.

He stared through the smoked glass of the limousine window at the hills north of Interstate 8, ghostly shapes in the faltering twilight. He took another swallow of the Macallan. After a few minutes, he began to feel calmer.

He had to stop Snake. For the moment, nothing was more important. Not because he was worried about Bradley's threat to tell the man how Kane had intervened to have him sent away. At least, that wasn't his primary worry. Next to the president himself, Kane had the best protection in the world. Still, he wouldn't have it forever. He wouldn't have it when he was no longer vice president. Which he certainly wouldn't be if anything came out about Bradley and that aptly named creature Snake.

When Noreen Prentis had gone missing, Kane suspected Bradley. When he learned Hope Jordan had been raped and murdered—the

Portland newspaper noting with infuriating coyness the connection to Bradley—Kane was nearly certain. And seeing Bradley tonight, seeing his reaction, confirmed it. Snake had cooked up a plan. With whatever level of support from Bradley, tacit or otherwise, Snake was eliminating the three women who might tell stories about Bradley from high school, and about how at the time Kane himself had engineered their silence.

Without more, those stories might have been survivable. After all, powerful men had beaten back multiple allegations of sexual impropriety before. What they hadn't beaten back were revelations that they had been killing the women who might accuse them.

It was maddening. Even as a boy playing Little League baseball, Bradley had ignored any coach who told him to go for the base hit, preferring to swing for the fences and take a chance on striking out instead. And certainly he had ignored his own father's attempts to steer him to Annapolis and the navy, preferring to seek glory as an enlisted man in the army instead. Kane supposed it was simply in Bradley's wanton, undisciplined nature to default to the high-risk, high-reward strategy.

On the other hand, he had to admit, in some ways Bradley's default settings had been working for him. "War hero" was a key element of Bradley's political brand, after all, and had been a huge asset in the special election that had earned him his congressional seat. Still, the success of Bradley's approach was more appearance than reality, because it had always depended on hidden assistance. First from Kane, who had bought off those girls. And now from Snake, who was killing them.

Maybe it was Kane's fault. He had been mortified when Bradley threw back in his face his own dictum about owing the bank a billion dollars. But he supposed his mortification was at least partly the product of the truth of Bradley's words. Because hadn't Kane continued to bail the boy out, starting with the girls he was indiscreet with in high school and continuing all the way to the present peril, getting in deeper and deeper until, indeed, Bradley's problems were no longer primarily his own but rather his father's?

Yes, maybe. But it didn't make a difference, either. He couldn't permit Bradley to go under. The debtor's bankruptcy would destroy the bank. Which meant there was nothing to be done other than another bailout.

He couldn't deny that it both enraged and disgusted him that Snake, through his current activities on behalf of Bradley, was in some ways part of that bailout. While also contributing to the bankruptcy Kane was intent on heading off.

But the emotion was irrelevant. So was the paradox behind it. What mattered was, there was a delicate sequence in play, and Kane needed to manage it. He had to let Snake finish quashing the women who could hurt Bradley. And then quash Snake.

Ordinarily, a sequence like that would present a challenge. But not this time. Because this time, Kane knew exactly where the man was going. The focal point of Snake's final service to Bradley, and the occasion on which he would present his last danger to Bradley, were one and the same.

The third woman. Sherrie Dobbs.

31

Livia looked through the window, watching the ground recede as they gained altitude.

Little figured his boss, Ronald Tilden, was still keeping tabs on him, so after extensive countersurveillance, they'd chartered a small plane from Sea-Tac to avoid having their names entered into the CBP system. The cost was $450 an hour, and the pilot, a guy named Dan Levin who exuded the kind of quiet competence anyone would want in a cockpit, told them he'd be happy to wait on the tarmac anywhere they liked, as long as they understood the meter was running. Little, saying that was what his 401(k) was meant for, accepted without hesitation.

Livia wanted to get in touch with the Kanab Police Department. Little had been opposed—he wanted to keep things as low profile and unofficial as possible. But Livia had asked how he was going to feel if Snake showed up and took Sherrie Dobbs while she and Little were in the air. At that, he relented. So as soon as they took off, Livia used the satellite phone and got ahold of the local chief of police, a guy named Cramer, who naturally wanted to know what it was all about.

"Just being cautious," Livia said. "I'm investigating a murder, and Ms. Dobbs has information material to my investigation. I don't think the suspect is anywhere near Kanab. Mostly I'd like to reassure Ms. Dobbs. She was feeling jumpy when I spoke with her on the phone. I should be there in about two hours, regardless."

"Well," Cramer said, "if it were tourist season, I don't know that I could spare someone. We've only got six full-time officers on the force, if *force* is even the right word for a police department that mostly hands out speeding tickets and deals with illegal camping. But this time of year? I'll be happy to park in front of the Dobbs house myself. Nice couple, by the way. Moved out here a few years ago and opened the kind of bakery I'll bet you don't have even in Seattle."

"What brought them to Kanab?" Livia asked, because you never knew what you might learn.

"Oh, the same thing that brings anyone who's not originally from around here. Mostly the great outdoors. We're a stone's throw from Grand Staircase-Escalante, Zion, the Grand Canyon . . . plus housing's affordable and the people are friendly. My wife and I fell in love with the area backpacking and rock climbing in college. We lived in Coeur d'Alene for a while, and it's beautiful out there, but with all the Californication a cop can't buy a house. So here we are. Got a great wife, two great kids, and I'm chief of police at thirty-two in a part of the world where nothing bad ever happens. You sold yet?"

Livia laughed, but his words made her uneasy. Maybe she'd tried a little too hard to downplay the danger to Sherrie Dobbs when she'd first described the situation. Maybe she should have told Dobbs to go to the station and wait for Livia and Little there. But no, the woman was on bed rest. "Listen, Chief Cramer—"

He laughed. "Tom, for God's sake. Barely anyone around here even calls me *officer.*"

"Tom, then. I told you, a patrol car in front of Sherrie Dobbs's house . . . it's more about reassuring her than protecting her. But the man I'm investigating is dangerous. You'll want to be cautious, okay? You said it's not tourist season. Good. If you see someone near Sherrie

Dobbs's house you don't recognize, or anything that makes you uneasy, get backup right away."

There was a pause. "How serious is this?"

"The man I'm looking for . . . he's killed at least two people. And he's got military training. Combat experience. It's great that nothing bad ever happens in Kanab. But if anything bad were going to happen . . . it would be this guy."

"You have a photograph or a description?"

She'd asked Fallon the same thing. He hadn't been able to offer much. "White. Wiry build. Five nine and maybe a hundred sixty-five pounds. That's all I've got."

"Well, it's something. If he shows up at all."

"You have a cellphone number?"

He gave her the number. "Thanks," she said. "I really appreciate the help."

"You bet. I'll see you at the Dobbs house. Two hours, you said?"

"Give or take. Thanks again, Chief. Tom."

She clicked off. The urban density of the Seattle metropolitan area was already behind them, the Cascade Range coming into sharp relief below.

She felt uneasy. How much pause would the sight of a patrol car give someone like Snake?

Some, at least. Noreen Prentis, Snake had disappeared into thin air. Hope Jordan, he'd made look like an ordinary carjacking that escalated to something worse. A tragic coincidence. But a dead cop in front of Sherrie Dobbs's house, with Dobbs dead or missing on top of it . . . how could they explain that? It would make Prentis and Jordan impossible to dismiss as unconnected. They wouldn't be that brazen.

She thought that was right. But of course she couldn't be sure.

Kanab, she thought. *Where nothing bad ever happens.*

She was going to do all she could to keep it that way.

32

Snake was proned out on a mesa overlooking Sherrie Dobbs's house, watching through binoculars. It was a good thing he'd reconnoitered before moving in. Because there was a cop parked in front.

The guy was in a pretty good tactical position, too—right at the edge of the corner lot the house sat on, away from bushes, parked cars, or anything else someone trying to sneak up on him might use for concealment. The guy looked alert—not snoozing, not reading a magazine, just giving the area a regular scan, making good use of his rearview and sideviews. And though Snake couldn't be sure because he could only make out the guy's chest and shoulders, he looked like a pretty solid specimen. Definitely not some weekend-warrior type, even though the town felt like a backwater.

What are you doing here, Mr. Policeman? Sherrie get the word about poor Noreen and Hope and then call you?

Or did someone send you?

Snake wasn't much of a marksman, but the cop was parked only about two hundred yards away, and Snake was in an elevated position with clear line-of-sight. If he'd had a rifle, it wouldn't have been a difficult shot. Unfortunately, he had nothing but the Ruger. If it had been night, he could have ghosted up on the cop no problem. Unfortunately, it was midday, and the sun overhead was so bright Snake could have stripped down and caught a tan.

Think there's another one inside?

He doubted it. The car was marked *Kanab Police*. Local. And how many local cops could there be in a town like this? A half dozen? Snake had a feeling the guy was here to humor someone, most likely Sherrie Dobbs.

What to do, what to do.

He supposed he could just wait. It would get chilly when the sun went down in a few hours, but he was wearing his homeless getup, including a watch cap, multiple sweatshirts to create the appearance of extra weight for any witnesses he might encounter, and tactical gloves to make sure he didn't leave fingerprints anywhere. Let it get dark, ease in, kill the cop then. It wouldn't be hard.

But waiting involved risks. Snake had done his online research, and made sure to walk by the bakery they owned. The husband had been behind the counter, and no sign of the wife. So a safe bet that right now, Sherrie Dobbs was home, and probably alone. Otherwise, why would there be a cop parked in front of her house? But in a few hours, who knew? Sherrie could go out. Her husband could come home. The neighbors might drop in for a chat. Anything was possible.

Plus, at night, people were less trusting about answering the door. Although in fairness, with a cop out front, it looked like that sort of trust would be in short supply regardless of the hour.

Snake watched the cop through the binoculars. The guy was still scanning. Snake wondered if he had any military training. Maybe. Or maybe it was just that he wasn't the complacent type.

Waiting felt like a risk. Now felt like an opportunity. The only impediment was the cop. Well, there were ways to take the man out that didn't involve a rifle or waiting for night. The problem was how it would look. Because the idea was that with two women missing and one raped and murdered, Boomer would be able to stonewall. But change that to one woman missing, one raped and murdered, and one disappeared with the cop guarding her house dead outside it, and stonewalling could start to get a little challenging.

On the other hand, hadn't Boomer's supporters already demonstrated their willingness—hell, their eagerness—to explain away Noreen Prentis? There were a half-dozen Facebook groups with thousands of supporters dedicated to the proposition that Noreen was a false flag, with her disappearance abetted by Boomer's enemies. One of the groups, and by no means the smallest, had even gone so far as to theorize that Boomer's enemies hadn't just assisted in her disappearance but had actually done her in. The controversy was causing some uncomfortable questions, sure, but only in media circles and among voters Boomer was never going to win over anyway. His supporters, by contrast, were fired up. Snake couldn't help smiling at the thought. Maybe he'd missed his calling. He should have been some kind of political consultant.

Not that whatever insights he had were rocket science. If there was one thing Snake knew about people, it was that once they got attached to a theory, it was hard to get them detached. They'd screen out unhelpful facts, invent favorable ones, and ignore contradictions in their own claims. Look at those Sandy Hook truthers, babbling about false flags and crisis actors and all the rest. When people were motivated enough to believe something, they were going to believe it no matter what. There was no such thing as a bridge too far.

Meaning . . . so what if a third woman were taken? So what if the cop who was parked in front of her house to protect her was killed? It would only show the lengths Boomer's enemies would go to in trying to discredit him. Because of his service to country. Because of what he stood for. Whatever. It didn't matter why. Boomer's people loved him, sure, but more than that, they hated his enemies. Snake figured the more threatening those enemies seemed, the more it would motivate Boomer's base.

Yeah, now that he was thinking about it . . . maybe a dead cop associated with Sherrie Dobbs's disappearance wouldn't be a bad thing at all. Maybe it would even be . . . an asset.

He imagined explaining it all to Boomer later. Boomer wouldn't like it, any more than he'd initially liked the way Snake had taken care of Hope Jordan. But he'd come around, right? He had when he'd seen Noreen Prentis, bound and gagged and ready for the two of them to enjoy. It would be the same with Sherrie Dobbs. Boomer might protest, but then he'd look at her, realize that Snake couldn't very well send her back, and fuck it, let the good times roll.

Okay. But none of it was going to happen if he didn't first deal with this cop. He'd have to adjust the approach, of course. Snake's car—a Toyota Corolla rented back in San Diego but with plates borrowed from another vehicle he'd found in a St. George office park on the drive to Kanab—was parked a quarter mile away in a motel lot. He'd planned to drive it to Sherrie Dobbs's house after reconnoitering, but that wouldn't work now. He might be able to pull up alongside the cop and get the drop on him. But doing it that way would mean an open approach from at least a block away. That was more time than Snake wanted to give the guy to get his game face on.

Presumably the guy had been briefed, and knew someone danger-ous might show up. But that wouldn't be a problem. Because when it came to danger, there was knowing, and there was *knowing*. So unless this cop had seen the kind of combat and killing Snake had, which was seriously unlikely, then no matter what he told himself, there were still going to be some background assumptions. For example, the assump-tion that violence always involved a buildup, an escalation, some kind of warning signs. Sure, violence might move fast, but not *that* fast, not so fast you couldn't anticipate it. People imagined even the worst violence would be like a sports car. There would be an engine roar, and squealing tires, and maybe the front would lift up a little because man, that baby is accelerating fast, you better jump out of the way. But in

Snake's experience, almost no one was prepared for his kind of violence, which was less like a car accelerating than like an IED you didn't even know was there before it blew up in your face. Good luck getting out of the way of that.

Meaning he could imagine a number of ways to get to the cop. But in the end, he went with the most straightforward.

He dropped back to the north side of the mesa and circled clockwise until he was out of sight of the cop's position. Then he scrambled down the side, his boots sending rivulets of red sand ahead of him and kicking up little clouds of dust into the dry air. It took him just a few minutes to reach the street parallel to the one Sherrie Dobbs lived on—another block of sleepy detached single-family houses, a few with cars in the driveways but most looking empty, thickets of trees casting shadows on the parched scrub lots, all of it surrounded by the desolate red mesas.

He walked along until he was about even with Sherrie's house and one block east of it. Then he turned right onto the driveway between two houses and slipped into the backyard behind one of them, zigzagging from tree to tree to maintain concealment from the cop's position. A dog barked from a house somewhere to his left, but Snake kept moving, and after a moment the barking stopped. There was the buzz of a lawn mower somewhere. That was all.

Within a minute, he had reached the back corner of the house directly across the street from the Dobbs place. He squatted and looked through the trees. There was the cop, still scanning, not fifty feet away now. His windows were open, maybe on account of the fine weather, maybe because he wanted to be able to hear the world outside the car. Snake would have left the windows up, himself. The glass would offer you some protection—say, from someone with a knife. And yeah, the glass would cut off some sound, but the tradeoff would be worth it.

On the other hand, the guy had parked the way Snake would have. Wrong side of the street, driver side facing the house. Meaning anyone approaching the vehicle from anywhere other than the house would be coming at the driver from across the passenger side. Not a huge buffer, but survival was a game of inches, and anyone who said otherwise had never been in the shit.

He waited, timing the cop's head scans. The guy was concerned enough to be doing the scans, but not concerned enough to be doing them randomly. Not a good idea. Sentries on regular patrols could be predicted. Sentries who could be predicted could be taken out.

Snake double-checked the terrain. To reach the cop, he'd have to cross a patch of grass, then the asphalt street, then a gravel shoulder. The only surface his footfalls would be noisy on would be the gravel. At that point, he'd be too close for the cop to effectively react.

He eased the Ruger from the small-of-back holster and watched, his stance forward and low like he was a sprinter at the starting blocks. The cop's head swiveled left. Swiveled right. Swiveled—

Snake exploded forward, arms pumping, legs churning. Over the grass. The asphalt. The gravel, the soles of his boots loud now, and the cop heard the sound and must have recognized the danger, because his shoulders were coming up, his head turtling in, his body spinning toward the passenger side, his left hand coming across to protect his face, his right going for his waist—

Snake skidded into the passenger side of the car, grabbing the window frame with his left hand and jamming the Ruger inside just enough to contain some of the noise if he had to fire but not so much that the cop could easily grab it. "Freeze, cop," he said. "I don't want to kill you."

Of course, that last part wasn't exactly true, but these things almost always went more smoothly if you gave the person a reason to cooperate.

The cop's right hand froze midway to the pistol holstered at his waist. His head continued to turn, though, and he looked at Snake. His expression was more angry than afraid. Snake didn't like that. He needed the guy to be compliant, because the plan was for him to drive Snake to the motel, where Snake would kill him and jump in the rental car, then drive back here and grab Sherrie Dobbs.

"Hands on the wheel," Snake said, the muzzle of the Ruger pointed directly at the cop's face. But his posture casual, just a passerby leaning in and chatting with the cop. "Slowly."

Still looking at him, the cop put his hands on the wheel. Yeah, he was solid, all right. Big hands, thick forearms. Maybe a rock climber or something. With all the mesas and national parks, there'd be a lot of that around here.

Snake didn't like the way the guy was looking at him. Like he was considering his options. The guy wasn't wearing a seatbelt, meaning he was more mobile than Snake would have liked, and the engine was running, meaning he could pop it in gear and be off in a heartbeat.

"Look the other way," Snake said. "Out the driver-side window."

"Why?"

Snake couldn't believe it. "Because I'll kill you if you don't. Any other questions, cop?"

"Yeah. What do you want?"

"I want you to drive me out of here."

"Why?"

That actually made Snake laugh. "You make me say it again, I might save us both the trouble and just fucking do it."

"No, I mean, why do you want me to drive you? If you want to get to the visitors center, it's not far. They close at four. You could easily make it."

Was this guy out of his mind? "Listen, you dumb shit—"

But he realized too late the question was just a distraction, because the guy lunged at him, his hands flying off the steering wheel and backhanding the Ruger away. Snake's fingers smacked hard into the window frame, and it would have hurt, maybe even caused him to drop the gun, but the glove was Kevlar-lined. The guy twisted and grabbed Snake's wrist, trying to control Snake's gun hand, knowing not to bother trying to unholster his own weapon, and using both hands to try to wrest Snake's gun away.

The guy was desperate, and his hands were fuck-all strong, too, but he was seated and hemmed in by the confines of the car interior, while Snake had complete leverage and mobility. Using his free hand for support, Snake yanked the Ruger back. But Jesus, the guy's hands were like a fucking bear trap. Snake tried turning the gun toward the guy's head, but the guy was too strong. The guy bellowed, a primitive roar of rage and determination, his teeth bared with the effort of trying to GET THE GUN, and in another second, the guy might grab the barrel, which would give him the leverage to twist it out of Snake's hands.

Snake shoved the Ruger forward, then yanked in the opposite direction off the guy's reaction. The move gave him just enough space to get a knee up against the car door, and to then use his lumbar muscles like a pry bar. The cop hung on gamely for another second, so tightly that Snake actually dragged him across the console and onto the passenger side. But the biggest forearms in the world were no match for a back, and when the guy's shoulder hit the passenger-side door it was enough for Snake to tear the gun free. The guy felt it coming a second before he lost his grip and started to turn to the driver-side door, maybe imagining he could scramble out even if his torso and the vest he was probably wearing soaked up a few bullets along the way. But Snake was faster, and trained to take out bad guys carrying hidden explosives, where center mass was nothing but a good way to get blown up. He brought the Ruger forward and shot the guy point-blank behind the ear. The guy's head jerked, then he slumped sideways in the passenger seat, his head coming to rest against the dashboard.

Snake heard the dog barking again. Fuck, he hadn't wanted to shoot the guy here at all, and if he had to, he'd planned to do it inside the car to keep the sound relatively muffled.

Well, probably anyone who heard the shot would tell themselves it had been something else. But you never knew for sure. And if Sherrie Dobbs had been concerned enough to ask for some kind of police protection, she wouldn't be dismissing a gunshot as a firecracker or backfiring truck. She might do anything—call the police. Grab the family shotgun. All of the above.

Snake glanced at the house. It didn't look like much. Just clapboard. He could probably kick in the door. He could certainly go in through a window. But between the gunshot and the sounds of his trying to gain entry, Sherrie Dobbs would have a lot of time to prepare. And that image of her waiting for him like Annie fucking Oakley wasn't a happy one.

Okay, Plan B. Or C. Or wherever we are.

He holstered the Ruger, ran around to the driver side, opened the door, and jumped in. He popped it in drive, whipped around to the right so the rear was facing the house, hit the brakes and skidded to a stop, threw it into reverse, and accelerated backward directly into the front door. There was a *boom!* and a huge jolt and the back of his head slammed into the headrest, but the car plowed through the door and the wall around it. He hit the brakes again and was suddenly, weirdly, in the middle of someone's foyer, albeit with a ton of wood shards and broken glass all over the place, and the air thick with dust.

He looked around but didn't see anyone, then opened the door and jumped out. "Sherrie Dobbs?" he called out. "Are you all right?"

There was a pause, then a woman poked her head from around the corner. Her eyes were terrified, but he recognized her instantly from his online research. Sherrie Dobbs.

"Who are you?" she said, her voice so high it was practically a squeak.

"Police," Snake said. "And we need to get you out of here. Right now."

"What happened to Tom?"

He could see she was struggling with her confusion and doubts. The trick was to keep things moving fast, so the person didn't have time to think. Didn't have time to listen to her gut.

"Tom's in the car," Snake said, heading toward her. "He's hurt and I need to get him to the hospital. But I can't leave you here alone."

The indecision in her eyes lasted another half second. Then it was gone, and he could see the doubt had won over. She disappeared around the corner.

Snake realized he had never seen her hands. *Fuck.* He raced to the corner and went around it—

And there she was, wearing a blue robe and hugely pregnant, holding a shotgun in badly trembling hands. Other than her swollen belly and the bizarrely bright yellow kitchen, the scene was right out of his imagination.

He knew without conscious thought that there was no turning back. The only way out was straight ahead.

He held up his hands and kept moving forward. "Are you out of your mind?" he said. "Don't point that thing at me. We need to get you out of here. Come on."

Her arms were trembling so badly she could barely keep the muzzle downrange. "Please," she said. "Please—"

He grabbed the shotgun by the barrel and snatched it out of her hands so fast she didn't even have a chance to get off a shot. The second he had the weapon, he realized how close it had been. If he'd so much as paused to think about it before acting, he never would have done it. Which was of course why he hadn't thought.

"Point a fucking *gun* at me?" he shouted, getting in her face. "I ought to shove it up your box and pull the fucking trigger!"

"I'm sorry," she said, holding up her shaking hands and crying. "I'm sorry, I don't know what's going on or who you are. Oh God, why is this happening?"

He threw the shotgun aside and grabbed her by the arm. "I'm with Tom," he said, struggling to get back in character and pulling her along. "I told you, he's hurt. You need to do what I tell you if we're going to get you out of this."

They turned the corner, and there was the cruiser, covered in plaster rubble and wood shards, the air around it swirling with dust motes caught in the sunlight coming through the windows.

Well, you don't see that every day. He had to stifle a crazy laugh.

He pulled her to the open driver door, reached inside, and pressed the trunk release. Nothing happened.

Are you fucking kidding me?

Must have damaged the mechanism backing up through the wall. Murphy. Every damn time.

But whatever. He reached into one of the pockets on his cargo pants and pulled out the handcuffs he'd brought.

Sherrie saw them. "What?" she said, her eyes freak-out wide. "What, why are you . . ."

Snake didn't even respond. There was no time. He just spun her around and shoved her facedown across the trunk. She screamed but he barely heard it. He ripped the robe off her back, tossed it aside, hauled her wrists behind her, snapped the cuffs on, grabbed the gag from a pocket, and tied it around her mouth. Then he opened the rear driver-side door, shoved her sprawling inside, and slammed the door closed behind her. He jumped in front, popped it in gear, and punched it. The engine roared and they blew across the lawn, the tires spinning clumps of grass and dirt behind them. A woman was standing in the doorway of a house across the street, watching open-mouthed. Snake cut the wheel right and the cruiser fishtailed and bounced over the curb, then the tires grabbed asphalt and they rocketed forward, and just like that the stupefied neighbor was in the rearview, obscured by a cloud of dust.

Snake gunned the engine, figuring if he was lucky he had maybe sixty seconds before whatever other cops Kanab could muster would be swarming all over him. He accelerated two blocks south, turned right, then forced himself to slow it down. He made another right. He was so juiced he didn't even see the car coming up behind him.

33

Livia and Little had jumped into the rental car they'd reserved at the airport in Kanab, just north of the Arizona border. Livia had felt lucky the place even had rental cars—the airport itself wasn't much more than a landing strip. The landscape was stunning, though—red mesas, endless sky, and a road stretching almost to the horizon—and she promised herself that one day, she'd take a vacation and ride out here on the Ducati. It made her think of Carl, who was also an enthusiast, albeit a Harley man. Maybe they could have taken a trip like that together. But it never would have worked. She'd done the right thing. Or, at least, the thing that had to be done.

Livia needed to be in control, meaning she always preferred to drive. But if they encountered any problems, she thought they'd do better with Little behind the wheel and her behind the Glock. So she agreed when Little had asked, obviously rhetorically, if he could do the driving. She hadn't offered her reasoning. He would have found it inherently insulting, in part because he would have recognized its fundamental accuracy.

She'd spoken with Sherrie Dobbs from the air, but wanted to let her know they were in the car now and just a few minutes out. She called. Four rings, then voicemail. She clicked off.

Probably it's nothing. Could be in the bathroom. Could be feeling ill—remember, eight months pregnant and on bed rest.

Still, it made her uneasy. She called Tom Cramer. And got his voicemail, too.

She clicked off and pocketed the phone. "No one's answering," she said. She pulled the Glock from the belly-band holster.

Little glanced at the gun, then at the navigation app open on his phone. "We'll be there in two minutes regardless."

Livia nodded, looking at the map in the navigation app. "Don't stop in front of her house. Go past it. We'll circle the block a couple times."

Little didn't argue—whether because he knew better than to try or because he agreed, she didn't know and didn't care.

They turned right onto Dobbs's street and drove north. Two blocks ahead, a Kanab police cruiser coming in their direction turned right. It was going fast, though without flashers, and was too far away for Livia to make out who was behind the wheel.

There were a dozen benign possibilities. She ignored all of them. "Did you see that?" she said.

"I did. You want me to follow him?"

She felt a small hit of adrenaline ripple through her torso. "Yes. But hang back. Give him room."

They turned left onto the street the cruiser had turned on just in time to see it making another right two blocks down. Little, who was obviously experienced with vehicular surveillance, sped up so they wouldn't lose visual contact for too long.

They turned right onto a four-lane street. No cruiser. "Shit," Livia said, scanning. Even if the driver had gunned it after turning the corner, they'd been close enough that they would have seen him turning onto the next block. There was some sort of park directly across from them, but he would have had to go straight, not right, to enter it. Two motels—the Quail Park Lodge on the left side of the street, a Days Inn on the right. An antiques store on the left side, but no cruiser in its parking lot. A restaurant called Sego to the right, part of another hotel called Canyons.

"U-turn?" Little said.

"Not yet." Her heart was thudding strongly now. Something was wrong here. She could feel it. "Turn right at the intersection. I think he pulled into that Days Inn and drove around back. Maybe there's a connecting lot."

Little turned right, then right again into the Canyons Hotel driveway. There was a parking area in front. Little drove past it, along the back of the hotel. To their right were more parking spaces, most of them empty, some occupied by empty vehicles. A few sedans. A U-Haul van.

They kept going. Straight ahead was a low concrete wall with a row of trees behind it.

"Not a connecting lot," Little said.

"Well, we can't drive through, but . . ." She pointed to the empty parking spaces along the back of the hotel. "Pull in over here. I want to get out and have a look."

Little did a three-point turn and stopped the car with the nose pointing toward the street they'd turned in from. A good habit—turning the vehicle around when you could was better than doing it when you had to.

They got out. It was quiet behind the hotel, just the muted sounds of traffic from the four-lane road they'd turned off. The air was cool and dry. Little unholstered his weapon. She was glad he needed no prompting. As the saying went: denial has no survival value.

"Hang back," she said quietly, dropping to a crouch and heading toward the wall. The trees running along it were good concealment, but she couldn't see what was on the other side, either. She was glad she was wearing her vest.

She came to the wall and dropped lower, thankful for the cover it provided. From the new position, she could see through the trees. And there. On the other side, not fifteen feet away. The cruiser. A sedan parked next to it, the back facing Livia's position. And a man stuffing a naked, cuffed, gagged, pregnant woman into the sedan's open trunk. Sherrie Dobbs. And Snake.

She felt a huge adrenaline dump. Her heart started pounding. Sound faded out. She put her sights on Snake's torso. "DO NOT MOVE!" she shouted.

Snake froze. He looked at Livia, his expression utterly surprised. His right hand drifted high, the palm forward, the fingers splayed, but his left hand remained pressed against Sherrie Dobbs's naked back. There was something disconcertingly protective about the way he was touching her—almost as though he cared for her, as though she was precious to him. Dobbs looked up at her, her face streaked with tears, her eyes so terrified that it hurtled Livia straight back to the boat, and the cargo container, and Nason—

She felt the dragon unfold inside her. *Shoot him, shoot him, KILL HIM—*

But she couldn't. The scrutiny she would face. The lost opportunity. To make a case against Boomer. To find out where they had taken all those girls. Where they had left them.

"Both hands!" Livia roared. "Show me both your hands RIGHT FUCKING NOW!"

Snake's left hand came up, too, palm forward, fingers splayed.

"Step to your right!" she shouted. "Away from—"

"Livia, down!" she heard Little yell from behind her.

She dropped instantly, and the concrete to the right of her ear exploded as a round punched into it, the sound of the shot reaching her just after. And then the sound of a fusillade of new ones. Little, returning fire.

She spun, brought up the Glock, and dashed along the wall, knowing she had to get off the X, trying to orient on where the shots were coming from. Another round hit the wall near her, and there, a man ducking back along the side of the U-Haul van, fifty feet away. More shots coming from behind the van—two sets, she thought—with Little returning fire using the door of their rental car for cover.

The geometry was bad—the van was the apex of a scalene triangle with Livia and Little at the base. What she needed was to widen the angles, and then flank the shooters. There was another concrete wall perpendicular to the one separating the lots and parallel to the back of the hotel. She reached it, dove over, and sprinted north, crouching to use the wall for cover. She heard more shots and ran faster. Any second, Little was going to have to reload, and even though if he was good it would take him only a moment, in that instant the shooters might try to leapfrog or flank him. She had to get ahead of that.

She heard an engine roar to life on the other side of the dividing wall. Tires squealing.

Sherrie Dobbs. Oh God.

For a bad second, she slowed, her body trying to drag her back almost of its own accord. But no. She couldn't engage Snake over the wall and take fire from behind at the same time. She couldn't help Sherrie Dobbs until the immediate threat was neutralized.

She forced herself to keep running. When she judged that she was sufficiently north of the shooters, she snatched a glance over the wall—

The man on the closest side of the van saw her. He brought up a pistol, his movements all slow motion—

She put her sights on his chest and fired. He jerked from the impact. She brought up her sights a notch and put a round in his face. He went down.

Little fired once more, then stopped. For an instant, everything was surreally silent. She heard the clink of metal on concrete—Little's spent magazine. The sound of a fresh one slamming into place.

She caught Little's eye and nodded fiercely. He nodded back, then turned and began firing furiously at the van.

Livia leaped over the wall and ran at a diagonal toward the van. She had no cover and no concealment. She didn't care. All she could think of, all she could feel, was Sherrie Dobbs, in the trunk of that car, helpless to protect the baby inside her, terrified, being driven to God knows where so a monster could rape and murder her and leave her body someplace where it would never even be found.

They must have heard her coming. One of them stepped out and fired at the same time she did. They both missed. She felt the bullet whiz by her. Another punched into the vest over her stomach. It meant nothing to her. Screaming, still running straight at him, she kept firing. Hit him in the chest. He fired again, his aim off now. She hit him a second time in the chest, still screaming, still charging forward, the dragon totally ascendant now, an engine of atavistic fury, enraged, fearless. He twitched and tried to reacquire her. She hit him again, this time in the neck. He staggered back spastically, his free hand flying over a crimson fountain suddenly pouring from his throat. Five feet away she put a last round in his face and leaped over his body as it hit the ground.

She saw Little closing, exchanging fire with a third guy. The guy must have heard her screaming on the way in and realized his partner was down. He started to turn but it was way too late. She shot him in the back of the head from so close she knew there would be powder burns on his scalp. His head snapped forward, his knees buckled, and he slid straight down like an imploding building.

She heard sirens. She was distantly aware that shooting while running was insane, and she didn't know how she'd come out on top—luck; rage; fear of her screaming, heedless charge; or some combination.

"That's three!" she called to Little. "Were there more?"

"I only saw three," he called back.

He came up next to her. They were at the back of the van now. Livia pointed to him, then to the passenger side. Then to herself, and to the driver side. He nodded. They each peeled off.

She came to the driver-side door. *One, two—*

She flash-checked through the window. Saw nothing. A longer look. Still nothing.

She pulled the door handle and shoved the door open and away from her. She heard Little do the same from the other side.

"Anything?" she called out, her back to the side of the vehicle just behind the door.

"Nothing!"

The sirens were much closer now.

"Ready?" she said.

"Yes."

"Go!"

She spun into position, the muzzle of the Glock up and pointed diagonally toward the back of the van. Little was doing the same from the other side. But the cargo space was empty.

She retracted the Glock. "We need to go!"

Little was breathing hard, his pupils massively dilated from adrenaline. "Where?"

"That was Sherrie Dobbs on the other side of that wall! And Snake, pushing her into the trunk of a car! Who do you think I was shouting those commands at?"

She turned and ran toward their car. Little followed her. "How the hell should I know?" he said. "Who were these three guys shooting at us just now?"

She did a perimeter check. "We'll figure it out later. Give me the keys. Come on!"

He dug a hand in his pocket, and—

Two patrol cars came barreling into the driveway straight at them, one behind the other. "Come on!" Livia shouted.

The cars stopped thirty feet away, blocking the driveway. Livia felt like she was in a cage, in that foul shipping container again.

Sherrie Dobbs, Sherrie Dobbs, I have to go, have to go, HAVE TO GO—

"Come on!" she screamed again.

"We can't!" Little shouted. "We're blocked in."

"Give me the fucking keys!"

"No! We have to stand down, now!"

Four uniformed cops jumped out of the vehicles, using their doors for cover, pointing their weapons at Livia and Little.

"Drop your weapons!" the driver of the first car, a pale white woman who couldn't have been twenty, shouted. Her voice was high and she was plainly terrified.

"We're on the job!" Little shouted. "Homeland Security and Seattle PD. We'll show you our badges. Let's all just slow it down here."

"Drop your weapons!" the woman shouted again, and somehow, the fear in her voice, and the determination, got through to Livia. Lowering herself slowly, Livia set down the Glock on the pavement. But her mind was screaming that she was being a fool, this was a trap, someone was going to hurt her now, her or Nason or both—

"You too!" the woman shouted at Little.

"It's cool, it's cool," Little said, bending down and setting his gun on the pavement.

Livia straightened, stepped away from the Glock, and raised her hands in the air. "A woman was just kidnapped," she shouted. "Sherrie Dobbs. Every minute we waste doing this dance is a minute farther her kidnapper takes her!"

"Prone out!" the woman called, her voice more confident now. "Face down, arms and legs spread, toes out, fingers splayed!"

"No," Livia said.

Little looked at her. "Livia, for God's sake—"

"I'm not proning out, or getting on my knees, or anything fucking else. I will show my badge and ID. Livia Lone, Seattle PD. Detective. If you want to shoot a cop, shoot me. Just make it fast because for fuck's sake *someone has to save Sherrie Dobbs!*"

The woman glanced at the cop on the opposite side of the patrol car, another young woman, this one black. The black woman nodded.

The white one called out, "Show me your badge. Slowly."

Livia took the badge from her pocket and held it out in front of her. Both women squinted. "I'll toss it to you," Livia said.

The white cop nodded. Livia tossed her the badge. The woman tried to catch it in her left hand, but was too adrenalized. She bobbled it, dropped it, then picked it up and examined it. "What about you?" she said to Little.

Little repeated the procedure. The black woman got back in the patrol car and spoke on the radio. They were being careful, checking Little's and Livia's credentials. But the time they were taking was making Livia want to jump out of her skin.

He's back on the highway now. He won't take a chance on speeding. Sixty miles an hour. A mile a minute.

It had been five minutes already. That was a five-mile radius they'd be working with. If this went on for ten minutes more, the radius would be fifteen miles. Over seven hundred square miles. And growing larger by the minute.

She wanted to scream. She would have begged, if she thought it would have helped. But she knew it would be useless. She would have to wait.

The white cop looked at her. Livia could tell from her expression that she believed Livia and Little were legitimate. But still she was being careful. Livia knew she would have done the same, but it didn't matter. In that moment, she hated her.

"We're trying to reach the chief," the woman said, a note of apology in her tone.

"Tom Cramer?" Livia said.

The woman looked at her, frowning in confusion. "Yeah. You know him?"

"I spoke with him earlier today. And I hope I'm wrong, but I think he's in the cruiser on the other side of that wall behind us."

34

Afterward, they regrouped at Kanab police headquarters. It had been as Livia had feared. Snake and Sherrie Dobbs were gone. Tom Cramer was in the cruiser, shot to death.

Both the Utah Highway Patrol and the Arizona Highway Patrol were searching, but they didn't have a lot to go on. Chief Cramer hadn't been wearing a bodycam—the town didn't have the budget—and the dashcam video in the cruiser was useless because Snake had never been in front of the vehicle. On top of which, Livia had gotten only a cursory look at the car Snake was driving. So what it came down to was, the state troopers were looking for a gray or silver sedan driven by a medium-sized white man. Eventually they might get photos from the military—assuming Boomer's father hadn't already found a way to deep-six them—but *eventually* was unlikely to help Sherrie Dobbs.

Worse, because of all the confusion at the scene, the checkpoints were getting set up late—over thirty minutes from when Snake had driven off. Even in a remote town like Kanab, hemmed in by various national parks and forests, that was a long head start. The closest interstate was I-15, about an hour's drive west, whether through Utah or Arizona, and the state troopers thought Snake would be heading that way. Livia doubted it. From what she could tell, looking at a wall map at the police station, Snake had at least seven routes out of town he could use, and she expected that with the military background he would have given a lot of thought to which ones would be best if anything went wrong. And that was assuming he even kept to the roads. Given his training and experience, Livia thought he'd have no trouble holing up for a few nights in the wilderness and waiting out a dragnet. His timing would certainly be good. The federal government was in the midst of one of its periodic shutdowns; the national parks closed, the park rangers all furloughed.

The Kanab cops were doing a good job of keeping it together, but they were all obviously in shock. As Chief Cramer had said, nothing bad ever happened in their town. And suddenly, their police chief was murdered, a pregnant woman abducted, and three mystery men gunned down by an out-of-town cop in a hotel parking lot. All John Does: no identification, the van they were driving reported stolen the day before in Flagstaff, Arizona. Nothing at all other than a video camera set up in the trees overlooking the area near where Snake had been parked at the motel, and a phone inside the van that was still receiving the camera feed when the local cops searched the vehicle. A useless feed, naturally, because the phones it was transmitting to were presumably the dead men's, and they were passcode protected.

Little came in from outside, where he'd been using his cellphone to talk to Homeland Security. "Any luck?" Livia asked.

He shook his head. "My boss, Tilden, is having a shit fit. Told me I'm AWOL. And he's way more concerned about what I'm doing out here than with the matter at hand. Told me to get my ass back to Washington and prepare to be grounded. I told him to fuck off and called the Salt Lake City field office instead. But Salt Lake City told me I'd have to coordinate through headquarters. That's Tilden, basically issuing an ICE-wide burn notice on my ass. Not that it matters. The field office is a five-hour drive from here. They couldn't help us right now if I were the pope instead of persona non grata. It's going to be the same with the FBI. It's all up to the state troopers."

He looked around the office. Livia knew what he was thinking—they were short on resources. The Kanab Police Department was just a storefront in a strip mall, alongside a liquor store and across from an insurance agency.

They were quiet for a moment. Livia felt horribly helpless. She had to call Strangeland, but she was dreading it. She wanted to go after Snake, but at this point he could be anywhere. The local cops had told her and Little to stay put—a compromise, given the exigencies of the moment, with what would have been SOP following an officer-involved, especially one where the shooter was an out-of-town cop. At least in the confusion and urgency surrounding Sherrie Dobbs, no one had tried to confiscate Livia's gun. Not that in her current state she would have let them.

Livia had briefed everyone on Stephen "Snake" Spencer, explaining that she suspected he was involved in the abduction and murder of two women who had gone to high school with Sherrie Dobbs, and that she had come to Kanab to interview Dobbs about Dobbs's fears of being next. There was no time to explain the rest, but she knew eventually she would have to. She couldn't prove any of it, and she could only imagine the shit storm Boomer's father would bring down on her for even trying.

They're going to throw you off the force after this, she thought. *Two bodies in an officer-involved just a month ago. The dead snipers outside your loft. Strangeland tells you in no uncertain terms to lay low for a while, so you charter a plane to Utah and gun down three more bad guys after the Kanab chief of police is murdered and a local woman is kidnapped. And the vice president and his congressman son are going to investigate you. Call you a psycho. Look into your past and dig up who knows what . . . and they'll attack the department, too. Lean on Best. Claim SPD hasn't been adhering to the DOJ consent decree. They'll put pressure on everyone all the way up to the governor to throw you to the wolves.*

She imagined herself saying *I can explain this,* and it almost made her laugh. Then she imagined Sherrie Dobbs, bound and gagged and terrified in a dark car trunk, and felt desperate tears welling up. She willed them back.

You have to think. The only way you can help her is if you think. THINK.

Of course, the woman might already be dead. Or would be, soon enough. But Livia wouldn't accept that. She'd never accepted it with Nason until she'd been proven wrong. And until she was proven wrong here, she would assume Sherrie Dobbs was alive. And that she could be saved.

Given all that had happened, the small office was less chaotic than Livia would have expected. The bodies of Chief Cramer and the three men Livia had shot had been transported to a nearby hospital, and several of the local cops were liaising with state troopers there. But the dispatcher, a young guy with a ponytail, was within earshot. And although one of the locals had gone to give the horrific news to Sherrie Dobbs's husband, the plan was to bring the husband back to the station. Beyond which, various people were coming and going—paramedics, a councilwoman, even the mayor. The department wasn't a great place for a private conversation.

"I need some air," she said to Little. "Come outside with me?"

He nodded, seeming to catch her drift, and they stepped out into the parking lot.

"He wasn't here just to kill her," Livia said as soon as the door was closed behind them. The sun was getting low in the sky now. If the state troopers didn't manage a lucky stop soon, they were going to have to figure out something else.

"Yeah," Little said. "If that was all he'd wanted, he would have shot her at the house, right after killing the police chief. Would've been a lot less trouble and a lot less risk."

"So why didn't he?"

"Because he's a rapist. Couldn't bear to waste the opportunity."

Livia didn't disagree, exactly, but she knew there was more to it than that. That thing she'd sensed she was missing. But she still couldn't see it.

"What about the three men?" she said.

Little glanced back at the entrance to the station. "Yeah, I was thinking about that. The camera. The way I see it, Boomer's father sent them. If we could figure out where Snake was going to show up, so could someone else."

Livia nodded. She was furious at herself for not having accounted for the possibility. Kane had been expecting Snake to make a run at Sherrie Dobbs, just as Livia and Little had been. What he hadn't expected was Livia and Little, any more than they had expected Kane. They had all been focused on Snake, and not on each other.

She knew Carl's friend Rain wouldn't have made the same mistake. One of the things that had impressed her about him was how thoroughly the man could put himself in the mind of the opposition. It kept him a step ahead. If someone like Rain, rather than Admiral Kane, had been gaming things out, it would have been very bad for her.

"So assassinate the assassin?" Livia said.

"That's my guess. After Noreen Prentis and Hope Jordan, Kane knows his boy Boomer is having Snake tie up loose ends. Kane wants the same thing, but he figures when it's done, convicted-rapist Snake, who's a known associate of his boy, becomes a loose end himself. So Kane sends his men to the known nexus—the third target, Sherrie Dobbs. They follow Snake, see where he parks his car, and set up a camera so they can keep concealed when he comes back. If he's alone, they figure he killed Dobbs already. They follow him regardless, though, just to be sure. And if he has her, they follow the two of them and take care of business on some deserted stretch of mountain road."

That sounded generally right. But something was still bothering her. "But then you and I pulled into the hotel parking lot . . ."

He nodded. "They came swarming out of the van the moment you threw down on Snake and started yelling commands at him. Which makes sense, because about the last thing in the world Kane would want would be Boomer's good buddy Snake in custody after attempting to kidnap the third girl Boomer raped in high school."

You should have just shot him, Livia thought for the dozenth time since Snake had driven away. Maybe they'd have a harder time making a case against Boomer if Snake were dead. But Sherrie Dobbs would be safe. And with the three men Livia had killed, and Boomer's father certain to be on the warpath, Chief Best was going to crucify Livia no matter what.

"Why didn't Kane's men just kill Sherrie Dobbs themselves?" she said.

"Like I said, they wanted Snake, too. If he's going to kill her first, why not let him? Either way, they follow him—"

And it hit her. "That's it! Follow him how?"

He shook his head for a moment, not getting it. Then his eyes widened. "You think—"

"A transmitter," she said, firing up the sat phone. "Why not? They were monitoring him with a camera, why wouldn't they have affixed something to his car, too? They know he's experienced and dangerous, they wouldn't want to have to follow too closely. That's what was bugging me—why just pistols, against a man like Snake? Why not assault rifles and armor-piercing ammunition? After all, Kane can get his people a fucking drone if he wants to. Why go in so light?"

"They wanted it to be low-key. And they knew they could. Because—"

"Because they'd be tracking him from a distance—see where he stopped, and when. Pick their moment. How could we not have seen it earlier? They'd be crazy *not* to use a transmitter. There must be one on his car right now!"

She got a signal and punched in Kanezaki's number. Per his habit, he picked up right away. Thank God.

"Tom, listen, it's Livia. It's an emergency. A woman named Sherrie Dobbs has been kidnapped. It's related to the drone you helped me with. I can't go into details now because there's no time, but I'll tell you everything I know later. All of it. The man who took her is driving a car I'm pretty sure someone affixed a transmitter to. Can you track it? Please."

There was a long pause. *Please,* she thought. *Please.*

"Maybe," he said. "Do you have any idea what kind of transmitter?"

She closed her eyes, willing away despair. "No."

"Do you know when it went live? Or where it was when it did?"

"I can get you an approximate time when it was placed on the vehicle. And an exact location, and an exact time when the vehicle started moving. Would that be enough?"

"Maybe," he said again, and she wanted to scream that she didn't want *maybe*, she wanted fucking *yes*.

She gave him the information. "Let me see what I can do," he said.

Livia closed her eyes again. "You have to find that transmitter, Tom. He's going to kill her. She's got a husband, she's pregnant, and her only crime is that she was raped twenty years ago by a man who doesn't want anyone to hear about it today."

"Boomer Kane?"

She opened her eyes. "How do you—"

And then she realized. Fallon was part of Kanezaki's network.

"Don't be mad at him," he said. "If I'm not in the know, I can't be very helpful. Think about that, next time you want to hold out on me. Now let me see what I can do about this transmitter."

35

Snake headed east on Route 89, surrounded by nothing but sagebrush and mesas and endless blue sky like he was in the middle of a cowboy movie. But he didn't give a shit about the scenery. This stretch of road was a choke point, and if the cops made a lucky guess, he might run into a roadblock at the other end of it. Once he made it past Page, they wouldn't be able to track him, but until then, he was going to be nervous. Nervous, hell, he was mildly freaked out, and if the car hadn't been equipped with cruise control, he probably would have been speeding. Because what the hell was that back at the hotel parking lot?

The Asian woman had been a cop, no question. Cop voice, cop commands. With the Kanab police? Possible, but he doubted it. Something about that woman seemed like the big time. When Snake had looked in her eyes, he wasn't sure if the bitch was going to arrest him, or smile and grease him where he stood. He didn't think the locals would have been half as confident throwing down on him, though in fairness, the guy outside Sherrie Dobbs's house had been no cupcake.

And then, just as Snake had been getting ready to go for the Ruger and shoot it out, someone had yelled for the woman to get down. Lydia? Livia? Snake hadn't quite caught the name. But a second later, the woman was taking fire from her rear, and then returning it. Snake hadn't known what the fuck was going on, he just finished stuffing Sherrie Dobbs in the trunk and got the fuck out of Dodge.

But if the woman was a cop, trying to arrest Snake and save Sherrie Dobbs, and if it was her partner who warned her about the threat from her rear, who were the others? It had been a lot of shooting, more than Snake could keep track of, especially focused as he was on saving his own ass. He thought at least two shooters, though possibly three. They hadn't been cops, that was for sure. No commands at all, just a straight-up ambush. But who were they there for? And who sent them?

Well, they'd been shooting at the woman and her partner, but that didn't mean those two were the primary targets. It seemed more likely that the primary target had been Snake, but then the other two had wandered into the picture.

Okay, but why Snake? Not to stop him from taking Sherrie Dobbs. The cop in front of her house had been for that. That parking-lot shooting team . . . they'd been waiting for him to show up. But they hadn't ambushed him there. It was only when the woman cop got there and tried to arrest him that they moved in.

Meaning they hadn't wanted him arrested. They'd wanted him to drive off. With Sherrie Dobbs.

Jesus, his wrist was throbbing. What the hell, did that cop have bionic hands? Snake looked at his shirtsleeve, and was surprised to see it was a little damp. He pushed it back and holy shit, his arm wasn't just bruised like it had gotten caught in a car door or something, the bruise was actually oozing. The guy had squeezed so hard it was like he'd given Snake an arm hickey. Must have been one of those freaks who sat around all day squeezing a rubber ball or something.

Anyway. Those three at the hotel were going to follow him. Presumably because they were planning to kill him. Your basic find, fix, and finish operation.

So who would want him to successfully abduct Sherrie Dobbs, and then kill him after?

Boomer?

No. Not after all they'd been through together. All they'd shared. It wasn't possible.

You sure about that?

Well, reasonably sure.

He ever try to help you out when you were in Leavenworth, on a fall that could as easily have been his, too? On top of which, almost seven years you were in the joint and he was living it up as a congressman. Maybe a senator next. With a rich family and a father who's the fucking vice president. You don't think guys have been thrown under the bus by a former friend for a lot less than that?

Yeah, but if Boomer wanted to kill him after Snake had finished cleaning up Boomer's three high-school messes, why wouldn't he do it when they met that night at the Salton Sea? Snake was bringing Sherrie Dobbs right to him. All Boomer would have to do was say, *Thanks, brother, and here's a bullet in the back of your head for your troubles.* Row the bodies out on the water, goodbye for good. God knows they'd done exactly that with enough girls when something had gone wrong.

Too squeamish, Boomer? Couldn't pull the trigger yourself on your own blood brother?

Maybe, although "squeamish" was about the last word he'd ever associate with Boomer.

But no, he was losing sight of something. Someone—maybe Sherrie Dobbs, maybe someone else, maybe both—had understood the Noreen Prentis–Hope Jordan pattern. Figured out Sherrie was on deck. That had to be why that cop had been in front of Dobbs's house. And it had to be why the Asian woman and her partner had been in town, too.

And if cops could figure out Sherrie Dobbs was some kind of focal point, why couldn't someone else?

Okay, that made sense. But why kill Snake? What had he ever done? He was just cleaning up Boomer's mess. Who would object to that?

Unless it was the kind of thing where after the fact someone might look at Snake as a potential liability. A loose thread, so to speak. Which took him back to Boomer.

He decided he'd be careful about what he told Boomer over the phone. That was good practice anyway, but even beyond communication security, Boomer sure had been upset about the way Snake had done Hope Jordan. So hearing about the cop in front of Sherrie Dobbs's house and the woman cop and her partner and the three shooters . . . well, it would all just freak Boomer out, wouldn't it? Maybe so badly he'd even take a rain check on tonight. Which really wouldn't be fair, after all the trouble Snake was going to in picking up Sherrie and delivering her.

It occurred to him that Boomer hadn't said anything about the woman being so pregnant it looked like the baby might drop in the trunk of Snake's car. He hoped that wouldn't happen. He had never done it to a pregnant woman before. He wondered what it would be like.

One thing was for sure. The adult diapers he'd brought for the woman were going to be too small. Well, they had adhesive strips, he could just stick two together. He and Sherrie had a long ride ahead of them. Couldn't very well have her messing up the trunk.

He wondered again whether Boomer was in the dark about those shooters. If he'd had anything to do with it, better for Snake to play dumb.

But damn it, it just didn't make sense. Boomer knew he could trust him. Snake had done nearly seven years and never said a goddamn word about anything or anyone.

Boomer's father?

The thought just popped into his head. He wasn't sure why. He started to think, *No.*

But . . . the guy was the vice president. You could see how a man like that would want someone to clean up Boomer's messes . . . and then want that someone cleaned up himself.

But shit, how would Admiral Kane even know about Snake? They'd never met. And the way Boomer talked about his old man, when he talked about him at all, it sure didn't sound like they were close. It was hard to imagine Boomer saying, *Hey, Dad, ever tell you about my good buddy Snake? Yeah, we share the same hobby, it's a hoot.*

Well, someone had sent those shooters. And the only realistic reason they could have been there was because they were keyed on Snake and intent on following him.

Wait a minute. Following how, exactly?

He felt a rush of fear. And started looking for a place to pull over.

36

Livia briefed Little. And then there was nothing to do but wait. And hope.

"Snake," she said. "You said he didn't kill Dobbs at the house because he's a rapist. Because he wanted her for later."

"That's right."

"But what was the plan, then? Disappear her, like Noreen Prentis? Because taking her from her house was never going to be explainable as an 'ordinary' crime, like Hope Jordan, even if he'd done it without leaving fingerprints. On top of which, he sees a cop in front of the house and still makes his play? Murders the cop, steals the cop's cruiser, backs it up into the house, and abducts Sherrie Dobbs . . ."

She stopped, trying to reason it through. Little watched her, saying nothing.

And then she realized. That persistent feeling she'd had earlier, that there was something she was missing. Suddenly she could see it. Not all of it. But an opening, at least. A doorway into the dark.

"It's not a plan," she said. "That's the wrong word. I mean, Snake and Boomer would think of it as a plan, but silencing these women isn't all that's motivating them."

"Like I said, they're rapists."

"Yes, but what I mean is . . . there are serial rapists I've caught because they engage in signature crimes. One guy who always used the same brand of surgical tubing to tie his victims' wrists. Another who would force his victims into identical humiliating poses and make them say the same words while raping them. Others who kept trophies—car keys, panties, jewelry—even though the trophies were a risk, even though the trophies in fact became key aspects of the prosecutor's case. And the thing is, rapists *know* these signatures are a vulnerability. And yet they engage in the behavior anyway. Do you see what I'm getting at?"

Little shook his head. "Like I said. A lot of these people have sick fetishes, even beyond the rape itself. They can't help themselves. The kink is too much fun, even if it's dangerous. Or maybe sometimes even because it *is* dangerous."

"Right. Like that song Grace Jordan told me about. 'Good Times Roll,' by the Cars."

"Boomer's rape soundtrack."

"Exactly. When he was in high school, that was Boomer's signature. He didn't just make every one of the girls listen to it. He put it in his yearbook. It was that important to him."

"But that was high school. Before he was trained in special operations, renditions, that kind of thing."

"Rapists improve their MO, yes. But the signature rarely changes. Like you said, they can't help themselves."

Little took off his glasses and scrubbed a hand over his face. She realized again how tired he looked. And drawn. It occurred to her that in all the time they'd spent together, she'd barely seen him eat.

She thought of the way Snake had been touching Sherrie Dobbs. Almost as though he was concerned for her. Cared about her. Felt some connection with her.

"Noreen Prentis, they disappeared," Livia said. "That fits the pattern. The signature—if the disappearances are a signature."

"Agreed."

"But not Hope Jordan. Her body was found. Along with her murdered son."

"True," Little said, "but these crimes are different. The primary objective is silencing these women. Snake still wants to have his fun, sure, but that becomes more a parameter."

"I think it's a little more than a parameter, given the way he just abducted Sherrie Dobbs. What he risked to do it."

Little shook his head. "I don't follow."

"What about Iraq?" she said. "They weren't abducting those girls. Or murdering them. There's no way Snake would have been court-martialed for a sexual offense—and a lesser one, at that—if the crimes had also included kidnapping and murder."

Little shrugged. "Crimes of opportunity. In Iraq, they didn't have to abduct their victims. They could just take them to another room to 'interrogate' them while the family is held at gunpoint separately. Poor girls were probably terrified to say anything to anyone afterward, too, out of shame, and fear of retribution."

Yes, she thought. She knew that shame well. And the fear. Fred Lone had loved instilling both.

"But then abduction itself isn't the kink we're looking for," she said. "Because in Iraq, Boomer and Snake were fine without it."

Little frowned. "You're saying—"

The sat phone buzzed. She pressed the answer key and snapped the phone up to her ear. "Yes."

"I have coordinates," Kanezaki said. "You ready?"

She felt a flood of relief so strong that for a moment it made her unsteady on her feet. "Get the Arizona Highway Patrol on the phone," she said to Little. Then to Kanezaki, "Go."

"It's an abandoned mobile-home park on Lake Powell, just over the Utah border in Arizona. Green Haven Estates, Green Haven two words. Bit of slick marketing there, given that the place is apparently derelict and in the middle of the desert."

She tried to suppress her excitement and only partially succeeded. She'd been right in thinking Snake would have a place in mind where he could wait out a dragnet. She repeated the information so Little could hear it, then said to Kanezaki, "And the coordinates?"

Kanezaki gave her the coordinates. She repeated the information again, and Little fed it to the Arizona state dispatcher.

"What about a satellite?" she said to Kanezaki. "Can you . . . do you have something you can use to see the place in real time?"

"We have that capability, yes. But I can't access it without getting asked a lot of questions I'm pretty sure neither of us wants to answer. And regardless, by the time I could get a bird in position, I think you'd already have people on the scene."

Okay, it had been a long shot, but worth asking. "Thank you," she said.

"Don't thank me. Next time, just tell me."

"Yeah, I get that."

"And if anyone asks how you came up with the location—"

"I'll tell them it was a lucky guess. I know you'd deny it regardless. But seriously—thank you."

"I hope you get her back. Let me know, okay?"

She felt tears wanting to come and shook the feeling away. She cleared her throat. "You're a good man, Tom."

"Yeah, that's what Dox always says. Right after I've done something I'll regret."

"You won't regret this. I'll keep you posted." She clicked off.

Little said, "Arizona Highway Patrol Division just sent units from Page. Should be on the scene in under ten minutes."

Livia nodded, not trusting herself to speak. *Hang in there, Sherrie,* she thought. *They're coming. They're coming.*

"Tell me again," Little said. "What we were talking about a minute ago."

She tried to get back on track. She was so distracted by the thought of the Arizona troopers taking down Snake and rescuing Sherrie Dobbs that for a moment she couldn't.

"I was saying . . . what if we've been looking at it backward? We've been assuming the disappearances are the point. A signature as much as an MO. But they weren't the point in Iraq. Because . . ."

She paused, imagining Sherrie Dobbs again.

Come on, come on . . .

"For all these years," she said, "you've been thinking about the men who took Presley, right?"

He nodded. "Every day."

"Even when they were faceless, you fantasized about killing them? Torturing them?"

He clenched his jaw for a moment. "Every day."

"Of course you did. But you see, for some rapists, that's not an artifact. It's the whole point. Some serial rapists are also serial murderers, yes. But others don't kill. Or they kill only rarely. Only when something goes wrong."

Little shook his head, plainly at a loss, and she went on. "What I'm saying is, for the kind of creature I'm describing, it isn't about killing the victim. It's the dominance, it's knowing that the rapist is part of the victim now, knowing that every night that girl goes to sleep remembering and every morning she wakes remembering. They're inside her mind the way they were inside her body. They cherish the memory of raping her because they know she shares that memory, and that for her it's a torment."

"You mean like . . . sending cards to the victim afterward. Or the victim's family."

"Exactly like that. What they crave almost more than the act itself is the aftermath. The way they matter to that girl now, forever."

His face contorted. "You're saying Snake and Boomer keep them alive? You're saying—"

"No," she said quickly, realizing she'd inadvertently fueled a hope he couldn't let go of. "No, the logistics of that would be impossible. The ones they've disappeared are dead. To a near certainty. I'm sorry."

He clamped his jaw and managed a nod, and she went on. "But why have we been assuming the disappearances, and the killings that must be part of them, are the point? Isn't it at least equally possible that the disappearances are a subset of something else?"

He shook his head, not getting it. She understood. When Nason welled up in her mind, it made clear thought nearly impossible. Being this close would be overloading all his Presley circuits exactly that way.

"Of what?" he said.

"Of raping teenaged girls they planned to release. Why always black and brown girls? We've been thinking that's a signature, but it could as easily be part of the MO. I mean, if they plan on killing and disappearing the girls, what difference would it make if the victims were marginalized? There would be nothing to go on, no matter what. We talked about this—they made a mistake taking Presley because her father is an HSI agent. And it still didn't matter. They could have taken a rich girl, a white girl, they could have snatched a princess off her throne—none of it would have mattered. If disappearances were the point."

He looked at her. "You're saying . . . they only disappeared them when something went wrong. That the disappearances were a Plan B."

"I don't know for sure. But . . . think about it. Forensics was a total loss with Hope Jordan. Now Hope, they had a specific reason to kill, but in general, if they're confident they've left no evidence, why not let the girl go so she can spend the rest of her life remembering them? Boomer let them go in high school. And reminded them, with that yearbook entry. They both let them go in Iraq. They're not afraid of risk—if they were, Snake would have killed Sherrie Dobbs at her house, like you said. I think these two have raped a lot more girls than we first thought."

He pressed his fingers to his skull so hard his arms trembled. "I was only looking at the disappearances. All these years, I was only—"

She surprised herself by taking hold of his hands. "It's not your fault, Little. A child disappearing is a parent's worst nightmare. A good parent, like you. How could that not eclipse everything else? Especially when you found other crimes with what seemed to have a similar signature. And you weren't wrong. You just missed that the disappearances were a subset of something else."

"You're saying that when they're confident they've left no evidence—no witnesses, no DNA, just a marginalized teenaged girl with a story probably no one will even believe—then they go with Plan A: let her go. Because they love knowing their victims can't stop thinking of them."

She nodded, hating what this was going to do to him.

"But if there's a problem," he went on. "A girl . . ."

His voice caught. He made a sound that was somewhere between a sigh and a whimper. Then he said, "A girl fights back. Maybe gets some of their skin under her nails. Or gets too good a look at them. Or"—tears started flowing down his face—"or calls for her daddy in a way that makes them worry this child will be believed, and protected, and that if she ever tells her story, someone will hunt them down to the ends of the Earth and never, ever stop."

He turned away and sobbed. She waited. She knew there was nothing else she could do.

After a moment, he pulled out a handkerchief, wiped his face, and blew his nose. "Sorry," he said.

She shook her head. More than that would have been too much.

"They're methodical," she said. "Not just with the Plan A. With the Plan B as well. Including where"—she paused, not wanting to say it, then went on—"where to dispose of a body if they need to. Someplace it won't be found."

"But if things go well . . ."

"Then they let the girl go. Degraded. Humiliated. Traumatized. A good chance she'll just live with what they did festering inside her and not even report it. But if she does report it, so what? They know the girls they choose won't be taken seriously."

"Or even if they are taken seriously—"

"Right," Livia said. "Even if they are taken seriously, when the girl and her family realize what it's like to be in the system, maybe the victim just retracts her statement. You know how many times I've seen that happen? And even in those rare cases where the girl is taken seriously, and is determined to see things through, there's no evidence. Because these guys are careful. Condoms. Bleach wipes. Maybe masks for themselves, hoods for the victims."

Little's cellphone buzzed. Livia's heart leaped.

Little raised the phone to his ear. "Yeah."

He frowned and pursed his lips. And the surge of elation she felt was suddenly extinguished.

"I understand," Little said. "It was just a lucky guess." A pause, then, "I can't talk now. I'll explain later. Thank you for following up. I'll let you know if I think of anything else."

He clicked off. "Snake dumped the transmitter at the mobile-home park. It must have occurred to him, based on what happened in the hotel lot, that someone could have placed something on his vehicle."

"No sign of him?"

"None. And that close to Page, he could be anywhere by now. North to I-70. South to Flagstaff and I-40. Or staying on back roads. Or holing up for a while in the backcountry."

Livia pressed a hand over her mouth, feeling sick. She'd thought they had him. But he'd stayed one step ahead. Again.

You should have shot him. You should have shot him. You should have—

"Hey," Little said, his tone sharp. "Stay with me now. We're not done here. If what you've said is true, Snake hasn't killed her yet."

"How do you know that?"

"I don't. Not for sure. But . . . look, we've been talking about patterns, right?"

Livia nodded, not sure where he was going, but hoping he could bring her along.

"Well, here's a pattern. Noreen Prentis disappears into thin air. SOP for these guys, right?"

Livia nodded again.

"And then Hope Jordan. That's a departure. An escalation. Because Hope gets found. Along with her toddler son."

Livia looked at him, beginning to see it, trying not to hope. "And Sherrie Dobbs is even more of an escalation."

"Hell, yes. This time, Snake murders a cop in front of Sherrie's house and then crashes the cop's own cruiser through the front door to abduct her. That is off the charts for these guys. You said it yourself—he wasn't just here to kill her. But now I'm thinking, it wasn't just to rape her first, either. Because when all Snake and Boomer want is to rape someone, we know how careful they are to make sure it might as well have been a ghost that did it. And okay, let's say for the sake of argument that, yes, Snake is a rapist and that's why he didn't just kill Sherrie Dobbs. But he still could have been more careful here, more low-key, no?"

That made sense. Even though it scared her to hope.

"You're right," she said. "Snake isn't stupid. This is a small town. He knows they don't have law-enforcement resources. They couldn't keep a cop on Sherrie Dobbs twenty-four seven."

Little nodded quickly, obviously excited at the way he was seeing it. "He could have come back at night, or the next day."

She was trying to stay calm, but his excitement was infectious. "Okay," she said. "Why's he in such a hurry?"

Little leaned closer. "Because he wants to share her. Like a dog bringing its owner an animal carcass. Share her with Boomer."

Livia looked at him. "Not because he wants to share her. Because—"

"Because they have *a plan* to share her."

He was right. She could feel it. The escalation. Whatever weird psychosexual bond there was between Boomer and Snake. The timing. All of it.

"Then if we track Boomer—"

He shook his head. "Find me anyone who's going to agree to sign a warrant for surveillance of a sitting congressman, war hero, and son of the vice president. Not going to happen. At least not within a time frame that would save Sherrie Dobbs. And we can't do it ourselves. Just the two of us, staking out and trying to follow a former Special Forces combat veteran career criminal on his way to commit another crime? He'll spot us before we even get our cleats on."

Livia wanted to disagree, but she knew his assessment was accurate. Still, there had to be another way. There had to be.

"Where would he take her?" she said, as much to Little as to herself. "You said they have a plan. That's who, what, when, where. *Who* is Sherrie Dobbs. *What* is they're going to share her like they do. *When* is soon, otherwise Snake would have waited out Chief Cramer. But where are they planning on meeting?"

Little pulled off his glasses and scrubbed his face. "Boomer's campaigning in California. That'll be his alibi, if he's ever questioned about Noreen Prentis or Sherrie Dobbs. But it also means that if they're planning to meet, it has to be somewhere convenient for Boomer."

"Yes. Snake's going to Boomer. Not the reverse."

"Do we know where Boomer lives?"

Livia had done all that research and then some. "A town called Alpine. East of San Diego."

Little smiled grimly. "That's at least an eight-hour drive from here. A lot more, if you're keeping to back roads to elude a dragnet and making sure you don't go a mile over the speed limit."

"What if Boomer's campaigning somewhere else?"

"Even better. Anywhere else he'd be campaigning in California would be an even longer drive. The southeast of the state is mostly desert. National parks like Death Valley, Mojave, Joshua Tree . . . thin populations. He wouldn't waste his time."

Little seemed to know the region well. "You've been there?" she said.

He grunted. "A long time ago. Family trip."

She should have realized that. She was tired. "I'm sorry."

He shook his head. "Plus his district is in Southern California. That's his base. You don't waste a lure on the fish you've already caught. Either he's home in Alpine, or he's visiting some population center at least that far away. Either way, we have time."

Livia pulled out her cellphone. "His campaign schedule. Maybe it's online."

It took her less than two minutes. "Palm Springs tonight. Some kind of thirty-thousand-dollar-a-plate thing."

Little groaned. "Outside Palm Springs, there's nothing but trackless desert and national forests. They could meet anywhere."

Livia thought. Almost certainly, they'd be too smart and experienced to have their cellphones on them when they were active. But also almost certainly, they'd have burners.

"What about Kanezaki?" Little said, seeming to read her mind. "They won't have their own phones, but with a program like God's Eye, Kanezaki might be able to zero in on their burners. Or what about a satellite?"

"I already asked him about satellite surveillance. He told me it was a no-go. And that's when we had exact coordinates. This time, like you said, we're going to be looking at thousands of square miles of desert and national forests. It's a needle in a haystack. We need a magnet, and I don't . . ." She balled her fists in frustration.

"Maybe not a magnet," Little said. "Maybe there's another way."

"What?"

"Reduce the amount of hay."

"Okay, but how?"

"By using the proper inputs."

She looked at him, too distressed to follow his meaning.

"You said it yourself," he said. "I was looking for disappearances and not realizing the disappearances were part of a larger puzzle. In fact, the disappearances were preventing me from seeing the real nature of the crime. What I should have been looking for were all the same aspects—the minority girls, the time of day, the walk to the convenience store. And a perfectly executed abduction, of course—but *without* the disappearance. I was seeing a piece of it, yes, but I might as well have been looking through a straw. But now we can widen the aperture. See the pattern clearly. We're looking for serial rapes, not serial murders. And we have one more thing we didn't have before."

She still didn't follow. "What?"

A hateful smile spread on his face. "A song."

37

Kane was in his private bungalow at the Avalon Hotel in Palm Springs. He'd told his chief of staff to cancel all appointments and hold all calls—to free up Kane's schedule for everything but the fundraiser for Bradley. And to have someone get him some Dramamine or other antinausea medicine. But the Dramamine had been as much of a failure as everything else, because as soon as he was alone, he'd vomited into the wastebasket, his stomach rebelling so suddenly he hadn't even been able to make it to the marble-lined bathroom.

After vomiting, he felt somewhat better. Part of it was knowing someone would clean out the wastebasket. Or better yet, replace it. With no questions asked. Just a mess cleaned up, gone, as though it had never happened.

He might have laughed if he hadn't still felt queasy. The operation in Kanab was another disaster. Snake had been there, as Kane had hoped and indeed anticipated. But so were Lone and Little. Kane's attempt to have the Seattle Police Department rein in Lone had been a total failure. It hadn't even slowed the woman down. And that feckless moron at HSI, Tilden, who was supposed to be controlling Little, hadn't even known where the man was until Little himself had called Tilden from Kanab.

At first, reports had been confused, and Kane thought it was Snake who had killed the OGE team Kane had sent. But no, it seemed it had been Little and Lone who had done that. If he had realized the two of them might put together the Noreen Prentis–Hope Jordan–Sherrie Dobbs pattern and themselves go to Kanab to try to anticipate Snake, Kane would have sent a much larger and more heavily armed team. Once again, he'd sent a force just large enough to fail. And fail spectacularly.

Well, it could have been worse. From what Kane's people were telling him, Snake had killed a local cop and abducted Sherrie Dobbs. He'd gotten away, at least, which was a thousand times better than if he'd been taken into custody. But Little and Lone had given his name to the Utah and Arizona State Police. That was bad, but still containable. Another team could find him. Fix him. Finish him. There would be questions, but Kane had battalions of lawyers, and public-relations specialists, and media people, and shock jocks, and wizards skilled in the darkest arts of social-media manipulation, all of whom would spring into a coordinated counteroffensive if anyone mentioned so much as the possibility that Bradley could have had anything to do with Stephen "Snake" Spencer's alleged crimes. Not to mention Bradley's own shock troops and rabid supporters, who Kane had to acknowledge were even more willing to slash and burn their way to victory than the more professional cadre Kane was accustomed to dealing with.

All right. How to find Snake didn't present an insurmountable challenge. The last time, Kane had found him through Sherrie Dobbs. This time, he would do it through Bradley.

Because Bradley was going to meet Snake somewhere. Kane knew that, though the thought disgusted him even in ordinary times and at the moment brought him dangerously close to vomiting again. This . . . thing of theirs. They obviously enjoyed doing it together. In Iraq and all over America, before Kane had Snake sent away. And then Hannah Cuero, after Snake got out. Plus the girls from high school, of course—most recently, Sherrie Dobbs.

Maybe they were planning to share Dobbs even as soon as tonight. After the fundraiser. It was just a gut feeling, but if Kane was wrong, his men would follow Bradley to Snake another time. It was why Kane had taken the expedient course of having his security people, in the guise of searching vehicles for explosives, affix a transmitter to Bradley's car. At some point, whether late tonight or late some other night, Bradley would go out. Kane had purchased another OGE team that would follow the boy. Urban-ops people. Military trained, combat and CIA joint-ops experience, currently in the private sector. Exceptionally capable men. Equipped with the latest night-vision, and more.

Bradley wouldn't like any of it, of course. He'd been upset to learn that Kane had engineered Snake's prison sentence, and he'd be upset at the knowledge that Kane had arranged this more permanent solution, too. But what could the boy do? He'd have to live with it. Adjust. Hate his father, possibly. But that happened between fathers and sons from time to time. And probably more often between kings and crown princes. It was all right. They'd get past it. And eventually, Bradley would realize his father had acted only out of love. And that it had been for the best.

Yes. Bradley would understand. Especially when he learned that the team's orders weren't only about Snake. Because Kane had of course tasked them with taking out Little and Lone as well.

38

Little and Livia had Dan Levin fly them to Jacqueline Cochran Regional Airport—at thirty miles southeast of Palm Springs, the closest they could get to Boomer. Slipping out of Kanab hadn't been illegal, exactly, but it wasn't entirely aboveboard, either. Still, they already had so much explaining to do that disappearing in the confusion following Chief Cramer's murder, Sherrie Dobbs's kidnapping, and the three men Livia had killed afterward felt trivial by comparison.

Little used his laptop in the air to query ViCAP again, this time with the proper inputs. But he found no entries for rapes with a signature song, and the number of rapes without the song was far too large to associate with Boomer and Snake.

Fortunately, there was another way. Boomer and Snake had disappeared girls all over the country. But those crimes had all been associated with stateside military training and deployments. As far as Livia could tell, the first time they'd raped together after Snake was released from Leavenworth, and while Boomer was a congressman, had been Hannah Cuero in Campo. Campo, which was barely thirty miles from Boomer's home in Alpine. It was only a hunch and certainly a long shot, but Livia and Little had drawn on a map a circle with a fifty-mile radius that had Alpine at its center, and had then begun calling every local police department within the circle. As far west as San Diego. As far north as Carlsbad and Escondido. All the tiny towns along the Mexican border. Anything about a teenaged girl, probably black, brown, or Native American, abducted and with a report about her rapists making her listen to a certain song.

Again and again, they got nothing. It was maddening: there was no time for in-depth conversations about who am I talking to, how long have you been on the force, who would be most familiar with the relevant records. Every negative might have been false. They had to just ask their questions as carefully as they could, ask if there was anyone else there who might have relevant case knowledge, and move on.

They landed. Rented a Jeep—the rental-car place seemed to specialize in four-wheel-drive vehicles. Stopped to buy ammunition at a gun shop, because after Kanab they were both getting low. Parked themselves at a place called Vintage Coffee House near Coachella and kept at it. Nothing. Nothing again. Nothing.

Livia was close to despair when they finally got a hit: an elder with the Mesa Grande tribal government named Gray Eagle Sanchez. Eight years earlier, Sanchez explained, a girl named Eva was abducted, though she never saw by whom. She'd been hooded. Driven an hour, maybe two. Raped repeatedly. She thought by white men, from their voices.

And the whole time, the men had played a song.

"What song?" Livia asked, gripping the phone hard. "Did Eva recognize it?"

"Yes. It was a famous song. 'Good Times Roll.'"

Livia nodded at Little fiercely. She said, "Is there anything else you can tell me? Anything Eva remembered, anything you think could help?"

"Yes. The hood they put her in. It stank of rotten eggs."

"Rotten eggs?"

"Yes."

"Do you have any idea why?"

"No. Maybe they had used it for garbage. Maybe to worsen her ordeal. Who can say why men do such evil things?"

"May I ask, sir, how you know all this?"

There was a pause. Then, "Eva is my daughter."

Livia needed a pause of her own. She said, "I'm sorry."

"Eva can't hear that song anymore, or songs like it. Or endure strong smells. There are a lot of things she can't do now."

"I know," Livia said, her voice not much more than a whisper.

"Are you going to catch these men?"

"I'm going to try."

"I wish you could bring them to me."

She looked at Little. "I don't think I'll have to."

A pause. "Will you tell me, then?"

"Yes."

"Promise."

She thought of Hope Jordan's sister, Grace, who had asked the same thing. Gray Eagle Sanchez deserved the same response. So did Eva.

"I swear," she said.

They drew another circle on the map, this one with its center at Mesa Grande. And because the surrounding area was so sparsely populated, they made the circle a hundred miles instead of just fifty.

More negatives. And more. Outside, it had long since grown dark. *Boomer is still at his fundraiser,* Livia thought. *And Snake couldn't have made it yet. There's time. There's still time.*

They got another hit: Palm Desert, just a twenty-minute drive west from where they were sitting. Seven years earlier. Another girl, Linda Haywood, this one black. The song again. And again the garbage-reeking hood.

They looked at the map. They were likely missing far more data than they had gathered. The results could easily be skewed. Still, the locus seemed to be east of Alpine. But what did it mean?

"Joshua Tree?" she said, thinking aloud. "The San Bernardino National Forest? What's out here that makes the area good hunting grounds? Are they just being careful not to make Alpine the center of the circle?"

Even as she said it, it didn't feel right. There was something else. But what?

Little was looking at the map intently. "The Salton Sea," he said.

"What about it?"

"The drone man. The body I had to get rid of in Seattle. I looked for a reservoir. A place to sink it. Faster, easier, and safer than digging a hole. Maybe . . . if something goes wrong, and they have to go with their Plan B, they have the water right there. And . . . wait a minute."

He worked the keyboard of his laptop for a moment. "I remember reading something about it. It's not really a sea, it's a lake. The largest in California, I think. Caused a long time ago by a flood or something. And evaporating, dying, ever since. So . . ."

He stared for a long moment at his screen, nodding. Then spun it around so Livia could see it.

He had Googled *Salton Sea smell*. There were over eighty thousand hits. All about hydrogen sulfide.

Livia looked at Little. "Rotten eggs," she said.

He nodded. "The kind of smell a victim would notice. And remember."

Livia's heart was pounding. "They like taking them there. And why not? Reeking like that, it's probably deserted. If something goes wrong, they dispose of the girl in the water. But if nothing goes wrong . . ."

"Then the hood. That's all the victim smells, from the moment they put it on her."

They brought up a Wikipedia entry, and then news articles and images. The place was all decaying structures and toxic dust. Weird algae blooms and avian die-offs. Beaches made of the pulverized skeletons of millions of long-dead fish.

Little blew out a long breath as though trying to calm his own excitement. He looked at Livia. "The song is a signature," he said. "The hood is an MO. Because they can't risk the girl identifying the place by its smell."

"You're partly right. The hood is an MO, but also an artifact of another signature."

Little nodded, his expression grimly determined. "That's right. That's a better way to put it. Because Boomer and Snake *like* the Salton Sea. That hellscape is their home."

39

Livia called Kanezaki. She told him the transmitter had been a bust. But that there was another breakthrough, if he could help her just one more time.

"How?" he said, his tone decidedly neutral.

"That program you have. The one you used to help me catch the park rapist. Guardian Angel."

"Livia, you're not even supposed to know about that program." He paused and added, "Assuming it even exists."

"I don't need much," she said. "I might not even need anything at all. I'm pretty sure I know where Boomer is going to meet his partner, Snake. The man who abducted Sherrie Dobbs. But I don't know when. And I don't know exactly where."

"You're asking me to track the cellphone of a sitting US congressman?"

"No. All I'm asking is that you locate a burner. It's a burner, who can say who it belongs to?"

There was a pause, and she thought he might be smiling. She hoped so.

"Tell me more," he said.

She briefed him. When she was done, she added, "I can give you the dates and places where Eva Sanchez and Linda Haywood were abducted. I'm pretty sure they were then taken to the Salton Sea. If you can access cellphone-company records, can't you pick out whatever phones took those routes on those dates and at those times? Especially because the phones in question will almost certainly have been activated not long before, and will almost certainly not have been used to call any other phone but each other."

"In theory, yes, I have the access. But do you really think men like Boomer and Snake are going to use the same burner twice?"

"I doubt it. But if they used burners for the other crimes, it's a safe bet they're using them now. Snake wouldn't have turned on a phone in Utah. But he might have turned it on briefly somewhere on the way to the Salton Sea. If he did, whatever number he called is going to be Boomer's burner. But even if Snake hasn't called yet this time, if they used burners to coordinate before, they'll use them again."

"How can you know that?"

"Tom, what the fuck do you think I do for a living? Do you know how to recruit an asset? Well, I know the freaks. Better than anyone would ever want to. And I'm telling you, when these guys find something that works, they just keep doing it. Okay?"

There was a long pause. He said, "I'll call you back."

Little had heard only her side of the conversation, so she filled him in on the rest. Then they waited, studying maps and images of the Salton Sea, trying to figure out where specifically Boomer and Snake might meet. Probably the northwest side, because it was closer to Boomer. But if they were wrong, they were looking at a circumference of about a hundred miles. They might still find Sherrie Dobbs, even without Kanezaki to help pinpoint the timing and location. But doing so would take an uncomfortable amount of luck.

Between the attempted drone attack and Kane's men in Kanab, Livia had been afraid to turn on her cellphone, so she couldn't know for sure—but she guessed by now there must be dozens of calls and texts waiting for her. The Kanab police would have gotten in touch with SPD and informed them that one of their detectives had been in an officer-involved and had then more or less fled the scene. Lieutenant Strangeland would be flipping out, and probably Chief Best was assembling a firing squad, figurative or literal. Livia didn't want to know the specifics. All she wanted was to save Sherrie Dobbs. But the thought of Donna twisting in the wind was too much. She called her from the satellite phone.

Strangeland picked up instantly. "Hello?"

Her voice was worried. The sat-phone number was blocked, but she must have been hoping it was Livia.

"LT. It's me."

"Livia. Jesus God almighty, are you all right?"

If only Strangeland had berated her. But the woman was primarily concerned about her welfare. Livia had to swallow before saying, "I'm okay. I'm sorry I didn't call earlier."

"Where are you? What are you doing? SPD got a call from the police in Kanab, Utah. Are you with Little? Is what they're saying true?"

"It's true."

"Honey, this is bad. Chief Best is out-of-her-mind pissed. I can't even count how many times I've heard phrases like *fugitive* and *rogue cop* and *Office of Police Accountability* today. And that's not the half of it."

Livia looked at the smiling customers at the register, ordering their vanilla-bean lattes and almond roca mochas. She felt the tears coming and this time didn't try to stop them.

"I'm sorry, Donna. You've been so good to me, and I don't want to create a problem for you. But if the Kanab cops told you about Sherrie Dobbs—"

"They did."

"Well, I've got some leads, and . . ." She stopped, unable to explain, maybe not even to herself. "I just have to try. I know Best is going to crucify me. I don't care about that. I just don't want her to crucify you."

"Don't you worry about me. What are these leads? Where are you?"

"LT, the man who abducted Sherrie Dobbs, and the man he's taking her to . . . if you go up against them, you're going to wind up as fucked as I am."

"You let me worry about that. Now you tell me what's going on."

Livia thought for a moment. Little had said they would get no help from HSI or the FBI. But what about . . .

"LT, I know where they're taking Sherrie Dobbs. At least to within a hundred miles. And I should know the time, too—could be in as little as two hours from now. But if the information I'm hoping for doesn't get more precise, Little and I, just the two of us . . . we might not be able to cover the ground that needs to be covered. We can't get help from the feds. But what about the California Highway Patrol? I'll tell you, I could really use a SWAT team."

"You're in California?"

"Yes."

There was a pause. Strangeland said, "I could try making some calls. But no one's going to send out a California SWAT team on the say-so of an SPD lieutenant. At a minimum, someone's going to insist on talking to the chief. And at this point, you get her in the mix, that SWAT team is probably coming for you."

"Okay," Livia said, not really surprised. Suddenly she felt strangely calm. Even clear. "It's okay. Little and I will do it ourselves."

"Do what? Livia, talk to me."

"I can't now. We don't have much time. Look, I'll send you an email, okay? To your personal account, not through the department. So you'll at least know what this was all about."

"Honey, you're scaring me now. I want you to tell me, right fucking now, what the fuck this is about so I can help you. Do you understand me?"

"I can't, LT. You can't help me now. And I can only hurt you. Which I never wanted to do. You've always had my back, and it's meant a lot to me. I'm sorry I turned out to be such a shitty friend in return."

"Livia—"

"I'll send you the email."

She clicked off, feeling strangely numb. It didn't mean the feelings weren't there. It just meant she was anesthetized. She knew that. Just like she knew that later, the anesthesia would wear off.

If there was a later.

She briefed Little on why they wouldn't be getting any help, then composed the email to Strangeland. She set it up so that it would send automatically the following day. Were the lieutenant to receive it now, in her current state, there was no telling what she might do, and Livia couldn't risk Chief Best getting involved. As soon as the email was taken care of, Livia felt calmer. Another *just in case.*

Kanezaki called back. "Okay," he said. "I concede. You do know the freaks."

And the anesthesia was suddenly receding, forced back by excitement. "Tell me."

"Both the abductions you mentioned were associated with burners. Two for each abduction, the units purchased shortly before the abductions and shut off and presumably destroyed immediately after. Each used only several times, and only to call the other."

She nodded at Little. Her heart was pounding. "What about now?"

"You were right about that, too. Three hours ago, a unit was switched on in the Coconino National Forest. I'm guessing there's not much signal in there, but it's on one of the routes from Kanab, and Snake must have found a spot that gave him a few bars."

She relayed the information to Little, who started working his laptop. She said to Kanezaki, "Has it been turned on again?"

"No. But the unit it was used to call is on."

"That's Boomer. He must be waiting for another update. Where is he?"

"We don't know that it's Boomer's. Remember, I'm just tracking a burner."

Little said, "Coconino National Forest three hours ago . . . I'd estimate ETA at two hours from now."

Livia nodded and said to Kanezaki, "Right, right. Where is the second burner?"

"The Avalon Hotel in Palm Springs." Kanezaki paused, then added, "It seems Boomer is holding a fundraiser there tonight."

"What a coincidence."

Livia repeated the information to Little, then said to Kanezaki, "Can you tell us when the Avalon burner is moving? Little and I have been learning everything we can about the terrain around the Salton Sea. Our guess is that the meeting will be on the northwest shore, because it's closer—less than an hour from the Avalon. Maybe on Salton Sea Beach. But it could be on the northeast shore—maybe Bombay Beach. That much ground we might be able to cover. But if it's somewhere else, we're talking about a hundred miles' worth of beach, and as much as we've narrowed things down, we're unlikely to have narrowed them down enough."

"If it gets left on," Kanezaki said, "I can tell you when the Avalon burner is moving. But from what I know, a lot of what surrounds the Salton Sea is wasteland. More iguanas than people. When it comes to cellular service, I'm guessing there are going to be a lot of dark patches. Your sat phone will work fine, so I should be able to reach you. But whatever burner I'm tracking—again, assuming it gets left on at all—is probably going to go dark."

"Good point. Still, the closer you can get us, the better. Judging from where he used his burner to make the call, we estimate Snake is a good two hours away now, probably more. Little and I are going to be in a Jeep near the town of Mecca. That's just northwest of the Salton Sea, and it's where Boomer—sorry, the guy coming from the Avalon—will have to break due south on Route 86 if they're meeting on the west shore, or southeast on Route 111 if they're meeting on the east shore. We'll follow from a distance for as long as you have a signal. Okay?"

Kanezaki sighed. "What if Boomer turns off the burner before he leaves the hotel? Or somewhere on the way?"

Livia had already thought of that. Well, at least they'd dropped the dumb word games. "Then it's going to be a long shot," she said. "Little and I will try to pick him up on whatever route is our best guess at that point, and follow him. And Sherrie Dobbs will probably die horribly."

There was a long pause. Kanezaki said, "It seems I'm not the only one around here who knows something about recruiting an asset."

She waited, trying not to hope. After a moment, he said, "Do you have the Azrael with you?"

She felt a surge of excitement. "Yes. Like you told me."

He sighed again. "It's not a surveillance drone, but given the distances and speeds we're dealing with, it ought to work as one. It's easy to operate. I'll tell you how."

She felt the tears again, the anesthesia completely gone. "Thank you, Tom. You're a good—"

"Don't say it. It makes me nervous."

"Well, it's true."

"Listen. Even if we can fix their exact location. You know how well trained these two are. Special Forces, six tours in Iraq. Out in the desert . . . it's going to be like home to them. And not just in a general way. If you're right, they've used the Salton Sea many times. They'll be familiar with the specific terrain. You're not. Surprise isn't going to be enough. You ought to have backup."

"I tried. No one wants to risk taking on Boomer or his father. At this point, you're about our only friend."

"You have other friends."

She understood his meaning. "No. Don't even think it."

"He'd help you. You know that."

"Forget it, Tom. There's no time, anyway. Just . . . please. Tell me when Boomer's moving. And how to use that drone."

40

They drove to Mecca, a sparsely populated agricultural town that some-one had figured out how to make blossom in the desert. Everything about it was silent and empty, and while there were houses and some lonely streetlights, it felt like an edge place—forgotten, cut off, even abandoned. And Mecca, from what she'd read, was one of the more populous areas surrounding the dead lake. If isolation and privacy were Boomer and Snake's objectives, she could understand the attraction of the Salton Sea.

They stopped on one of the countless stretches of empty, cracked roads, dry arteries that simply petered out at the edges of desert hills, with nothing but sand and waste beyond them. Kanezaki explained how to use the drone, and Livia practiced with it. It was simple to oper-ate, as he had assured her. In fact, it was a lot like a video game. There were only two controls: A joystick that controlled speed, direction, and altitude. And a red button, covered by a clear plastic flip-up protector. Naturally, when she asked Kanezaki about the button, he said, "You know what the button's for. Please don't press it." Which she decided to interpret as "Unless you really have to."

The screen readout was as simple as the controls. There was a feed from the unit's cameras, of course—two each in the nose and the belly, regular and night vision. Readouts for speed, direction, and altitude, and also ones for battery life and geographical coordinates to help locate the drone if it went down. But Kanezaki assured her a crash was unlikely. The unit's built-in avionics and sensors wouldn't allow the operator to maneuver it in a way that would result in a crash, and if for any reason the control signal were lost, the drone would fly back and circle to reacquire it.

The biggest danger, really, was that the drone's battery life would be insufficient. Kanezaki had told her its top speed was close to sixty miles an hour, and she was confident Boomer wouldn't exceed any posted limits, so keeping up wouldn't be a problem. But the unit had only about an hour of loiter time, and flying full-out was going to drain the battery far faster than loitering. They'd have to hope that once they acquired Boomer, he wouldn't be going far.

And then there was nothing to do but wait. They parked in a dusty lot behind a boarded-up church, the engine off, the windows cracked. The night was hot and dry, and even miles from the water the air smelled vaguely putrid. A waxing gibbous moon had risen above some rocky hills in the distance, and but for its weak illumination there would have been no light at all.

Little dozed, and Livia was glad he was able. Several times he grimaced and twitched in his sleep, and she imagined his dreams were as bad as hers. She sipped from a bottle of water they'd bought in Coachella, which seemed a long time ago, and waited, and tried not to think about Sherrie Dobbs and how terrified she must be. Livia didn't know why the woman had been put on bed rest. She hoped it wasn't life-threatening.

Eventually, she nodded off herself, awaking with a start at the buzz of the sat phone. She clicked the answer key and brought the unit to her ear. "Yeah."

"I think he's on the way," Kanezaki said.

Livia's heart started pounding and she sat bolt upright. "What do you mean, you think?" Little was awake now, looking at her intently.

"Five minutes ago," Kanezaki said, "Snake's burner got switched on and was used to call Boomer's burner. A minute later, both burners got shut down. My guess is, the call was of the nature of 'I'll see you soon at the place.' At which point, Boomer shuts down his unit because although he doesn't mind having it on when he's stationary at the hotel, he doesn't want to take a chance on anyone using it to track him to the crime scene."

Boomer's phone was off. How the hell were they going to track him? She tried to think. "Where did Snake call from?" she said.

"From outside a town called Westmorland. That's about forty-five minutes from the northwest shore of the Salton Sea, and past the point where he would have turned north if the plan were to meet on the eastern side."

"So Boomer . . . if he takes surface roads, and they're meeting on the western side, we're too high up. We'll miss him."

She checked her watch. It was nearly two in the morning. She'd been asleep longer than she realized. Her shirt was damp from sweat.

"I already thought of that," Kanezaki said. "Look at the map. The last of the surface roads Boomer could conceivably take run into Route 86 just south of the Torres-Martinez Reservation. If you set up there, then it doesn't matter which road he takes, or even if he takes the interstate. He still has to pass your position."

"What if they're meeting farther north?"

"Then Snake will pass you going the other way. Look, the bad news is, at this hour there are going to be zero cars on those roads out there, so vehicular surveillance, especially against men like Boomer and Snake, is going to be impossible. The good news is, if you see a car, you can be pretty sure it's them. And with the Azrael, you should be able to follow it without revealing yourself."

That made sense. She should have seen it herself. She needed to get out of the Jeep. Clear her head.

"Just south of the Torres-Martinez Reservation," she said so Little could plug it into the navigation app. "We'll get in position. If anyone's burner comes on, call me, okay?"

"Don't worry," Kanezaki said. "I'm not going anywhere."

41

Boomer was in his minivan, on his way to Salton Sea Beach. It had been a miserable evening and he'd had way too much to drink. But Boomer could drink and drive with the best of them, always could. And the hell with it anyway, because being drunk felt good, and fuck anyone who had a problem with it, California Highway Patrol included.

The admiral had skipped a bunch of the festivities, claiming some kind of stomach flu. Which left Boomer to deal with all the glad-handers alone, even though everyone knew the admiral was the real attraction. Maybe the old man was demonstrating how much Boomer needed him. Yeah, maybe it was that. And maybe that's why Boomer had gotten so obviously lit up, so word would get back to the asshole and show him that the bank really didn't want a default on this particular loan. He remembered how freaked out the admiral had been when he'd thrown the old man's own aphorism back at him, and he laughed.

After the guests had left, Boomer had gone back to the hotel room. Even drunk as he was, he was too keyed up to sleep. He'd checked the news from Kanab, and it was crazy—a dead cop, a kidnapped woman whose name the authorities hadn't yet released but who had to be Sherrie Dobbs, a shootout in a hotel parking lot. But he didn't even care. Snake knew what he was doing. And there was no way to connect any of it with Boomer.

All he cared about really was that he and Snake were going to meet later at the Salton Sea—the best thing in the world under any circumstances, but especially so tonight, because Snake was bringing him Sherrie. They'd do her together, get rid of the body, and Boomer's damn Me Too problems would finally be over.

Or, if not over exactly, at least contained. He knew there would be speculation, and questions, and even accusations. But he was getting good at dismissing the speculation and questions as conspiracy theories and fake news. And the accusations he almost welcomed, because they all came from the other side, and the more outraged they got, the more it fired up Boomer's base.

Boomer's wife didn't much care for any of it, that was true. She wasn't doing so many events these days, and had skipped Palm Springs tonight. Well, that was fine, actually. She'd been giving him a hard time about the drinking, and he was getting tired of it. And anyway, it would have been hard to explain why he was going out at two in the morning.

He tried to focus on where he was heading, and what it would be like when he got there. Noreen Prentis had been so much fun. They'd taken the gag off and she'd begged a lot. Boomer had just laughed and told her it was her fault, she shouldn't have said anything, and she agreed with him, telling him he was right, it was her fault. But he and Snake had done everything to her anyway, everything and then some. And when they were finished, maybe an hour before dawn, they pulled a plastic bag over her head, which was how they did it when they had to disappear someone because a bag didn't leave much evidence in case anyone ever found the body. And they'd sunk her in the water with weights, and man, it had been a night to remember.

And tonight would be another one, wasn't that right? Yeah. It would be. It was just . . .

He was beginning to realize he hadn't been happy in a long time. Ever since Snake went to Leavenworth, and Boomer left the army and got started in politics. And then Snake was out, and everything was all right again, so Boomer thought that was all that had been missing, his buddy and the good times they had together. But now he realized that wasn't quite right. It was the politics that was making him so miserable. It had started when he ran for Congress, and got worse when he'd won, and now he was running for the damn Senate and if the polls were right it looked like he might even win. Which should have made him happy, but instead made him almost want to puke.

When did things get so complicated and messed up? He wished he could just make it all go back to how it was. Simpler times. Happier times.

He laughed at how maudlin he was being. Because wasn't he on his way to see Snake right now? So fuck all the rest, he'd worry about it tomorrow, and he'd figure something out.

He laughed again, feeling a little better. Well, his mom had always said he was good at cheering himself up.

He'd left his regular cellphone back at the hotel—routine security precaution, because how many bad guys had they killed or captured in Iraq by locking onto a cellphone?—so he didn't have his playlists. But that was okay, he had the CD he'd burned ages ago, which was still his favorite way to listen. He popped it into the minivan's drive and cranked up the volume. *Yeah, baby,* he thought. *Let the good times roll.*

42

Little was tired and trying not to show it. He'd been going for weeks now on not much more than adrenaline and coffee, and while he'd been able to manage bursts like that just fine back in the day, lately he was realizing it was a younger man's game.

He parked behind a stand of fruit trees on a dusty strip of road called Eighty-Fourth Avenue. As though they were in the middle of a city and not the middle of nowhere. But the hell with the street names. If Boomer were heading south, he'd have to pass them here. And the same for Snake heading north.

They each took a bathroom break among the trees, and then there was nothing to do but wait again. Little wanted to get the drone aloft, but Livia cautioned him about the battery. If Boomer was the one they picked up, as they expected, and he used surface roads, it would take him an extra twenty minutes compared to the interstate. So they had to time things carefully.

The good news was that the area was about as deserted as anything Little had ever seen, the moonlight falling weakly on idle fields, and roads so still it was hard to imagine them ever having been used. One of the family trips he had mentioned to Livia was to the Badlands in

South Dakota, and for sheer emptiness that was his only analogue. The three of them had gotten in late, on a moonless night, and had to pass through the park to get to their hotel. His wife was sleeping, and Presley had leaned forward from the back and asked quietly if they could stop and get out. And even though Little had been paranoid about bears or God knows what, he did as she'd asked. He parked and turned off the headlights and the two of them stepped out of the car. Once the doors were closed, the darkness was so total they might have been in a cave, the night so soundless the silence wasn't an absence but rather a presence, an infinite, solemn entity pressing close from all directions.

He'd shone a flashlight around, and they saw they'd been driving through a canyon of prehistoric rock formations to either side. The night was so black the car's headlights hadn't even illuminated them.

Presley had whispered, "Daddy, it's beautiful!" And that sweet girl had hugged him tight. And he would have given anything, truly anything, to have that moment with her again. That moment, and nothing ever more.

Livia, maybe sensing his mood, looked at him. "You okay?" she asked.

He nodded. "Just remembering something nice."

She paused, then said, "You looked sad."

"I always look sad when I remember something nice. Is it not the same for you?"

She chuckled at that, and he was glad. He himself had an easy laugh, which he'd cultivated because it disarmed people. But she wasn't like that.

"You know," he said, surprised to feel his eyes filling up, "I think Presley would have liked you a lot. And she sure could have done worse for a role model."

She gave him a small smile. "I would have liked to have known her."

He sighed and the tears spilled over. "I wish you could have taught her some of your skills, I'll tell you that."

She nodded. Someone else might have given his hand or knee a squeeze, but Livia didn't like that kind of contact. He understood why, though of course she'd never told him and he'd never asked.

"Listen," she said. "We need to talk about our objectives tonight."

He thought he knew where she was going. He'd already been thinking about the same.

"I get it," he said. "You're thinking that, because we have that drone, I'm going to want to just kill them. Unless I'm looking for an opportunity to torture them first."

She didn't answer, and he knew that was exactly what she had been thinking.

"I don't blame you," he said. "And you're not exactly wrong, either. But the main thing, and if need be the only thing, is that we rescue Sherrie Dobbs. Sherrie, and her baby."

"That's right."

He nodded. "I know it's right."

"I want to kill them, too. But with Sherrie Dobbs's testimony, they're done. Kidnapping, murder, conspiracy, everything. I'll put them in separate rooms and interrogate them, and I promise you, by the time I'm done, they'll have fucked each other so badly they'll both be spending the rest of their lives in prison. With Boomer's father for company. But you know what I want almost as much as that?"

He didn't answer, and after a moment she went on. "I want them to give up where they left all the missing girls. I want you . . . I want you to be able to bury Presley. To take care of her, one last time. Like I did for Nason."

That made him cry again. "I'd like that, too."

They were quiet for a moment.

"I appreciate what you're doing for me," Little said. "And . . . for Presley. And I'm sorry for getting you into it."

She looked in his eyes, and he thought he had never known anyone so formidable.

"I'm not," she said.

"I shouldn't have made it your fight."

She looked as though she was considering that. But all she said was "It is my fight."

And then they waited again, the digital clock in the Jeep marking down the minutes.

At 2:50, Little said, "You know, I did a little research on the name Azrael."

She looked at him. "Yeah?"

"Azrael was an angel. In the Koran, the angel of death. But in the Hebrew Bible, the name translates as 'angel of God,' or 'help from God.' And you can call me foolish, but I'm going to take that as an omen."

"That's fine with me," Livia said, opening the case and taking out the drone. "Because we're going to need all the help we can get."

43

Boomer headed south on Route 86, the four-lane road running along the western shore of the Salton Sea. He was feeling good now, the discomfort and bullshit of the fundraiser behind him, the excitement of seeing Snake and everything else just ahead. The stink of the water was overwhelming, and it was like a promise of what was to come.

He wasn't used to driving from this direction, and drunk as he was and without the usual landmarks like the Red Earth Casino, it was a little confusing. The road ran closer to the water here—he could see ripples glittering in the moonlight. But other than that, it was nothing but sand and scrub and rock formations, and never-ending telephone lines paralleling the trackless highway. If anyone ever figured out how to get a colony going on the moon, and it failed, he imagined this was what it would look like.

He thought he'd passed a Jeep a few miles back, parked behind some trees. Maybe some kids getting high or making out. He'd checked the rearview, and even pulled off the road and cut the lights for a minute, but there was no one trying to follow him. Yeah, just some kids.

He passed a tiny town on the left—Desert Shores. Nothing but a gas station and *For Rent* signs and graffiti-covered walls. A few small houses that looked ready to give up the ghost, and not a light on in any of them. And then it was gone, and he was back on the moon again.

A few miles farther along, he saw it—the streetlight, and the fading welcome sign by the rusting electrical pole. It looked more like a warning than a welcome if you asked him, but that was for the day-trippers who came to gawk at the ruins when there was sunlight still in the sky. No one ever came here at night.

He cut the headlights and made a left onto a paved road that soon became gravel and sand, his heart rate kicking up a notch. There was a garage he liked to park in, and he headed slowly toward it. Well, *garage* was probably a strong word, the thing was really just three disintegrating walls at this point, but it served to conceal the vehicle. Whoever of he and Snake got here first always scouted the area, just in case there were any homeless lurking. They were yet to encounter one—there was no one you could panhandle off in this ghost town—but still, you never knew.

He laughed, feeling good. *The Salton Sea,* he thought. *Shunned even by the homeless. But not by us.*

44

Livia watched on the screen as the Azrael tracked Boomer's minivan. The drone was incredibly easy to use, and so far it was working perfectly. It was strangely compelling to imagine that when Boomer stepped out of his car, all she'd have to do was fly in close and press the button.

She wished she could. But that wouldn't help Sherrie Dobbs.

Little made sure to stay several miles back. The road was desolate, and they didn't want to take any chance on Boomer seeing them.

"There he goes," Livia said. "Salton Sea Beach. Like we thought he might."

Little blew out a breath. "Okay. I know the drone isn't loud, but you might want to pull back before he gets out of his car. Just in case."

She appreciated the respectful way he'd suggested it. "Will do."

"We're almost at Desert Shores. Stick to the plan?"

"Yeah, make a left when we get to it. We'll cut the lights and drive in along the beach for a few minutes, then hoof it for the last half mile or so. Can't take a chance on their hearing or seeing the Jeep."

"Any sign of Snake?"

It was a little hard to tell. The beach was dotted with abandoned structures, ghostly in the green glow of the drone's night vision.

"Not yet," she said after a moment. "Boomer's pulling into . . . I'm not sure. Some sort of abandoned structure. Give me a second, I want to fly over to see if Snake is already in there . . ."

She could see on the screen that it was just Boomer. The drone was incredibly useful. She'd had no idea.

"It's just him," she said. "Okay, I'm going to take the Azrael higher. We'll get a better view. How have I gotten by without one of these my whole life? I told Kanezaki I'd give it to him when this was done, but now I don't know."

Little chuckled. "How are we doing on battery life?"

"Getting low. Following Boomer drained it fast. Down to thirty percent."

"Well, if this is where they're meeting, we should be good to go, Azrael or no."

She nodded. She knew he was right, and she'd been joking about keeping the drone. But still, it was weird how quickly she had grown reliant on it. Being able to see remotely was game changing.

Little turned left and drove through the town, over cracked roads sprouting with weeds. No curbs, no sidewalks. There were telephone poles, but no streetlights. The houses were small and unlit. It was like something from a dystopian movie.

"They could have filmed *Mad Max* out here," Little said, reading her mind. "Or the movie version of Dante's *Inferno*. And my God, the stench."

The road ended at the beach. They drove on, the tires crunching and crushing what Livia knew from their research were fish skeletons, not sand. At the water's edge, they turned right.

Livia watched the screen. "I'll tell you why they like this place," she said. "All the deserted structures. I'm seeing garages, burned-out trailers, abandoned houses . . . They have their pick of places to take their victims, and then take their time. Rusted-out vehicles, decaying furniture . . . it's like a postapocalyptic junkyard. We knew they'd be at the Salton Sea, but even so, if we didn't have the Azrael, we never would have pinpointed them."

Little drove on. About a half mile north of where Boomer had parked, Livia said, "We better stop. I don't know how sound carries here."

Little did as she asked. They got out. The air was dry and hot and stank so strongly it made her eyes water, as though someone had opened an oven with a burned animal carcass still smoking inside it. It was impossible to imagine anything ever having thrived here—the ground itself seemed to exude nothing but desolation and death and despair. Livia thought of the painting *Saturn Devouring His Son*, and wondered if Goya had known a place like this one.

They'd already turned off the interior lights, and they left the doors open to keep noise to a minimum. They started walking, keeping close to the water because the pulverized fish bones were damp there and more tightly packed, and made for quieter footfalls. Little had his gun out. Livia couldn't yet because she was still operating the drone. She kept circling it. And—

"There he is," she said in a low voice. "Snake. I don't see his car. He's walking north by the water."

"Maybe he left the car in one of the structures with a roof?"

She circled the drone wider. "Maybe. Come on, Sherrie, where are you?"

"She can't be far," Little whispered. "And worst case, if we can't find her directly, Snake and Boomer will lead us to her."

She hoped he was right. But she was getting a bad feeling. The battery was at ten percent now.

"There's Boomer," she said. "Walking east toward Snake. Yeah, this is their place. They know exactly where they're going to meet."

"We could take them out," Little said. "And search for Sherrie Dobbs after."

"And if we don't find her?"

Little didn't have an answer for that.

She thought of how much she regretted not having killed Snake in Kanab, when she had the chance, and hoped she was making the right call now. "Remember, it's not just Sherrie," she said, as much to herself as to him. "It's all the girls they've disappeared. If we kill them now—"

"I get it. Let's keep going."

She looked at the battery readout. "Shit," she said. "Five percent. I need to bring it back."

Less than a minute later, the drone descended in front of them, not much louder than a big fan at a high setting, and landed at her feet like a pet bird. She picked it up, shut it down, put it in the case, and drew the Glock.

They were close enough to see Boomer and Snake now, about fifty yards away, walking toward each other in the faint moonlight. The two men reached each other and embraced. Livia and Little crept closer and paused at the edge of a rusting trailer. Furnishings that had once been inside littered the ground like viscera. Concealment, but not much cover—Livia doubted those rusting walls would stop a rock, let alone a bullet.

Boomer and Snake stood talking for a few minutes, close enough for their laughter to be audible, though Livia couldn't quite make out their words. Snake had a bottle, which they started passing back and forth.

Livia set down the drone case. This was their chance. She leaned close and said in Little's ear, "We take them here, okay?"

He nodded. "If we have to drop one . . ."

"Make it Boomer. Without Snake, we might not be able to find Sherrie Dobbs."

"Got it."

After a few minutes, Boomer and Snake started walking toward the trailer. If they had guns, and Livia assumed they did, they were holstered. They were laughing, excited, distracted. She and Little were going to be able to take them totally unawares.

Just twenty yards away now. Livia's heart was pounding. She breathed slowly, noiselessly, through her mouth.

Ten yards. Snake and Boomer came to a pile of junk—broken chairs, tractor tires, a wheelbarrow dissolving like something from a Salvador Dali painting. And just as they passed it—

Some of the shapes moved, seeming to unfurl. Livia thought, *What the fuck?*

Men. Three of them, in ghillie suits. She could make out the shape of night-vision goggles, the silhouettes of suppressed machine pistols.

"Holy shit," Little breathed.

Boomer and Snake sensed the men, or heard them, but too late. One of the three, farthest to the left and taller than the others, said, "Freeze or you're dead right there."

Boomer and Snake froze. The tall man and the one farthest to the right immediately fanned out, their machine pistols up and planted firmly against their shoulders, their heads close behind their gun sights. The practiced confidence and coordination of their movements looked military—and not regular military, either. "Hands high," the tall one said. "These are suppressed MP7s. We have night vision. We're not going to miss."

Again, Boomer and Snake complied. "Do you know who I am?" Boomer said, his voice slightly slurred.

"We do," the tall guy said. "It's why we're here."

The third guy came in smoothly from behind, and quickly extracted a pistol from the small of Snake's back, and knives from both Snake and Boomer.

Little looked at Livia and mouthed, *What the fuck?*

She shook her head, stuck for an answer. She had no idea what this was. All she could think was *Where is Sherrie Dobbs?*

A voice came from behind them. "Drop your weapons. Same drill. Same MP7s pointed at your backs."

Livia felt a huge adrenaline surge. She wasn't going to give up her gun. For anything. She took a breath—

There was an explosion of light behind her eyes. For a moment, the world disappeared. Then she was on her knees, dizzy and shaking. The Glock was gone. She felt hands probing her pockets, and groped for the Vaari. But her coordination was off. She felt the knife being yanked from its sheath.

"Jesus," came a voice from behind her. "I'll be keeping this."

Her head was throbbing. She felt something trickling down the back of her neck. They'd cracked her in the head. The trickle was blood.

"It's not personal," another voice behind her said. "The word was to not take chances with you."

She tried to stand and was hit with a wave of nausea. "You're all right," one of the voices said. "Just a little love tap. Let's walk."

She managed to get to her feet. Little was beside her, his hands up, empty. He looked at her and shook his head. "I'm sorry," he said.

They walked. Once she started moving, the nausea abated. But she made sure to keep the unsteadiness in her gait. She didn't know what else to do but try to make them underestimate her. It was hard to believe it would make a difference, but knowing that she was working even the smallest angle kept the fear at bay. She thought of Sherrie Dobbs, and that helped, too.

They stopped a few feet from Boomer and Snake. The two men were on their knees, facing the first three ghillie-suit men, who were standing with their machine pistols at low ready. The sight of it took her back to the cargo ship of her childhood, and Skull Face and Square Head and Dirty Beard, and what they had made her do.

She worked to force it all away. She wasn't that helpless girl anymore. She never would be. No matter what.

Little was trembling, staring at the two kneeling men. She knew what he was thinking: if he could just get his hands around one of their throats—

"Don't," she said. "Not yet. Sherrie Dobbs."

Little groaned with the effort of not launching himself. He stared at Snake and Boomer and said, "You took everything that beautiful child was ever going to have. If I don't kill you here, I swear to God I will find you in hell."

Boomer and Snake didn't answer. The two men behind Little and Livia walked over to their three comrades. One of them was carrying the drone case. He set it down. "The drone," he said. "Gonna be a nice bonus."

A car drove past along the dead-fish beach. No headlights. It stopped. The driver got out. He was wearing a ghillie suit and night vision, like the others. He opened the trunk. Livia heard a muffled whimper.

Sherrie Dobbs.

45

"She's here," the driver said, moving around and joining the others so that the six of them faced Boomer, Snake, Little, and Livia from a few yards away. "In the trunk. We're good."

The tall man gestured to Little and Livia. "On your knees."

Livia looked at him. "Fuck you."

The man laughed. "Yeah, we were told you were a hellion. You want to get smacked again?"

They hadn't underestimated her. The opposite. They were keeping their distance. But maybe she could goad them. It wasn't as though she had anything to lose. Compared to getting on her knees, she didn't care if they killed her.

"Try it," she said.

The man laughed again. "Whatever. You want to make a run at me, go ahead. Congressman Kane, you're free to go back to your vehicle. The rest of you need to stay."

Boomer said, "What?"

Snake said, "What the fuck is this?"

Boomer said, "My father sent you, didn't he?"

The tall man nodded. "That's right."

Boomer laughed. "I should have known. Well, tell him to go fuck himself."

"You can tell him yourself," the tall man said. "Maybe I wasn't clear when I said you were free to go back to your vehicle. What I meant was, go back to your vehicle. And drive out of here."

"Fine," Boomer said. "Snake comes with me."

The tall man shook his head. "Everyone else stays. You go. That's the deal. And believe me, that's how it's going to happen. One way or the other."

Boomer said, "Okay, fuck you too, then." He started laughing.

The men looked at each other, plainly at a loss. Boomer laughed harder. He threw back his head and shook with hilarity.

The men were distracted, she could feel it. If she launched herself at the closest, Little would see his opening, too. So might Boomer and Snake. It could turn into a melee. Far from ideal, but at this point chaos would be a lot better than order.

She braced to make her move. But then a strange thing happened. The tall man's head snapped back, as though someone had punched him. For a weird second, he remained upright. Then his arms relaxed, his weapon fell, and he collapsed, his knees folding up beneath him.

Livia blinked. And in that instant, the head of the man to the left of the tall man also jerked, and then he went down, too.

Carl. Kanezaki must have—

"Sni—" a third man started to shout, and then his head snapped back and he collapsed like the others.

For a surreal instant, everyone and everything seemed frozen. And then it all exploded:

Boomer leaping to his feet—

The three remaining ghillie-suit men scrambling in different directions, scanning, trying to locate the direction of fire—

Little, who had played football at Florida State, flying forward and blasting into Boomer with a berserker roar—

Snake jumping up and running to the driver side of his car—

Livia bolted after Snake. One of the ghillie-suit men heard her coming and started to turn, his machine pistol coming around—

Livia grabbed the suppressor with both hands and twisted hard. A staccato burst of rounds stitched across the fish-bone beach. She kept twisting. The man screamed as his finger broke inside the trigger guard. Livia spun, popped in her hips, and threw him with *ogoshi*, a basic judo throw, ripping the gun loose as he flew past her. He hit the ground and she stepped back, aimed at his face, and pressed the trigger. There was a long burst of fire and the man's head exploded.

She checked her flanks. Little was on top of Boomer, bellowing with rage. Boomer was shrieking. She didn't see the remaining two ghillie-suit men.

She brought around the MP7 just as Snake's car disappeared behind a building, the trunk still open. She screamed in frustration and dashed away from the water, trying to get a better angle. She saw the car again. Aimed for a tire. Fired. The rounds landed short—she was being too cautious, unfamiliar with the weapon and afraid of hitting Sherrie Dobbs—and then the trigger clicked back, inert. She was out of bullets.

She screamed in rage, dropped the gun, and ran back to where they'd been standing. There—the drone case. She grabbed it. She heard the machine pistols. She couldn't tell if they were firing at her or engaging Carl. She ran for the wall of a collapsed shack, dropped to her knees, and opened the case. She took out the Azrael, powered it up, and set it on the ground.

More suppressed fire. A scream. It sounded like Carl had hit one of them. The Azrael whirred to life and lifted off. She worked the toggle and watched the screen. She got it twenty feet in the air and punched it. The battery was at three percent.

Please, she thought. *Please.*

She watched the screen. The beach raced by. Two percent. She saw Snake's car, slaloming along, beach detritus shooting up behind the spinning tires. *The engine,* she thought. It was far enough from the trunk. She hoped. One percent. She brought the drone around in front of him and flew it full-speed directly at the grille of the car, afraid the anticollision sensors would override her. The battery indicator went to zero. She flipped up the plastic and pressed the button—

The screen went black. She heard an explosion a hundred yards away. She dropped the case and charged down the beach.

She saw the car, stopped against the side of another abandoned structure, smoke pouring from under the hood. The door opened. She kept running. Snake got out. He coughed and wiped his face. He looked up and saw her.

"You want me?" he snarled. He held his arms out, palms up, the fingers rippling inward in a *Come on* gesture. "Well, here I am, bitch. Come and get it."

Livia was too enraged and adrenalized to even slow down. All she wanted was to get her hands on him—

At the last instant he stepped offline with his left foot and caught her with a sharp right jab in the jaw. She saw stars. She tried to pivot and get a hold of him, but he was fast. He sidestepped again and this time caught her with a left hook that staggered her. She stepped back, breathing hard, her hands up, thinking *boxer.*

He smiled as they circled each other. "You like that? I hope so, because I have a lot more. Maybe they'll all kill each other back there. Maybe it'll be just you and me and Boomer. Think you'd like that? A threesome, how does that sound?"

"What's wrong?" she said, her breathing ragged. "Can't rape by yourself, Snake? You need your friend?"

"Oh, I've raped plenty of bitches without Boomer, don't you worry. And I'm going to do you either way. Gonna do you so—"

She darted in. This time she was ready for the sidestep and the jab. She turtled her head, got her arms up high, and absorbed the impact along her bicep and forearm. Just as fast, he retracted the arm and went to dance away—

She snagged his left sleeve at the wrist. He was fast again, coming in with the other elbow. She didn't care. She had him now. She turtled tighter and sidestepped to the right. The elbow glanced off her head. She yanked his arm down hard with her right hand, pushed his head the other way with her left, and leaped over his shoulder with her right leg. His balance broke and he went down onto all fours. She stayed with him, transitioning to *omoplata*, a jiu-jitsu arm bar. He must have had some ground training in addition to the boxing, because he tried to roll out of it.

Here it comes, you rapist motherfucker—

She gripped the back of his belt with her right hand and scooted left. His base broke and he collapsed to his stomach, his left arm trapped between her legs. She leaned forward, clasped her hands around his neck and far armpit, and scissored her legs violently. His face plowed into the fish-bone beach and his arm went high. There was an instant of resistance—then she felt his shoulder separate and his elbow break. He screamed, the sound muffled by the fish bones.

His newly fractured arm flopped loose, and for a crazy second, she remembered something an instructor had once told her—*Actually, the knee bends in both directions, it's just that one requires a trip to the hospital.* She planted a hand on his head, shoved his face into the ground, and swiveled across his back. He tried to turn in to her, showing some training again, but she flowed with him easily, catching his good arm and dragging it toward her. He clasped his hands together, but his left arm was useless and the grip meant nothing. She caught his good elbow in a figure-four Kimura lock, twisted hard, and broke it. He shrieked again. She disengaged and stood. Snake writhed on his back, his face a rictus of agony.

She barely heard his screams. The dragon's voice eclipsed them—

Kill him. Kill him. Take his back, spine lock, neck crank, cripple him, KILL HIM—

And then another sound cut through all of it. A woman's voice. Muffled. Agonized. Desperate.

Sherrie Dobbs.

Livia ran to the open trunk. The light was on inside it. Sherrie Dobbs was on her side, naked, bound, and gagged, shaking, almost convulsing. A pair of wet diapers lay next to her. They must have come off somehow. The trunk was soaking wet, and it took Livia a second to realize why.

The woman's water had broken.

46

Livia reached for the Vaari so she could cut away the gag and the cords around the woman's wrists and ankles, but of course it wasn't there—the men had taken it.

"Sherrie," she said, her voice quavering. "Sherrie, it's me, Livia. We talked on the phone. You're going to be okay."

Livia leaned into the trunk and tried to untie the gag, but her fingers were shaking too badly and the knot was too tight. *Come on, come on* . . .

A smell cut through the sulfur stink of the air. Blood.

Not just her water, she's hemorrhaging.

"Sherrie, listen to me," Livia said. "I'm not leaving you. I'm going to look inside the car. I need a knife. To cut off the gag and the cords. Do you understand? I'm not leaving."

The woman moaned and her eyes rolled in terror. Livia couldn't spare another second to reassure her. She dashed around to the passenger side. It was locked. She screamed in frustration and ran back toward the driver side.

Somehow, Snake had gotten to his feet and was staggering away. She braced to go after him, thinking *You should have broken a knee—*

And then his knee did break. It seemed to shatter, like a sapling hit by an axe, and he went down.

Carl.

She got in the car and popped the glove compartment.

Come on, come on, these guys are pros, there's going to be a knife in the car—

There was. A black folder. She grabbed it, jumped out, and ran back to the trunk.

"Sherrie. Hold still. I'm going to cut off the gag. I'm getting you out. You're going to be okay."

She got the blade up alongside Sherrie's jaw, sliced through the gag, and pulled it free. Sherrie drew in a huge, agonized breath and retched as though she might vomit.

"Hang on," Livia said. "Hang on." She cut the cords around Sherrie's wrists and ankles.

She heard footsteps, coming fast from behind her. She spun, bringing up the knife. It was Little.

"What's going on back there?" she said.

"They're all dead. Sniper."

"Boomer?"

"Alive. But he's not going anywhere."

Ten yards away, Snake writhed on his back. "Get me a fucking doctor!" he yelled. "I know my rights!"

Little strode over. "Little, don't!" Livia called after him. "Presley. And the other girls."

But if Little couldn't help himself, there was nothing she could do.

He paused and looked down at Snake. "You're lucky I don't put you out of your goddamn misery," he said.

"Get me a doctor!" Snake yelled again.

Little stood looking at him for another second. Then, bellowing a cry of pure, primal rage, he raised a leg and stomped Snake's groin. Snake shrieked and tried to wriggle away, but between his arms and his knee he could barely move. Little went on stomping for a few more seconds, and then stopped. Snake lay there, whimpering.

Little came up alongside Livia. "He'll live," he said.

Sherrie moaned. She was very pale. "It hurts," she said. "Oh God, it hurts."

It was horrible, there wasn't even anything to cover her with. "We need to get her to a hospital," Livia said to Little. "The Jeep is too far. Can you get Boomer's keys and drive his minivan over here?"

"On it." He took off running.

"Sherrie," Livia said, reaching into the trunk. "Take my hand. Come on, let's get you out of there."

She heard a voice from the other side of one of the dilapidated structures, the Texas accent unmistakable. "Labee? It's me, Carl. Okay to come in?"

She felt a huge surge of relief. "Yes," she called back.

He came around the building and jogged over, a suppressed rifle cradled in his arms. "You all right?" he said, with that supernatural calm he got when he was sniping.

If things were surreal a minute ago, she didn't even have a word for this. "What are you doing here?" was all she could manage.

"Old Kanezaki told me. I'll explain the rest later. What do you need from me?"

"Are they all dead?"

"As Julius Caesar. Except for the two I understand you're interested in. The one I just disabled, and the other it looks like your partner already did the same."

He set the rifle against the car and looked in the trunk. "Oh, damn." He was wearing some kind of tactical vest over a long-sleeved shirt. He stripped off the vest, dropped it, then got the shirt off and handed it to Livia. Livia went to cover Sherrie with it, then stopped.

The baby was crowning.

"Sherrie," she said. "We need to get you out of the trunk. That baby is coming right now."

"Oh, damn," Carl said again, for the first time since she'd met him apparently stuck for words.

Livia looked at the ground. She couldn't imagine a less sterile place. "We don't even have anything to put down," she said.

"Floor mats?" Carl said.

"Good idea. Hurry."

Carl ducked into the car. A moment later he was back with four floor mats.

"Spread them out," Livia said.

He kneeled and arranged the mats. He looked up at her and said, "You know how to do this? 'Cause I sure don't."

"Cops get trained, yeah."

She left out the part about never actually having done it.

She handed the shirt back to Carl. "Put this on the mats." Then she turned to Sherrie. The woman was so pale. And her breathing was rapid and shallow. She was covered in greasy sweat.

"Sherrie," Livia said, reaching in and taking the woman's hand. "I need you to sit up. Can you do that for me?"

Sherrie shifted and cried out. "It hurts!" She started crying.

Livia felt her composure slipping. "Carl, get her out of there."

Carl stood and leaned into the trunk. "Ma'am, I'm going to slide my arms under you and pull you right out. I think if you could hold onto my neck, that might make for a smoother ride. Can you do that?"

Sherrie groaned and panted. "I think so."

Carl got in position. Sherrie put her arms around his neck. "Okay," he said. "One, two, three."

He lifted her out. She screamed. Her thighs were covered with blood.

"Set her down," Livia said. "Hurry."

Carl set her down on the pallet he had made and moved aside.

"Do you have a flashlight?" Livia said.

"You bet." He pulled a mini-light from a pocket.

"Hold it for me. I need to see what I'm doing."

Livia kneeled and furiously wiped the sweat from her eyes. "I need you to push, Sherrie. Okay? Your baby's almost here. I'm going to help you. But you have to push."

Sherrie groaned. "Oh, God," she said. "God!"

Carl shone the light. Livia got her hands in position. She reminded herself of what they'd told her at the academy: *Don't pull the baby. Just support its head. Remember, it'll be slippery. Don't drop it.*

"That's it," Livia said, and she realized she was crying. "That's it."

More of the baby's scalp emerged. Sherrie screamed.

"Almost there," Livia said. "You got this. You made it this far, Sherrie, you can do anything. Come on now."

She heard a car behind them. Carl said, "It's Little. We're all right."

She saw a miniature face. She got her hands under the head.

"Looking good," she said. "Just a little more. Push, Sherrie. You're so close. Just—"

And then the shoulders slipped through, and suddenly the whole baby was on the way, sliding out so rapidly it almost went right over Livia's hands. *Don't pull, just support, don't pull, just support—*

And then the baby was out, in Livia's arms. It was so tiny, and its eyes were closed—

Is it breathing?

She wasn't sure. What was she supposed to do?

Check the cord. It shouldn't be around the baby's neck. If it is, unwrap it.

She looked. Oh God, the cord was around the neck. She unwound it carefully. The baby's little mouth and nose were covered in mucus or something. She wiped it away as carefully as she could—

Come on, baby, come on, come on, COME ON . . .

The baby sucked in a huge, whooping breath, then gave an outraged cry ten times too big for such a little body.

Sherrie Dobbs looked up, crying. Livia was still crying, too. "It's a girl," Livia said. "Here. Here's your brave little girl." She placed the baby on Sherrie's breast. Sherrie held it and shook with emotion, alternately laughing, cooing to the baby, and sobbing.

But the woman was still bleeding. And she was so pale.

"Sherrie, listen to me," Livia said. "You're bleeding. We need to get you to a hospital. And that means we need to get you in a car. A minivan. Can you do that?"

Sherrie looked at her baby, then at Livia. Her face was pale and exhausted, but her eyes were fierce.

"I can do anything," she said.

47

When they arrived at the hospital in Palm Springs, Sherrie Dobbs was seizing and delirious. Doctors took the baby to the NICU and Sherrie into emergency surgery.

Livia had initially insisted on driving, but Carl had said, "Your head's bleeding. You might have a concussion. You stay in back with Sherrie and her new girl, okay? Leave the driving to me for a change."

She wanted to argue, but she knew he was right. And maybe it was past time she found a way to accept a little help.

Just before they left, Little had said, "The stereo was on when I got in. Keep it off."

Livia looked at him. "The song?"

Little nodded. "She doesn't need to hear it again. But the CD is still in there. That'll be evidence."

"Does it have gas?"

He smiled grimly. "Yes, it does. Boomer was a careful criminal."

Livia had to give Carl credit—he drove like she did, covering the forty miles to Palm Springs in less than twenty-five minutes. Livia called the hospital on the way to make sure they were ready. Also the Kanab Police Department, so they could get word to Sherrie Dobbs's husband.

And finally Kanezaki, who said he would send a team to retrieve the truck Carl had been driving, and the rifle.

Little stayed behind. He was going to secure Boomer and Snake, bring up the Jeep, and throw them in the trunk. And then drive them to the Palm Springs Police Department, which Livia agreed would be better than the California Highway Patrol or the San Diego County Sheriff's Department. Safer to keep it as local as possible for now, away from the reach of Boomer's father.

The doctors wanted to examine Livia, too. She knew they should—the danger past and the adrenaline faded, her head was throbbing, and she thought Carl was probably right about a concussion—but she told them she needed to make a few phone calls first.

She went out to the parking lot. It was still full dark, but the air was early-morning cool, and after the Salton Sea everything smelled wonderfully fresh. The lawns around the lot were startlingly dense and well manicured. The city must have been wasting outrageous amounts of water to create such lushness in the desert, but for the moment, the sight of so much vibrant green was nothing but beautiful.

She saw a man leaning against a tree on the other side of the lot, just beyond the ambit of a streetlight. Carl. She walked over.

"She going to be okay?" he asked.

"They don't know yet."

"The baby?"

"I'm not sure. I think so."

They were quiet for a moment. There were so many things she wanted to say to him, and they were all so confusing.

"You make me nervous when you stare at me like that," he said. "I can't tell whether you're going to hug me, or punch me."

She wasn't sure herself. She managed to say, "Thank you."

"Don't mention it. Next time, you could even get in touch. You know if you do, I'll come running."

Maybe that's the problem.

"How did you find me?" she said.

"Kanezaki called, thinking you might need backup."

"You couldn't have gotten here from Bali that fast."

He smiled. "Right, I forgot I was talking to an ace detective. Well, you got me. I was already here. Old Fallon got in touch, told me you were taking on some powerful opposition, so I flew to Seattle, thinking I'd be close by just in case. But you were already on the move. Luckily, Kanezaki was able to have a plane pick me up. You know, he's a fine travel agent, but it occurs to me you could save everyone a lot of trouble just by being more up-front."

She knew he was right. Knew her stubbornness could have gotten her killed. And Little. And Sherrie Dobbs and her baby.

But she hated the thought of needing help.

"Don't be mad at them," he went on. "There are people who care about you, that's all. And you know what? Maybe you inspire people, too. Maybe they want to be part of your work. You ever think of it that way?"

The truth was, she hadn't. Her work was her work. She didn't expect anyone else to see the world the way she did.

"How did you know where to find me at the Salton Sea?" she said. "You didn't follow our car. I would have seen you. And Boomer and Snake would have seen you if you'd tried to follow them."

"All true. In this case, credit for my prescience about your location must go to Kanezaki's Azrael drone."

She realized she should have known. "It has a transmitter?"

"I think it communicates with a satellite or something. I don't know the details. Kanezaki doesn't generally share information except in exchange for information, and I'm currently light on anything new to offer him. I guess I could have asked about the drone anyway, but I was about maxed out in the favor department on account of his flying me on private airplanes and equipping me with badass sniper rifles and all that. But yeah, as soon as you turned it on, old Kanezaki knew exactly where you were and relayed the information to me. Which was all for the best, I'd say."

She didn't respond, and he went on. "Is this why you told me to get lost last time we talked? 'Cause you were afraid of needing someone?"

She didn't answer.

"Why does it have to be so hard?" he said. "I mean, if you hadn't come to my rescue in Thailand, I'd be dead twice over. And the second time, I'd told you not to, remember?"

Again she didn't respond. Though of course she did remember.

"Not to press," he went on, "but do you ever wonder why you're so driven to help other people but so stubborn about accepting a little help yourself?"

She wanted to answer. She hated that talking about these things was so hard for her.

She settled on "You're a good friend, Carl."

He looked down, then back at her. "Is that all I am? A friend?"

She shrugged. "I don't know. I don't have . . . a lot of experience with these things."

"Yeah, me neither."

She looked at him, and after a moment he gave her a small grin. "Okay, maybe a little experience. But not, you know."

She thought maybe she did. And it was nice that it was as hard for him to talk about it as it was for her.

"I want to stick around," he said. "But you're probably facing a lot of questions, and I think it would be better for both of us if they didn't involve me."

She nodded. But she didn't want him to leave.

"But how about this," he said. "When you're done with the questions, and all the paperwork and whatever, let's talk, okay? I mean, if we really are friends, we can do that, right?"

She nodded again.

"On the other hand," he went on, "if that's as much talking as you're willing to do, it might be a short conversation."

She laughed. She so loved the way he could make her do that.

He smiled, maybe loving that he could do it, too.

She reached out and touched his cheek. She knew he liked that. And the strange thing was, she had come to like it, too.

He put his hand over hers. "Of course, if you're going to do that, we don't need to talk at all."

He leaned in and kissed her softly. She didn't mind. Not even a little.

"I'll stay for a while," he said. "Call me when you're ready, okay? Don't make me kill a bunch of bad people again just to get your attention."

She laughed. And then she kissed him back.

48

Sherrie Dobbs's bed rest had been due to preeclampsia—high blood pressure during pregnancy—and when Livia reached her, the condition had escalated to eclampsia. Her placenta had separated from her uterus before labor, and she was hemorrhaging even as she had the baby. Just a little while longer, and she would have died.

But she didn't. She lived. And so did her baby girl.

The day after her ordeal, she and her husband gave a press conference right from her hospital bed in Palm Springs. Sherrie told everything: How Congressman Kane had raped her when they were in high school, including the song he had made her listen to and then put in his yearbook entry to taunt her—her and Hope Jordan and Noreen Prentis. How she had spoken with Hope after Noreen had disappeared, and how afraid they had been. How the other man in custody now, Stephen "Snake" Spencer, had abducted her from her house after murdering Kanab Police Chief Tom Cramer and then driven her to the Salton Sea. Sherrie made sure to thank Seattle Police Detective Livia Lone and Homeland Security Investigator B. D. Little by name—thank them for the personal risks they had taken, and for saving both Sherrie's life and the life of her newborn baby.

And there was another man she thanked. No one knew his name or what he had been doing on the poisonous shores of the Salton Sea at three in the morning, and Sherrie Dobbs had been delirious and remembered only a little about him, but he had shown up at just the right time to help Detective Lone deliver Sherrie's baby and then race mother and daughter to the hospital. The media was referring to the man as the Good Samaritan, and he was urged to come forward and be recognized for his heroism.

The sight of that determined woman—alongside her supportive husband and their new baby—relating such a horrifying tale from her own hospital bed was spectacularly telegenic. Livia watched on the cable stations and knew that, despite all his power and connections, Boomer was done.

Ironically, even as Sherrie told her story, Boomer and Snake were being treated at the same hospital. Snake had two broken arms, a separated shoulder, a fractured pelvis, a shattered knee, and two ruptured testicles. With enough physical therapy, one day he would be able to feed himself. But he was never going to walk again, at least not without pain. As for Boomer, in addition to various more superficial injuries, he had two ruptured eyeballs. He was facing multiple surgeries, and doctors were optimistic that he might retain some degree of vision in at least one of his eyes.

Little and Livia had talked that night at the hospital, and Little explained that he had gotten on top of Boomer and managed to get his thumbs in the man's eyes. Boomer was younger and stronger, and had all the martial-arts training, too, so in the immediate aftermath, Little had attributed the outcome to a surge of ferocity boiling up out of a lifetime of pent-up hatred and rage. But in considering it afterward, Little wondered whether Boomer had been fighting as hard as he might have. Maybe it was because he was drunk. But Little sensed also that for whatever reason, something inside the man had already given up.

"Oh, and I almost forgot," he said. He reached into a bag he was carrying and took out something wrapped in Carl's bloody shirt.

"Your knife," he said. "Didn't have anything else to wrap it in. I searched the bodies before I left. Didn't take long to find—that thing has quite the profile. Anyway, it belongs with you."

Livia went back to Seattle. She had called Strangeland, who told her she better report immediately to a very agitated Chief Best. And so the following day, Livia found herself back in the chief's office—the view again, and the photographs, and the courtesies. They sat as they had last time, and after a brief attempt to wait Livia out, Best broke the silence by saying, "When I told Lieutenant Strangeland you had forty-eight hours to put the toothpaste back in the tube, this isn't exactly what I had in mind."

Livia nodded. "It wasn't what I was picturing, either."

Best gave her a tight smile. "Last time we spoke, it was about the ambush at the martial-arts academy, and the mysterious dead snipers outside your apartment. Seems almost quaint now, doesn't it?"

Livia didn't respond, and Best continued. "You're lucky Sherrie Dobbs is such a powerful presence on television. I heard she's being booked on all the big shows. And other women are coming forward now. Even some from Iraq. I don't see how Boomer Kane survives this. The FBI is looking into his father now, too. Gonna be quite the circus."

"Good."

Best sighed. "You have anything to tell me, Detective Lone?"

"I'm not sure what you mean, Chief Best. Charmaine."

"Oh, I don't know. Any notions regarding who those six men were, for example. The ones that were all shot, apparently by someone with a high-powered rifle."

"I'd have to defer to the FBI on that. It's their case now, because of the interstate aspects."

"I assume your thoughts will be the same regarding the three men you killed in a gunfight in Kanab."

"I have no idea who they were. I hope the FBI can find out."

"Any thoughts on what caused the explosion that stopped Snake Spencer's car? San Diego County Sheriff's Department says they think it was some kind of miniature drone."

"I wish I knew. I'm just glad something stopped him, whatever it was."

"And this Good Samaritan. Do you think it's possible he was the one who shot the six men?"

"I guess so. I'm glad someone did."

"It seems the shooter also crippled Mr. Spencer. Quite the marksman—six headshots, but one knee shot. Why would that be?"

"I guess no one's perfect?"

Best gave her the tight smile again. Livia felt so drained, it didn't faze her. If the chief wanted her scalp, she was welcome to try. She might even get it. Compared to Sherrie Dobbs being safe, Livia didn't really care.

"You're going to receive an award for valor for this," Best said. "At the rate Sherrie Dobbs is going, you might even become famous. How does that feel?"

The truth was, it felt awful. She hated the attention. And feared it.

But she couldn't tell Best that. The woman might use it against her in some way. Or, her imagination circumscribed by her own political ambitions, she might think Livia was lying, and feel even more threatened as a result.

So all Livia said was, "I'm just glad Sherrie Dobbs is safe. And her baby. And I hope the Bureau is able to find out what happened to all those other girls."

Best set down her coffee cup. Livia took that as her cue and stood. Best followed suit and walked her to the door.

Best put her hand on the door handle, then paused. She seemed to be struggling with something. After a moment, she looked at Livia and said, "I'm glad about Sherrie Dobbs, too. And her baby. And everything else. You did well, Livia."

Livia was surprised—surprised enough to be a little touched. "Thank you, Charmaine."

Then the moment was gone. Best straightened and opened the door.

"But watch yourself, Detective Lone. Because I'll certainly be watching. You can count on that."

49

After seeing Best, Livia took the stairs to the fifth floor. Homicide and Sex Crimes. When she walked into the office area, two cops at their desks stood and started clapping, slowly and in unison. Livia felt herself flush. She kept walking. Other cops stood and joined in the tribute. Livia nodded because it would have been disrespectful to do nothing in acknowledgment, but all she could think was how much she wanted to be alone.

And then Suzanne Moore, another sex-crimes detective who, like Donna, had early on taken Livia under her wing, came over. She put a hand on Livia's shoulder, leaned close, and whispered, "I am so fucking proud of you."

Livia continued on. She made it into Strangeland's office and closed the door, and the applause was mercifully over.

Strangeland came around the desk and looked at her. "You okay?" she said.

Livia nodded. "Concussion. I'll be fine."

Strangeland paused. Head injuries obviously weren't what she had been talking about, but she let it go.

"You talked to the chief?"

Livia nodded. "I think she's feeling a little . . . ambivalent."

Strangeland laughed. "What she's feeling is confused. She thought you were some kind of threat. Now she's wondering if Livia Lone, hero cop of the Seattle Police Department, might be a political asset. Probably she's worried it's both."

Livia looked at her. "I don't care if I'm a threat to Best. But I want to be an asset to you. I'm sorry about all this, LT. For the position I put you in."

"You did your job, Livia. I'll never ask you to do anything else."

"Thanks."

"Except maybe tell me about it. Off the record."

Livia laughed. Having avoided the exigency she had feared, she'd canceled and deleted the email to Strangeland that otherwise would have gone automatically. Still, she thought she could tell the lieutenant some of it. But only some.

"Coffee?" Strangeland said. "What do you say?"

"Starbucks?"

"Nah, we'd probably run into that guy who was hitting on you. Let's go to your place. Caffe Vita. I'm buying."

Livia smiled. "Deal."

"Oh, one more thing. But this one I'm not asking. I'm ordering."

Livia waited, and she went on. "You're taking a vacation. A real one. Away from Seattle, away from the job. I don't care if you need to be sedated the whole time. You're taking one, understand? And not just because there's going to be mandatory administrative leave and another officer-involved investigation, which even as those words leave my mouth I find I can't quite believe. But because you need one. And this time, you're going to do what I tell you."

Livia thought of Carl. She said, "I think a vacation might be good."

Epilogue

One month later, Livia was back in Kanab, riding the Ducati, the end-less sky a vibrant blue, the desert wind warm against her leathers.

Despite Strangeland's insistence about the vacation, there had been a lot of paperwork to fill out, and countless interviews with various federal, state, and local law-enforcement agencies. Not to mention another Force Investigation Team convened, and another Force Review Board, and a lot of interagency bullshit because Livia had killed those three men in Utah, and dealing with multiple jurisdictions gummed up the works considerably. But in the end, she'd been cleared of any wrongdoing. The press she was getting, courtesy of Sherrie Dobbs, didn't exactly make her untouchable, but it gave potential enemies pause. And Livia's refusal to do any interviews herself only burnished her stature. A cop who didn't care about publicity, who cared only about saving lives. In the end, she was awarded for valor, as Chief Best had predicted, or maybe as she had feared.

Kanezaki was sanguine about losing the drone. In fact, he told her, he was glad it had been so useful, even instrumental, in saving Sherrie Dobbs.

"You're not sorry about Boomer being exposed?" Livia had said.

"What do you mean?"

"If it's public knowledge, it's not useful to you. Or at least not in the same way. I think in the end, I got more out of this exchange than you did. I mean, you're a spy, right?"

There was a long pause. Kanezaki said, "Yeah, I'm a spy. I'm also a father."

Maybe the line was manipulative. But she decided to take it at face value.

"I'm glad you told Carl," she said. "Dox."

"Believe me, so am I. If you need me again, holler, okay?"

She smiled. "You're a good man, Tom."

There was another pause. He said, "I'm trying."

She'd taken a leisurely three days to cover the eleven hundred miles from Seattle. The country was beautiful—forests and mountains and finally desert. But not a desert wasteland like the Salton Sea. More a different kind of life—the cloud-studded skies, the twisting canyons, the long red mesas with their timeless, brooding patience. The ride was good. It gave her time to think.

Snake had lawyered up, but Boomer was cooperating with authorities. The remains of the nine girls they disappeared had been recovered—the nine, and four more who had never been entered into ViCAP. Presley had been found at the bottom of Lake Needwood in Maryland's Rock Creek Park. It wasn't just the Salton Sea—it seemed Boomer and Snake liked to have a body of water nearby if things went wrong. Little had buried his daughter with her mother, and, except when he was traveling, had visited her grave every day since.

Vice President Kane had stepped down—to "focus on my family," as he put it at the press conference announcing his departure from public office and public life. After what had happened in Kanab and at the Salton Sea, Livia wondered how long Snake would keep his mouth shut, and when he might decide Admiral Kane ought to be going to prison, too. Where Snake might have access to him.

Livia had personally called Grace Jordan, Gray Eagle Sanchez, and Hannah Cuero's parents. None of them would ever be the same. Livia knew that. But she also knew there was something to closure. To just . . . knowing. And, for people like the Cueros, and Little, and Livia herself, to being able to care one last time for that person you loved, to put her bones to rest and tend properly to them afterward.

Little had come to Seattle—to testify, but also just to talk. "I told you I was sorry I involved you," he had told her. "But I'm not now. Finding Presley . . . I needed that. More than anything in the world. More than I'll ever have a way to express."

Livia nodded. She knew. And he knew that she knew.

"And not just for me," Little went on. "We eased a lot of people's pain, didn't we? And prevented a lot more."

She was glad he was thinking that way. He'd once confided in her that if he knew for sure Presley was dead, he would end himself.

"I told you," Livia said. "I was never sorry."

Before he left, she asked if he was going to be okay. "I think so," he told her. "What we did . . . it feels right. Not just finding Presley and the other girls. Taking down those devils. I don't want to stop doing that. I'm not sure if I even could."

She wondered about his boss, Tilden. At a minimum, the man had been obstructing Little's efforts. She asked if he was going to do anything about that.

"No," he told her. "Maybe I would have before. But now . . . Tilden doesn't matter. And he's afraid of me. Afraid of what I might do to him, professionally or otherwise. He's more useful to me in place than he would be in the ground."

She had nodded, glad he was able to see it that way. Even if she herself could not.

From Kanab, it was only about an hour's ride to a place Carl had told her about, called Amangiri. "Beautiful country to ride in," he'd promised. "And a hot tub with a view of the desert sunset at the end of every day." They'd be sharing a room for four nights. The thought of it made her nervous, as always. But also excited. And maybe even . . . happy.

She'd be there soon. But she had two more stops to make beforehand.

The first was the Kanab City Cemetery. Livia had wanted to attend Tom Cramer's funeral, but was tied up in Seattle with everything that was going on in the aftermath. So she would pay her respects belatedly, to the man who had provided posthumous evidence in the case being assembled against Snake and, by extension, Boomer. Because it seemed Cramer had struggled with Snake before Snake had shot him, and had squeezed Snake's wrist so tightly that there had been some transfer of DNA. Sherrie Dobbs's testimony was already going to be devastating, but that DNA would be another nail in Snake's coffin.

The city cemetery was a patch of grass at the foot of a towering red mesa. From the little Cramer had told her about his feeling for the area, Livia imagined he would have been pleased.

His grave was adorned with dozens of flower bouquets, many of them obviously fresh. Livia knelt and placed a hand on the earth above him. Already it was sprouting with grass.

"I wish I hadn't called you," she said. "I'm sorry."

She knew one day someone might be saying the same to her. She knew if she could, she would tell them it wasn't their fault. She knew none of it would matter.

She got back on the Ducati. One last stop, also in Kanab. Sherrie Dobbs and her husband. And their month-old little girl.

They were in another house—modest, like the previous one, and rented with the proceeds from a nationwide GoFundMe campaign while the home Snake had plowed into was repaired. Their bakery had become something of a tourist attraction. Financially, at least, they were going to be okay.

Sherrie Dobbs cried when Livia came to the door. She hugged Livia tight, and it was all right, all right enough for Livia to hug her back. Then Sherrie took her hands and pulled her inside. The house smelled deliciously of fresh bread.

A man came from the bedroom, holding an infant girl in his arms. Livia recognized him from television—bald and a little chubby, with a wispy beard and the clearest, bluest eyes Livia had ever seen. Sherrie's husband. *A baker,* Livia thought. *Yeah, I can see that.*

He gave Livia a radiant smile. "I'm Calder," he said. "We spoke on the phone." Then he turned to the baby. "Look who it is, hon. Do you want to say hello?"

The baby had her father's startling blue eyes. But not, at the moment, his smile. She started to cry. "Oh, here we go," Calder said, and handed her off to Sherrie.

Calder went to the kitchen and returned with a tray of croissants. They sat in the living room, and while Sherrie fed the baby, they talked about the case against Snake and Boomer, and what a relief it was that the interviews were starting to die down. Sherrie was having nightmares, but she said focusing on the baby helped. The croissants were the best Livia had ever tasted, and she could easily imagine where Calder's extra pounds came from.

Her belly full, the baby had stopped crying. She seemed on the verge of sleep. Sherrie looked at Livia. "Do you want to hold her?"

Livia wasn't sure. She hesitated, and Sherrie added, "You have before. You held her even before I did."

Livia thought of Rick, and of how, when Livia had been a teenager, he'd told her about a little girl named Lucy he had rescued from nearly being beaten to death when Lucy was seven. Lucy had called Rick on her eighteenth birthday to tell him she was going to be a nurse. She said she would never forget him, would never forget that she wouldn't be alive if it hadn't been for Rick.

She looked at Sherrie. "Okay," she said.

Sherrie got up and sat next to Livia. She handed her the baby. Livia looked into the little blue eyes and was surprised to feel herself smiling.

"What's her name?" she said, realizing she had been remiss in not asking sooner.

Sherrie looked at Calder. For a moment, neither spoke. Then Calder said, "We named her Livia."

Livia was so surprised, and felt so stupid for being surprised, that for a moment all she could do was shake her head.

"We want her to be a fighter," Sherrie added. "Like you."

Livia, overwhelmed, managed to say, "Like her mother."

Calder beamed at his wife. "Like her mother, too."

They asked her to keep in touch. To come back and stay with them anytime. Livia told them she would, but it was hard to imagine.

She went out, got on her helmet, fired up the Ducati, and rode off. Soon the small town was behind her, lost in a plume of dust, and it was just the sky again, and the road, and the endless, peaceful mesas. Carl had been right. It was beautiful country to ride in.

She thought of Rick again. *Sometimes you get to really save someone,* he had told her. *Makes all the bullshit worthwhile.*

Yeah, Livia thought. *It really does.*

Or at least it did sometimes. She wished sometimes could be enough.

NOTES

PROLOGUE

A brief history of the Salton Sea:
https://www.vice.com/en_us/article/9bz5b7/i-went-to-californias-post-apocalyptic-beach-town-salton-sea

And some haunting photos, too. Careful of the Lost America site—it'll suck you in.
https://www.katherinebelarmino.com/2016/07/photographing-salton-sea-ghost-towns.html
https://lostamerica.com/photo-items/the-salton-sea/
http://www.jimriche.com/salton-sea/

Great six-minute documentary film about the Salton Sea:
https://www.youtube.com/watch?v=otIU6Py4K_A

And the 2002 Tony Gayton noir film *The Salton Sea* is wonderful and surprisingly not well known.
https://www.imdb.com/title/tt0235737/

CHAPTER 1

Some tips on how cops interrogate suspects, and why the deck is stacked against you:

https://boingboing.net/2018/10/03/why-cops-beat-you-in-the-inter.html

If you doubt Livia's backstory (told more fully in *Livia Lone*) in which her parents sold her and her little sister:
https://www.theguardian.com/global-development/2019/jan/14/indian-village-where-child-sexual-exploitation-is-the-norm-sagar-gram-jan-sahas

CHAPTER 4

Signal, the end-to-end encrypted calling and messaging app:
https://signal.org

CHAPTER 5

A photo history of the slow disintegration of Aliquippa, Pennsylvania, the former steel town where Stephen "Snake" Spencer had his childhood:
https://www.washingtonpost.com/news/in-sight/wp/2015/11/04/the-former-steel-town-that-dimmed-its-light-to-help-pittsburg-shine

The old-timer who taught Snake dirty boxing might have been Champ Thomas, who wrote *Boxing's Dirty Tricks and Outlaw Killer Punches*.
https://www.amazon.com/dp/1559501472

CHAPTER 7

A CIA primer on disguise:
https://www.youtube.com/watch?v=JASUsVY5YJ8

The movie Snake is thinking of is Steve Barancik's *The Last Seduction*. Came out in 1994 and hasn't aged a bit.
https://www.imdb.com/title/tt0110308/

Some thoughts on women's self-defense that Livia would agree with, from a woman:
https://www.jiujitsutimes.com/self-defense-seminars-arent-preparing-women-violence

What Hope Jordan missed, you can be aware of—by reading Gavin de Becker's excellent *The Gift of Fear: And Other Survival Signals That Protect Us from Violence*.
https://www.amazon.com/dp/0440508835

CHAPTER 8

Shortcomings of ViCAP:
https://www.theatlantic.com/politics/archive/2015/07/vicap-fbi-database/399986/

Racial disparities in media coverage of, and law enforcement resources devoted to, child abductions:
https://www.teenvogue.com/story/what-happens-after-a-minor-goes-missing

More on "forced teaming":
https://en.wikipedia.org/wiki/The_Gift_of_Fear

Names change; programs continue:
http://en.wikipedia.org/wiki/Information_Awareness_Office#Components_of_TIA_projects_that_continue_to_be_developed

CHAPTER 10

If you don't think Livia could have taken out the fake cop with a knife before he could deploy his pistol, check out the Tueller drill. I've done it with Simunition, and it is eye-opening.

https://www.wideopenspaces.com/tueller-drill-need-train/

And a video:

https://www.youtube.com/watch?v=jwHYRBNc9r8

Arguably the Vaari would be too much knife for everyday carry for someone like Livia. Still:

http://www.somico-knives.com/the--vaari-.html

CHAPTER 16

The relentless miniaturization of drones:

https://www.economist.com/science-and-technology/2018/05/17/the-worlds-lightest-wireless-flying-machine-lifts-off

"The US Army Is Equipping Soldiers with Pocket-Sized Recon Drones":

https://futurism.com/the-byte/us-army-pocket-sized-recon-drones

Yes, the US government really does call assassinations "dispositions" (for when even "targeted killings" is just too gauche). When Kanezaki explained to Rain in *Winner Take All*—all the way back in 2004—that the government called its assassination list the "International Terrorist Threat Matrix," he was pretty close to the actual, subsequently revealed "Disposition Matrix" terminology. To paraphrase H. L. Mencken, no one ever went broke underestimating the euphemisms of the US government.

https://www.theguardian.com/world/2013/jul/14/
obama-secret-kill-list-disposition-matrix

Kanezaki would neither confirm nor deny the existence of insect-sized drones. But:
https://www.youtube.com/watch?v=8cJv4O2zEOw

CHAPTER 18

The Ukrainian journalist who handled death threats by faking his own death:
https://www.theguardian.com/world/2018/jun/05/ukraine-presi-dent-petro-poroshenko-backs-faked-murder-of-russian-journalist

If you think six combat deployments is a lot, note that America's forever wars can mean far more than that—here, fourteen total, in Afghanistan and Iraq:
http://www.nbcnews.com/id/45066961/ns/us_news-life/t/
us-soldier-killed-th-deployment-war-zone

"Decorated Navy SEAL Is Accused of War Crimes in Iraq":
https://www.nytimes.com/2018/11/15/us/navy-seal-edward-galla-gher-isis.html

Shining a spotlight on rape in war:
https://www.economist.com/international/2018/10/13/
the-nobel-committee-shines-a-spotlight-on-rape-in-conflict

CHAPTER 19

"Rules of Ranging":

https://www.goarmy.com/ranger/about-the-rangers/rodgers-orders.html

CHAPTER 20

It's not just Livia who's rolled with Dave Camarillo and Rene Dreifuss—it's her author as well. Two outstanding teachers and technicians:

http://www.guerrillajiujitsu.com/dave-camarillo

https://radicalmmanyc.com

CHAPTER 24

More on victimology, modus operandi, and signature aspects of serial crimes:

https://www.psychologytoday.com/us/blog/take-all-prisoners/201003/catch-serial-criminal

"Justice was her vehicle, and hate was the fuel it ran on" is yet another aspect of Livia inspired by child advocate and novelist Andrew Vachss:

http://www.vachss.com/av_interviews/case_2004.html

CHAPTER 29

I didn't get to visit Sherrie Dobbs's and her husband's bakery when I was in Kanab, but the Kanab Creek Bakery is one of the best I've ever been to.

https://kanabcreekbakery.com

"Rapists don't stop raping on their own. They stop when someone stops them."

https://case.edu/socialwork/about/news-publications/research-reveals-new-insights-into-rapist-behavior-assists-rape-investigations-and-prosecutions

CHAPTER 32

"When people were motivated to believe something, they were going to believe it no matter what. There was no bridge too far."
https://www.snopes.com/fact-check/sandy-hook-exposed/

CHAPTER 36

Sexual trophies:
https://www.psychologytoday.com/us/blog/in-excess/201607/sexual-trophies-murder-and-addiction

More on trophies:
https://www.propublica.org/article/false-rape-accusations-an-unbelievable-story

Humiliating a victim as both signature and disincentive for the victim to come forward:
https://medcraveonline.com/FRCIJ/FRCIJ-02-00077

Tormenting a victim by contacting her afterward. I wish I were inventing these things for the story. I'm not.
https://www.sacbee.com/latest-news/article209917839.html
https://www.dailymail.co.uk/news/article-2692829

Victims sometimes recant true allegations:

https://www.propublica.org/article/false-rape-accusations-an-unbelievable-story

"Today, a $3 million satellite that weighs less than 10 pounds can capture significantly sharper images than a $300 million, 900-pound satellite built in the late 1990s . . . What began with satellite cameras is rapidly expanding to infrared sensors that detect heat; 'hyperspectral' sensors that identify minerals, vegetation and other materials; and radar scanners that can build three-dimensional images of the landscape below."
https://www.nytimes.com/2019/01/24/technology/satellites-artificial-intelligence.html

CHAPTER 38

More haunting photos of the Salton Sea, this time Bombay Beach on the northeast shore:
https://www.nbclosangeles.com/multimedia/Salton-Sea-San-Andreas-Fault-Earthquakes-California-504858882.html

And Charles Bukowski's poem "Dinosauria, We," which makes me think of the Salton Sea. Beware, it's a little depressing
https://www.youtube.com/watch?v=HDiLfQUBnyA

See also this haunting passage from H. G. Wells's *The Time Machine*:
https://www.mun.ca/biology/scarr/Time_Machine.html

CHAPTER 40

This is just a fraction of the ways the government can monitor cellphones:

https://www.eff.org/deeplinks/2013/10/nsa-tracked-americans-cell-locations-two-years-senator-hints-theres-more

CHAPTER 44

It's a good thing Livia has trained with Dave Camarillo, because that's where she learned flying omoplata. For this and much more, see Dave's excellent book *Guerrilla Jiu-Jitsu: Revolutionizing Brazilian Jiu-Jitsu*, a must for any serious grappler.

https://www.amazon.com/dp/0977731588

ACKNOWLEDGMENTS

Thanks to the Legislative Drafting Institute for Child Protection—an organization that does work Livia would be proud of, and that deserves your support.

https://ldicp.org

And a particularly easy and effective way to support the LDICP is through AmazonSmile. It's simple to sign up and have Amazon donate 0.5 percent of your purchases to the LDICP (or other charity of your choice).

http://barryeisler.blogspot.com/2018/11/if-you-buy-from-amazon-do-it-at.html

Thanks to former prosecutor Alice Vachss for *Sex Crimes: My Years on the Front Lines Prosecuting Rapists and Confronting Their Collaborators*, which I continue to draw on in researching this and the other Livia Lone stories.

https://www.amazon.com/dp/B01FTBDKJM

Thanks to child advocate and novelist Andrew Vachss for, among other things, compiling a comprehensive list of resources I have drawn on in researching this and the other Livia Lone stories.

http://www.vachss.com/help_text/index.html

Thanks to Daniel N. Hoffman, retired CIA clandestine-services officer and former chief of station (among other things), for his fascinating and helpful primers on intelligence work in war zones and on the exigencies of "strike to develop" and "develop to strike."

Thanks to Mike Killman for sharing his knowledge about and experience with combat deployments and rotations home—information that Fallon then passed along to Livia and that was vital in her efforts to crack the case.

Thanks to thirty-three-year law-enforcement veteran Randy Sutton for his always-solid advice on all things cop—and for the critical work he does through the Wounded Blue foundation to bring attention to a nationwide lack of support for wounded police officers.

https://thewoundedblue.org

Thanks to Dan Levin for helping Livia and Little charter a plane safely, quickly—and accurately.

Thanks to Dr. Peter Zimetbaum and Nurse Practitioner Lindsay Harris for their steadfast reluctance to contact the authorities regarding my, shall we say, offbeat how-to and anatomy questions, which in Peter's case go all the way back to "Hey, could you remotely short out a pacemaker?" in the very first book. Remember, they did it in *Homeland* and then–Vice President Cheney was worried about it in real life, too, but Rain got there first.

To the extent I get violence right in my fiction, I have many great instructors to thank, including Massad Ayoob, Tony Blauer, Alain

Burrese, Loren Christensen, Wim Demeere, Dave Grossman, Tim Larkin, Marc MacYoung, Rory Miller, Clint Overland, Peyton Quinn, and Terry Trahan. I highly recommend their superb books and courses for anyone who wants to be safer in the world, or just to create more realistic violence on the page.

http://www.massadayoobgroup.com

https://blauerspear.com

http://yourwarriorsedge.com/about-alain-burrese

http://www.lorenchristensen.com

http://www.wimsblog.com

http://www.killology.com

http://www.targetfocustraining.com

https://www.nononsenseselfdefense.com

https://www.chirontraining.com

https://conflictresearchgroupintl.com/clint-overland

https://conflictresearchgroupintl.com/terry-trahan

https://mastersofmayhem.info

Thanks as always to the extraordinarily eclectic group of "foodies with a violence problem" who hang out at Marc "Animal" MacYoung and Dianna Gordon MacYoung's No Nonsense Self-Defense, for good humor, good fellowship, and a ton of insights, particularly regarding the real costs of violence.

Thanks to Phyllis DeBlanche, Wim Demeere, Grace Doyle, Alan Eisler, Montie Guthrie, Meredith Jacobson, Lori Kupfer, Laura Rennert, and Paige Terlip, for helpful comments on the manuscript. Apologies to Montie for the lack of a love scene in this story, because those are his favorites and never cause him any psychological damage whatsoever. Special thanks once again to Mike Killman for never letting me get lazy about creating action scenes that are both dramatic and tactically correct, and for his fascinating, discursive editorial comments generally. If you like the Bukowski and H. G. Wells notes for Chapter 38, Mike is the guy to thank.

Most of all, thanks to my wife and literary agent, Laura Rennert, for being such an amazing daily collaborator and otherwise doing so much to make these books better in every way. For anyone else grateful for the increased pace of my writing, Laura's the one we owe it to. Thanks, babe, for everything.

ABOUT THE AUTHOR

Photo © Naomi Brookner

New York Times bestselling author Barry Eisler spent three years in a covert position with the CIA's Directorate of Operations, then worked as a technology lawyer and startup executive in Silicon Valley and Japan, earning his black belt at the Kodokan Judo Institute along the way. Eisler's award-winning thrillers have been included in numerous "Best Of" lists, have been translated into nearly twenty languages, and include the #1 bestsellers *The Detachment, Livia Lone, The Night Trade,* and *The Killer Collective.* Eisler lives in the San Francisco Bay Area and, when he's not writing novels, blogs about national security and the media. www.barryeisler.com.